CW01335793

MR. GRAYSON

BILLIONAIRES' CLUB BOOK 4

RAYLIN MARKS

WWW.RAYLINMARKS.COM

Copyright © 2021 by Raylin Marks

All rights reserved.

No part of this book may be reproduced in any form or by any electronic or mechanical means, including information storage and retrieval systems, without written permission from the author, except for the use of brief quotations in a book review.

INTRODUCTION
BREE

I sat perfectly still while my best friend and makeup artist, Cassie, did a complete makeover on my face. My mind was reeling with how I would handle this night—the night that Mitchell and Associates celebrated the merge of two highly-acclaimed architectural firms.

I wanted to chew my dad's ass out for being charmed by Alex Grayson—letting the perks of Grayson's investment company seduce him into allowing this merge—but that would be impossible since Dad's Alzheimer's took a turn for the worst two years ago. Dad had set up this merge without telling me, just like he waited until the last minute to tell me about his diagnosis. I supposed he was trying to protect me, but his lack of faith in me was a tad bit soul-crushing. Why couldn't he trust that I'd keep Stone Architects Group moving forward and expanding globally without the help of Mitchell and Associates?

It didn't matter anymore because Mr. Alex Grayson no longer worked as the vice president for that company anymore, anyway. Now, Alex would be my *partner* because he'd recently become the owner of the architectural firm that was intended to merge with mine. My partner. God help me. I should've taken more time to research this man, but I was too busy losing my London deal instead. Another story for a different day.

"All right," Cassie said, stepping back and taking in her artwork. "The highlights in your hair were needed big time." She tapped the back of her makeup brush to her glossy lips. "The eyeliner works," she paused and arched her eyebrow in some kind of warning, "only because it's an *evening party*. This shade of eyeshadow makes your green eyes pop too."

"You're acting like I'm walking a red carpet, Cass," I laughed.

"You are. The fact that this celebratory event is being held at the Beverly Wilshire makes it so," she said, grabbing my silk gown. "All right, then. The pale color of this strapless dress sets off the hints of red in your auburn hair." She helped me into the gown and stepped back after ensuring it fit as if I were one of her models that she was prepping for their photoshoot. "Yeah, you're lucky your boobs don't sag because you're not wearing a bra with this dress. We can't have lines."

"Hold up," I sighed. "What if the spotlight falls on me while I'm on that stage? Have you thought of that? This dress could be see-through, and I don't need my *high beams* becoming Mitchell and Associates' newest headline because they're throwing this unnecessary merge party for Brooks Architectural Firm and us."

"James Mitchell would never allow that," she said, more worried about ensuring the dress hugged every curve in my body. "Perfection." She smiled. "Now, you're ready to show your new partner how lucky he is to help run your company."

I arched an eyebrow at her. "I think you have that one backwards. I'll be helping him run *his* company."

"You'll both be running the company together," my assistant, Nicole, spoke up with a sigh. She sat cross-legged on the sofa in my dressing room, scrolling through her phone. She pulled her reading glasses off and eyed me. "Sheesh, if you can't accept this merge by now, all you're going to do is make the man hate you, and then neither of you will be getting anywhere with two great companies merging."

"Yeah, yeah," I exhaled. "I'm the artistic one, and he's the businessman."

"Exactly," Nicole said while she shot me her usual smug grin. "Keep that in mind tonight, please."

"Hard to do when Theo and I have been the ones running my family's company since Dad left," I answered, grabbing my clutch. "But I'll be a good girl and do my best to accept Alex Grayson as my new business partner."

I left my best friend and assistant in a rush, knowing I was pressed for time already, and I headed straight to the elevators that led out of the luxurious apartments that my dad helped design years ago.

I loved my home. It would've been nice to have a place near the beach, but that wasn't in the cards since I didn't want that crazy of a commute to work. I would rather stay close to my business and fully immerse myself into the company—that I suddenly felt I was losing in this merge.

Shit, don't think like this, I had to remind myself, knowing I was already missing the first part of this event, and showing up late was *not* what I'd planned on for first impressions while meeting my new business partner.

Buzz! Buzz! Buzz!

I glanced at my phone, knowing I was minutes away from the Beverly Wilshire where the party was taking place. "Hey, Theo," I answered my vice president and the man who was as close to me as a brother. "I'm almost there. An accident jammed-up traffic, and now I'm seriously late, I know."

"For God's sake, Bree," he said. "Why would you choose tonight—of all nights in history—to be late to something? Why?"

"No shit. I'm sorry, but I don't control the traffic. Also, I had a client go over this evening, and I wasn't about to drop them because of a company merge that would happen whether or not I was at this stupid party. Besides, we both know this is just a bragging event for Mitchell and Associates. The official merge is when we start collaborating on Monday."

"Damn it, Breanne," he practically growled. "I know you're

deliberately avoiding this, but you've screwed yourself by not getting your ass here when the press was snapping pictures of us all walking in. You also missed the *official* announcement that Mr. Mitchell made to all those cameras for business insiders. The best part came when I had to stand in your place alongside Mr. Grayson while the man was forced to make a speech in his *new partner's absence* tonight. Well done, you've officially dodged all the important reasons for this event."

I felt a knot tighten in my stomach. Theo had every reason to be pissed at me after all the work that'd gone into this. "All of what you just said is the reason I hate this. It feels like they slipped this all under my nose. It's like every other thing that's happened with this freaking merge."

"Listen up," Theo said. "I know the *personal* reasons why you're not mentally on board with this, but you need to snap your ass out of this fast. You're never late to *anything*. Ever. You're the face of Stone Architects Group, and it was sort of a slap in everyone's face that you weren't here for the kick-off of this merge."

I felt tears of frustration start to surface, and I *never* cried. This was the last thing I needed. "Well, I didn't realize they'd make the *official* announcement tonight," I said, trying to defend myself and keep the tears back.

"That's because you're in denial," he said. "You've been avoiding this all month. Now, you missed your time to show them they are fortunate that Stone is merging with Brooks. And let me reiterate the fact that you're not just a little bit late. Dinner has come to an end, and the dancing has commenced." He exhaled. "You know what? I'm done lecturing. I'm exhausted. Just get here, Bree. I think Mr. Mitchell already took off, and Grayson with him too."

I sensed his frustration, but what was I supposed to do? Did he expect me to get out of the car on the gridlocked freeway and run there? I had to defend myself and lack of professionalism. "It looks like the traffic has forced me to meet Mr. Grayson on Monday, which was when I genuinely believed this would all be considered official."

"I want you to listen to me when I tell you something. Okay?"

"Okay," I sighed, pinching the bridge between my nose.

"This merge is a good thing for you, us, and our company. Primarily, it's a blessing for *you*. You're our imaginative and overly creative dreamer; you always have been. That part of your happiness in this field was stolen when your dad was diagnosed, and we lost him soon after that. You not only had to grieve his death, but you also had to ditch your dreams of designing amazing shit when you had to take over the business side of everything. Mr. Grayson will take over in those areas, and you will be free to go back to your first love of creating, imagining, and engineering again. It's a gift, and you keep kicking it in the balls."

After tipping my driver, I stepped out of the car, and I glanced up at the magnificence of the Beverly Wilshire Hotel. "You're right," I said. "I'm sorry I let you and everyone down tonight. I am Theo."

"Just get your ass in there and mingle a little bit. The big guys are gone, but that's not who you are anyway. You're the one who sees eye-to-eye with the employees who are the core of our company. Enjoy being with them and show them that you are just as *thrilled* about this merge as they are."

"Get my ass *in there*?" I questioned. "That sounds a lot like you're not *in there* as I speak to you. Don't tell me you left, too?"

"I handled all of your important business. You know, making excuses as to why you weren't here for the ceremony and shit like that? My part is done, and I'm leaving now that you're here to take over. I have a headache, and I told Stanton it's his turn to rub my feet after the night I've had. He's already drawing my bubble bath, waiting for me at home."

"God, I feel like I wasted Cass's time with this whole dress-up stuff."

"There are still some suits here with eyes on everyone. Flash that pretty smile of yours at them, and do your part."

"Go enjoy Stanton and your bath. I'll do my part." I rolled my eyes, looking for the signs that led me to the ballroom. "I'll see what I can salvage after being Mr. Grayson's flaky new business partner tonight."

"That's my girl." Theo laughed. "Owning up like she always does. See you tomorrow at lunch."

"See you tomorrow," I said, ending the call.

I walked in, music playing loudly. For the first time since Dad passed, I felt almost anonymous in a room full of peers. At least, it didn't appear as if I were running one of the best architect firms in Southern California, and I didn't feel like the woman who ran the company. I was a—

Nope. Get out of your head. You're Breanne Mother-Fucking Stone, and even though you're late, you're still one of the executives. Time to woman-up, I thought, hating that I'd put myself in a position to look bad at this event.

Instead of cowering, I raised my chin and smiled. I wasn't going to allow being late to break me down in front of mixed company— Brooks Architectural Firm employees and my very own employees. I was a tenacious woman who ran a badass firm, and I was late because I wasn't about to tell a client they were interfering with my party time.

Sphere Company was expanding on the coast, and I needed them as my clients. They would be my gift and show of strength that my company carried with them into this merge. I worked overtime, showing them my plans and visions for the hotel resort they were planning to build in Malibu. I was their girl, and I landed the deal—I just needed to seal it. That's why I was walking in late.

It was a shame that Alexander Grayson couldn't be bothered to hang around a little longer to meet his new partner. That was on him, and I'd question his priorities with this *partner* stuff when I met the man on Monday. The fact that he left early tonight was a slap in my face, actually. Would he have treated a man with the same lack of respect? Doubtful. But that was the price of being a woman in a man's world. Unfortunately for him, the *patriarchy* could kiss my ass. I deserved my spot at this table.

Theo was right. These employees were *my people*, the ones who were the core of the company. I wasn't a stuck up *suit*, and I didn't act like one either. Now, it was time to interact with these new faces and enjoy mingling with the employees who kept these two firms running.

You know, the important ones behind the curtain that business executives never gave too much credit. People like Alexander Grayson, my new partner, who left early, would differ from me in this merge. He'd be the stuck-up jerk in a suit, and I would be the down-to-earth boss they all could relate to.

After an hour of laughter, new faces, and meeting the lively group who'd received the exclusive invites to the event tonight, I felt quite satisfied that I'd done my part. Everyone enjoyed themselves, and after the room started to empty, I felt the need for a stiff drink. I remained at the party with the small group who'd stayed behind for the free drinks and dancing, and I found myself at the bar.

I ordered a gin and tonic, with no desire for my usual martini. After the stress of this night, I downed my cocktail faster than I expected and called for another.

Damn, I needed this drink like a month ago. I felt my nerves unwind with the first cocktail down the hatch, and it was the most relaxed I'd been since finding out about this merge.

A slight buzz washed over me just as I spotted my ex-fiancé with an animated, leggy blonde hanging on his arm.

Of all the times and places. What the hell is he doing here? I thought, knowing I wasn't ready to see this man again. I would *never* be ready to see this man again.

I squinted my eyes to be sure. Yep, it was Max.

Oh, hell no. He was *not* seeing me sitting at a bar and drinking alone. I had the upper hand on this jerk since our split, and I wasn't about to lose that.

Yet, here I was. And there he was with some beauty on his arm—it was as if the devil himself had sent my ex to ensure this night was a complete failure.

Maybe I was getting payback for the way I called it off with Max? I *did* ditch the bastard at the altar on our wedding day, but it was after I saw a video of him cheating on me, so I figured I wasn't the monster in the situation, but it's not like blaming him made me feel any better.

Now, here he was with a perfect-looking broad? She was stunning and dressed in a tight black dress, complete with bouncing boobs nearly spilling out of it. Seeing them together made me feel sick to my stomach.

Why the hell do I suddenly care about what this miserable prick does and who he does it with? It was a year ago, Bree. You're over this loser, I reminded myself when I saw him beaming, and then they turned and moved toward my direction.

Goddammit. He can't see me drinking alone. That asshole would just fucking love that. No way. Think of something, Breanne. You're creative. It's what you do, create shit.

When Max smirked like a cocky asshole when our eyes met, I reflexively turned to my left and saw a young man. I sized him up quickly. He was about my age and dressed sharply in a crisp white shirt, suspenders, and a bowtie.

This could work, I thought as he ordered a bourbon sour.

I was running with enough liquid courage that I did something that my sober mind would have never considered. This wasn't creative; this was beyond being desperate to hold my own against my ex, who was currently heading my way.

I grabbed the man's sleeve. When he turned to me, my eyes widened when I saw how out-of-this-world beautiful this guy was.

"Oh, Jesus. You are quite handsome," I spoke the truth out loud like a crazy woman.

He smiled at my bluntness, thank God.

"Breanne Stone," the striking man said with a grin that made the liquor in my system fuel this insane idea even more. "Lovely to meet you."

His assertive voice carried a deep scratch to it that was as hot as he was.

The liquid in my system told me I didn't have time to gawk.

My proper mindset told me just to walk away.

Buzzed Bree didn't listen to her practical mind, so I accepted the man's gesture and pressed on.

"I'm happy you feel that way," I answered with a rushed smile. "Listen, I don't have time to explain, but I need you to do me a huge favor and go along with me on something," I begged, turning to see that Max and the blonde's pursuit to the bar had been interrupted by a brief, passing conversation. Max's eyes moved over to where I was again, and I was not letting this asshole have the upper hand of happiness on me.

I turned back to the guy who seemed pleased to meet one of the new partners in this company merge. "Okay. Question. Do you know that man over there? The one in the burgundy button-down and gray slacks with that blonde woman on his arm?" I asked.

My victim's humored green eyes peered around me as he took a casual sip of his drink. "I'm not sure about the gentleman, but the blonde woman he's with works for Mitchell and Associates."

"So I assume you work for them as well?" I asked. "Please tell me she doesn't know who you are."

"No," he chuckled. "At least not that I'm aware of." He eyed them, playing along with whatever in the hell I was doing to his poor, handsome self at the moment. "I just know that she's new to the company."

"Good, then you're my boyfriend." I locked eyes with his wide and playful ones. "Can you go along with that lie for me? I promise I will make this up to you somehow, but that's my ex, and it's quite a long story." I cringed at what I just asked of the guy.

As I took the time to reflect on the fact that I was obliterating any chance of this divine man ever thinking I was a normal human being, his lips turned up into the most deliciously devilish grin. I had to admit that I loved the fact that he might play along with my immature, liquor-driven idea.

The shadow along his cheek and jaw created a razor-sharp chiseled face that I couldn't help but stare at. His face was well defined, and his hair was cut longer on the top than the back and sides. He must've been a model, hired to be a seat-filler at this party. Mitchell and Associates had models that covered their magazines, and I knew for sure this guy wasn't one of my employees.

"Bree?" I heard a familiar laugh come from behind me.

Max.

"Hey," I said as I turned around. "Why are *you* here?" I thought I'd play it cooler than cutting right to the chase, but apparently not.

"My girlfriend. Bree, this is Haley. Haley's company invited her to attend this event," Max said, smiling at the woman. He looked at me smugly, like the fucker he was. "Drinking alone, I see. It looks like you've turned into the lonely CEO I'd always knew you'd become, huh? As they all say, must be pretty lonely at the top."

I sucked in a ragged breath, but I suddenly calmed down when I felt the dreamboat of a man beside me pull me into his sturdy side. "My lady, a lonely CEO? Hell no," the man I'd pleaded to roleplay with me scoffed at my dumb-ass ex. "I would hardly call what we have going *lonely*, would you, Breanne?" The man's voice was authoritative, mature, and confident.

He was perfect for this, and I owed him big time.

"Hardly lonely…" I looked back at my savior. *"What's your name?"* I mouthed, and he smiled some cheeky grin in return to me.

"I'm Logan," he announced to Max as he pulled me closer to him and extended his hand to shake my ex-douchebag's hand. "I worked at Mitchell for a time," he said, looking at the blonde who was just as taken by this stone-cold fox as I was. "You've been pretty high-spirited tonight that you work for them. I've heard you talking about it."

"Oh," she snickered as she blushed. "I love it there. Do you still work for the company too?"

Dreamy eyes looked at me. "Not anymore." He arched an eyebrow that would make any woman melt and smiled at me. "Now, I'm Breanne's number one man, and soon to be…" He stopped. "Should we tell them, darling?"

Darling? I smiled, then turned back to my ex and his arm ornament. "Why not?" I ran my hand down the center of dreamy eyes' shirt. *Damn!* All muscle. I pulled it together and smiled and Logan's sexy grin. "Logan and I are going to be tying the knot?" I looked back at Max. "Poor Logan had to deal with me turning him down a couple of times—you know, due to all the past traumas and insecurities I have from being cheated on—but in the end, I said, yes." I smiled sweetly at Logan, who was watching me ramble.

"You're still not over that?" Max asked defensively. "Three years ago and—"

"She is now," Logan spoke for me.

Max eyed Mr. Hotness. "How long have you two been..." he stopped watching me with some cowardly look.

"God," Logan said with a dramatic sigh and a shit-eating grin. "It certainly has been in the works for a while. Call me a sappy romantic..." He locked eyes with me. "Nonetheless, since the moment we announced the engagement, the time has practically flown by." He took a sip of his amber drink and looked at Max. "Now, it feels as though this festive event is pretty much celebrating us," he said and clinked his glass of bourbon to mine. "Cheers to us, Breanne."

"Cheers." I grinned at his excellent response.

I turned fully to him, my eyes thanking him for the fact that he was going along with this charade for my benefit.

I certainly didn't expect a demon from my past to join me in my night of fuckery after showing up late to this important event, and I didn't expect for it to have *this* effect on me either. Max was a worm, and I *knew* my sober self would've walked the hell out of here without a word. But here we all were. Thanks a lot, gin.

"I heard you are working with the former VP of Mitchell," the blonde said, cutting through the silence of my locked-up thoughts and the tangled mess I'd pulled myself into. I looked back at her. "Sounds like you're the lucky one," she said. "From what I understand, Mr. Grayson is pretty hot." She wiggled her eyebrows, making me furrow my brows in response before I looked at Max.

I hope she cheats on your ass, too, slimeball.

"What?" Max questioned, stepping up to the bar and guiding the blonde to sit next to him.

I almost answered, but instead, I looked back at the poor guy I'd roped into my drama. I hoped I never saw him again. This scenario couldn't have been any more humiliating. What happened to the bold woman I was? Where the hell did she go? I was so out of character that I couldn't think straight, and my buzz was propelling me further into this flaming pile of garbage. So, naturally, I downed the last of my third cocktail.

Bad idea? Meh. Fuck it.

"Hello? Are you still on the planet with us? God, you still space out like a weirdo, Bees," Max insulted me with the name I hated most. "Are you jealous of my new girl?"

"You have seen the man she's spending the rest of her life with, right?" Logan said about our fake engagement. "I hardly believe jealousy is what is on my girl's mind."

"Then why are you acting so fucking weird?" Max asked.

"It's been a long night with the company merge…" I started.

"Rumor has it that you weren't even here and that Grayson dude had to do your job too," Max clicked his tongue after he cut me off. "Bad timing on that unprofessional slip-up."

All of my witty comebacks, which were usually at the tip of my tongue, were frozen by the fact that this was getting messier and uglier and more mortifying by the second.

"I'm sure Mr. Grayson will forgive me for working late tonight." I smiled. "You wouldn't know the first thing about working, much less working late, though, would you, Max?"

Max rolled his eyes. "We weren't here for Mr. Grayson's announcement, but word is floating around that he expected nothing less from a woman like you."

I felt my fists ball up in response. "I was certain Mr. Grayson was especially happy Bree was late," Logan said. "In fact, after seeing him tonight and listening to him speak, I'm going to worry about that man working so closely with you." He looked at me and pursed his perfect lips. "Alexander Grayson is quite the catch, and I can't lose you completely to that appealing businessman."

I smiled, somehow my nerves chilling under this man's steady gaze. "Kiss me," I softly said.

Did I just ask him to kiss me? Was my drink spiked? What the hell am I doing? Self-sabotaging?

"Kiss you?" Logan softly questioned, capturing me with his daring smile and perplexed expression.

Max and Beach Barbie were distracted by her cosmopolitan not being made to her liking, and I was in awe of the perfection and beauty bottled up in this man in front of me. I was confident I must've been possessed earlier and didn't realize it until now—possessed by the old, wild and daring side of me that'd been stifled since my parents died and I had to become the responsible CEO.

Between losing my parents and Max's final nail in my coffin, I'd turned into a stiff businesswoman with blinders on, but at this moment, I felt like my old self. The fun, friendly, silly, goofball. The alcohol was the culprit for taking it to extremes with a stranger, but there was no turning back now. The guy seemed like he might *actually* kiss me, so I pressed for more, not even remembering the point I wanted to make with the gesture.

"Yes. I said, kiss me." I arched an eyebrow at him, my eyes playfully drifting back to my idiot ex.

He took a sip of his bourbon sour and nodded. "Do you want a peck or a show-stopper that'll rid you of the douche bag who's starting to piss me off with all of his derogatory comments at your expense?"

My eyebrows rose with my smile. "I mean, when you need to make a point, it seems like you *have* to go with a show-stopper. Like it or not, I guess."

His laughter was infectious, and I couldn't help but join in happily. I hadn't been silly and laughed about something so frivolous in…well, way too long.

"The sacrifices we have to make sometimes, right?" he said, sliding the corner of his mouth in between his teeth and eyeing Max and Beach Barbie.

"So, when's the *big day* for you and Logan?" Max asked snottily, obviously seeing right through my stupid little game. Then he laughed, "You can stop acting like you both are together now. You look like an idiot, Bree." He looked at Logan. "Sorry, dude. She's sort of an odd one."

"Listen," Logan said, taking my hand in his, "your insults prove that you're the one having difficulty losing this beauty on my arm."

"You can't be serious?" he questioned Logan while I felt the need to run the hell out of here after asking him to kiss me, and now Max saw right through my game.

"I am," Logan said, steadying me on my feet, one arm gracefully sliding on my back and the other holding my hand. "I'm also serious when I say that you're a dick too."

"Bree, you're really marrying this asshole?"

I couldn't answer. My brain was mush, I was livid, and I was embarrassed.

"We're taking off," Logan answered for me. "I think my lady has had enough of her asshole ex questioning her. Hey, I know you don't work for either company present tonight, but it's a known fact that no one questions Breanne Stone. Goodnight."

"What the hell did I just do?" I said, feeling more clearheaded as we walked outside into the fresh night air. I looked at Logan's tall frame as he followed me out. "I swear to God that I'm not *that* immature in real life. I don't do shit like this *ever*. And—oh, my God—if you work for me? Totally unacceptable behavior to ask you to kiss me." I walked away from the front doors of the exquisite hotel.

"It was hard to resist, but if you caught my eye when you first walked in tonight, I'm quite sure all eyes were on you at that bar tonight too. It was for the best that nothing happened," he said, trying to make me feel more comfortable about my pathetic idea.

"Well, I'm sorry anyway," I answered. "If you work for me, that could—"

"Technically, I work for Mr. Mitchell," he said.

"Great. You're one of his models, aren't you? I knew it. This is right up there with the lamest way I've ever behaved in my life," I said, finding a bench and sitting on it.

"Well, I must say that finding Breanne Stone nearly fall victim to a complete douche bag tonight was not something I imagined her doing when I had the privilege of first meeting her."

I was so spun out. I was pissed at my lack of professionalism, the weakness I didn't realize I still had concerning Max, and this entire fuck-up of a night. There was no backing out of this and nothing to excuse my behavior.

"Listen, Logan, I don't know what article you may have read about me or what that man, Mr. Grayson, said about me tonight to put that in your head, but I'm human too. Human's crack sometimes." I leaned back, pressing my fingers against my forehead. "My God, what possessed me to fall apart like this? I'm so humiliated." I kept my eyes closed, willing this other-worldly, gorgeous model to leave and never see me again. "Please, God, can you keep this between us?"

I gained the courage to look over at him as he sat at my side. "I'm not the one you should worry about. It seems like your ex might have something to say about you wanting to kiss your handsome fiancé."

I grimaced. "I'm sorry I brought you into that and my demons from the past. There's nothing I can say to get you to respect the woman I *really* am, but hell, this has most certainly been a night I wish I could restart."

"Nothing wrong with wanting to kiss your future life-long partner," he smirked. "I'll keep it between us." He rose. "Hey, will you be okay? That man was a bit off-color in the way he should treat a lady."

I laughed. "I was a bit off-color the last time I saw him." I looked up and took in the man's muscular figure and what must've been all six-foot-four or so inches of him.

"Strange, but I can't imagine that from you."

"Neither could any of our wedding guests."

"That sounds like a story I want to hear," he chuckled, and it must have been because of my expression.

"Yeah, and I wish it was a story I could forget," I said, shaking my head and not wanting to get into it any further.

"Then I hope, for your sake, one day you will." He stepped back with a smile. "It was lovely to meet you, Ms. Stone."

"Hey," I called out as he strode away like the runway model he was. "It was nice to meet you too. Thanks again for roleplaying with me tonight."

He stopped and turned back. "You're going to be a damn fine partner for Mr. Grayson."

I stared at him as he walked off like he owned the world, and I couldn't muster the courage to chase him down. I could've used a night of letting that god kiss away all of this shit, but it was for the best to let him walk on. God only knew what the rumors would be on Monday if that man talked about what I had done.

Sneak Peek: Part II
 Bree

"The suits are here," Nicole, my assistant, proclaimed while I sat in our conference room, waiting impatiently. "Five minutes early, unlike you, who—"

"Nicole," I snapped, pulling my blazer down. "Thank you. I understand I was late for the gala. The entire room is aware of it, as well. We don't need reminders."

"Got it," she cringed. "Sorry."

"Don't apologize, just lead them in."

All right. Moment of truth. Time to meet my new business partner, who I needed to start appreciating for allowing me to go back to my focus on design and engineering.

"Are you ready to start the beginning of something new and exciting?" Theo asked, taking his seat next to me.

"As ready as I'll ever be." I smiled at my right-hand man. "Are you?"

"After I saw the smile that was plastered on your face at brunch on Sunday," Theo chuckled, "I'd think you'd finally—"

"Met her life-long partner?" a familiar voice rang out as a group of crisp suits walked into the room.

I looked up to see Logan. His smile was as radiant as mine must have been after telling Theo my dark secret of how I handled Max's unexpected cameo at the conference.

I observed Logan in his three-piece business suit and stared in confusion as to who the hell this man *really* was who was sitting across from me—because he sure as shit wasn't a model if he was in this meeting.

Mr. Mitchell remained standing and announced himself, but I couldn't peel my eyes away from Logan.

"Logan?" I finally questioned, lost in his dazzling smile highlighted by his gray suit and black tie.

I looked at Mr. Mitchell after he softly coughed out a laugh. He was as handsome as Logan was. For a brief moment I had to wonder where the hell these impossibly gorgeous men came from.

"Did I miss something?" I asked, seeing Mr. Mitchell was suddenly amused after I greeted Logan.

"And that's my cue." Logan rose, buttoned his suit jacket, and I didn't miss the humored eye contact he gave Mr. Mitchell.

I felt ice-cold panic shoot up my spine at the thought that the man I'd roped into an elaborate roleplay, ending with forced sexual advances, was a goddamn executive. What had I done? This couldn't have possibly gotten any worse.

"Good afternoon," Logan greeted us, his voice still that sexy deep rasp. "Most of you already met me when I introduced myself at the gala." He looked at me. "But for those of you who were late, allow me to introduce myself." His face was commanding, and I suddenly felt played. "I'm Alexander Grayson…"

That's all I heard after the ringing in my ears made me fucking deaf. Seriously. For the next hour of him talking, I couldn't focus on one single word. I felt like my head was in a barrel, and everything was muffled. How—of *all people on the planet*—was this man Alexander Grayson?

CHAPTER ONE

BREE

*T*he nightmare scenario of the other night—from being late to running into my ex-fiancé—wasn't truly mortifying or shameful until this moment when I got the whole picture. It was like the universe had made a massive joke at my expense that night, and I was only now realizing how bad it was. Dignity? Say goodbye to that, sister. It was nonexistent at this point, and good luck getting it back.

I cleared my throat, stared at Mr. Grayson, my partner—in crime and business, apparently—and I didn't let my expression waiver.

"And now I'd like to hear a few words from my new partner, Ms. Stone," he said.

I stood and walked to the front of the room, and I smiled at Mr. Grayson. "Lovely introduction," I said. "Mr. Mitchell, nice to have you join us today. I understand your time is valuable, and so I'll keep this short and sweet."

Mr. Mitchell nodded, his deep blue eyes glistening in humor that made me think this Grayson trickster gave him more information than I wanted him to have.

"Mr. Grayson," I leveled him with a daring smile, "I have to say, I'm beyond honored that our two companies have merged, and you and I are official now, aren't we?"

He nodded and stared at me.

You bastard, you allowed me to fall into your little game and capitalized on me being late? I thought as the room waited for me to thumb through papers I wasn't reading.

"Bottom line, everyone, is that I'm grateful to have such an *honest* man working as my new partner. He's essentially my savior," I said, cupping both hands together and bringing them to my heart, mocking him. "In fact, you have saved me from much more than I believe you actually comprehend." I raised my eyebrows and smiled at him.

"Good to know." He smiled that handsome smile I remembered when I was too dumb and buzzed to *walk away* after I'd seen Max.

I grinned at the executives in the room, and I cleared my throat, really trying to nail this asshole somehow. "Today, I'm proudly giving up the dreaded files of endless paperwork that I'm forever drowning in. All thanks to my *lifelong* partner *and* savior for taking on this task." I widened my eyes and brought them to the trickster in his pristine suit. "So, thank you, Mr. Grayson. I'm beyond elated to say that I look forward to this partnership and reigniting my engineering and designing fire and passion. It's been too long since I've been able to work closely with my design team. With Mr. Grayson joining us, I can do just that. With all of that said, I think you can see that I am eager to return to the second floor while Logan—" I cringed. *Oh, dear God. How stupid can you be, Breanne?* "Excuse me, *Mr. Grayson*, works with our marketers, our business development teams, and our finance department."

I saw Mr. Mitchell covering a smile with his fist and Mr. Grayson arching an eyebrow at me.

I never faltered against Alexander's expression, but why—of all the things adding to this shit-fest of him being my new partner—did he have to be so strikingly gorgeous?

Maybe it's because he was actually Satan in a suit.

Alexander leaned back in his leather chair, relaxing his hands on the leather armrests. "I'll gladly take on my duties so you can indulge in your passion, *darling*," he said with a cocky smile.

I ignored that and smiled at everyone in the silent room. "That is all I have. I'm truly excited about this new direction our companies are moving in together," I said, pulling up my files and tapping them on the table. "Any questions for Mr. Grayson or me?"

The room remained silent as to be expected. This was a merge, and they were waiting to see if they'd be keeping their jobs and continuing to work with the employees from Brooks Architectural Firm.

Truth be told, I should've been the one remaining silent. After behaving as I had with Alexander Grayson, I was lucky he was still okay to be the partner of a businesswoman who caved to her lame ex.

If only I could change the past instead of having to learn from it.

"I think we're all good here." Alexander broke the silence and was the first to stand.

The rest followed, helping to conclude our meeting.

"Theo," I said with a smile so fake I could tell it was freaking him out, "I think you and Mr. Grayson met the night I was regretfully late to his speech."

"We did," Theo answered, looking at me as if I'd lost my mind. "I'm delighted we're all off to a great start."

While Theo and I went to leave Mr. Grayson in the care of the suit army that followed in Mr. Mitchell, I overheard Mr. Mitchell speak.

"You gave her your middle name? Jesus Christ, Alex. You—"

"I'm sorry, what?" I stopped and turned back. "Logan? That is your middle name?" I smirked.

Alexander returned my grin. "I prefer Alex," he said.

"Ah, I see. Well, then, *Alex*. I'll be on the second floor if you need anything. Otherwise, Theo can help you with the stack of accounts and invoicing that I'm behind on. They'll be moved to your new office. It's got the best views of the alleyway. You'll love it, I'm sure."

"Delighted," Alex said. "Lovely to see you again, by the way. I look forward to you paying me back someday, also."

"Excuse me?" I asked.

"You, me," he said playfully with the most handsome smile, "that ex of yours and his girlfriend, who Jim had escorted out of his building this morning? It turns out her name is Haley Burns, and she was quite bold to show up to the gala without an invitation." He watched my expression, and his eyes glistened under the lights of the room. "She and your ex practically snuck in through the back doors." He slid his hands into his pockets, and his forehead creased in humor.

"Escorted out of Mitchell and Associates? She was fired?" I asked, knowing my expression that always gave me away probably had this liar ready to burst into laughter after he blasted me with another *gotcha!* Instead, he simply nodded to confirm the woman was indeed escorted out.

"On top of her attending the gala, we learned quickly that she was not an employee of Mitchell and Associates." His eyes narrowed some. "Looks like she slipped under the radar over at Mitchell and managed to procure a job in some filing room. With her mentioning she was an employee of Mitchell and Associates, Jim had his high-tech security detail locate the woman as she attempted to sneak into his building. So, unfortunately, the ex-boyfriend and this Haley woman were sloppy, up to no good, and engaged in conversation with the wrong people." The way he talked was so smug. "Looks like our covert operation to deflate the ex-fiancé did a little bit of good, I'd say."

"Why are you telling me this?" I questioned. "I'm not surprised in the slightest Max would stoop to this level. He certainly didn't act like the man I was engaged to when he behaved the way he did at the gala." I rubbed my forehead. "And as you are well aware..." I paused and sighed. "I wasn't quite acting like myself either."

He smirked. "Well, if it helps, from my vantage point, it wasn't you who showed up without an invite and through lies, of course."

"But I was late. That's almost as bad as sneaking in the back doors with lies." I widened my eyes and chuckled.

"You were late, yes," he grinned, "but sneaking in? Hardly. You stole the attention of the room from the moment you entered the building, Ms. Stone. In a good way, of course."

"Of course." I felt my cheeks flush and ignored it. "Well, I'm glad my unpunctuality didn't raise issues for either of our companies."

"Ms. Stone," he said, his tone changing to that deep baritone rasp he used when he spoke business, "aside from the gala occurrences, I wanted you to be aware that we may be raising security some. Your ex and this woman were there without an invitation for a reason. The woman he was with didn't seem as though she understood why her new boyfriend was insisting that she tell the entire room she worked for Mr. Mitchell's company after they seemingly snuck into the event."

"Was this woman questioned?" I crossed my arms. Then I sighed. "Not trying to defend the man, but Max wouldn't hurt a fly. I'm not sure why he was there. He was most likely seeking revenge for the way I left him at the altar, as I mentioned to you that night. Instead of him acting like a fool to embarrass me somehow, I did that to myself."

"The woman was questioned by security when Max and she made the mistake of approaching us, the two executives the gala was being hosted for," he answered. "I'm only making sure you're aware of that bizarre situation and what we learned."

"I appreciate the information," I answered. "I would have also loved knowing exactly who you were at the time that I dragged you into the middle of my charade that night. Why wouldn't you have just told me that you were Alexander Grayson?"

"Not to add more insult to injury, but if you were on time to the gala, you would have known that it was Alexander Grayson who you wished to kiss in front of our employees." He smirked.

My eyes widened, and then I exhaled. I encouraged Alex to follow me to a more private spot in the room. Theo had already been in conversation with Mr. Mitchell and some suits, so it wasn't too conspicuous.

"That was the booze," I quietly argued. "You understand that, right? I do not ordinarily behave like that."

"That's too bad because I was certainly hoping for that kiss as your new savior, of course."

"You lied about who you were," I said, trying to keep the conversation a little more proper to defend my actions.

"I withheld information." He chuckled. "And let us not cast stones, *Ms. Stone.* You obviously didn't do your research on your new partner as I had." He crossed his arms and grinned.

Do not get lost in this man's gorgeous looks, sexy smiles, and cunning words.

"We're done here, Mr. Grayson. Enjoy your office at Stone Company. As I said earlier, Theo will bring an overwhelming amount of paperwork to your new office. I'll be down on the second floor if you have questions or need my help figuring anything out."

He smiled. "I believe I will manage just fine. However, are you sure you don't want to go through this first part alongside me? Numbers? Spreadsheets? Expense reports? Revenue—"

"I trust you're an educated man," I said, cutting him off with a smile. "And if you must know, I did do a little research on your capabilities."

"And I trust you were highly impressed?" He was flirty, and I was struggling to remain firm in my business frame of mind.

Alexander was the opposite. He was relaxed and somehow seductive, and I didn't know if he was trying to charm me into some trap of his.

"Yes, I was impressed. I see it took three individuals to replace the one position you held at Mitchell and Associates. Not only that, but you're remaining on the board at Saint John's Hospital as well?"

"That's correct."

"Well," I said, "it looks like we'll hardly be seeing each other at the firm. As partners, you'll be doing your duties up here, and I'll be doing mine two floors down. If what you said is true, you will be kept quite busy in your office and behind closed doors."

I watched him eye me, but with the sound of someone walking over to join us, he opted to seal his lips instead.

"I see everything is working out between you two?" Mr. Mitchell said, joining our conversation. "Ms. Stone, it is great to have your artistic and creative dexterousness merging with Brooks Architectural Firm. This will be a monumental merge for both companies."

"Thank you. Now, gentlemen, if you'll both please excuse me. We are facing a deadline, and I'm sure you, Mr. Mitchell," I politely smiled at him, "would not be thrilled if we missed it."

"Then I won't be keeping you any longer," he said.

"Mr. Grayson," I studied his beautiful yet tricky eyes. "It was a pleasure to meet on a better day."

"The pleasure is all mine," he answered.

"Theo," I looked at my vice president, "if you don't mind, please introduce Mr. Grayson and Mr. Mitchell's team to my assistant, Nicole. She has information packets and everything else should any of you desire to take a full tour of the building."

That's when I took my exit. I rolled my eyes at how lame Max and I had both behaved, and Mr. Grayson officially had all that garbage and immaturity to throw in my face if he wanted to. I should have walked out with a good buzz and just went home. Now, Grayson had the upper hand, and I couldn't allow that. I wasn't allowing *a suit* to run my dad's company with an iron fist. I knew this merge would suck; all company mergers did. Let's hope the trickster of a man I'd met at the gala at least had a heart when it came to successfully merge the two companies.

CHAPTER TWO
BREE

One week had passed, and I officially hated merges more than I knew. It was no thanks to the rumors and whispers I'd been hearing and trying to ignore all week, and the one word I despised...*restructure*.

Alexander was starting in, and I swear to God that if one more employee walked out of this building in tears, I was done trusting his skills.

Mr. Mitchell had guaranteed this would be a fair and equal merge, but it certainly wasn't feeling as if that were the case. I had to trust Mr. Mitchell, who was known to be a fair and fantastic businessman. I also learned this week that he and Alexander were best friends, and there would be no way that Alex would make Mr. Mitchell out to be the fool.

That knowledge was the only reason I hadn't thrown open the door to Mr. Grayson's office...yet. I was beginning to think the man lived in his office, or at least, that's where it seemed Alexander Grayson's personality was transformed from a trickster and into the devil.

Alexander took no prisoners. I only thought this way because I'd been informed that it wasn't just Stone Company that was dealing with the good and bad of the merge. Theo confirmed Brooks Architectural Firm was going through this dreadful process too.

I was patient only because I knew I had a huge heart—a heart that would allow the companies to merge without a single person being laid off. I may have been a stiff businesswoman when I needed to be, but to pick and choose who remained employed during a restructuring wasn't my thing. Now, though, it seemed like every single day, someone was on the chopping block. Would it ever end? My emails this morning—with three more employees from marketing given their severance packages—told me the devil in his suit hadn't put the pitchfork down just yet.

It was as if a disease had entered our building, and our employees were dropping like flies.

On the positive side, Alex left the design and engineering teams alone. For how long, though? Were our architects up next? At this point, I wouldn't be surprised if *my* ass was getting sacked.

Stop being dramatic, Bree. You already agreed on restructuring this division together.

I needed to calm down. I understood restructures, I understood mergers, and I needed to refocus. Alex had already informed me he would interview all employees and go through resumes and work accomplishments before making these cuts. Even so, this whole thing was becoming too much for me.

I needed to eat something, get my coffee, and, for the love of God, stop letting that damn email with the newly dismissed employees get under my skin.

Once I'd eaten, I started feeling better. The coffee added to my encouraged spirits, and the barista's jokes at the coffee shop were a perfect way to lighten my mood.

Then I walked in the damn front doors of my firm.

I should've chanted away the evil spirits, but alas, the sense of gloom wafted over me anyway. I sipped my coffee, looked up at the glass dome in the ceiling, watching the sun's light shining down in our central atrium. I looked around the light and airy space, smiled at our security and receptionists, all while understanding today was the day I would most likely meet face-to-face with Mr. Grayson. The expressions on the faces of employees rushing around to get into the elevators were enough to tell me that everyone felt the unease that I was feeling.

Instead of ignoring the tense nerves of the office, today, I absorbed them. The fact that everyone's eyes were intense as I walked into the drafting room let me know that this shit was interfering with our creative designers, and, of course, it was on the day I was scheduled to give my final pitch to Sphere. If we lost this deal, we might as well go under. I knew the numbers weren't looking good for this firm, and Sphere was the deal I needed to right this ship. Now, I had my entire drafting team looking at me as if they'd caught some zombie virus and were waiting to mutate into the living dead.

Damn it, I thought. I felt deflated and more concerned about my employees' feelings than pitching this deal to Sphere and paying the bills.

The devil on the third floor seemed to have possessed the team I was working with inside the drafting room, and as we studied the final 3D images for the Sphere pitch, I noted all of their eyes were filled with dread.

"That's it!" I finally said, unable to focus on the computer screen that showed me the building's blueprints. "I'm heading to Grayson's office. We won't get anywhere if everyone's in *this* mood. All of you can take a break until I get back. Get some fresh air and take some meditating breaths or something."

"We'll be here. Unless, of course..." my head architect and designer, Danny, said before he stopped himself.

"Stay in here and keep going over the finals. I need these drafts, and you're coming with me to pitch this to Sphere. So, if you think you can focus, Danny, then please do," I answered him. "Just—just keep this moving forward. We need to be packed up and out of here by noon to be early and make this deal with Sphere happen today."

Danny was an asshole, and he'd always stared down his nose at me on projects Dad had put us on together. I bet the jerk was livid to see me on the second floor again, heading up our teams. The guy and I never got along, but he was a kick-ass architect, and I hoped we'd build a better relationship by me allowing him to oversee this project. We still butted heads, but that didn't matter right now. We needed to focus on our final drafts and get ready to pitch our deal with Sphere.

"Danny, I need you to dive deep into this final mock-up we're doing. I'm still finding mistakes as if it were our first pass."

"It'll be finalized. You worry too much," he said in a dismissive tone.

"There's a difference between worrying and finding errors in a final project," I snapped.

"Go deal with whatever it is Grayson's doing to piss you off today."

You're an asshole, I thought, knowing that Danny not finding errors on this project was the main reason I hadn't even spoken with Alexander since he started making cuts. I was in this room, fixing this prick's mistakes.

Here we were with a deadline, and I needed to speak with Alexander since he moved in and turned into Ebenezer Scrooge— Satan style. Too bad it wasn't Christmas, so he could be paid a visit by three ghosts. I'm sure the third and final, grim reaper ghost could give him a run for his money.

"Bree," Theo said. His voice was grim when it came from out of nowhere. "We need to talk." My eyes were pulled away from Danny's indifferent expression and turned toward my right-hand man, Theo.

Shit. My heart sank after seeing Theo's grave expression. No need to wait for the holidays. I'd play the grim reaper spirit and strangle Grayson myself.

"Don't tell me," I said, tugging at his elbow and leading him out of the drafting room, "you got yourself a sweet little email from Mr. Grayson, and now you're here to tell me that you've been replaced?" I opted to take the stairs up to Grayson's floor instead of using the elevator.

"Breanne," Theo said, keeping up with me as I took the steps two at a time.

"Let me guess," I interrupted him, "since you *didn't* tell me about this, and you haven't talked to me all fucking week, you want me to take this all casually, right? Responsibly, right? Hell no. I'm done with Grayson, and I'm not losing you."

"You've been working on Sphere, and it's a long week. You know why we haven't had two seconds to talk."

"It's been a shitty week, to say the least, Theo." I looked at him as I approached the hall that led into the devil's den. "Stay here, and we'll talk when I'm finished dealing with this man."

"Bree, I wanted to talk to you before he did—"

That was all that my vice president had to say. Grayson was mine. It was time he learned he was privileged to sit in that office and allow me to trust him on this end of this business. Now he was taking out *Theo?*

I pushed open the cracked door to Alexander's office. A smiling and cheerful tiny blonde with soft red lips was the one to greet me. "Ms. Stone," she said, shifting files to her left arm, "I'm Jacey. It is such an honor to meet you finally."

"The pleasure is mine," I said, maintaining my composure to the kind woman. "Would you mind allowing me a moment for a private meeting with Mr. Grayson?"

"Absolutely." She nodded. "If he needs me, I'll be next door."

"Wonderful."

Jacey closed the door behind her as I stood there and studied the tall man before me. Alex was on his phone. He had a hand casually slipped into his pocket as he stood facing the windows that overlooked the streets below our building. I was lying when I said his view would be an alley, but I wished it was. No. He would do better in the basement. That way, he could be closer to hell where his true throne likely was.

"That's fine. Will the interns be placed on the Berkenshire after that?" he asked. "I want their fresh minds, just as I know you do. There's a reason Brooks Firm in London is out there."

I took a seat as I heard him casually laugh. The blazing heat was surging in my veins as anger pulsated through me. I needed this fire out, and the only way to make that happen was to handle the freak up here, handing everyone severance packages.

He ended the call and turned back to me. "Well, to what do I owe this honor of finally seeing my business partner?" he asked, sitting at his desk.

The once empty office had been transformed. It was immaculate with computer monitors and flat screens hanging on walls. He'd certainly brought in some high-tech stuff that made even me a tad bit envious.

"I thought you and I agreed that this would be a fair restructure, and you would be considering *everything* about where an employee's talents were served best in this merge, Mr. Grayson."

"We did. That's exactly what I've been keeping in mind while I've been handling the restructuring. Is this why you've finally decided to grace me with your presence?" He tried to appease me with his charms.

Not today, Satan!

"Replacing nearly everyone who worked for Stone is *not* my idea of meeting in the middle on this merge."

"I understand," he said. "However, when you dropped all of the business side of Stone in my lap, I took charge. You, my *darling*, have let quite a bit slip through the cracks. I'm not even sure Mr. Mitchell or Mr. Monroe know the full details of these financial reports I'm seeing."

"Why are you firing Theo? My VP was not good enough for you, I assume?" I snapped. "Is that Jacey woman your secretary? Is she serving him with his final—"

"Hold up," he said, his face darkening, and goddamn if it didn't make him look sexier. "Theo came to me, not the other way around."

"Excuse me? Theo is practically my brother, so that is an outright lie."

"I think you and I should probably take our lunch together today. We have quite a lot to discuss, and I'm honestly surprised it took you a solid week to enter this office to question my decisions."

"I've been busy, and I don't have time for lunch with you this afternoon. I have a ready proposal, and—"

"I'll be going with you," he interrupted. "Unless, of course, you'd trust me in your place on that job as well. Dare I say that me going alone with Danny, who is costing you that job, would not end well for him."

"I will be there. How would you know about Danny costing us anything? Danny has done well with Sphere, and the bid is perfect. It's the reason we'll nail this deal today."

"Interesting." He eyed a paper on his desk. "Papers, numbers, and facts on spreadsheets all overrule your opinions about Danny and his bid for Sphere."

"Opinions?" I nearly screeched. "If you must be there, we leave at noon. I'll eat lunch and discuss business further with you after I secure that deal. So, yes, come along. By all means, I'd love to have your business mind there. Perhaps you'll ax that deal along with Danny *in front of me* this time."

"As partner," he grinned that damn sexy smile again, "I *will* be coming along. Danny has a lot to explain in the mock-ups I've seen, and especially with a multi-million-dollar deal on the line for Stone."

"Now that we've settled that," I said, watching him study the computer and fidget with his fingers, "tell me what's happening with Theo."

"Theo has requested he speak with you about his future with Stone. I encouraged him to do so," he answered. "I know you've only experienced a night of me *roleplaying* and not being my authentic self to you at that gala. I appreciate you being concerned for Theo, given this has been a week of me making executive decisions. In all of what you're most likely hearing, I can see why you're here and wondering about Theo's future."

"The way you said his name just now," I said, "it's almost as though I'm witnessing Mr. Ass-Suit himself feel bad about all these cuts he's been making."

"I understand you are prematurely judging me; however, I haven't seen you up here once until Theo approached you."

He grew bold, and I sat more erect in the chair I took across his desk. "That's on me," I said. "I'm just sad I've learned my lesson this late in your heartless game."

"This is not a game," he answered. "I assure you of that."

"You're right. Games are to be left back with me, getting buzzed and acting like a fool."

His expression was unsettling. What the hell was going on, and why in the heck did I think I could pounce off in rebellion and leave my dad's company at the mercy of this man?

I wasn't handling this merge well at all. I was trying to bury myself by returning to the design room, but ignoring the hard work was more than reckless.

All I could hope now was that we landed Sphere, and it would be worth the negligence on my part. I turned to leave, knowing I needed to speak with Theo.

"I will admit..." Alex started, stopping me from leaving the room.

"Admit what, Mr. Grayson?"

His smooth and sexy voice pissed me off the more I thought about what Theo would tell me.

"I wasn't lying when I mentioned you'd be a fine partner for me that evening at the gala. We need to start working together more. It will all be fine in the end. Trust me on that."

"Good. Anything else?" I said, trying to keep it together.

"Now that you mention it, yes. I will also admit that you're much more beautiful in person than online or in magazines. Also, your ex is a fool for letting you go."

I narrowed my eyes at his playful tone, knowing I was on my way to find out why Theo was most likely getting axed by this man.

"Thank God you're handsome," I managed to return. "I think, because of that, I'll never have to worry about my idiot of an ex ever again."

"Indeed, fine looks and a dapper man was all you needed to rid yourself of that lunatic."

"Dapper man?" I stared at him. "Interesting. I think even Satan's real name was Lucifer, right?"

"I believe that is correct, Ms. Stone. How this analogy has anything..."

He paused when I arched an eyebrow at him. "Lucifer was

beautiful, possibly even *dapper*, all while being evil as well. You're nothing more than a devil in a suit to me, Mr. Grayson."

He chuckled. "Well, then, at least you've formed some manner of opinion about me. Now, you and I can get to work, merging these companies as the devil and his mistress."

I rolled my eyes. "Way to spin that into something that makes absolutely no sense at all."

"Well, we are life-long partners, and you've associated me—your partner—as the devil. That makes you my lovely mistress."

"We have more pressing issues than this nonsense of referring to each other as diabolical entities."

"We do. Might I point out that *I* wasn't the one to bring up the analogy of evil creatures and being associated with them; you were."

"Then perhaps you should quit acting like an evil asshole, and those comparisons wouldn't enter my mind," I said. "I have to go. I need to speak with Theo and make preparations to meet with Sphere today."

"Fantastic idea. We have quite a busy day ahead of us. I'll have the car ready and waiting when we're set to leave and meet with Sphere."

I wanted to get out of here. Alexander Grayson was flirty, tricky, and I wasn't about to get caught up in his handsome features as he used my lame references against me. What I'd seemed to fail to get across was that it felt like our firm had been possessed by some evil entity, bringing about the gloomy atmosphere all around us.

I had to speak with Theo. I needed to regroup, get my head straight, and move forward. Alexander was probably right; I needed more time with him to form a better opinion of him. I certainly didn't want to continue to see him as a beautiful man who was nothing short of evil while he made cuts, handed out severances, and made life-changing decisions for both firms' employees.

I had to get to know him and understand how the man ran a business on top of adding my opinions about who we laid off in this merge. I would take full responsibility for avoiding this part, knowing I might have been able to save jobs if I'd stayed at this man's side while he made the hard decisions. I was blaming it all on him as if I weren't supposed to be helping make all the cuts.

After I left Alexander's office, I couldn't shake the way he mentioned Theo's name. That was what stuck with me. He was sincere, and I saw that in his eyes. I was too busy throwing insults around instead of appreciating that this man may have had a heart after all.

CHAPTER THREE
BREE

As soon as I walked out of Alex's office and Theo's phone went to voicemail, I was abruptly pulled aside by one of my architect designers on Sphere. Shelly insisted on talking to me, but I held a finger up when my phone rang in from Theo, and I answered the call.

"Hey, are you in your office? I just spoke with Mr. Grayson, and he's tightlipped about *your future* with Stone Company. We need to talk about what's going on and what he said to you."

"In my office, but you need to talk to Shelly. She's looking for you," Theo responded.

"She's right here, and I will, but I need to talk to you first, Theo."

"Our conversation must wait," he said. "Sphere just called *me*, and they're pushing up the meeting to noon."

"Why wouldn't they have called me?" I answered in confusion.

"No idea. Something's up. Are you taking Mr. Grayson with you to meet with them? You all need to leave right now if you want to make the noon appointment."

"Noon? You're right. Something isn't sitting well with me about them calling you to move up our meeting." I rubbed my forehead. "Alex and Danny are going to be there with me. About our conversation, that's on hold for the time being. Can we talk at lunch or something?"

"Yes, and don't you dare worry about me for a second. My situation isn't as urgent as saving this deal. You need to focus on Sphere. Get your eyes on whatever they must've seen on those mock-ups. Some errors must've slipped past you."

"What? Nothing *slips past* me."

"I know. So, make sure it's clean and ready to go for the meeting," Theo said.

"Got it. I'll call you when we're done."

"Good luck. You got this, Bree."

"Thanks."

I felt like I walked out of Alex's office, and a tornado ripped me out of the hallway and threw me into the middle of chaos.

"Shell," I looked at my designer, "send me over everything. Is Danny bringing the—"

"I've got everything we need. Thank you anyway, Shelly," Alex said as he approached, calm and assertive. "You ready to do this? We need to leave."

"I know. I need to get to my office, grab my stuff, and I'll meet you out front. Can you call an Uber for me? I need to—"

"I've got it all taken care of," Alex said as I looked up at the man who towered over me in heels.

I held onto his smooth vibes. This guy was calm, cool, and collected amid a brewing storm. Then again, he wasn't likely losing his vice president or, from what Shelly's expression told me, a multi-million-dollar deal due to errors *I* apparently missed in our final mock-up.

After grabbing my briefcase, I left my office and moved through the building with a steady foot, ready to head out.

I wasn't going to freak out that we were possibly going to lose this deal, or about the errors on our final project that were missed, the reason Sphere moved our appointment up, or, most importantly, the fact that it felt like everything was falling apart all at once. Theo and I would work things out later. Now, it was time for me to focus on *keeping* this deal no matter what I did. I was known for fixing last-minute errors, and for all I knew, Shelly was overreacting. The vibes in the office these days made it seem like everything was going to hell, so it was my job to rise above and handle business.

When I walked out of the front doors and turned to the parking structure, I spotted Alex first. He stood in conversation with a man who appeared to be the driver of the fancy Rolls Royce parked outside the parking garage.

I didn't have time to argue that this wasn't the particular Uber I would have expected, but who cared? It was transportation. I had to sit down, go through these mock-ups, and, hopefully, fix errors during the drive to our appointment.

Alex turned to me, easily matching the beauty and stateliness of the Rolls, and before I could sit in the car, Alex moved to where the chauffeur had greeted me and offered his hand to help me into the back seat of the vehicle.

I stopped and turned back when I heard Danny approaching from behind us, whistling like some high school guy who was checking out a hot chick.

"Sorry I'm late. What the fuck with this badass car?" He smiled and clapped Alex on his arm. "It's pretty damn good to have you around, Mr. Grayson."

"I know," Alex answered as he looked at Danny over the silver rims of his Ray-Bans. "We'll see you there. You're in the car behind us." He nodded toward a microcar car parked behind the blacked-out Rolls Royce, and I wondered how the driver could sit inside it without getting leg cramps. "We're running late." Alex grinned at Danny, whose cheeks were red with anger, as Danny squared up to him. "Is there a problem?"

"Yeah, there's a fucking problem," Danny said, trying to size up Alex, who was at least three inches taller than the six-foot man. "I'm not riding in that tiny-ass car. I'll sit in the front seat of the Rolls."

"Bummer for you," Alex dismissed the confrontational tone with a sigh. "Because you're not riding in the car with Ms. Stone and me. Breanne and I have quite a bit of business to go over with our pitch to Sphere before we arrive at this meeting."

"This is bullshit." Danny looked at me.

"Just get in the other car, Danny," I said, looking at the guy acting like an overgrown toddler, throwing a fit. I'd trusted Danny with this project, and he dropped the ball at the last hour on me, and now he was looking at me for help? I don't think so. "And by the way, I just want to thank you for not catching errors in our final project. This should be *super* easy to fix in a damn car on the way to our appointment. This is our *last and only* chance to nail down this deal."

I was furious that this man was more worried about the car he was driving in than the fact that we had errors in our presentation.

"I'm sorry I didn't get the finals over to you until today." He exhaled, annoyed.

"*Sorry* doesn't pay the bills," I said as I slid into the backseat of the Rolls.

"I couldn't have said it better," Alex said. "We'll see you at the site. I would suggest taking the car I called for you. We're already pressed for time and now having to fix last-minute errors, thanks to you..." Alex paused while taking blueprints that were shoved into his chest by Danny.

"I'll take my car, thanks."

"Good luck finding parking in Malibu during lunch hours. If you don't make the meeting, I will make sure it will be the last one you miss."

"Are you threatening to fire me?" Danny snapped.

"After learning *you* moved up the appointment with our clients, and now, Ms. Stone is the one having to fix *your* errors—possibly resulting in losing this deal altogether—what would you suggest I do?" Alex asked as I was logging into my account to pull up the drawings. "You're coming with us, and *you will* sell this client."

"Wait, *what* did you just say?" I seethed from the backseat, watching their exchange. "What did you do, Danny?"

"Danny has plenty of time to think about what he did in his own car." Alex sat in the car next to me. "We need your pretty little eyes on this project and making it shine before we get to our clients."

I watched as Danny stomped to the little car behind us and crawled inside, and then our car took off, the microcar following behind.

"What did he do that I don't know about?" I asked Alex.

"It's nothing that won't be handled *after* we fix errors and save our client." Alex nodded toward my laptop and iPad. "We need your eyes on those building designs. I can't pitch this and make it work without you fixing the errors and making last-minute enhancements. I've researched your talents, so it's time to turn water into wine, Ms. Stone," he said with a grin before continuing. "The team on this project found errors. While I may be a genius with spreadsheets and such, I will admit that I'm not an AutoCAD person. I need you to translate to me what we're looking at and how I'm to pitch it to Sphere."

"Shit," I said, rubbing my forehead.

He glanced over his sunglasses that defined the sharp features of his face. "Take a breath. Do what you do best. Let's fix the issues and get ready to land a multi-million-dollar deal, Breanne," he offered with a smile that comforted my frazzled nerves.

"Got it," I said, then I intently focused in silence as the car moved toward the traffic on the freeway.

Oh, my God.

"What the hell? Is this a last-minute addition? We didn't go over this in the original plans," I whispered as if I were the only one in the car. "No." I slid to the next diagram. "How did he slip this in under my nose? Oh, my God." The car was quiet and barely moving, still jammed-up while I was finding critical errors that Danny had snuck in. "Of all the people who should've been given a severance package." I chewed on the corner of my cheek. "That son of a bitch cut corners. His cut sheet is filled with cheap shit. Fuck!" I said, my eyes wide in disbelief at how my beautiful vision had been destroyed overnight and by the jerk driving in the micro-car behind us.

"Okay, the suspense is killing me," Alex smoothly cut in. "What have you found? I need to know what we're dealing with here. Do I need to call in the top architects from Brooks to look at this? We may need their eyes if the fixes are that difficult."

"Let me think." I kept looking at the unjustifiable inaccuracies that had me sick to my stomach. "I can't believe I trusted Danny to supervise my vision and ensure this…" I paused in disbelief. "All of the sketches that I stayed up until two or three in the morning drawing up —I can't believe this. My work had to be translated into our programs to make this vision come to life, and now, it's as if Danny didn't use my sketches or design maps at all," I said, pissed and intently studying the shortcuts and flaws. Why weren't these discoverable until now? There's no way I missed this shit. I looked over at Alex's concerned expression. "We can't pitch this project. I can't show these building designs to them. We have to cancel this meeting. Holy Shit. This is a goddamn joke."

This was a huge blow, and I was crushed that Danny had the audacity to destroy this project. Was it done intentionally? Shit, I knew he was an asshole, but I couldn't imagine him wanting to sabotage the *one thing* that would put our company in a good financial place. I was baffled at how Danny took such a detailed and beautiful vision and ruined it by being cheap, sneaky, and sabotaging this entire project with errors.

"We're not canceling the meeting with Sphere," Alex said. "From what I've learned about you, you're not a woman who quits, either. There are plenty of articles out there, proving that you are indeed a woman who overcomes obstacles, not a woman who is defined by them."

"You think I can overcome *this* disaster in the next hour or so? It's like he deliberately sabotaged this."

Alex casually leaned his arm on the armrest that separated where we sat as I zoomed in on the pillars that would've been disastrous with the way Danny *redesigned* what I sent him months ago.

"You can and will overcome it," Alex said. "However, I do need to know and understand what you're seeing. Give me something, Breanne. I've seen where your bid is at least three million under what should've originally been pitched. With the numbers alone, this is going to put the firm under. When it is all said and done, you'll be paying *them* to build this. I have seen that no one else has been able to match your bid, and it's in the bag, yes?"

"Yes. You're right about all of that." I looked over at Alex. "And the deal is *in the bag* because we're going under by shorting ourselves on the bid. Why am I *just now* seeing this? You and I both know that there's no fixing this without convincing them to give us at least four million more, and that's *after* I tell them we fucked up the designs. That's not even hiring the contractors, purchasing the *correct* materials, drafting new bids with real estate. I can go on and on."

"I can handle the negotiations of all of that," Alex said, his voice relaxed. "Nevertheless, I need to know exactly what I'm negotiating now that you've noticed the errors." I could tell he was making an effort not to escalate my panic. "Breanne, I understand that you're frustrated, but if I'm going to nail this down, I need you to show me the flaws that you see through your design programs. What is going through the designer's mind?"

I rested my head against the seat. "What is going through my mind right now?"

"Yes," he answered.

"Titanic."

"Titanic? As in that's how monumental you see this mistake is?"

"No, the ship that sank. You're a numbers man, correct?"

"Yes," he said in a curious voice. "I'm now struggling to figure out if we're building a ship and heading to a shipyard?" He chuckled.

"Do you find this funny, Mr. Grayson?"

"I find the creative mind intriguing, and now, you have my full attention. Please explain why you've questioned me being a numbers man while bringing up the Titanic. I must know what *that* has to do with a superlative ocean liner."

"Well, that's what this entire project and everything in my vision will turn out to be if it's built," I said. "There's no last-minute fix to these flaws in the design. It will look grand and beautiful yet flawed and built so damn cheap that it won't ever be what it was intended to be. So, this reminds me of Titanic, of all the things I could compare it to. Titanic sank for the same reasons."

Alex readjusted himself, his long legs seeking comfort in the back seat of the car. "I find your mind to be as brilliant as it is somewhat wild, but I'm struggling to follow. Am I to believe that you're expecting us to land this deal and build this magnificent building, then after it has been built, it will take the lives of those who spend time there?"

"So, back to numbers," I said with a sigh. "I'm sorry, my mind is all over the place."

"Talk it out. We're stuck in traffic, and I'm quite interested in how you're tying this to a ship sinking in 1912."

"Okay," I said. "The Titanic was the most glorious ship, and first of its kind, in the year it was designed and engineered. It was fashioned to captivate the world with its size, grandeur, and its speed. And it did captivate the world."

"With its sinking, of course. It still does captivate most, and I see that it seems to have *you* especially captivated."

"Back to numbers," I went on. "With a crew of nine hundred people, the Titanic's capacity was brought to more than two thousand souls on board; some say three thousand. Yet more than fifteen hundred people lost their lives in that disaster."

"And from what I recall, it was deemed the unsinkable ship."

"Correct." He was humoring me, but I had a point. "They were careless and too confident, so they didn't allow for a proper number of lifeboats to satisfy saving all lives on that ship should it come into trouble."

"And now there are laws in place due to that."

"My point is that they were rushed. All of them," I said, knowing this was what was happening with my company and this bid. "From what I learned growing up, the ship sank because the architects and the company were in fierce competition with others...they rushed everything. They took short cuts; they were faulty in their designs. On the outside and the inside, that ship would've never felt like it could sink. But it could. In fact, if it wasn't rushed, or if cheap parts hadn't been used in critical areas, that ship would have been able to limp back to—" I was going into too much detail. "Bottom line. It was rushed and pretty much staged to appear to be unsinkable. How could anyone have known the owner of White Star Line at the time was rushing all of it? Because of that, the Titanic was doomed before passengers ever boarded it. This project is following the same pattern." I looked at him and shrugged. "We can't pitch this. It may look as beautiful as Titanic did, but the engineering shortcuts and cheap materials will force Sphere to shut down their new hotel chain for safety reasons alone. The glass walls? They won't stand safely in their frames with weight on them like this. They may last for a good six or seven months, but they could easily explode under pressure." Alex had the most curious look on his face, but there was something else behind it. He probably thought I was a nutcase. "That's just one wall in a dining area. I'm not even pointing out all of the other intricate details I designed to help their patrons feel as though they were in a hotel that was virtually on the sea. The illusions are still designed well, but they're more deadly than anything now. This is a hazard zone, and the building, though beautiful, should be condemned if it's ever built in this manner."

"All right. I think I may be following you some now," Alex responded. "So, this project is doomed before we even start it? You might feel that way, but we can make modifications so long as you're finding mistakes. I'm not letting this go. I'm not letting Danny, the lead architect, off that easy."

I felt tears stinging my eyes, and it wasn't due to my lifelong obsession with why such a unique, state-of-the-art ship sank either. "We have to reject this Sphere project, Alex," I said.

"Hold up." Alex draped an arm over the seat behind me and looked at the models I was flipping through. "I admit I love the creative mind and listening to the way you see the world and designs. It's intriguing to see things in a way I have never perceived them before."

"We're doing the same thing they did with that ship. Danny led us all to believe it was coming together, but we rushed it." I handed him the iPad and closed my eyes. "Danny was in charge of this. He was cheap on the bid and materials. It's not designed to be constructed well." I stopped babbling and shook my head. "The bathrooms are even hazards."

"Well, shit. *That's* a damn problem." He winked at me and took the iPad. "Let me see this."

"I should have never trusted him. He always hated me when I was head architect, and my dad ran the business side of things."

"Well, that's what Brooks' engineers will help fix, and, of course, the permits and inspections in California will never allow a building of subpar work to be erected." I watched as he studied the raw numbers instead of the images. He glanced at me and flashed a smile. "They also would never allow us to pass inspections that would lead to the untimely demise of hotel occupants. Especially while using the bathroom."

"I'm serious," I said, somewhat smiling at him, lightening the mood.

"Hey, I am too. Especially if this hotel is going down as if it were the great tragedy of losing the Titanic." He grinned. "I hope you can loosen up a little and understand that we will make the revisions that are needed. It's not all lost. This won't be a repeat of the year 1912. I promise you that."

"Funny." I rolled my eyes. "I wouldn't even know where to start fixing this. We're coming in with a bid that is undercutting everyone. We *will get the deal* and then end up delivering subpar work and cheap materials. I won't allow my dad's company to put its name on that, and I won't allow the late John Brooks to have his company's name put on this either."

"That's why you have me as your partner because I'll ensure that won't happen."

"So, you'll walk away from this multi-million-dollar deal?"

"No," he answered resolutely. "I'll inform Sphere that we have their best interest in mind and that we have noted that such a highly acclaimed company would want nothing but the best for their newest hotel chain. Then, if I feel like we're losing them, I'll bring up the Titanic sinking. I'll have the number of the lost souls, and after I relate their hotel's future to that, they'll be writing us another check and keeping our design."

"Really?" I said dryly as I eyed his handsome and dazzling smile. "Do you even comprehend why I even brought the Titanic into this?"

"Not really, but I will accept you've seen the comparison. I'm not questioning your upset with this—well, perhaps I'm humoring you a little bit."

"I don't need humoring, Mr. Grayson," I said. "I need you to understand that we're acting like desperate fools. We're rushing the finish date. We're delivering on a project that will fall apart within a year. It's a joke."

"Well, I did notice that you were utilizing cheap materials for an extremely luxurious company and nothing that would compare to the models I've seen once it was built. I read through the multiple bids that were pitched aside from yours and noted that Stone was well under the three million it's *worth* to see this particular vision come to life."

"Well, I've noted it's all dog shit. It's a disaster, and I think I hate Danny for being a prick and even considering short cuts, cheap materials, and rushed dates of completion. We don't deserve their business if we believe we're worth nothing more than cheap bids to get them, or anyone else for that matter."

"Well, you're certainly thinking along the same lines as I am. It only took a dipshit screwing up to help you realize I'm not the devil in a suit." He smirked at me. "We will meet with Sphere, and we will ensure Danny will explain why he did a subpar mock-up to our clients."

"I don't want him there," I spoke. "I'll face this myself. Good, bad, and ugly."

"Speaking of cheap and shortcuts. I believe you're taking your own."

"What is that supposed to mean?"

"Well, first of all, you're letting Danny off easy by facing this alone. Make that asshole face the people he tried to fuck over. Fire his ass and quit taking the shortcuts. It's business, Breanne. It's not personal.

You have to make this man accountable for costing this firm time, energy, money, and possibly our reputation."

"I just want this over with."

"Then let's fix this shit and go over the flaws you're finding together while we still have time. I need to make a few phone calls to some contractors while you point out the errors as I speak to them on the phone. When we meet with Sphere, I'll inflate the bids to give us some room for error and possibly earn back money already lost. Your job is to sell *your* creation and vision. Then, if you nail this down," he smiled at me, "I'll gladly fire that asshole myself for making you give me a history lesson on the Titanic's demise."

I grinned. "Probably dumb, but the point was there. That ship sank for the same reasons that I have no faith in this horribly planned-out model."

"The project is rushed, we're in a competitive market, and using subpar materials, yes? Titanic all over again," he said with a silly and fun expression.

I grinned. "So funny how you can sum that up so quickly." I leaned my elbow on the window. "I can't think or easily explain things like that sometimes. Actually, it takes someone telling me to *get to the point* when I talk out my thoughts."

"You're painting an image." He smiled, looking ahead. "And to get some people to visualize what your artistic mind sees, I would imagine that, occasionally, it takes some elaborating on the matter. It's also helped keep my mind off traffic." He softly laughed.

"So, what are you visualizing after this crazy revelation, and me, trying to relate it to the Titanic's flaws?"

"That if I were a man on that ship, I'd be pretty pissed off that I was dying because some asshole like Danny took a short cut. And then, when it was too late, and I found that ship had flaws after I was told wouldn't sink," he looked at me with a raised eyebrow, "frankly, it would just suck. The worst of it all would be if I had a beauty on my arm, such as *you*, and I had to put you into the lifeboat, never to see you again. Hell, now that this has all been brought up, I'd be fucking livid at the designers of that ship."

I shook my head. "You question what goes on in my mind, and yet I do wonder what goes on in yours."

"Numbers, of course." He winked. "That and the fact that we need to handle this error, fire the asshole who made it happen, and then to enjoy that I get to watch you bring it together and win Sphere over today. More than all of that, I believe you're due for a solid and resounding compliment and a win. When they accept our amendments and new bid, which they will, you and I will celebrate over dinner tonight. You still owe me for that night when I assisted you in running off your ex."

"I already have a date with Theo. He's coming over, and we'll be talking about what the hell is going on with him too." I arched an eyebrow at Alex. "God, I can't think about Theo right now."

Alex nodded. "One thing at a time," he said with a slight grin. "Then, dinner tomorrow night? You and me to celebrate you winning this bid."

"Wow." I laughed. "You're that confident about all of this? That we'll get this deal after putting them in a position to think we lied to them?"

"Of course, I am."

"Well, at least one of us is. I feel like I'm going to barf. This is like bringing in a project only to watch the model fall apart when you touch it."

"How about this? Let's leave the Titanic analogy out altogether, and we'll be on point. In fact, bring *that* analogy up to Danny after he asks why the asshole in a suit fired him. You can also let him know I got the last lifeboat because we needed my muscles for rowing, and he was a worthless and self-centered man who tried to steal a seat from a lady."

"In other words, you'll fire him, and I'll explain our reasons as—"

"He sunk your luxurious ship, of course. I have to admit, in watching you speak and study the errors in that project, I don't believe I ever wish to see you this upset over your vision being destroyed by an ass that you trusted again. That's straight-up, fucking bullshit."

"I'm shocked you're not firing both of us."

"See, I'm not the devil after all, am I?"

"No, but you're not to be trusted, either."

"That I can agree with you on, Ms. Stone." He grinned. "Perhaps at a later date, you'll learn you can trust me. I would hope my undivided attention during history class today would be good enough to gain your trust after I deceived you at the gala. I certainly did not think I'd wake up this morning, go out to this project, and become educated on the Titanic as it relates to signing papers on a multi-million-dollar deal."

"God, stop." I smiled. "You sound like my dad. Funny story about me? I always brought up that ship when I saw design flaws in any of our projects." I laughed at how I drove Dad insane with my obsession with that ship.

"Why is that? Are you a woman who loves ships?"

"I just think of it because it sank due to greed."

"That's a conspiracy, you know?"

"That's my take on it, and I'm sticking to it." I grinned. "And yes, I love taking cruises and being out at sea."

"I'll take note of that."

It was the way he said that last part that made me stare at him as if he'd build a ship and let me set sail. I couldn't figure this guy out, but I liked that he was a fun, mysterious, and—from what I'd experienced thus far—a kind but firm businessman. He could have ripped into me for not overseeing this project better, but instead, he offered help. He listened to me, crazy assumptions or not. He actually heard and added some input.

Perhaps we'd work well as partners. In the drive down here, he'd humored my creative mind, and he also found a way through my confusing analogies, something that I used to bore my dad to sleep with at night. Now, time would tell if we could truly work as partners with our talents and save this deal.

CHAPTER FOUR
ALEX

*M*y phone was blowing up with details about this project, but I ignored the incoming calls. Instead, I got my construction engineer, Adam, on the phone and started relaying information to him as Breanne walked me through the different aspects of this project. I'd worked with the man on various projects after Brooks Architectural Firm became my responsibility. He was a master of his trade, and he would put this shit together as fast as I spouted off numbers to him.

I had no time to think, just to give information as I watched Breanne work magic with her adjustments to the joke of a project Danny had messed up on every level.

If I hadn't had a taste of the woman's fiery side, her vulnerable side, and learned about her true passion for designing, I would have called in for the head architects at Brooks to salvage this chaos.

Before taking ownership of Brooks Architectural Firm, acquiring businesses for Mitchell and Associates was my expertise. I lived and breathed to land million-dollar projects like it was nothing. It was all second nature to me. Never once, though, had I been put in a situation where it seemed my company had lied to entice a client. This was an entirely different level of *dirty business*, and it was why I had to have

Breanne in the car with me. I had to see her reactions to what I'd learned an hour before Sphere unexpectedly moved up our appointment.

My conclusion? She had nothing to do with this shady shit. I felt for the woman, but I wasn't going to let her cave under pressure. Breanne Stone was known for her creative skills, and she'd helped Stone Company make a solid name under her father's guidance. Sadly, she sat in the business department for too long, and now, we had an underhanded snake trying to destroy both businesses' reputations as they were merging.

Hell no. Not on my watch. No way would I allow anything to go sideways on this. This shit didn't fly with me, nor was it excused. Danny was about to wish he could travel back in time to undo the shitshow he'd orchestrated.

The bottom line was that I wasn't losing this client. Even though I witnessed my business partner, Breanne, deflated, I could also see that something had come alive in her just now. Once she got past her wild idea of comparing this to a 1912 disaster for a ship, she refocused, and I watched magic move through her fingertips as she started to create an even better blueprint of this hotel.

It was intriguing to watch her design, and what she was tweaking and creating was badass.

This three-story hotel would be built on the oceanfront, spanning for at least a block, and then it would follow regulations to allow for a private, exclusive pier.

This was something you'd find in some tropical resort location, not Malibu Beach. Honestly, I was shocked this had made it past city regulations, but it was easy to see it would bring fantastic revenue to the city and increase home values.

This would be the first of its kind if we could manage to keep this deal. If not, I'd find a way to salvage Breanne's project, and we'd move this innovative design to a location in another state or some tropical area.

I was never one to leave a good deal sitting on the table, though. We would salvage this with Breanne's work and my sales pitches.

They'd be fools to walk away, even with our bid increase, and I would ensure they recognized that.

My phone kept blowing up, and Breanne's phone started in next.

"Mr. Nazari," I answered a call from one of the business owners of Sphere. "We're almost to your site, and—"

"Mr. Grayson," he interrupted me in a pissed off tone. "The deal is off. We just spoke with Danny, the man who is in charge."

"Excuse me? Danny is merely a contracted architect. He's hardly in charge, sir," I said while Breanne's face was black with anger after she ended her phone call.

"Then that is yet another lie that your company has communicated to us, Mr. Grayson."

"Another lie?" My voice became firm. "Allow me to explain something, Mr. Nazari," I said, hoping I'd keep this upset client on the phone. "We understand your grievance with Danny, and God only knows what else that man has said to you. Allow me a chance to rectify all of this. I assure you that you will not only approve of our alterations to your astounding project, but you will also accept our deepest apologies for any issues that may have forced you to believe that we have *lied* to you." I rolled my eyes at the garbage coming out of my mouth.

Lied to them? What the fuck did that asshole do?

"What do you plan on doing to help restore our faith in your company?"

"I'm changing the meeting location." I instantly went into another gear—time to bust ass, think, and save this shit. "We'll be meeting at Esprit in Marina del Rey. I'll send for a driver to pick up you and your team so we can meet. Suppose you are not impressed with us after we've clarified things and made accommodations to express our apologies for your inconveniences. In that case, I will arrange for Mitchell and Associates' luxury jet to fly you home."

"We have our own private jet."

Not like ours, chump, but okay.

"Very well, then. Allow me to gain your trust by insisting that we buy your property site in good faith that we *will* deliver on our designs."

"We're not selling our beachfront property. We will be moving forward with another architectural firm."

"Is this other firm willing to purchase that property and then sign the deed over to you?"

Breanne looked at me as if I were more insane than comparing this to the Titanic. I smiled to reassure her I knew what I was doing to salvage this part of the deal.

"I'm sorry, but did you say you would sign over the deed?"

"Paid in full. All yours. Now, you're just fronting the investment and capital on our project to give you the grandest hotel on the Malibu shoreline."

"So, you're willing to front the money for our property?"

"Correct. Paid in full, as I just stated."

Silence on the line made me glance at Breanne's panicked expression.

"We'll wait for your driver," he finally came back. "We are pressed for time, Mr. Grayson."

"Is there another arrangement or business dealing you are required to be at, or can I make this right by providing at least two days of relaxation after we agree on this project?"

Silence again. I needed these guys to myself until this was a signed deal. Just the mention of his interest in another firm told me I couldn't let him jet-set off to meet with someone else.

"What the hell are you doing? It's over. Danny's going home," Breanne whispered.

"*The fuck he is*," I mouthed as I winked to help settle her down.

I put the call on speakerphone. It was time to find out the name of the Uber driver for the chickenshit who'd fucked us in the ass and bounced.

"Give us a moment," Mr. Nazari said.

"Take your time," I answered while taking down the license plate of the Uber behind us.

While our friends, who currently hated us, deliberated on the other end of the phone, I began doing a data lookup on the Uber driver behind us.

This Danny character was about to see a different side of me— Breanne was about to see a different side of me too.

The poor woman would probably never come to a healthy assessment of who I really was, and maybe that was for the best. I was her partner, and she needed to understand I knew how to run global empires and business deals…shit like that.

I wasn't just a *devil in a suit*. I was a bastard in a suit.

For that reason alone, I handled business dealings as if I were playing cards with kids. It was second nature to me. We would get this deal, and the price of the property I just agreed to purchase would be inflated and placed in the final bid. First, it was time I used my methods of persuasion to finesse Sphere with words, money, lavish lifestyles, and the temptations that I knew greedy elites loved. They wouldn't be going anywhere when I was finished with them.

Even Jim would be outraged that we were losing this company. There was a lot on the table with them in future dealings. Mitchell and Associates were waiting patiently to invest in Sphere, and the new vice president, Spencer Monroe, was also awaiting my call to inform him that we'd sealed this first deal, and Mitchell had the green light to invest.

We wanted more from Sphere on the architectural side, and Mitchell wanted in on their holdings, shares, and the potential of new money coming to Southern California.

Sphere wasn't going anywhere so long as I was on the phone with them. I would charm them, and they would be the happiest sons of bitches on the planet when they signed on the dotted fucking line.

"There will be five of us," Nazari said when he finally came back on the line. "How many days of apology do you plan on giving us to relax?"

"As long as you desire. If you have significant others, bring them along too."

"Don't get too far ahead of yourself. We'll await the driver. This better be worth our time, Mr. Grayson."

"I assure you it will be. Where am I to send the driver to pick you up?"

After I worked out the details of picking up the five brothers from Sphere's headquarters in Laguna Beach, I dialed the number I'd found for the Uber that was no longer following us.

"Henry, change of plans. Take us to Esprit, please," I said to my driver.

"Sure thing, Mr. Grayson. We'll be there in about an hour. We have to reroute—"

"Doesn't matter," I interjected. "I need that time to pull some things together anyway."

"What the hell is going on?" Breanne asked with a growl I never imagined her to have in her voice.

I held a finger up when Sam, Danny's Uber transport, answered. "Sam?"

"Yes, who's this?"

"Mr. Grayson, the superior of the man you're currently driving."

"Oh, yes," he answered. "Would you like to speak with him?"

"I'd rather not," I said. "I'd like to let you know that we lost you driving behind us, and your passenger is unaware of our new destination." I inhaled. "Listen, it's the poor man's birthday, and we've got a surprise for him. So, whatever or wherever he's told you to take him, go ahead and cancel that. We'll be at Esprit in Marina del Rey awaiting you. I'll ensure your tip is healthy for the last-minute change of plans."

"Not a problem, sir. So, not a word?"

"Not a word. I'm sure he won't even ask, but if he does, inform him that Mr. Grayson has quite the surprise for him. If he becomes obnoxious, please call me back, and then I will speak with him."

"He's staring at a computer and a phone, sir." The driver's voice lowered.

"Good, he won't have a clue, then. Thank you and see you there."

I hung up and opened my texts. "Can you keep Danny on the phone and busy? He's not getting out of this as easily as he thinks," I said to Breanne.

"Yes, but I have no idea what the heck is going on."

"We're salvaging what Danny did after he called Sphere and chased them off for one reason or another," I said. "Just keep him busy with emails or texts. I need his eyes off the road. Fight with him or something." I grinned at her.

I needed to text Jake, one of my best friends, to get this ball rolling and fast.

Alex: *I need a favor, Jakey. What company did you use to print that name on your yacht?*

Come on, Jake. Fuck.

I was texting him during work hours, and since he was a cardiovascular doctor, that meant he could be in surgery, with a patient, or busy as hell.

Thank God, I thought when the three dots popped up on my phone.

Jake: *I can't remember. I have them in my contacts. Why do you need their number?*

Alex: *Business. Send it over to me*

JAKE FORWARDED the number to me, and I dialed out. Time to name a fucking yacht I hadn't seen since Jim and I bought the thing, and it arrived last week. Jim said it was great when he and Avery took it out for the weekend, but they didn't bother to name it. So, here I was, and naming a four-hundred-foot superyacht wasn't something I would typically do—I wasn't that freaking creative.

"This is Falcon," a woman said.

"Falcon," I answered. "You come highly recommended by Dr. Jacob Mitchell. He's a good friend of mine, and I need your talents. Can you be in Marina del Rey in five minutes to get a name on a yacht?"

"I'm out here printing a yacht name now. What slip?"

"The one I need you on is too large for a slip. Can you reach the A location? There will be an individual in a small boat who will bring you to my yacht. You can name the price, and I'll have you covered before I arrive. I need this done and finished in thirty minutes."

"Fuckin' executives," I heard her sigh.

"Are you willing to do the job or not? I won't listen to your insults if I'm letting you name whatever price you wish."

"Sorry. Fine. One thousand dollars, and I'll have it done in thirty."

"The man in the boat will cover your *generous* deal. Thank you."

I hung up with Falcon and heard Breanne going off on Danny over the phone. I was handling a lot of business and fast, so I was grateful they were both busy. Now, it was time to call the main man.

"Jim," I said when the CEO of Mitchell and Associates—and my best friend—answered my call.

"I heard we're losing Sphere," he said, unamused.

"Unless you hear it from me, don't believe it. I'd suggest you stay away from the gossip that's coming from Stone Company."

Jim laughed. "What's up, and how are you salvaging it?"

"Since you're somehow up to speed, I need you to call in our catering team—the one that we used for conducting business on Jake's yacht."

"What are you doing? I thought you were—"

"Can you please have your secretary handle this for me? I'm saving a goddamn project for you, so your VP, Monroe, won't have an aneurysm if we lose Sphere altogether."

"What happened?" Jim asked.

"I'll tell you later tonight. Now, I need shit pulled together fast. I need that yacht up and running as if we'd planned for a week trip on the coast. Can we make that happen?"

"I'm on it," Jim said. "Alex, don't fuck us over."

"Have I ever?"

"No," Jim chuckled. "I'll handle all of it."

"Thanks. Oh, call the marina as well. I have Jake's yacht lady who needs to be picked up. I'm naming the damn boat."

"What?" Jim laughed.

"Hope you and Avery like it."

"You better hope Addy likes it. She thinks it is her boat."

"Let's hope the client likes it. It ran well, though, right?"

"Avery and I couldn't have been more impressed."

"Great. Talk to you later."

DING!

My phone alerted a new text just when I thought all was settled and I could finally talk to Breanne. I wanted to try and catch her up with the whirlwind of changed events, major ass-kissing in our future, and Danny being my only target for all of this as I worked to save this deal.

I checked the phone.

Falcon: *I need the name for this badass boat.*

I SMILED at her changed tone and swiftly accepted my phone's prompt to add her name to my contacts. Funny how money made magic happen with moods and loyalty. I hated seeing shit this way, but in my line of work and with the people I dealt with, it was money and luxuries that kept the large and small fish taking my bait.

Alex: *Give me a second to think. Shit. What do people name yachts?*

Falcon: *You can always use the first name Jake used for his yacht. Sex Sea?*

I SMIRKED at the picture that came through with this chick's contact info, showing a young, hot blonde. It was a pity that I was on a mission for business, not pleasure. I could use a drink and a lady in bed after this day. *Think, Alex.*

I looked over at Breanne. Her Titanic history lesson made my mind jump to using the luxurious yacht to keep these men as clients in the first place. She studied the drawings, and her auburn hair hid her face from me. Just as well. I had no business going *there* with my new partner. I couldn't even allow my mind to go back to the gala when I observed her in such a desperate state, not knowing who I was. I didn't want to think about the kiss that was so damn difficult to resist after seeing her plump lips and emerald eyes begging me for it.

Shit. Stop! I ordered myself. I had to come up with a name, or I would be stuck with the name Jake used to name his yacht when he was drunk.

Stone? Bree? Sea Stone? Stone Sea? Stoned...? What in the hell do I name a goddamn superyacht?

Alex: *Made in Stone?*

Falcon: *Heavy, but it needs to be creative. Like Lady Stone?*

Lady Maiden...Iron Maiden? Maiden...fuck! Stone Maiden?

Alex: *What about Maiden Stone?*

Falcon: *Sweet. That's what's up.*

Alex: *Thanks. Handle it quickly, please*

Fantastic. I'd officially named the business and family yacht after Breanne. She had no idea we were about to do a sales pitch and wine and dine a deal on it, and I had to hope all of this looked and felt natural to our clients.

I couldn't have them questioning my last-minute idea, wondering why I'd bring them out on a multi-million-dollar yacht. I needed to land the deal, fire Danny after making him look like the jackass he was, and then explain all of this to Breanne.

I had to prep her that more was on the line than her vision of this one hotel. There was a reason I was about to go full-blown businessman on this woman, and I wasn't sure she'd enjoy *this* side of me. It seemed slimy, greedy, and disgusting, but I had to inform her that you met fire with fire when it came to these sorts of people.

These weren't victims. These people took you as their victim if you let them.

I'd met with worse, though. If I could survive my childhood—living with the most wretched man alive until my grandfather rescued me—then no man could intimidate me. And no man ever did. Not anymore. Breanne might have her *Satan in a suit* opinion of me return after everything was said and done today, and maybe she'd be right.

Strangely enough, though, I didn't want her to see me as a just another dick in a suit. Who knew, maybe she'd like that I'd named Mitchell and Associates' superyacht after her? That might help keep that lovely smile of hers present while she boarded a yacht instead of sitting at a table in a conference room with Sphere.

Why was I thinking about any of these things? I needed to leave the nightmares of my past in the past and stop worrying about Breanne's feelings about me. It was time to get her on the same page with me in business, and that was it. I needed her game tight, not falling apart after Danny screwed multiple deals with Sphere. This sorry idiot was about to wish he'd never tried to end this without talking to Breanne first. What a colossal asshole.

I had a good feeling that a deep dive into Stone would uncover the fact that this jerk was the reason the company was upside down financially, and we were scrambling to climb out of this hole fast. I was calling bullshit on Danny. Too many strange events had happened in too short a time.

Sphere was our answer, and my game to seal this deal was just getting started.

CHAPTER FIVE

BREE

*I*f I'd walked into work today naked, I would've probably felt less humiliated than I did at this moment. On top of the final specs that were engineered having unforgivable flaws, the pitch meeting with Sphere getting bumped up, and Danny trying to ditch us in the process, I'd reached my absolute limit.

Then there was Alexander. This man wasn't letting it go, and we were officially boarding a goddamn superyacht to save this deal. Maybe this was Alex's cocky way of bringing this disaster of a proposal full circle on me. I wouldn't know. I hadn't talked to the man since one of the Nazari brothers who owned Sphere called Alex instead of me.

Alex slipped his phone in his suit pocket and lent a hand to help me out of the boat we'd taken to get to the yacht.

"Follow my lead, and we'll save the deal. Easy as that," he said, releasing my hand and turning back to tip the people who'd brought us to the vessel.

I eyed the name of the boat. *Maiden Stone?*

"The clock's ticking, and the Nazaris don't seem as though they like to be kept waiting," Alex insisted when I glanced over at him, climbing the spiral staircase.

I followed him, hugging my iPad and laptop to my chest.

"What is all of this, and why are we on a luxury yacht?" I asked as the man took two flutes of champagne from a hostess and turned back with a smile.

"Cheers," he said as he continued walking ahead. I could tell the man was in business mode, but my brain hadn't entirely caught up with him yet.

I took the champagne and glanced up to where I heard music playing on one of the top decks of this insanely elaborate yacht.

I reached for his elbow, stopping the tall man who was taking long strides toward the interior of this floating hotel. "I'm not sure this will work. Danny tried to ditch out, and I have no idea where he is. The final designs have been redesigned to the point that I can't fix the fucking things, and—"

Alex's light green eyes leveled me. "Excuses, Ms. Stone?" he asked as if I were the architect and engineer who'd screwed up all of this. "Is that what we're going to talk about while we keep our clients waiting —clients who are trying to fire our asses, I might add?"

I glared at him. "I don't plan on keeping them waiting. I don't plan on keeping them at all. I can't fix this shit," I growled. "Danny sabotaged this." I eyed his impatient expression. "There's something more. You know more, and you're not telling me."

"All you need to know is how you're going to use your creative mind to build a vision on the Nazaris' real estate that we are going to see from the yacht in about an hour. I need your brain working, and I'll close the deal that Danny sabotaged."

"If it's obvious to you that Danny did this, then it should be obvious to the brothers who own Sphere."

Alex sighed. "If it were obvious that we had an architect who was planning on stealing Stone Group's design while he decided to jumpstart a new business in the architectural field, we'd be having a different discussion. I wouldn't have gone through the trouble of securing this yacht and bringing Sphere out to sea as a way of kissing their ass and giving us one last chance to keep them as our clients."

"Danny wouldn't steal my vision and my work."

"Newsflash!" Alex's eyes widened. *"That* mother fucker was already in the process of doing precisely that while you were enjoying a latte this morning."

"I can't do this," I said in full honesty. "Danny has always hated me as head of the engineering department while Dad was running the company." I was speaking my thoughts, and I didn't care who heard them. "Why would he do this? We pay him well. Well above what architects and engineers would ever make. He was always compensated nicely."

I ran my now sweaty hand over my forehead, fighting back tears of anger and disbelief. Alex was brutally honest about something I should easily have known Daniel Kyle would do to me. It was a matter of time.

"Forgive me if I am not one to waste time on this episode of *Coworkers Behaving Badly,*" he interrupted me with some humor and a cocky way of mocking my current situation, "but let us be the ones who nail this bastard in the end. We certainly can't do that here on the helipad of the yacht. We need to be up *there,*" he pointed toward the upper decks, "charming the shit out of the Nazaris, who decided they'd call *me* up and try to fire my ass."

"None of this makes sense," I said, feeling like my blood pressure spike was either going to make me pass out or jump ship. Literally. "Why would they call you?"

Alex ran a hand impatiently through his hair. "The simple answer is that they don't trust you," he said. "Now's the time to regain that trust."

"I don't want their business. Not like this." I spun away from Alex's intimidating businessman expression. "Goddammit. I can't believe this."

"What can't you believe, Ms. Stone?" Alex questioned, stepping around to make me face him again. "You can't believe that someone who's never liked you would sabotage you and steal your business and designs?"

"Precisely that," I said, annoyed as hell that this man was so fucking sarcastic when I could hardly contain my anger as it was.

"Well, get used to it. It sort of happens in a cut-throat business. Even I could tell that prick was a piece of shit the first time he shook my hand. Let's move forward and save this as partners. You understand I know very well that Stone needs Sphere, correct?"

"How would you know that?"

Alex's eyes narrowed. "Because after you bounced on my ass all week, allowing me to run this fucking business and complete this merge, I found out rather quickly that Stone is upside down in just about every fucking aspect. If it weren't for this merge with my firm, you'd be filing bankruptcy within the year."

It felt like my blood was boiling beneath my skin. I was so pissed that I didn't know where to direct my anger anymore. Who was I angry with? Was it Danny for fucking me over, Alex for speaking to me this way, or myself because none of the above would be happening if it weren't for me?

"While we're on the topic," he continued, "you've yet to prove to me that you're even interested in working as my damn partner at all. All I've witnessed so far is a woman who has her head buried in the sand, allowing the financial directors of Stone to mismanage funds— financial directors who I fired, by the way. You're welcome for that. And what about your vice president, Theo?"

"Don't you dare."

"I will fucking dare," he said. "You're falling apart on me, and if I can't get you to step up and own this shit like the badass businesswoman I've *heard* so much about, then I'll kindly ask you to step down while I save Sphere, and you can work for me instead of pretending to work with me."

All of the feelings of humiliation and betrayal that Danny had caused today dissipated that second. As pissed as I was at Alex for speaking to me like a condescending bastard, he was one-hundred-percent right. I left him to run this company alone as if I were playing some silly game. I knew I needed Sphere because our debts were burying us, and I chose to trust my financial department and directors to ensure we stayed afloat. Hell, I'd sacrificed numerous personal paychecks and *donated* them back into the company to keep the lights on. I avoided difficult decisions like the plague. That was Dad's specialty, not mine.

"Theo is quitting on me, isn't he?" I asked, jumping straight to the only question that mattered to me.

"No one likes to work for free, Ms. Stone," Alex said, seemingly loving to drive the point home that I sucked at running a business. "I tried to keep him, letting him know that he would actually have a *boss* to work for."

"Enough!" I seethed. "We stay here until Danny boards this fucking yacht." I unlocked my phone and called Danny's phone. "How do I get Danny brought out to this ship? He's going to explain everything to you and me and the Nazaris for putting us in this situation."

Alex smirked. "Wow." He took a sip of champagne. "It looks like we finally have someone who wants to run the company."

"I've had enough of you and your bullshit for one lifetime, Alex," I said. "Again, how do I get Danny on this boat?"

"Three steps ahead of you, Breanne." He tipped his glass toward the stern of the boat. "The engines aren't firing up until after that snake boards the yacht."

I saw nothing but red, and I was ready to bury Danny for stealing Sphere—or trying to, anyway. In reality, I was angriest at myself. I'd acted childish about this merge ever since I found out about it. I was so smug about wanting my rightful seat at the table, but I'd shirked all of my responsibilities and let so many other things slide, and Alexander wasn't about to baby my ass. He should've been firing me after I let Stone Company go to hell by not holding my employees accountable since Dad died.

What hurt the worst was knowing what I'd put Theo through. Theo had offered advice on handling everything, he even told me to fire Danny, but I was too stubborn to listen. He'd been my right-hand guy for so long, and I'd been so wrapped up in my self-pity that I hadn't bothered to make sure he was okay. Obviously, he wasn't. It was no wonder Theo had been so grateful for the merge and Alex joining me as a partner. I'd overwhelmed my dear friend and burnt him out while I pretended to be some incredible businesswoman.

It was all biting me in the ass at this very moment. Alex was officially seeing me at a low point for the second time, but this time wouldn't be like the last. *This time* I was going to do what was expected of me. I was about to save Sphere and own up to everything I'd created while playing the *avoidance* game after taking on this company.

Instead of cowering, I knew I had a fire in my spirit. I hadn't been acting like it, but I knew I deserved to remain as Alex's partner—I just needed a little nudge. The nudge of Alex being a complete jerk and enjoying it a little too much, if you ask me. He wasn't wrong, though. Nothing he'd had to say about me or my actions was wrong, and I needed him to say it all.

Dwelling on the past and my mistakes would *not* save Sphere for me. I had to save it by accepting full responsibility for what I'd allowed to happen. That would be my starting point.

"Looks like your personal Judas is about to board. Suit up, Breanne. It's time to save Sphere," Alex said.

"Good." I nodded at Alex. "We're going to use that son of a bitch to make our case to the Nazari brothers."

"Now, we're thinking like partners." He clinked his glass to mine. "Nice to have you with me, Ms. Stone."

CHAPTER SIX
BREE

 *W*hen Danny appeared through the luxurious entrance at the back of the yacht, I could only stare in disgust that he'd deliberately put me in a position to fail. While Danny walked over to join us, Alex called up to the captain to get the yacht moving.

"Mr. Kyle," Alex said, ending his call and using his sharp features to level the man, "I do hope you gave Bradley a fat tip for chartering you out to our yacht."

"Why would I do that?" He waved his hand around the opulent deck we stood on. "I would imagine that Mitchell and Associates would take care of my expenses for me."

"You're a creep, you know that?" I said, unable to keep my mouth shut.

"I think he knows that well enough," Alex said dismissively. "But no, Mitchell will not be paying for former employees to be collected from the ship once we're done saving Sphere in an hour or so."

Danny laughed off Alex as we turned to walk into the yacht. Marble floors greeted us, and my eyes were drawn to a grand staircase with polished wooden rails. It was as glorious as a magnificent hotel or resort. From where we walked, it was evident that this yacht had been designed with a taste of elegance that weaved itself around you and filled you with a sense of grandeur and importance. I had to keep reminding myself this was a yacht and not some trillionaire's toy.

"You realize that the Nazaris no longer want Stone Company's bid, correct? You're out, Bree. They're moving on," Danny said smugly.

"It's just a matter of who they're moving on *to*, isn't it, Daniel?" I said.

"Daniel?" Alex quipped in a way that snapped my attention over to him after we walked into an area where the elevators were hidden. "Damn." Alex hit the button to open the elevator doors, and he looked back at Danny. "Ms. Stone seems to have moved on from the friendly nicknames to the *your ass is mine* names."

"Bree," Danny started.

"That's enough," I interrupted. "Both of you. I've met with the Nazaris on multiple occasions. I can easily say that when our tardiness adds their reasons for trying to fire us, this magnificent yacht is only going to prove we're desperate to keep them."

"But we sort of are, aren't we?" Alex leaned down and whispered in my ear, taunting me.

I glanced up at him and back to Danny as soon as the doors opened to reveal the insanely awesome party deck at the top of this boat. "Desperate or not," I tugged on Danny's arm, "we're going to be honest and do what's right since all we've done is waste their time and insult them. You'll be speaking up first," I told Danny, then looked at Alex, who had a shit-eating grin on his face. "The games are over. Mr. Grayson, please show us to where the Nazaris are and pray to God that the staff on this boat has kept them—"

"They've been taken care of," Alex assured me. "Ms. Stone, *Daniel*," he mocked Danny's name, "if you'll both follow me."

I sucked in a breath, keeping my heart rate down as we moved past a sparkling pool, rounded a corner to see a fully staffed bar, hosts and hostesses, and, at long last, the five extremely wealthy brothers from Dubai—the Nazaris.

I took the lead once the men rose from the posh lounging sofas, and I smiled at the one brother who always seemed flirtier and more agreeable than the other four men.

"Xavier." I smiled, locking eyes with his stunning amber ones. "Damien, Latif," I nodded at the two always stiff brothers after Xavier met me with a smile. "Malik and Cyrus." I sighed when the last two brothers smiled and greeted me with a *Ms. Stone* in return.

"Who are the gentlemen with you?" Xavier questioned, sizing up Alex's six-foot-four frame. Part of me was shocked that he'd already forgotten what Danny looked like.

"This is my partner, Mr. Alexander Grayson," I introduced Alex, who practically hopped with a smile to shake each of the men's hands firmly. "This is the head architect and engineer, Mr. Daniel Kyle—or Danny." I watched as all five brothers smirked along with Danny. "I'm surprised you've forgotten him already?" I questioned, feeling like these dickwads were in on whatever Danny had done behind my back.

"Jesus. Don't insult the Nazaris, Ms. Stone," Alex said in a cocky voice as he raised his eyebrows at me, then leered at Danny. "It's effortless to forget a man like Daniel. I almost left his sorry ass on the shore when I was taking a call from—" He stopped himself as he pointed around at the men. "Well, you'll all have to forgive me," he was using some assertive yet condescending tone, "which one of you called to fire *me* again? And behind Ms. Stone's back?"

"That was me," Damien said indignantly. "And for good reason too."

"I would imagine. Let's have a seat. I believe that we all need to clear the air," Alex said, nodding toward a woman who held a tray of food. "Please, after all of you."

Alex sat next to me, and I looked across at the other bastards, who were smirking in some knowing game. It wasn't hard to pick up on the idea that no matter what Alex did for the Nazaris, Danny would walk away smelling like roses, and we would be left to look like lying shitheads.

I glanced at Alex as he casually crossed one ankle behind the other and saw that this man wouldn't be made out to be a fool. His Italian leather shoes, his bespoke Brioni suit, his fancy-smelling cologne being blown around by the sea breeze, and his unshakeable confidence…all of it assured me that I sat next to a powerful man.

I glanced at the smirk on his face. I could instantly tell that this man lived for shit to go south so that he could come out on top in the end. As intimidating as Alex Grayson could be, I was his partner, and we were both going to bury Danny here and now, just as Alex said when we boarded the yacht.

"Gentlemen," I spoke after everyone settled into their seat. "I will admit that there are errors in your final specs and the drafts of the hotel resort you entrusted us with at Stone Company."

"To say the very least, Ms. Stone," Latif said. "It seems as though all of Stone Company has fallen apart. If what I've heard is true," he looked at Danny, "Stone Company will be going under soon enough. It will be our company that saves you."

"Excuse me?" I looked over at Danny.

"You heard my brother," Cyrus said.

"Loud and clear," Danny smirked. "Sorry, Breanne, but you and I both know that underbidding this job to save Stone's ass will only put you under that much more."

Everyone snickered as fire surged through my veins. Well, everyone but Alex, who remained attentive and unexpectedly quiet.

"In the end," Xavier said with a kind smile, "you'd be paying us to build our dream hotel. I'm sorry, but we'll be taking Danny's bid instead."

"Danny's bid?" I looked over at that Judas-ass mother fucker. "Well, this is news, isn't it?"

"Bree, it's not what you think," Danny said, seemingly shocked that Xavier admitted that Danny was stealing my clients.

"Please explain, then, because what I'm *thinking* is that you're in violation of Stone Company's—"

"Violation my ass," Danny interrupted. "Stone Company is gone, Bree. Accept it so we can be done here."

"Yeah, can I get a bourbon sour," Alex said to a host who stood next to the bar, utterly off-topic from what was going on. He looked at me. "You look like you could use a stiff drink too. The bartender is phenomenal here. In fact, I'd hire him as my personal bartender if James Mitchell wouldn't kick my ass for stealing him away."

"I'm good, thanks," I stammered, caught off-guard by his question. "Can we focus on—"

"How about you, gentlemen?" Alex ignored me and looked at the arrogant Nazari brothers. "Beers all the way around?" He wound his finger through the air then looked at Danny. "Sorry. That was rude of me to interrupt your thought as if we're not going to sue your ass for stealing our clients." He took the bourbon that was quickly brought to him and sipped it. "Go on. This is fascinating."

Danny leaned his arms on his knees. "It's no secret that Stone is going under. We've talked about how Breanne allowed the engineers to cut corners, the contractors who are known to ghost on projects—"

"Mr. Vallance," Alex interrupted, calling over a steward. "I'm going to need another bourbon. It seems I'm thirstier than I realized." He blew out a breath and reclined against the cushion of the sofa. "Tell, Anthony we're thrilled he's behind the bar again," he continued in some damn world of his own. "Just keep the booze coming." He looked over at Danny. "It seems like it's going to be a while of listening to your lies."

"Wait," Malik spoke up. "Who exactly are you?"

Alex licked his lips and smirked at me. "No wonder you're all being duped into doing business with a fool. Everyone in this business knows who I am." He eyed each of the Nazari brothers. "I'm sorry you men haven't done your research on the most influential and powerful men in business. It's a shame because if you had, you'd already know that my company has merged with Stone, and the financial concerns Danny has brought to your attention are no longer valid."

"Stone merging with another firm? That is a lie. No company would merge with a firm that is going under," Xavier looked at me. "Danny sent the numbers to us to prove Breanne's firm is not to be trusted."

"Wow," Alex said. "You're *full* of surprise betrayals today, aren't you?"

"The merge is not official," Danny blatantly lied.

"Bullshit," I snapped. "You know goddamn well it is. Now, tell me why you believe it's okay to go behind our backs and lie to our clients to secure them as your own."

"We're keeping the original design," Latif said, "and we'll be entrusting Daniel Kyle to deliver on his promises."

I wanted to punch Danny in his face, but my angered reaction was stopped when Alex used the back of his hand to stop himself from spitting out the bourbon he'd sipped. I pursed my lips and refocused on the shit that'd just rolled off Latif's tongue.

I glared at him. "Unfortunately for you, *Daniel Kyle* does not own the designs for the hotel," I confirmed. "The designs you wish to keep are the property of Stone Company whether you believe we're going under or not." I sat up. "You gentlemen appear to be intelligent; why else would you be firing a group that you believe is going under? Am I correct?"

"Correct," Malik answered.

"If that is correct, I cannot help but wonder why you would trust an employee of that company," I said. "Regardless of where you believe Stone is, you will need to decide for the vision you have with your grand hotel. With that said, you need to choose here and now if you want *my* design that encompasses your dreams for the resort in Malibu, or if you want a knock-off from a startup company." I glared at Danny. "A company ran by someone who's using Stone's reputation and numerous awards of recognition in concept and architectural designs to build a company of his own. I will tell you," I eyed each of the five men's dark expressions, "if I find that Daniel Kyle and Sphere has taken so much as a millimeter of my design detail for your hotel in Malibu, there will be legal action to follow."

"You can't afford to retain the lawyer," Danny sneered.

"No, but the man who owns the Stone firm, this yacht, Mitchell and Associates, and everything that goes along with *that* company *can* afford it, and he will procure a legal team with fervor," Alex chimed in. "I struggle to imagine what your corrupt little self will do once the big guys step in." He looked over at the Nazari brothers, who were no longer amused. "I also wonder how you'll fare when you see us building *your hotel's vision* on Malibu's shore for ourselves, and then kicking your asses right out of my house when we're taking a hell of a lot of business from whatever Daniel Kyle designs for you."

"That's our vision, our hotel, and our agreement," Xavier snapped.

"Not if you go with this twisted chump." Alex sipped his bourbon and pointed toward Danny. "It's Breanne Stone's concept and vision. In fact," he sat up and moved his glass between his palms, "it's the only reason Mitchell and Associates merged my company with Stone. You see, gentlemen, Mr. Monroe and Mr. Mitchell are enormous fans of Breanne Stone's ideas so much so that they'll gladly keep her as my life-long partner, even after they both willfully accepted the debts of Stone group." He looked at Danny. "Debts you must know that Breanne's dishonest employees caused. But that's office drama, gentlemen. The yacht is stopping here, and a charter boat is on its way to retrieve the six of you if you decide to continue on this foolhardy path." He casually took a sip of his bourbon. "Or you can choose Stone to bring your vision to life and let the charter collect Danny's deceitful ass. You've got five minutes to make the right call."

"The right call?" Cyrus spoke up.

"How are we to be assured that if we go with Stone and not Daniel Kyle that our vision will be put on the shore in Malibu?" Latif questioned.

"You're Alex Grayson, the former executive at Mitchell, aren't you?" Xavier asked as if he'd had a revelation.

"The one and only. Now, are you going to play with the executives who have the financial backing to see your vision through, or are you going to go dream under stars with Danny?"

"Dream under stars?" I softly said to Alex.

"Four minutes and we've got transportation arriving to bring you back to the docks, gentlemen," Alex said, ignoring me.

"We want the best."

"You obviously can't afford the best," I said to Malik. "If you could, you wouldn't have accepted Danny's bid, knowing he was burying my company with it." I exhaled. "And you sure as hell wouldn't be going with some lying piece of shit employee who works for a company that was *going under*. If you want our business, the bid increases by ten million," I said, going for broke. Fuck it and fuck them. I didn't care. This meeting was insulting enough.

"Jesus Christ," Alex whispered under his breath, sitting up and looking at me in humor and shock.

"We were told you'd buy our real estate, and it would only cost half the original amount due to errors."

"That's before I found out that you were leaving my firm for Danny's offer," I said. "If you want my design and my vision, you will trust that I will reengineer a bigger and better hotel, and you *will pay* the ten million extra. I know very well as I sit here and quote you on this higher bid that James Mitchell will snatch up the designs in a hot second if you pass on them."

"What are you doing?" Danny seethed.

"Stating a fact." I smiled at him and the five brothers who were now at the mercy of paying for my design and work.

"What makes you so sure that Mr. Mitchell or Mr. Monroe will buy your design?" Xavier asked, more agitated than I'd ever seen him.

"Because they bought a company that was going under for my design and engineering talents alone." I looked at Alex. "Isn't that what you mentioned?"

"I'll call Jim Mitchell right now and tell him the offer is officially on the table." Alex licked his lips in humor. "I'm confident he'd gladly pay an extra ten million to build a new resort on California's coast. Well, done," he mused.

"No. This is our hotel, and the blueprints are what we want. There are no other designs that have captured what we wanted as this one has."

Alex stared at his phone and clicked his tongue, feigning horror or whatever he was doing to increase the dramatics on this. "I'd hate for my best friend to miss out." He sighed. "How about a good faith deposit, and we keep Mr. Mitchell's grubby little hands off your design?"

"We'll give a fifty-percent down-payment now to secure you as the firm we'll be working with," Malik said, looking at Danny. "You will hear from us on a better day, Mr. Kyle. For now, I hope that boat is here to bring you off this one and back to shore."

"Boat's certainly here," Alex said. "Unlock this for me." He reached for the iPad that I didn't realize I was holding with white knuckles. "I need that fifty-percent deposit on the Nazaris." He looked at Xavier. "I trust you can have it wired to Stone Company by the time we remove an unwanted rat from the yacht. Then Breanne can use her talents and help you see *your* innovative hotel come to life."

"You're all damn fools," Danny said as he rose.

Alex waved over security. "Get this idiot off the yacht and stay with him on the charter until he's seen to shore."

"Yes, Mr. Grayson."

I watched in shock as Danny tried to walk with his head up and disappeared through the private area that hid the elevators in the lavish yacht. Did I just upsell myself by ten million and seal the deal without ever addressing or fixing the errors?

"What the hell just happened?" I questioned Alex after the men picked up their phones to make contact with their bankers.

"You just blew my fucking mind," Alex grinned. "Ten million additional dollars?"

"I should've gone for twenty," I said with a smile.

"Jesus, woman," Alex chuckled. "Now I know why Brooks lost out on a couple of projects. It turns out you know your worth. That's highly admirable."

"I don't need your approval," I said.

"No shit." He nodded with a coy smile. "Let's go grab a quick drink, settle the Nazaris in to enjoy this yacht for a few days, and I'll call for the chopper to pick us up and get us the hell out of here. It looks like I didn't need the yacht after all."

Talk about getting burned and then rising out of the ashes. I was prouder of myself than I'd ever been, and I couldn't wait to tell Theo, Cass, and Nicole about this.

CHAPTER SEVEN
ALEX

*B*reanne Stone had proven to me that it wasn't wise to piss her off, especially regarding personal matters.

The Nazari brothers put the ass in asshole, but Breanne put an abrupt end to their scheming smiles when she highlighted her value as a talented woman. The confidence I observed from her rose far above their petty deceit. So instead of us begging to keep them as clients, Breanne kept their lips firmly planted on her ass and with the healthy *perk* of paying her an additional ten million dollars to do so.

Impressive.

Once the Nazaris were tucked in for a four-day cruise—which they were lucky I allowed after the shit they pulled by trying to fire us and hire Danny—Breanne and I left them in the care of the yacht's personnel.

After boarding the chopper, I studied Breanne as she gazed intently out her window. I handed Bree a flute of freshly poured champagne and sat down across from her.

From the moment we'd left the Nazaris and yacht staff, Breanne's demeanor had changed entirely. The woman who'd worn a smile that was more fake than Daniel Kyle's Rolex now sat rigidly with an intimidating expression.

Being one to never waver in the company of pissed-off individuals, I didn't let her current disposition faze me.

"You handed everyone their balls on a platter today, and I'll gladly drink to that. Nice work." I raised my glass. "It's just a shame that you didn't make all those pricks sit through a history lesson about the Titanic to sell them on your designs."

Breanne turned to me, and her jade eyes narrowed. "You mentioned that my finance department heads were all fired?"

"Yes. I figured that you and I would talk about that on Monday, but if we're going to talk shop instead of celebrating," I sipped my champagne, "then let's talk."

"Why were they fired?"

"They worked with your architects, engineers, and marketing groups to steal from your company."

Breanne closed her eyes and rubbed her forehead. As an individual who read body language like poetry, I knew this reaction was because Breanne had reached her mental limit with bullshit.

"Perhaps this is a conversation for Monday," I advised.

"I need to know what you found while I spent the entire week with my *head in the sand*," she said, bringing up my accusations from earlier. Her left eyebrow rose. "I want to know how you discovered my employees were stealing from me while I didn't have a clue about it."

"You didn't have a clue because they worked the system and did a damn fine job of it."

"But *how*?"

I could sense Breanne was feeling me out. She was too protective of her company and seemingly blinded by the idea that the only person who would fuck her over was Daniel Kyle.

"No." She held a finger up. "Why don't we start with *who* worked the system?"

"Your architect, financial, *and* marketing teams. And with smiles on their faces, I might add. They worked together with subcontractors who were giving them kickbacks to underbid the hell out of legitimate companies and ensure you never saw the losses."

"But *you* did?"

I nodded, keenly aware that she was apprehensive to believe that I'd caught it, but she didn't.

"It helps to have a sixth sense for sniffing out hyenas who like to steal from companies. If you must know, these dicks were sloppy and gave themselves away almost immediately."

She smiled, and it was the fake-Rolex smile from earlier. "Thank God for you and your sixth sense. I'm sure that will hold up when lawyers are involved after I fire employees for you *sniffing* them out like a dog."

"After I sniffed the bastards out like dogs," I eyed her challenging gaze with a smirk, "I gained hard evidence about why your company was in the red with nearly all of your clients. With the right digging and prodding, one of the lower-level employees came clean and basically handed me the whole scheme. The documents that came to you and Theo had been manipulated to show profits instead of loss. Falsified documents, forged signatures…" I took another sip of my champagne. "It all appeared to be profitable when it crossed your desk, so you signed off on it, but in actuality, every contract that crossed your desk was costing you hundreds of thousands in kickbacks and sub-par bids."

I watched her lethal expression die. "Who came forward?" she questioned meekly.

"Ryan Miller."

"Wow. He was extremely loyal to my father and this company." Her eyes were brimming with tears when she directed her gaze out of the chopper window. "You're sure Mr. Miller's statement is true?"

"Beyond a shadow of a doubt. The man showed me how they worked the process and offered up documented proof."

"He will face the consequences for being involved," she said, wiping a tear away as swiftly as it rolled down her cheek. "Why would he come forward? Why would he do this?"

"He came forward to save you and Theo from facing legal action with Mitchell and Associates. He wanted to ensure that you and your VP weren't implicated in the embezzlement."

Her bottom lip quivered. "Why would he even think to steal from my company?"

"Greed has a way of making people become the worst versions of themselves. Breanne," I said, taking the champagne from her trembling hand, "I'm sorry this has happened. However, we can work together and get Stone Company financially topside again."

"I'm just in shock that I never knew *this* was the reason I couldn't get Stone's numbers in the black. I had no idea that while I was working myself to the bone, sacrificing my paycheck, these grifters were eating steak and lobster."

"And buying designer handbags." I hoped the levity would let her know I had her back personally and professionally. "Sadly for them, they'll be trading their tailored Tom Ford suits for a county jumpsuit. Those soft hands and toned asses should be a big hit on the convict catwalk."

Her lips tightened, so I went on.

"To get you up to speed, legal action is being taken, and Mr. Mitchell already has investigative teams and lawyers involved. Daniel Kyle's little *ship-to-shore* excursion will likely be the last of his adventures in crime."

"Fucking unbelievable!" she hissed. "Do you know how hard I've worked to run this company only to look like a bag of dicks as a CEO?"

"Well, if you think employees using shady tactics to steal from you makes you look like a dick, then James Mitchell is the biggest mushroom tip of us all," I teased. "This kind of thing can happen in big business. Take a breath. Now that you're up to speed, what I need from you is to get over being pissed off so can we start working together to fix the last of the merge."

"Forgive me, but I can't just *get over* shit like this," she seethed. "Oh my God. Everything I've busted my ass to do to keep my dad's company going after he died, and now—"

"And now you have greedy employees taking advantage of that and trying to bury you and your dad's company with him."

"Precisely," she answered. "I need to know if this is the reason Theo is leaving."

"No, it's not the reason he's leaving. I would let you in on his situation, but I promised to take a back seat and let him fill you in."

"This helicopter can't land fast enough." She tucked a strand of hair behind her ear. "I'm sorry if I'm not one for conversation at the moment; not only did Daniel Kyle succeed in destroying my day, but it seems I can't trust any of my employees anymore either."

"Let's summarize. Your workers are thieves, your clients believe their lines of bullshit, and your company is under investigation for embezzlement. Though," I held up my hand to keep her from losing her shit, "if you're up for it, we can fix these matters with our legal teams and keep Stone and Brooks out of the media."

"What do you have in mind?"

"You up for playing the devil's mistress?" I smirked.

She smiled in return. "Roleplaying?"

"Why not? We did it so well to ward off your douche of an ex, didn't we?"

For the first time since boarding the chopper, Breanne's posture relaxed. "If only this situation were as *serious* as that," she mocked.

"I don't think you and I will ever be involved in matters more serious than getting rid of a bastard of an ex while you're buzzed at the bar."

She chuckled as her cheeks turned a healthy shade of red. "How mortifying." Her eyes widened, and the most charming, dimpled smile appeared on her face. "Do you realize that since first meeting you, I've encountered nothing but humiliating situations?"

"Now that you bring *that* up, I'm totally fucked."

"Exactly." She was finally lightening up. "How are you ever supposed to find me undeniably attractive?" she asked coyly.

"Sucks for me. After all this, and I'm still stuck with you as my life-long partner."

"Dreadful." She smiled and rolled her eyes. "Now, back to dodging the press. What's your plan?"

The fun and games were over, but at least she didn't collapse into a puddle of tears after finding out her employees had completely screwed her over. She was ready to take action on the thieves, and that's where I needed my new business partner.

"Now that I've got you in the game, this is how we'll do it," I said. "It's rather simple. The company is restructuring, right? Your architects, engineers, and marketing team already know I'm hot on their asses, so we're going to move into the Brooks Firm building on Monday."

"No wonder they were all uptight when I walked in today." She exhaled. "So, move our entire business? As in..."

"As in, Stone Company will have its front doors locked, building vacated, and a bunch of confused employees will be left to wonder what happened to the company they tried to bury. They'll soon learn they didn't get the exclusive invite to the new business address. I'll have my VP send out the memo for the employees who are moving with us as soon as we land, and they'll have offices ready for them on their respective floors at Brooks on Monday. For the others, they'll get an exclusive invite to meet with our legal teams at Mitchell and Associates."

"You honestly think we can move everything over to Brooks by Monday? That's three days from now, and tomorrow is Saturday."

"That superyacht isn't the only perk of having Mitchell and Associates as our parent company. I'll hire a moving company to bring everything over, and I'll even give you a lovely office with a corner view..." I paused. "A corner view of the alleys, of course."

"God, I was such a bitch to you. I'm sorry for that."

"I've dealt with worse," I teased. "Though it was obvious you weren't thrilled about the *family* business merging with another firm."

"I wasn't. I had my reasons. I'd like to say they were all valid, but with you doing some investigative work, it looks like I have to accept that this was the best thing for my company."

"Personal question before the chopper lands, and we part ways until Monday."

"No, I will not date you."

I smiled; she was back. She took the news better than I'd imagined, and I saw determination dominating her expression. She'd been fucked over by the people she trusted, and it was apparent she wasn't going to allow them to have the last laugh.

What started as an interrogation from her was ending with her flirtatious grin. "You won't date me?" I laughed. "But you're thinking about it. I can see it in your smile." Her cheeks tinted red again, and I crossed an ankle over my knee. "Back to my personal question. I'm curious if you enjoyed being the one to fill your father's seat after he passed?" Her expression darkened after I brought up her late father. "Breanne, I need to know. Do you *enjoy* this part of the job—dealing with the bullshit?"

"I hate it more than anything. I went to college to become an architect, not to major in business management."

I grinned. "We need to restructure the company during this merger accordingly then. I'll handle the *dirty* side of the business, and you can return to doing what you enjoyed before your father left his company to you."

"Trying to steal my company, Mr. Grayson?"

"Perhaps I'm trying to steal its owner, Ms. Stone." I arched an eyebrow and watched her eyes widen at my response.

In the end, it was good to know that a bomb like this being dropped in Breanne's lap did little more than draw a misty-eyed rant and a few four-letter words. She was tougher than she realized, and it was fucking impressive.

The helicopter landed, and I knew Breanne and I would have a lot of shitty details to tackle in a short period. Monday couldn't come fast enough, but for now, I would fill in Jim on everything from randomly naming his yacht to saving Sphere and getting Breanne ready to face the thieves in her company head-on. Being the CEO of our parent company and my best friend, Jim would undoubtedly be interested in this day's events—events which nearly cost him ten million in a bidding war sparked by Breanne to check-mate the Nazaris.

CHAPTER EIGHT
BREE

Once the helicopter reached the landing pad on the top of Mitchell and Associates' Howard building, Alex confirmed that his driver was waiting to take us to Stone Company's offices.

As much as I appreciated the offer, I was in desperate need of fresh air and alone time before I met with Theo. With Stone's building being only a block away, I chose to take the short walk to stabilize my thoughts about today's disastrous revelations and events.

Instead of feeling weak, mortified, and broken, I felt a wave of confidence overrule all of that. I'd love to say my change of attitude was fueled by the cocky poise that Alex displayed from the moment we stepped on the yacht and up until we landed, but I knew that wasn't it.

At first, I didn't believe the man when he started throwing out accusations about my employees, but as much as I appreciated Ryan Miller, I'd noticed the man's attitude toward me change a while back. He went from being a fun, friendly, and admirable architect to a cocky bastard who spoke to me like I were an ignorant child. I was never overly familiar with the man, but he *was* a respectable employee, which made me question what I'd done to piss him off. The only time I'd ever asked him why he'd talked down to me, he quickly apologized and blamed his uncouth behavior on *personal issues*. I should've kept my eye on him then, and that's why it all clicked into place when Alex laid the truth bare.

I owed Alex a debt of gratitude for not judging my character after all of the embarrassing shit he'd witnessed since we first met. Instead, he asked the one question that only Theo cared to know—was I happy running this company that I inherited after Dad's passing?

If I hadn't known that Alex was on my side after seeing the Nazaris and Danny exchanging their smug glances at my expense, I probably wouldn't have trusted the man with my answer. Instead, Alex ran significant interference by obnoxiously ordering drinks and cutting off Danny's lies about my company and me. That slimy bastard had intentionally underbid, and then he underhandedly placed flaws in all of my final concepts so that Sphere wouldn't trust me.

What a fucking unbelievable son of a bitch to have the audacity to pull that shit off in front of *my* clients and me. I had no idea—nor did I give a damn at this point—why Danny had the nerve to do what he'd done. The man would answer to my lawyers for his actions. I had to wash my hands of all of this and move forward with Alex. God only knew what the man's genuine opinion of me was, but after I loosened up and began to appreciate my new partner, it seemed we were on the right path.

In the presence of the ridiculously handsome man all day, I held my own against his sexy appearance and the enticing tone of his voice. Not once had I gawked or *lost myself* in Alex's deep green eyes, not until his tone changed and he grew sincere about the one thing Theo knew too well about me. He understood that I wasn't programmed to run the company while dealing with bullshit, but I was primed to immerse myself in designing concepts that blew our clients' minds when I captured their visions.

When Alex said that he'd handle the administrative stuff and allow me to do what I do best, my love for being an architect came rushing back to me, and this time it was without the threat of a merger stealing my company away. I didn't know what Theo was about to tell me, but thank God I had the renewed hope of wholeheartedly *appreciating* my job again.

I rolled up to Theo's place around seven in the evening and walked into his pristine Beverly Hills home. The only thing that was different about his and Stanton's mansion was the *For Sale* sign that'd been planted near their curb.

"Honey," Theo used his usual nickname for me, "get your ass in here and tell me everything."

I walked through the open foyer and into the den where Theo had candles lit and my favorite lavender tea was steeping in a glass pot. He poured me a cup and sat in the bend of his sectional, eyeing me for all the dirty details. Without hesitation, I offered up all the specifics from the minute I left the office this morning until I parted ways with Alex.

"So, that's everything from Daniel Kyle openly revealing how he'd undermined us to Alex delivering the behind-the-scenes dirt on half of our employees stealing from us," I said, finishing off my second cup of tea and dropping my head back against the leather sofa. I turned my head to him. "All right, you've kept me talking about this for at least an hour. It's your turn to tell me what is going on with you."

His lips turned down, and he glanced over at his unique black and white cat sculpture. "I want to say I would have gone to you before Alex on this matter," he looked back at me, "but your head hasn't been in the right place since the merge was announced."

"For that, I'm so damn sorry." I felt tears stinging my eyes for behaving like such a selfish bitch about the merge. "I don't have the right words to apologize, but I love you, Theo, so much it hurts."

Theo rose and walked over to me. It took the familiar fragrance of one of my best pal's cologne and his firm embrace for me to finally come to reality. I'd been too absorbed by my issues to check in with those who mattered most. Poor Theo never had a chance to talk to me about what was going on with him because I'd been dodging just about everyone.

I pulled up and brushed my hand over his soft, cotton shirt. "Damn it. This shirt must've cost you a hundred bucks, and I've ruined it."

He smiled, offering me some tissue from a box. "And from what Alex has uncovered, it seems you can't afford to replace it either."

I chuckled. "That's the damn truth." I dried my wet cheeks and sniffed. "All right, spill it. You have to tell me what's going on."

"Stanton was offered an amazing opportunity to model in France for a huge agency."

My eyes widened, knowing this was a profound dream come true for Stanton. "Oh my God! How long have you known?"

"He's been working with agents, the agency, and numerous others to secure a six-figure deal per shoot on this. They wanted him, and Stanton made them pay for it." He grinned proudly.

"Well, with a body like that man has combined with his good looks," I poked Theo in his chest, "you're lucky he'd rather have you instead of me."

He chuckled, and I nestled securely in his side.

"So, that's why the house is up for sale, I'm guessing." I paused, unprepared to say the next words. "You're moving?"

"To Paris, my darling. The city of love and fashion."

"And what will you do while your man is posing for all the camera peeps to drool over?"

A smile spread on his face. "I spoke with Alex about resigning my position, knowing Alex already had an amazing VP, and there was no need for a company with two VPs. Alex came back the next day with an offer I couldn't refuse whether or not Stanton had gotten the job in Paris."

"What?" I asked with a bashful smile, thinking that maybe Alex Grayson was starting to shed the devil horns, and a halo was about to replace them. "An offer? Was this before or after he found out that everyone we've ever known has been stealing from Stone?"

"It was after he and I discussed things, and I sat in on that snake, Ryan Miller, as he confessed." He held a finger to my lips when I went to speak. "You weren't going to learn about any of this until *after* you finalized Sphere, and I told you I was moving. The last thing Alex and his sexy-self needed was you blowing up like a volcano over nonsense."

"I was in a bad place."

"And it took you finally behaving like Alex's partner for you to appreciate him and this merge?"

"Pretty much," I said.

He shook his head and smiled. "Well, after I declined Alex's offer in the Brooks Architectural Firm London office, Alex nearly grilled my ass and raked it over hot coals." He smirked. "In a good way. He wanted to know all of my history with Stone, your dad, and *you*," he gave me a playful wink, "and I gave him my credentials. So, now, it looks like I'll be replacing the VP of Brooks Firm in London while they prep to merge the London offices with Stone down the road."

"They're merging us with Brooks in London?" I said with shock. "That's quite the commute from Paris. How will you manage that?"

"Stanton and I have kicked it around, and it'll be easiest if we live in Paris. I can spend a few days per week in London for work. It'll be long hours and one hell of a commute, but we both adore Paris, and—"

"Won't that put a strain on your relationship? Only seeing each other on the weekends?"

"The perk of having a top model as my boyfriend is that Stanton can travel to London and stay with me there if he only has a couple of days of shooting, and there are sister agencies he can book shoots for in London anyway. We're both pretty flexible, not to mention there are plenty of things I can do remotely on a swing day here and there."

"Alex understands that you'll live in Paris and not London?"

"Alex wants Brooks and Stone to get their hands dirty in Paris too," he said. "I'll be heavily involved in opening doors for us to begin designing in France. It's something Alex said that John Brooks was throwing around before he passed. Brooks lost their fire after that, and Alex saw something in me to help reignite those passions while he busies himself with you out here."

"This has to be a dream come true for both of you." I hugged him and held back my tears, feeling that this was worse than Theo leaving the company—he was moving out of the damn country. "I'm going to miss the hell out of you," I said. "As Alex's partner," I playfully crossed my arms and smiled at his beaming expression, "I'm going to insist that I visit you to make sure you're not, you know, embezzling company funds and things of that nature. It's going to be imperative that I keep a close eye on you."

"God, I will miss you and your adorable Jen Aniston style, girl," he chuckled, referencing the celebrity he always compared me to.

"You better quit comparing me to her. What will the people of Paris and London think when I show up to visit, and I'm nothing like that lovable actress?"

"My darling, you've got nothing but lovable energy surrounding you. You get emotional if I swat a fly, and your heart is always overjoyed for other's happiness as if it were your own."

"You think you have me all figured out?"

"I've known you for twenty years now; you're practically my sister. I *know* I have you figured out. Though I have to say, it's nice to have you back. This bitchy-Bree business was hardly tolerable for the last month."

"More like over-dramatic Bree," I teased. "Gosh, so you're really going to leave me, huh?"

He started humming *Somewhere out There* as if we were in the cartoon, An American Tail, with the two mice living under the same sky but still being worlds apart. The man always knew how to get an unexpected laugh out of me at the drop of a hat.

I continued to smile at Theo's humming, and I determined that any crying I might do for the remarkable life change that awaited Theo and Stanton would be here and now. It would be reasonable tears of happiness and not me *losing it* again. Sure, I'd let the tears rip when I saw them both off at the airport, but I wasn't going to allow this to deflate me.

It was time for all of us to turn a corner in the right direction, and I planned to do just that. Tomorrow night was Cass's birthday, and we were going to spend it at the exclusive club, Tobias, where all the little socialites loved to come out to play.

Life moved forward, and I understood that well. It was time to move forward with open sails and welcomed breezes.

CHAPTER NINE
BREE

I probably looked like any one of the wealthy socialites who sat around me in this bar; however, I was far from that. I couldn't even afford to eat from a value menu at a fast-food restaurant thanks to the pricks who'd been stealing from my company.

Because of my bullheaded determination to keep my dad's business afloat, I'd sacrificed my paychecks to pay the bills at Stone Company instead of my own. Every last dime I had saved was gone, and I'd been a complete fool to allow things to go on in this way for so long. I'd been running with some blind mentality that if I didn't cut myself a paycheck, we would lock in a promising deal to get Stone back in the game.

Sphere was that deal and thank God that we landed it because my bank account desperately needed to see some money again. Now, all I had to do was pay off all the debt I'd accrued since I went flat-ass broke. Hopefully, I'd be back on track in a month or ten—I was in a pretty shitty, *delinquent* situation.

I wanted to stay home and wallow in my pity after surrendering my leased car to the dealership, but I'd made a promise to Cass that we'd celebrate her thirtieth birthday as if we were all turning twenty-one again, and goddammit, that's what we were going to do.

Turning a new corner and having the wind in my sails was what I was working with tonight. I had to remind myself of the positive thoughts I'd left Theo with last night, and even if I'd gotten a brutal slap in the face from the dealership wanting their car back, I had to remind myself that shit happens. Life fucking happens—to the best of us.

I should've never allowed myself to get sucked into the personal side of the company and sacrifice my paychecks, but I did. Why? Because I couldn't bear to see any of my hard-working employees do what I did today—turn in their car and pray to God they could scrounge up enough cash to get their utility bills paid to current.

It was so damn hard not to bring my anger with me tonight. All I could think about was that after all the monetary sacrifices I'd made for my employees, they'd been stealing from me. I'd been worried sick about their welfare, and they were the reason we could never pull off a profitable job. So, from here on out, lesson learned. Time to adopt the saying that I'd always felt was so cold: It's not personal, it's business. It was business. It had to be only that.

"Bree," Natalia, one of my three very close girlfriends, said. I looked to my right, where the beautiful blonde raised her cosmopolitan toward me. "I know you had a couple of shitty days," she smiled as she used her usual sultry voice on me, "but tonight is Cass's night. Smile, babe."

I raised my martini glass to her and grinned. "Sorry. I was mentally working on that before you interrupted me." I took a sip and then spooned a bit of caviar on a cracker and took a bite.

"We'll talk it out later. We gals are all here for you, and you know that. I'm just pissed you never told us *this shit* was happening too."

I softly laughed and rolled my eyes. "The *one day* my best friend shows up to buy a Mercedes, and I'm there turning mine in."

She gave me a fun, challenging expression. "Well, thank God you've merged with Brooks, cleaned out the garbage who tried to bankrupt you, and have that *fucking hot*," she leaned over and purred those last words in my ear, "Alexander Grayson as your new partner."

I smiled at the patrons who were starting to filter into the place.

The entire area was set up beautifully. Pink roses placed in beautiful glass vases were the centerpieces and theme for each table at Tobias tonight. Cass worked with the owners and somehow enforced that anyone who went to the lavish hot spot tonight would enjoy the splendid décor of Cass's choosing. The candlelit table was a great finishing touch, and our table—positioned next to the large window overlooking the ocean below—couldn't have been more perfect if I helped design the layout myself.

This was the restaurant portion of Tobias, and the next building over was where their club was—a club that everyone stood outside in line for hours with the hope that they'd be lucky enough to get inside. I'd never visited the nightclub here before, mainly because the nightlife seemed to be a thing of the past for me once I noticed Stone Company was going under.

Tonight, I would have to put on a brave face when we migrated to that section for the second part of Cass's birthday celebration. God only knew how that would work out. I was rusty and in no frame of mind to mingle with the single elites of Southern California. I was thirty-one years old, for Christ's sake. You'd think my friends and me would've been over this lifestyle by now, but alas, we were diving into it while we celebrated the last of our group turning thirty.

The night was for Cass, and I wasn't going to argue with how she wanted to spend her birthday, even if it meant acting like we were twenty-one again while screwing off in a club. So, I wore my best smile and my best strapless dress to match. A new chapter might as well start with a bang.

"Ladies," Sammy, a best friend I hadn't seen in too long, announced. "Well, well," she looked at me with her radiant smile as she sat, "look at you finally out of leggings and hoodies and joining us with a smile. I've missed the hell out of you, Bree."

"I've missed you all more. Let's just say this last month took its toll on me in more ways than one."

"Well, you've heard it from Theo, Stanton, and all three of us a million times," Cass said, joining us as she sat across from Nat and me with a cheeky grin, "the merge was a good thing, and from what we're all aware, thank God it happened."

Cass arched her eyebrow at me at the same time as Sammy, and Nat peered at me knowingly as she sipped her cosmopolitan, making it evident that my friends had learned that not only was Stone going under, but they knew I was in financial trouble for the time being as well.

"Yes, thank God." I tried to ignore all the expressions.

"You are dead meat for not telling me that you're completely broke," Cass said, ordering another round of drinks for the table. She sat perfectly erect in her chair and folded her arms. "Spill it."

"Spill what? How about this? Happy birthday, Cass." I smiled at her authoritative look. "We're all here to celebrate your big day, and I'm feeling more like myself again and hoping to add some cheer to the festivities."

"More like yourself, eh?" Sammy sipped her cocktail. "Were you feeling more like yourself when you handed that dealership the keys to your car today?"

I sighed. "Thanks, Nat." I looked at my no-nonsense friend. "What would I do without you helping to get *that* out in the open for me?"

"No, no, no, babe," she said as she took a bite of her caviar cracker. "That's not how this shit works between all of us, and you know it. We're all as close as sisters here." She gave me her warning look with a smile. "You also know we confide in each other when things go wrong. No one here is ever on her own."

When I exhaled and looked at Cass, she looked at me with a guilty frown. "We could have done pajama night like when we were in college instead of doing all this. You know, staying in and hanging out. That would've been fun too."

I laughed. "Pajama night in college was like a lingerie show for Nat to bring frat boys back to our place." I glanced over at Nat's glossy and proud lips as she nodded shamelessly. "And so—"

"And *so,* what?" Natalia covered her full cleavage. "We were in college, and there were gorgeous men on campus. How else were we supposed to survive USC?"

I shook my head and instinctively fixed a loose curl on her shoulder-length blonde hair. "Natalia, you got us in trouble more times than we could count. We're lucky we didn't get thrown out of college."

"I say I did all of us a favor—all those raging hormones needed to be released somehow. I was just doing my part to keep everyone balanced," Nat said with a devilish grin and a laugh. "And as much fun as lingerie and men in a dorm room sound, we're all *finally* out together after Bree has come up for air from that suffocating company. So yes, we're celebrating Cass, good friends, and great conversation tonight." She gracefully lifted her chin and then raised her glass to Cass.

"Cheers to that!" I held my glass up for Cass. "Shall we kick off the celebration with the fact that you're the last of us four to leave the *roaring twenties* behind?"

"We shall." Cass raised the martini she'd just ordered. "All of us together, and Bree finally dolled up for a great night out too." She eyed me. "After learning about what happened with that fucker, Daniel Kyle, and that big heart of yours bankrupting you, I'd like to thank you for coming out. But know this: we'll all be here to help you get through."

"I know. It's why I love you three." I tipped my glass. "To new days ahead as we pull Cass across the line into her *dirty thirties!*"

Toasts went up, and we enjoyed laughter, silly talk, and a few drinks to loosen up. Being out with my friends felt renewing to my soul. Even if I was in a pitiful place in my life at the moment, I knew it would pass.

"That one there," Natalia started sizing up someone behind me. "That man is a good prize for Bree." She sipped her drink as if she were tasting the dark-haired man herself.

My girlfriends were daring and full of nonsense once the booze kicked their brains into another gear. Nat undoubtedly trailblazed into flirty and frivolous behavior, which always led to a good laugh. She seemed to oddly balance out the four of us—in her own crazy, horny way, of course.

"No, not him," Cass laughed along with the rest of us at the table. "He's too proper with that polo shirt tucked into his khakis." She winked at me. "Our Bree is looking for someone a little more put together, maybe someone in a nice button-down shirt and black slacks."

"True," I teased. "I'm officially a gold-digger tonight, so sniff that one out with your constant wondering eyes, will you, Nat? I'm sure he'll join us when we head over to the club after dinner."

"Ask and it shall be given," Sammy teased, knowing Nat would take this as an open invite to find the man for me. "Probably shouldn't take the leash off Nat while we're still in the restaurant, though, Bree," she played along. Then her eyes widened, and she gulped down a sip of her cocktail. "Dear God in heaven."

Sammy paused like a deer caught in headlights, and then it felt like the entire room paused with her—the whole area except for the six men who'd just moved through it like they were the owners. It was James Mitchell and company, so they probably did own this place in one way or another.

All six men grabbed the attention of the room like A-list celebrities, and Mother of God, they were all agonizingly gorgeous. Smiles were flashed around from a blond man and a dark-haired man —the dark-haired man being Dr. Jake Mitchell. We all knew his face and story too well after the paparazzi had taken an interest in the hot, chief heart surgeon at Saint John's Hospital. The others, aside from Alexander Grayson and James Mitchell, were unknown to me.

"Well, Jesus, Mary, and Joseph," Natalia said. "Your new partner is hotter in person than in those business magazines." She leaned into me. "And you're telling me that you despised him being your partner?"

"It was personal." I smiled, enjoying that Alex was oblivious to the fact that I was sitting a few tables away from him.

"Yeah, we all officially now know what *personal* gets you, don't we?" Cass raised that damn eyebrow at me. "Thank God for those men at the table. They're saving your dad's company," she reached for my shoulder, "and your adorable, perfectly plump ass."

"Cheers to that," Sammy nodded as she sipped her martini.

"Now, who's going over there to thank them?" Nat asked.

"No one," I interrupted with a smile, holding onto Nat's arm with a death grip. "And if you so much as move a muscle to get up and go over there, I will break both of your kneecaps. Shattered bone, do you hear me?"

"Relax," Nat countered with an eye-roll. "As a matter of fact, excuse me?" she called for the server. "We need to kick this off with a round of shots." She slid her arm out from my grip and placed it on my shoulder. "Make them all blow jobs." She winked at the young man and then carefully sipped her drink.

"Oh, Christ. You're going to get us all in trouble," I answered.

"You'll all thank me in the morning."

"While nursing hangovers?" Sammy laughed.

"Or maybe waking up in some stranger's bed?" Cass chuckled.

"*That* will never happen again," Nat said, referencing the worst experience she'd had during a weekend in Vegas. "I still have nightmares about that pitiful situation."

"We all broke our promise of never going to another club again after that happened to you, and here we all are." I chuckled.

"Well, we did mature, I think," Sammy said with a laugh. "So, we're safe tonight."

"Yes, and how are we supposed to accept our *maturity* while we have blow jobs for shots in a fine restaurant?" I couldn't help but look at Nat and laugh.

"Just like this," Nat answered me when she took her shot glass, knocked it back, then slowly used her tongue to lick her upper lip seductively.

We all laughed while I raised my shot toward Sammy and Cass. "To maturity and Nat insisting we're still the girls gone wild in college."

"Cheers," Cass and Sammy said in unison while we downed our shots.

I couldn't help but smile when Alex Grayson's eyes met mine at the very moment I set my shot glass on the table. He raised his bourbon, winked, and then flashed a smile that made my insides warm before he brought his attention back to his group.

I noticed how strangely beautiful the man suddenly became to me at the current moment. It wasn't the booze, either. I'd already encountered the strikingly good-looking man with enough alcohol in my system to understand this was different from that.

"Breanne," I heard the girls laughing, their voices ringing through my head while my brain misfired because of that charming smile of Alex's.

"What?" I asked, our delicious dinner plates being placed in front of us.

Sammy's lips were tight with humor, Nat had her head down to prevent bursting into laughter, and Cass wore a sympathetic grin while she raised her cloth napkin to her upper lip.

"You have whipped cream all over your lip." She covered her smile with her napkin.

"And if I were going to point out a *fact*, I'd say that Alexander Grayson was certainly appreciative of the white-lipped smile you just gave him," Nat said with a soft laugh while pushing the tomatoes around in her salad with her fork. "Too bad you missed the opportune moment to lick that off your lip for him."

I shook my head with embarrassment. "I seriously can't win with that guy. Swear to God," I said while briskly wiping the cream off my face. "Now, not only did the man find my employees stealing from the company, but he's also watching his business partner act like she's a—"

"Hot piece of ass who most likely gave him a stiffy that he has to hide under that table," Sammy chuckled.

"I saw that smile on that devilish face of his," Nat nudged me. "Nice work, Bree."

"Change of subject." I handed Cass a tiny jewelry box. "I had this made for you," I said as I pushed my dinner plate to the side, folded my arms, and leaned on the table.

"Bree!" She grinned. "You know I love gifts, but I was serious when I said that coming out and being with you girls was all I wanted."

"Open it." I smiled.

She did and gently pulled out the delicate charm of the sun I'd designed and had a jeweler create. The engraved lines were meant to reflect light as if the charm itself were shining. It was simple yet unique in how the jeweler had fashioned it. I was quite blown away when he held it up, and rays shone as if I were looking into the splendor of a diamond under bright lighting. I always referred to Cass as our beam of light, and I couldn't help but design and have the jeweler create something symbolic that represented our Cass.

"That's positively stunning," Nat said, she and I being on the receiving ends of the light hitting the charm.

"I love this," Cass said, holding it out, all of us impressed by the prisms beaming from the dainty charm. "How in the world..." she stopped and looked at me. "You are amazing, Breanne Stone. You designed this yourself, didn't you?"

"Bree, how do you come up with this stuff?" Sammy asked, touching her fingertip to it.

"Well, it was your thirtieth, and I got a little sentimental with ideas this year. Better than a gift card, eh?"

"It's the most beautiful gift ever, sweet Bree." She blew me an air kiss, and then we all returned to our meals before moving the party to the club in the next building.

While we went straight to dancing, laughing, and forgetting the world around us, I found my spirit again. I was sparked with energy and filled with revitalization. I loved it, and I'd missed this.

The girls and I must've spent an hour on the dance floor between drinks and laughs before I needed a break to catch my breath.

"Damn, I'm out of shape," I laughed when Cass joined me at the bar.

"What do you say we go back to my place, do pajama night, and... hang on," Cass stopped and took a sip of the cosmopolitan she'd ordered. "We can do pajama night and use that brand new lingerie to do *The Catwalk* as we did in college."

Cass danced where she stood while I ordered water, seriously in need of hydration and catching my breath. "Why don't you take your tipsy-self back out to the dancefloor? The Catwalk will have to wait for another time."

"We're doing it, Stone," she arched an eyebrow at me. "Even if we have to take a few cuties home with us tonight to be our judges."

"You're drunk," I laughed.

"You're proposing a damn good idea," the low, scratchy voice of Alex said from behind me.

"Right?" drunk-Cass answered Alex. "You can be Bree's judge." She laughed then chewed her lip after my eyes widened to what she'd said and the fact that Alex was *actually* in this club. "Off to dance…"

I turned on my stool to face Alex as he sat next to me with his drink.

"You and I are not having this conversation," I said. "I'm drinking, have been drinking for a while. We're not doing *this* again."

"I figured I'd use this opportunity to get my kiss from you finally." He sipped his drink, then looked back at the dance floor. "I was also quite tempted to steal you away from a few men out there."

"Right," I nodded. "So, what brings Mr. Suit into a club?"

His expression succeeded in reviving all of the once dead sexual parts of my body. "Well, after you teased me with that shot at dinner tonight, I figured I'd stalk you like a crazy man into the club."

My body wanted to believe he was serious—and the liquor in my system would have helped my brain believe it if I hadn't been cautious about not getting wasted tonight—but the man was enjoying teasing me, so why not play back?

"I don't do one-night stands, sorry." I shrugged and drank my water. "Might have to keep a wandering eye on that dance floor, though."

"That's good to know," he said. "Now I won't have to worry about taking you back to my place, you know, because it wouldn't be for just one night."

"Ah," I answered. "Sounds like you want to cross some serious ethical work boundaries, eh?"

"Nah," he shrugged that sentiment off. "You're my partner—life-long, as I recall—and therefore, ethics go out of the fucking window when you own the company *with* me and don't work *for* me."

"Goddamn," I said. "You've done a little research. It seems you have it all figured out with our life-long partnership, don't you?"

"Well, there was no way I wasn't going into a relationship for life with a beautiful woman and not having sex with her."

"You're insane," I finally laughed. "Seriously, what brings you in here?"

"Just finishing up dinner and thought I'd congratulate you on a job well done again. Also, it appears you're doing well with the news of Theo moving?"

I nodded and smiled at him. "What you did for him was a very kind thing. He's a great man and deserves nothing less than the offer you gave him."

"So, you're handling the move well?"

Suddenly, Alex and I transitioned into a more casual and friendly conversation, and I sensed his concern about my mental state more than anything else. I couldn't blame the guy. He'd seen me stupid drunk, crying, and insecure, and he'd also seen the bitch side of me. He was probably wondering if Theo leaving was going to be what made me finally break.

"I'm looking forward to better days for all of us," I admitted. "And for you and me as partners. Tonight is my best friend's birthday, and what better way to turn the page in one's life than to celebrate the happiness of another?"

He licked his lips, his eyes seemed to swirl in their emerald color, and he let out a breath that made me believe he wasn't expecting to hear that from me.

"You're a unique woman, Breanne Stone," he said, before he finished the last of his drink. "I believe my car is awaiting me, and I'm glad you're doing well."

"Turning the page." I smiled at him.

"That's an ideal way to look at it. Enjoy the rest of your evening, and you have my number if some douche wants to try anything stupid with my girl."

"*Your girl*, huh?"

"Lady? Life-long partner? It's all the same." He arched a friendly eyebrow at me. "And in all of those things, you're most certainly mine."

"For life," I softly said, my brain trying to process his expression, tone, and gentle nod.

"Absolutely," he affirmed.

As quickly as Alex Grayson appeared from out of nowhere, he disappeared in the same manner, walking through the crowd in the massive club area, and I was left to wonder what the hell had just happened.

CHAPTER TEN
ALEX

I had watched each of my close friends have life-changing occurrences which led them down a path of finding love in the most peculiar ways. As a bystander who'd watched everything my friends had gone through, I decided long ago to take what I deemed was a more straightforward route—not allowing a woman in at all. Quite frankly, I enjoyed the less problematic method of happiness by *not* bringing a complicated woman into my life.

I could never become *that man*, the one I'd watched all of my buddies transform into. The man who was blindsided by love and all of the complications that waited on the other side of that word. Don't get me wrong; what my friends found with their ladies was priceless and worth it for them. I was a pragmatist, however, and there was no way the lucky lightning could strike all four of us. I suppose they had what I don't, though, which is a willingness for love to find me in the first place.

My childhood was made up of horrors I wouldn't wish on my worst enemy, so the idea that I might have to share those experiences with another was a reason for me to avoid relationships like the plague. The pieces of the trauma I hadn't blocked out were enough to make me suffer from night terrors for as long as I can remember—

night terrors that made me jolt awake, drenched in sweat and feeling like I'd been trying to outrun the hell hounds that tormented me endlessly. I didn't want to have to explain the occurrence to anyone. Weird things like night terrors led to questions, and questions led to the truth. And the truth was something my family didn't talk about.

I tried to make things work with Summer, but ultimately, my attempt at that confirmed what I've always known: I don't have it in me. In the end, I looked like the asshole I was because she desperately tried to change the game on me. We were supposed to be having casual fun, but it didn't take her long to sink her claws into me and try to transform me into the perfect boyfriend material. That's when it all went south.

What started as fun with an uncomplicated woman ended up being a suffocating relationship driven by her insecurities and desire to *fix* me and make me into the man of her dreams. I moved on from that for her and myself. If she wanted a man to share forever with, she should have easily known I could've never been that man.

Now, I was dealing with Bree. From everything I'd come to know about her, she was my definition of a complicated woman. She'd had a messy, wedding-day breakup, she was a mess at work half of the time, and I'd seen her on the verge of falling apart more times than I'm sure she'd have liked. And even though she's everything I usually steered clear of when it came to women and my so-called version of a relationship, I'll be damned if she wasn't drawing my sorry ass in despite the walls I'd built to keep myself guarded. I wasn't entirely her victim, though—well, perhaps I was because Monday morning couldn't have come fast enough after I saw her out with her friends.

I'd seen many different faces of Breanne Stone and was either annoyed or amused by her shifting moods. After seeing the veil of the woman's business side dropped and catching a glimpse of the lovely demeanor she displayed with her friends, I knew I was headed down a road I swore never to travel—taking an interest in a woman who I could never make happy. Why was I fascinated by her so suddenly, the most complicated woman I'd encountered in far too long?

She's your fucking partner, that's why, I reassured myself before shaking this wild tangent of thought from my head. This was the last possible thing I needed to be thinking about.

Ring! Ring! Ring!

I glanced down at my phone after stepping out of my car and seeing that Breanne's new parking space was empty.

"Hey, Theo," I answered. "Everything good on your end?"

"I'm going through the proposals and wanted to thank you again for this. Should I drop it by Stone or Mitchell?"

"Fax it to Mr. Monroe at Mitchell. He's handling the restructure in the London office while I deal with the shit that went south with Stone." I glanced at my watch and then back to Bree's empty parking space. "Quick question," I said to Theo while shouldering my leather briefcase.

"Anything. Is everything okay? Bree told me you guys are opening up in the Brooks Architectural building today."

"Yeah," I answered, still confused as to why the hell she wasn't yet here. "I'm curious about whether or not she's a creature of habit, and maybe she showed up at the wrong building this morning. She's not here."

I heard a sigh on the other end of the line.

Complicated women. And this is who you thought about for your entire commute to work this morning? I thought with a roll of my eyes.

"What's up, Theo?" I became more direct. "If something is going on with her, I need to know. I'm getting ready to head up to my office, and I wasn't expecting her to be late on a day when her faithful employees are here to report for work."

"I shouldn't say anything, but..." he paused.

"I'm a man who doesn't beat around the bush. Tell me what is going on with Breanne."

"She's at work. She's already there and said she loves her office. She's been there since six this morning."

"Ah," I answered, listening to the man stammer, holding something back. "Why isn't her car here, then? Is she so humble that she parks on the second floor in the garage with the rest of our employees?"

"She'll *kill me* if I told you, but after the way you've taken care of me, I know you'll understand her unfortunate situation."

I stopped from entering the front doors of my building and walked toward one of the pillars that faced the valet stand.

"*I'll* kill you if you *don't* tell me," I teased. "Seriously, I need to know what I'm walking into. What kind of *unfortunate situation* is Breanne facing?"

"She's broke as hell," Theo sighed while my eyes widened in shock.

"Broke as hell?" I repeated. "As in living on the streets? I saw her at a ridiculously expensive restaurant on Saturday night. What'd she do, gamble her life away in Vegas on Sunday?"

"Alex, I can hear the humor in your voice, and this is why she would kill me for letting you in on this."

"It's not humor. It's more like disbelief," I answered. "What are we looking at? The woman is an executive for a large architectural firm. On top of that, Mitchell and Associates pay rather well as our parent company."

"Well, after her girlfriends told me she surrendered her car to the dealership on Saturday, I wanted to chew her out. Her best friends are very close and will help her financially until she can fix this."

"I need direct answers, Theo, not gossip column BS. How *broke* is she, and how did this happen? Does she not understand the meaning of investing money? Paying bills? What?"

I was becoming firm because this was the most insane thing I'd ever heard in my entire life. At this age, and with all of these opportunities that'd been made available to her, how the fuck could she be flat broke?

"Bree has a huge heart. All of the money she had to her name, down to every last penny of her father's inheritance, she invested into her father's company. She was determined to keep Stone afloat and save her father's legacy. This is why I hope you bury every last son of a bitch who stole from her. While they pillaged, she was donating her paychecks, life savings, and selling off stocks so they wouldn't lose their homes or cars."

I could hear the man choking up.

"Jesus Christ," I finally said.

"Don't you dare be an asshole to her," Theo's voice sharpened. "I *don't* need that job in London, and I will risk losing it to tell you that I will kick your ass if you tell her you know and if you're a condescending dick to her about this."

I smiled. Someone threatening to kick my ass while talking business was normal, but a CEO being flat broke after *donating* their assets? That was *not* fucking normal.

"My lips are sealed," I assured him. "I am in shock that she considered doing that shit, but my new partner never ceases to amaze me. Don't worry about Breanne. I'll manage to get her to tell me, and we'll ensure the woman isn't auctioning off her belongings at high noon today."

"This isn't a joke, Alex," Theo said. "Breanne may have a huge heart, but the woman is as stubborn as a mule."

"Got it," I responded. "Maybe over a few *Moscow Mules* this afternoon, she'll confide in me, and we'll get the bills paid and a *company car* offered in her new bonus package."

"She'll see right through that," Theo warned. "She won't drink during business hours either. She stated that after her run-in with you while she was drunk at the gala. She vowed never again to let liquor interfere with her thoughts while in your presence."

"I'll find a way. I always do." I smiled, knowing there hasn't been one woman or business transaction that I couldn't have my way with. "Take care, Theo, and fax over the details. Spencer Monroe will be working on your transfer and ensuring you're taken care of."

"Not a word to Bree," he warned again.

"Her dark secret is safe with me," I teased.

"I don't like that tone."

"And I don't like keeping secrets," I answered. "However, I'll get the news directly from the woman. Rest easy, friend." With that, I hung up.

Breanne Stone may be a complicated woman, but she wasn't complicated enough that I couldn't manage to sneak this out of her. I was her partner, and I would do anything to help her rise from the dust pile her employees threw her in. For the love of God, who in their right mind would allow themselves to go bankrupt with their company? That shit would have to be explained to me because I would never figure it out on my own.

Failing businesses either close up shop or get sold to the highest bidder, eager to take them on—I'd never heard of a CEO going bankrupt along with the company. Executives could usually see a bad thing coming, and they'd jump ship long before they went down with the damn thing. This woman was dangerously attached to her father's company, but to the point of bankruptcy? What the living fuck?

My new mission today—on top of shaking the last of the rotten apples out of the tree from Stone and the joys of sitting with HR and legal at Mitchell this afternoon—was to crack Breanne Stone. The woman had done the most mind-blowing thing I could imagine, and I *was* going to get it out of her. I knew trust was something she needed to find in me, so I'd start there. I sure as shit hoped the friends she was out with on Saturday were helping the woman because I couldn't lend a hand unless I confessed that Theo had sold her ass out.

With a new smile of determination on my face, I walked into the magnificent entrance of Brooks, happy to be back in the intricately designed building—designed by John Brooks himself—and eager to get some coffee and meet with my destitute business partner.

Strangely, I welcomed this because I had a feeling the woman was going to lie at every angle to save herself embarrassment, and I wasn't going to let up on her. It's how I was programmed—to find answers and seal deals at any cost.

MY VICE PRESIDENT, Jacey Grant, was the first to greet me after slamming into me with a pile of papers, which exploded all around us, falling like feathers to the ground. I laughed as I always did when Jacey's mind was spinning, and she was trying to handle shit behind the scenes.

"I thought we were going *green*, Jace," I teased her, seeing her hair falling out of its once intricately styled bun, her cheeks heated, and her eyes pleading with me to leave her to the day that was trying to go to hell on her.

"This is bullshit," she said. She was never one to cuss, around me, anyway.

I knelt and started to gather the papers that were scattered in the hallway. "What's bullshit? What happened?"

"I'm getting calls from Stone Company employees asking why their place of business has locked them out."

"Why haven't you directed them to Breanne or me?"

"Bree jumped my ass for it earlier." She smirked and raised her eyebrows. "She certainly has fire in her spirit."

"Jumped your ass?" I frowned, off-put at the idea of Breanne being a bitch to the woman we shared as a vice president.

"In a good way. She wasn't mean," she said, looking over her glasses at me. "She told me to block their numbers from my cell and that they were her problem, not mine."

"Here's the deal," I handed her the last of the papers and stood with her, "they're neither yours nor her problem. Unfortunately, these fuckers who robbed Stone blind didn't get the memo that Lexi sent out on Friday night."

"You're playing it too nice, if you ask me," Jacey eyed me. She was unbelievably gorgeous, albeit a bit neurotic for my taste. She was also completely off-limits if I wanted to keep a good vice president running this place.

"Well, you're a big, bad New Yorker," I said. She'd come from a badass firm in Manhattan, and she proudly graduated top of her class at NYC, and being a native East Coaster, she didn't mince words. "Sometimes, we Californians don't operate as boldly as you."

"You take the easy route," she chuckled.

"We tend to play the long game and give you enough rope to hang yourself," I countered. "While you blast people with truth bombs, I'm more inclined to put someone in the hot seat and watch them squirm and suffer a little bit."

"Whatever. Because you love watching people squirm, I'm left to deal with their BS in the meantime. I say cut and run."

I grinned, then nodded toward the papers she held. "What's with all the papers? Did our marketing team start printing flyers?" I pinched my lips, trying not to laugh at her rising frustration.

"They're the last of the papers we're inputting from Stone," Breanne said, walking up to us. "Here, Jacey. I'll take those."

I eyed Breanne, and though I loved her Michelle Pfeifer-esque mysterious eyes and lips, my primal male instincts begged me to see if the cleavage that was alive and well in her cocktail dress was still pronounced to perfection. This woman hid a body underneath that business attire that I wanted to discover in more ways than one.

She wore her usual pencil skirt, and I could tell her matching suit jacket was draped elsewhere while she and Jacey were up here busting their asses, making me feel like I was the schmuck who was late for work. With her business jacket abandoned, my eyes were grateful she wore a fashionable pink silk blouse with a loose, v-shaped neckline. I could tear this woman up if I wanted to destroy my business relationship —and part of me was starting to believe it would be worth it.

"You look pissed off," Jacey said, eying Breanne, then me.

"I'm sort of feeling like I'm late to the party," I looked at Breanne. "In fact, I was about to jump your ass for being late on your first day here when I noted your car wasn't parked next to mine in executive parking."

"Oh," her eyes widened, cheeks turned pink, then she looked at Jacey for help. "My car is in the shop."

I slid my hands into my suit pockets, realizing that Jacey and Breanne had already formed a little womanly bond and most likely about Bree being broke. Their body language and eye contact— Breanne thanking Jacey and Jacey giving a quick nod in response— confirmed it.

"Your car is in the shop?" I interrupted the women's telepathic glancing. "Oil change?"

"Nah. It broke down." She blew out a breath.

I refrained from smiling. "That sucks. Where did it leave you *broke* down at?" I toyed with the word broke, seeing her eyes narrow at me.

"Does it matter?" Jacey shot off, jumping on Bree's bandwagon. "How about we talk about the fact that we're moving Breanne out of the dark ages and teaching her to *go green* for the environment by inputting all of this into the computer?"

"How about that," I smiled at the two. "Let's spend the entire day inputting jobs into a computer instead of allowing our PAs to earn their paychecks."

"Confidential paperwork," Jacey said. "So, we'll see you later."

"Hold up, both of you." I turned to face where they were headed. "Let me see the papers."

What the hell were they all secretive and girlfriend-ish about? Who knew, maybe Jacey and Bree both preferred women—each other—and in the end, I'd be the damn joke.

Jacey shoved the papers into my hands, and I started to fan through the pages. Most were outdated projects, bids that needed approval, and some were mock-ups that the architects had fucked us on that would require the legal team.

I eyed Breanne. "First of all, you'll have to ignore Jacey and her love for the environment at times, especially when it comes to us needing this hard evidence in the hands of legal for this afternoon when we meet with them." I looked at Jacey. "I'm hoping this is why you're acting out of character and suddenly so skittish."

"We're trying to handle the last of the business. You're slowing us down," Jacey said with an arch of her eyebrow.

"Breanne and I have a meeting with some new department heads today." I smiled at Breanne. "Well, one head, anyway. I think they're all mostly losing their heads with those papers as proof that they robbed you of virtually everything."

"True," Breanne said.

"All right, get the papers secure and in my office," I said to Jacey. "You're in this meeting too. It seems that you and Breanne have become close enough for you to learn how we will be handling the merge moving forward."

"You're too nice by allowing them to step foot in the Howard building and giving them a chance to defend themselves in front of James Mitchell and Spencer Monroe," Jacey said.

"I told you that I like to put people in the *hot seat* earlier, and Mr. Monroe prefers to sit their asses on hot coals. The man has a way with words that will make the litigators take notes on how to improve their interrogation skills."

"I heard he's an absolute son of a bitch," Breanne said. "I'm not in the mood for assholes today."

I noticed her demeanor change when her eyes moved toward the wall I stood next to. "Well, with your car being *broke* and leaving you stranded, I can imagine."

"You say the word *broke* as if it's supposed to mean something else," Breanne snapped.

"I'm bringing these to your secretary," Jacey said. "I'll let Spencer know we have more documentation heading his way too."

"If he gives you shit, give him Bree's number," I said with a grin. "He needs to be checked by the woman who's not in the mood for assholes today."

She smiled while Breanne laughed. "Yeah, if Spencer Monroe wants to be bitchy about this, I can certainly handle him," Bree said.

"Have you met my buddy Spencer, or are these rumors that Brooks' employees have delivered to your itching ears today?"

"I was told that he's a no-bullshit man. He's James Mitchell's VP, so I can guarantee he's a hard-ass."

"I'm all those things as well. Does that guarantee me a seat at the table where you prematurely judge people?"

Her lips twitched. "I'm sorry. I'm being rude. This whole day has been hell from the minute I woke up and realized I didn't have my ca—"

A smile spread across my face when she stopped herself from telling the truth about not having her car.

"I'm sorry, are you from Boston all of a sudden? You didn't have a *cah* when you woke up this morning?" I teased.

"Alex," she tucked her hair behind her ear, ignoring my question, "our meeting is in fifteen minutes. We should probably go over notes and how we're going to roll out all of this."

"I'm more curious as to how you went from having a car in the shop to waking up without one altogether."

"Long weekend." She threw up that excuse next. "I'm not getting into it. I need to get my head into the game so that we can kick off this meeting properly."

It was bugging me that she wouldn't come out and tell me that the sons of bitches who had been stealing from her were the reason she was fucking broke. Time for the trust game. "I'm hoping your weekend wasn't long because some dick ruined it for you. You never called the one man who promised he'd take care of what was his."

Her eyes diverted from mine. "You can think that all day long, but no man owns me."

"So, you didn't go home with some dick who promised you what only I could give?"

Her eyes did that sexy wide-eye look. "Good God, Alex. We're at work, not at the bar."

"We're on the executive floors," I smiled, leaning my shoulder against the wall. "And I want to know the truth about your car. You're covering something up, and I'm not one for secrets."

"Well, instead of you believing I'm holding in a deep, dark secret," *which you are,* I thought while I nodded along to her proclamation, "it boils down to one thing." She arched a cocky eyebrow at me. "It's personal and none of your business."

"Now you've got my full attention, and I won't be able to focus in that meeting until I know the truth about why you and Jacey seem to be having a day from hell, and we're only thirty minutes into shop time."

"There's a lot ahead of both of us. My car not being parked next to yours should be the last thing on your mind."

"Just trying to make sure we're all merging, trusting each other, and two business partners are helping each other get through it all."

She inhaled and put on the smile that shut my ass right up. The goddamn dimples that popped in her cheeks would certainly fuck me over if I allowed them to latch onto me.

"Well, if you need any help," she said, "I'll be right at your side as you announce the new changes to our department heads and tell them why we're all moving into their building."

"When you smile like that..." I stopped myself immediately and simply nodded in agreement with her, ending the conversation. Shit. That one smile was enough to make me have to fight to ignore my impulses. She was smiling *at me* as she had her friends at dinner the other night. She was goddamn beautiful, and I was the most dangerous creature she could ever meet.

I was so fucked because I knew I wasn't wired to keep that smile on her face. I was a heartless bastard because, as my father always loved to remind me, I wasn't capable of love. Still, that'd never stopped me from pretending I could be Mr. Right for all the wrong girls.

But now, my voice was nearly cracking as I let her know that her smile does something to me, and the baffled, bashful look on her face —probably the knowledge that she knew I was smitten by her, and she liked it—sucked me in even more.

For someone who didn't let anything stand in his way—business or pleasure—I sure was having a hell of a time with this woman today.

CHAPTER ELEVEN
BREE

*M*y morning was a disaster so far, starting with me walking out to my car only to be reminded I didn't have the damn thing anymore. After spending all day Sunday, half hungover, going over the jacked-up paperwork from my embezzling employees, I could safely say that the last few days had been less than ideal. Regardless, I had all my paperwork ready for Mitchell and Associates' legal teams, and that's all that mattered.

I secured an Uber to take me to the office, and instead of feeling sorry for myself that I'd lost my car because of my dickhead employees, I used it as fuel to ignite a fire under my ass to handle business with those thieves.

I was doing great until Jacey overheard Theo on my speakerphone, asking me about the car. With perfect timing, she walked in as he mentioned my unfortunate financial situation. She was an angel when I ended the call right then and there with Theo and explained in vague detail how managing shitty employees had bitten me in the ass. With some resistance—and I'm sure confusion—she agreed to keep it between her and me. She tried to urge me to inform Alex, but when I explained that my new business partner didn't need to know about my crappy financial problems while dealing with my sleazeball employees, she backed off. We left it at that.

I wasn't used to being broke or accepting charity of any kind, so when Natalia offered to let me use her BMW—one of her *extra cars*—to say I was humbled was an understatement. Maybe a bit of my pride was bruised, but that was no one's fault but my own. I was wholeheartedly grateful to have such understanding friends in my life. My only problem was that I wouldn't get the keys until today, and it wouldn't have been a problem if good old Alex hadn't been prying into the whereabouts of my car all fucking morning.

He was the last person on earth I wanted to know about this. Learning my company was upside down because I'd been a spineless leader was more than he needed to know about me. My financial situation, however, was probably enough for him to walk away entirely. Someone like Alexander Grayson would never understand why I put everything back into the company because I was determined to keep my dad's legacy alive. Shit. I can't even imagine trying to explain that to Mr. Business in a suit.

After pushing his nose out of my business, ignoring the dark three-piece suit that served to enhance his fine figure and beautiful face, I was prepped for our first meeting of the day with our heads of marketing and sales.

While Alex talked and seven other men and women sat around the conference table, I watched their reactions to his words. Some seemed annoyed at the changes that were taking place in the company, and some seemed confused. They listened to Alex as he explained the finalization of the merge. After rounding everything out with my company moving into this building, the only thing left to do was to continue to shake things up, push out complacent employees, and perhaps find some dirty ones working for Brooks Firm too.

As he spoke, I studied the real estate company Brooks had been using—the agents and the land they scoped out for their customers—and I found a potential issue that could be a problem.

"Mr. Grayson," I spoke after he asked for input before moving forward, "I know we're going over in time here, but I've found something that's bothering me."

Alex smiled and nodded. "Take all the time you need." He took his seat at the head of the long glass table while I stood and walked toward the middle of it with my iPad. "Would you like to share what you have on our big screen?" he asked, trying not to laugh at my lack of technology savviness, coming from a company that didn't hold meetings in such a way.

"Go ahead." I handed it to him.

After he ran his fingers over the touchscreen, the corner screen in the room projected the real estate that one of our team members was working on for a project. It was a horrible plot, not at all acceptable for this project, and I was shocked marketing and sales had allowed it to move forward.

"What are we looking at here?" a man named Greg asked.

"We're looking at a project site for a brand-new outdoor mall," I answered, walking over to the screen that displayed the images of the land. "This isn't good real estate, and I wonder if the architect who's working with this client understands that."

"That site was the best in the valley, according to the agent. Our clients want an outdoor mall on a larger scale, and this was the biggest piece of land. It came at a great price," a woman named Tish answered.

"I didn't ask *why* it was purchased; I asked if the architect who's designing an outdoor mall with a waterpark included in this unique design knows about this site."

"No. We purchased it, and the client agreed."

"Why didn't you work with the client's architect?" I asked in confusion. "Shouldn't they have a say in where their design will be?"

"What's wrong with the site?" Alex asked.

"For starters, it's next to a sewage treatment facility, not to mention the tangle of freeways intersecting around it. Would you shop anywhere *outdoors* near that?" I looked at the expressions of realization popping up on everyone's faces except for Tish, who defended the site location.

"Perhaps the agent left that part out?" Tish said.

"Perhaps that is why you got such a fantastic deal as well, Tish," Alex eyed the woman. "Find out which sales member on your team approved the purchase of this shitty site, pun intended, and then we'll discuss why we've encouraged our clients to build a fantastic outdoor mall next to a goddamn toilet."

"We need to make sure that we're visiting the sites we purchase; this shows me that no one went to the site with their client. I know we're all living in a digital age but visiting sites that we're to build on isn't just good client business, it's also necessary for us to see the grand scale and do the best job possible. It's got stay in the—"

"Excuse me," the door cracked open, and my secretary Nicole had a look of horror on her face that forced me to pause in the same manner. "Natalia is here with a car."

Oh, for fuck's sake! I thought, remembering Nat was dropping the car and keys off at noon so we could grab lunch. Unfortunately, this meeting had run right into the lunch hour, and my stunning blonde best friend was waiting behind where Nicole stood, dangling keys as if she were my transportation fairy godmother.

"Show her in," Alex said with that sly smile of his.

Natalia walked in. Being a real estate agent for a top broker in Beverly Hills, she was dressed and coiffed immaculately, and I watched her air of confidence fill the room along with her rich perfume.

"Sorry to interrupt. I hadn't a clue Bree was still in a meeting," she said in her usual commanding voice. "I just need to hand off these keys…" she stopped when she saw the look on my face—a look that would've turned her to stone if it could've.

Nat was caught in the crossfire of Alex's smirk and me looking at her with a death stare at the same time as she locked eyes on the sewer property.

"Keys for Ms. Stone's car? The one that's broke down and in the shop?" Alex pressed.

"Yes," Nat smoothly said. "I had no idea where to park the thing. Forgive me, but I can't help but notice the construction site next to that wretched sewage treatment plant." She smiled at the room. The men sitting around the table were damn-near drooling over her, and the four women sat there with challenging expressions. "I'm in real estate, and I know this site well. I would never allow any of my clients to purchase it. Please God," she looked at me, "tell me this isn't another situation that occurred at Stone."

Alex smiled. "This is a lapse in judgment that occurred within the Brooks Architectural Firm that Breanne spotted with her eagle eyes. Tell me, Mrs. Hoover, or is it Miss?" he inquired as Nat relaxed into her usual real estate agent pose.

"It's *Ms.* Hoover." She glanced at one of the young, hot guys in the room. "And I plan for it to be *Ms.* Hoover until the day I die," she added while my mouth dropped. "Call me Nat, though. I prefer that method when I'm in a conversation."

God, Natalia. I will kill you.

"Good to know," Alex answered while everyone around the table watched this theatrical event playing out. "I won't look for a wedding invite anytime soon." He smiled while Nat eyed me with a look that said, *if you don't fuck this man, I gladly will.* "Now, you mentioned you wouldn't allow your clients to purchase this real estate?"

"I'm with J&R Brokerage. I'm sure you've heard about us?"

"My friend, Spencer Monroe, had a great experience with your firm with the purchase of his two homes," Alex said.

Nat nodded and smiled in her sultry way. "Mr. Monroe was one of my most enjoyable clients," she added. "We had a brilliant—"

"Nat," I interrupted my best friend, who was likely about to announce that she'd screwed mine and Alex's boss to a room full of employees. "Perhaps you would like to meet me downstairs. I'll only be a moment."

"Of course," Nat smiled. "I do hope no one signed on the dotted line for that property."

"It's for an outdoor mall," Alex said, keeping Nat in the room.

Is he trying to give me a fucking heart attack? The smile on his face told me he loved every ounce of this shit.

"I would like to offer you an exclusive opportunity to work as our sole agent for Brooks and Stone. I should hope you specialize in commercial as well as residential properties?"

"You're talking to the finest real estate agent in Beverly Hills, Alexander Grayson."

Fuck. Fuck. Fuck. Leave, Nat. Please, God, just go.

"I could sense that from the moment you walked into the room," Alex said. "How about this," he looked at the department heads around the table, "we'll meet tomorrow in the first-floor conference room. I want each employee on your team present as we introduce Miss Hoover to them. She will be their new contact for properties, so we don't end up building a children's museum next to a nuclear reactor."

"I'm the girl for the job." Nat smiled at me.

"Would you recommend Miss Hoover's services?" Alex asked me with a shit-eating grin.

"She's who we used at Stone, and she comes highly recommended." I smiled at my best friend. I should not have been surprised that after spending a handful of minutes in the room, Nat's sass had landed herself a job as our exclusive agent. She was nothing if not charismatic. "It was her work that brought us that remarkable piece of beachfront property for Sphere before it even hit the market. She's skilled, she's fast, and she's worth far more than I'm sure we're willing to pay to secure her."

"Oh, I think she'll like the package I'm willing to offer." Alex smiled at me before he looked around the room. "Any questions before we all meet again tomorrow with all teams present?"

"None," Tish said flatly.

"Good," Alex narrowed his eyes at her. "I expect you'll fix this purchase error, apologize to the clients, and work swiftly with Natalia tomorrow to find a better location for their mall in the valley. I don't settle for shit, and all of you are keenly aware of that. Especially you, Tish," his dark stare softened her stiff posture. "Fix this by the meeting tomorrow. I want to see that the property is either back on the market or sold by then. This error is egregious, and I hope we don't uncover anything else like this under mine and Ms. Stone's watch again. You may all go and grab some lunch."

I FILTERED OUT with the rest of the room and took Nat's elbow in my hand, leading her directly into my office.

"Nat," I sighed, then hugged her. "You know you'll be the *end of me,* right?"

"Good Lord, this is the end of you? This room is fucking heaven on earth!" She raised her hands and walked toward the corner of my office that had floor-to-ceiling windows.

She stepped forward, leaning into the way the windows were fashioned to slant outward, giving an optimum view of the garden area located next to a small boutique mall and cafe.

"Speaking of—"

"Gloria's!" she smiled back at me. "We're shopping there. I'm sure you can use some leather and lace in your wardrobe. It's expensive, but..." she paused, and her coy smile spread on her lips when she looked at my door.

"I'm sure that since we caught thieves in Stone and landed the Sphere account," Alex said, stepping in behind where I stood, "Breanne could afford to purchase some of that fine Italian clothing for all of us."

I pursed my lips and eyed my best friend, then turned around. "Not while my car is in the shop," I reinforced my lie.

"Right," Alex slipped his hands into his pockets, a gesture that shouldn't have done anything to me whatsoever, but it served to keep the man as sexy as sin. "Strange." He looked at Nat. "The keys that you delivered, aren't they for Breanne's car?"

"Listen," I held a finger up to keep Nat's lips shut and looked at Alex, "I have a hefty bill to pay for repairs, so no, I'm not going to be buying you lace underwear for your wardrobe today, Alexander."

He playfully smiled at me, and I knew the man wasn't done with his quest to find out I was broke as fuck. Why the hell did he care to find out so much, anyway? Jesus Christ, turn a blind eye for God's sake. Something told me that it was probably morbid curiosity—like watching a horrible reality television show—that kept his attention. The constant, shitty drama in my life was like a train wreck he couldn't look away from.

"Dammit. Maybe on a better day, then," he said. "So, Miss Hoover, I must know the details of your friendship with my good friend, Spencer Monroe."

"Spicy Spence?" She did her sexy yet contagious laugh. Then she caught herself when she realized she'd revealed her sex name for our boss.

"Spicy Spence?" Alex laughed a laugh that made this stressful situation fade in that instant. "God in heaven. I thought I would never have anything to hang over that man's head."

"I don't plan on seeing him again." Nat's eyes darted to me for help, but she walked into this game I'd been in the middle of since Alex and I first met. I might as well watch her squirm in her confidence a bit. "So, please, do not mention I'm working as your agent."

"Was he a dick who dumped you? Don't tell me that because of his lack of good judgment, I'm going to lose my partner's friend and someone who appears to be an excellent real estate agent too?"

"Natalia might not be our number one choice here," I interrupted. "If she's had a relationship with Mr. Monroe, then that could potentially be a problem, and we can't have any more drama than we already have." I looked at Nat. "You'll most likely be seeing him again; are you up for that?"

She chewed on her bottom lip. "Monroe was a great time, but the man answered a call in the middle of…" she paused while Alex softly laughed.

"Sex?" Alex said.

"Yes," she answered. "It doesn't get any more humiliating than that. I'm an amazing—"

"Real Estate agent," I finished Nat's sentence, stopping her from treating Alex as if he were Theo or one of the girls, "and I would like to keep you involved. We need to find a way to have you help us secure deals, but not quite working with a man you screwed."

"If I weren't allowed to work with men I screwed, I'd never have any work at all!" Nat said with a laugh.

"And there it is," I added, covering my face with my hand as Alex laughed loudly at my shameless friend.

"Well, I'm starving," Alex said, breaking up this conversation. "Breanne, I would take you to lunch to discuss what Mr. Mitchell and Monroe have planned, but I believe you and your friend here have some job details to work out." Alex rocked back on his heels as I nodded. "The lawyers and Monroe are set to finalize the things, and we're just going to be there for the entertainment. Enjoy your lunch, ladies. I'll see you at the Howard building at two o'clock." Alex nodded, and then he left like he magically floated on air.

"Nat, what the living hell?" I said to her.

"What? I screwed Monroe, and I thought I was amazing, but the son of a bitch still stopped in the middle and answered a goddamn phone call."

"That's what you get for screwing wealthy businessmen to close deals."

"Breanne Stone," she snapped, "he signed the agreement first, then we had cocktails, and the liquor drove me into his bed."

"Being in my boss's bed is bad enough."

She looked over at my door. "I can tell Alex is still part of Mitchell and Associates, and he's more of a boss to you than Spicy Spence could ever be."

"What does that mean?" I asked, closing my door.

"It means I have a suspicion that Alex—your partner—not only works here, but he also has his tight connections with your parent company. He's best friends with the owner, for Christ's sake."

"I'm so done with this day, and I haven't even met with lawyers and ex-employees yet." I rubbed my forehead. "I have no appetite, and I probably should go hunt Alex down and figure out exactly what's going to—"

"You're having lunch with me. You're going to relax, and you're going to appreciate that I see how Mr. Alex Grayson looks at you.

Your cute little expressions? Your horrible poker face? All of it fuels that man to *want you*, and in delicious ways, I'm sure."

I smiled at her. "Everything is sex to you," I grabbed my purse, "and I'm not you. So, if Alexander Grayson thinks he and I are going to have sex while he answers his phone, then he is sorely mistaken."

Nat chuckled. "I highly doubt he will be answering phones while you're riding him to the extreme heights of ecstasy."

"We're walking out of my office now," I warned her. "No more sex talk, and no talking about the loaner car you brought me—which, thank you again for that."

"No problem," she said. "Ronaldo is my partner at the agency. He's the one I'll have rep for us over here if you and Alex still want our real estate services."

She was more professional now that we were in public again, mostly because she was on her way to eat. I loved the girl, but God almighty, she had a knack for fucking me over in the worst ways possible. There was never any gray area with Nat, though. Everyone knew exactly where they stood with her, and at times, I felt like I would be wise to learn from her fearless nature.

CHAPTER TWELVE
ALEX

*B*ree and I sat quietly while Spencer and Jim made these bottom-feeding thieves confess their wrongdoings through tears or out of fear of the police being called.

It was quite enjoyable to watch Spence and Jim play *good cop, bad cop,* but I could see that this shit was taking its toll on Breanne. I tried to empathize with her, but since I was the guy who caught the assholes and not the victim of their maliciousness, I struggled to give a damn about how these sneaky fuckers felt.

Breanne was face-to-face with the people who'd all but bankrupted her, believing that she was to blame for her company not paying its bills. That's the main reason I was enjoying watching Jim and Spencer ream these pathetic losers. The woman who sat stiffly by my side couldn't pay her bills because she thought she needed to protect these sons of bitches, so these people deserved every ounce of karma that was about to crash down on them.

Any other day, I would have happily jumped in alongside Jim and Spence to make these dicks suffer more guilt and fear for what they'd done, but oddly, my gut told me to sit this one out. It was more useful in this situation for me to be a bystander with Breanne and offer her smiles of reassurance that Jim, Spencer, and the lawyers were going to fix the problem.

After the last jerk-off walked out in tears, offering Breanne one final pathetically guilty nod, I rose and thanked the lawyers for their time. Breanne was behind me, and I could sense the woman was utterly drained after listening to this shit for four hours.

"You okay?" I quietly asked after the lawyers left me, Jim, and Spencer with her.

She lifted her chin. "I'm good," she said, fake-Rolex smile plastered on her face.

I glanced at her hands. "Your hands are trembling." I instinctively covered where she folded them together to prevent Jim and Spencer from seeing her at a breaking point. "Tell me this is from nerves of excitement and not guilt."

I sucked in a breath when her eyes lifted to mine. Of all the emotions I'd seen in her, I'd never seen this expression. It was as if she were holding back tears, but her eyes seemed to plead with me to hold her as if the woman were mine to protect. The act of covering her hands with mine brought about a revelation that damn-near struck me upside the head: I *loved* the idea of her being mine to protect from any shady bastard who would dare to hurt this woman in any way. The sentiment was a total shock to me, but it wasn't unwelcome.

"Nerves of excitement." She pulled her hands away from mine after we shared some weirdly intimate eye-locking moment. "That's all."

"Liar," I teased, resorting to humor, knowing that if Spence and Jim had seen this thoughtful and un-business-like situation I'd lost myself in, I'd never hear the fucking end of it.

Jim was the first to walk over while I turned to see Spence on his phone, finalizing the details of the pricks we'd spent the last of the workday dealing with. "Jesus Christ," he said with a half-smile. "I can't believe that shit was going on at Stone." He looked at Breanne. "You had no idea this was happening?"

"No idea," she answered firmly, holding her own against Jim's usual no-bullshit expression. "And if I'm honest, it was difficult to keep my mouth shut while they made their excuses."

"Well, I'm glad you did," Jim answered with a smile. "Sometimes, disgruntled and lying employees have a way of turning their former boss's words on them."

I grinned. "You're not alone, though," I said, gripping my best friend's shoulder. "Jim has had his fair share of sitting with lawyers while I was the one doing the interrogations of the shady employees."

Jim softly laughed. "From the sound of it, it seems like you had difficulty sitting through it and keeping your mouth shut too."

"Nah," I half-lied. "It was quite enjoyable to watch your dick-side surface when those thieves started to use Breanne as their excuse for *not understanding* why their fuckery got them fired, and some of them facing jail time." I glanced at Breanne, the woman still holding a stiff business posture. "The best of it all was watching Monroe blast their asses with facts and making them all feel like the pieces of shit they are."

Jim glanced back at our friend from college. "I don't even want to think about the years I wasted with you doing that man's job instead of him."

I laughed. "Nice try, fucker…" I paused my bantering with Jim when Breanne's demeanor proved she wasn't in the mood for it.

Strangely, I gave more of a damn about her current state of mind than I did catching up and throwing jabs back and forth with Jim at the moment. Nailing these bastards to the wall for the last four or more hours should've made her relieved it was over so she could move forward. It should've cued that dimpled smile that was sure to be the death of me.

Instead, the woman was expressionless and unwavering in this death stare that seemed to be looking at something other than Jim, and I loosened up and in conversation. Who knows, Jim was *Mr. Mitchell* to her, and she was standing in the largest conference room at the headquarters of the man's global empire.

"All good?" I asked her.

She blinked, the fake-Rolex smile reappeared, then she turned back and grabbed her purse. "If that's all you need from Alex and me, I have some other pressing issues to finalize for a project," she said to Jim, lying through her teeth.

"We're all good here," Jim answered with a smile. "I will say that it's good to see things cleaned up and moving forward. May I inquire as to how you're faring with the idea of closing Stone Company's building?"

"It'll take some getting used to, but after what went down today, we certainly needed to make that change." She forced that smile again. "It's a good change," she said with no emotion.

Jim eyed me as if I'd fucked the woman and sent her packing directly after. Being businessmen who dealt with dirtbags daily, both of us were trained to read people. It was vital to make sound business transactions, and Jim knew what I was currently picking up on. The woman didn't want to be in this room another second.

"Breanne Stone," Spencer walked up right before Breanne could squeeze in another exit attempt. "It's nice to meet you finally." He reached his hand to shake hers.

Breanne's eyes carried a hint of a sparkle in them, and thank God for that too. She and I were both given a little insight into Spencer, who had the ladies worshipping at his feet with just a friendly wink. One of his admirers being Breanne's very forward friend, Natalia. How on earth he managed to answer the phone while fucking her, I'd never know. I thought I was a dickbag when I had a fling, but I'd never pull that number on someone, even if they were terrible in bed. One thing was for sure: *Spicy Spence* was never going to hear the end of it after the guys and I went out for dinner.

"What the hell is that look, Alex?" Spencer asked after Breanne blew his ass off in her business frame of mind.

I eyed Breanne, and her eyes flashed a warning that she would hand me my balls later if I dared to bring up her friend—*which I would* —but not now. It would be best if Breanne knew the men as I did, and that wouldn't have been the best icebreaker. So, using my best effort to shut the hell up about *her* friend fucking *my* friend, I remained tightlipped about Natalia Hoover.

"You kicked ass, man," I diverted Spencer's probing eyes. "It's good to watch you in action again."

"That was a shitty situation." He looked at Breanne. "I trust you're feeling somewhat better now that your company, along with Brooks, will remain profitable. The bottom-feeders are no longer in a position to hurt you or your father's incredible legacy. I have to say, you've done an effective job of running that company, even if there was financial trouble due to the issues we uncovered."

"I'm glad it's over, and they're gone." She smiled at him stiffly. "All of you were great today. I'm grateful we have you on our side."

"The feeling is mutual, Ms. Stone," Jim reverted to a more solemn demeanor. "If you'll all excuse me, I have to attend to a few business matters with Mr. Monroe." He nodded to Breanne and then to Spencer. "We have a few things to go over before we can get out of here."

With a glance of concern from Jim to me, the men made their exit. Jim knew Breanne was not fucking around at the moment, and he knew it was up to me as her partner to ensure the woman didn't have ill feelings about the fallout that'd taken place. My expression answered him with a look of knowing that I could handle Breanne; at least, I thought I could. If the woman would bust out the truth on me, she'd quickly learn that she was in the presence of three powerful and wealthy men who would do anything to help her, especially after listening to all the hell these idiots put her through. All she needed to do was say was the word, and she'd be taken care of.

I remained quiet as I trailed Breanne to a red BMW. I would have ordinarily walked to my car and allowed her time to cry on her friend's shoulders, but no. One damn sniff, watching her fighting with her key fob, bubbled up some unfamiliar emotions inside me.

"The unlock button should be easy to find on a vehicle I assume you own," I said.

I was in uncharted waters of actually giving a damn about someone being emotionally affected by business matters, so I didn't know how to be of support, but here I was trying.

"I know," she sniffed again. "Thanks."

"What the hell is going on with you?"

That was probably too harsh, but she was a businesswoman. She could handle the harsh shit.

"What the hell is going on with me?"

I was now asking myself if *I* could handle the harsh shit, standing on the other side of a woman's expression who was simultaneously pissed off and hurt.

"That is what I asked. You should be walking with a smile on your face and a spring in your step, but instead, the tears are back." I was a dick, but I couldn't help but react to her cold, bitch behavior.

"I'm not going to lose my shit."

She glanced toward the expensive cars in executive parking at Mitchell and Associates. "Certainly not in this parking garage, and certainly not in front of you again." She eyed me, and her mysterious glare was sexy as fuck. "I'm not a weak person, Mr. Grayson, but I've spent the better part of the morning here, listening to those fuckers finally admit that they stole from me. After all the goddamn, mother fucking hard work I've done to take my father's seat and all the personal fucking sacrifices I've made for *their* families, their betrayal cuts deeper than ever."

She was officially breaking, and I would be a liar to myself and the rest of the world if I said I wasn't breaking with her. She was a strong woman with a huge heart, and that heart had cost her fucking everything. This shit was real, and it sucked to see a good person go down like this. So, if she was going to lose her shit either through profanity or tears, I wasn't leaving until she understood that I was a man who gave a damn about her well-being.

"Breanne," I said, reaching for her elbow, her lips tight and eyes fierce, "I was in that room too. I can't imagine how you're feeling, but I need you to know more than anything that I'm here for you if you need to let it all fucking go."

"I appreciate the sentiment, Alex. I do." She smiled while a tear slipped out of the corner of her eye. "But I swear to Christ, I've also reached my limit with you seeing me like this."

"Like what?" I answered. "Get your ass over here."

That's when I did the last thing I should've ever done. I pulled her stiff body against mine as if she were my girl, and I would never let so much as a fly hurt the woman.

Breanne was smart in resisting the gesture at first. I was not programmed to act this way. I was the man who was programmed to bring out her tears and exacerbate her feelings of brokenness, as I had with every other woman I'd been with. And God knew I could easily do that. I had nothing to offer but disappointment and a tortured past. I had no business trying to be happy or make anyone else happy.

My toxic thoughts were washed away once her rigid body relaxed into mine, and her fresh scent filled my senses. Maybe I was possessed? Who knew what the fuck I was, but this felt good. It felt right. She rested her head against my chest, and her hands held onto my back while she broke down in tears, and my anger toward those snakes who'd caused her pain flared up even more. I ran my hand over the top of her head and managed to resist kissing the woman as if she were mine to protect.

Hell, if this was the answer to finally gaining her trust, I was doing it like a fucking champion. I loved holding her, smelling her, and feeling her trust me enough to cling to my back while she let out the last of her shitty week.

"We're going to get through this. I promise you that. I could kill a mother fucker for hurting you like this," I said without thinking, lost in this trance that'd come over me.

I felt her laugh. "It looks like we're both going to jail for murder, then." She briskly rubbed my back and pulled away.

Fuck. As if I hadn't already fallen into the sap-trap, she finished me off with the dimpled-smile.

"That smile will be the death of me, you know?" I grinned.

"Great. Then add another dead body to my list of casualties."

I chuckled. "I'm serious, though. It's over. They're gone. It's you and me now, and we're going to kick ass together as partners."

Her eyes were glassy as she smiled up at me. "You're damn right we are," she said. "Sorry I ruined your expensive suit."

"I'll charge it to Jim. He's the one who made sure I had an emotional business partner," I teased.

"I swear that I'm not usually an emotional person. You have met a side of me I don't think I've ever let any man see except for Theo or Stanton."

And you've just met a side of me that I didn't think I would ever see.

"Well," I answered, moving past the supportive man I'd suddenly transformed into, "I believe you owe me dinner now." I knew she was broke as fuck, and I wasn't going to let up on that until she gave it up and I could find a way to help. "Tobias is my restaurant of choice as well."

"Bummer for you." She smirked. "I'm in no shape to pay for a dinner that expensive."

"I'll take care of the mechanic's charges for the car. You'll take care of my appetite."

"Nice try." She flashed a new smile, one that sealed the deal on the fact that I wanted this woman on a personal level and now.

"You at least owe me a kiss," I pressed. "Or ten, now that you've destroyed my suit."

She pressed her lips together. "Oh, God. We'd be in trouble." She then gave me a flirty smile and opened her car door. "Because I don't think I could stop at one kiss with you and that gorgeous Johnny-Depp look you have."

My face fell. I hated that everyone always insisted that I could be the man's doppelganger. It wasn't a bad thing to be compared to the finer-looking Johnny Depp, but Jesus Christ, were there any women out there who could see past it? Maybe it'd just gotten old to me by now. Perhaps it was because my stupid friends always suggested I dress up like Jack Sparrow or Edward Scissorhands for Halloween. All I knew was that I despised it.

Breanne's laugh was the most beautiful noise to enter my sudden thoughts of frustration. "Oh, damn. That does piss you off, doesn't it?" She laughed again. Then her hands ran up the side of my cheek. "Don't worry, Harrison Ford is my Hollywood crush."

"Who told you I despise being compared to him?" I asked.

"A little birdie." She gave me a silly look, slipped into the car, and winked at me. Then, the woman I slowly desired now more than ever drove off, leaving me to wonder which one of my idiot friends managed to put that shit in her head.

Women talked, and after meeting her friend Natalia, I would guess that if I said something while I was drunk to an ex, then the rumor of me hating being compared to an actor was probably still out there and she knew about it. That and the goddamn Billionaires' Club rumor. That ridiculous tag would never die no matter how many of my best friends got married, had kids, and went to hell and back to prove we didn't screw women who were wealthy because we were guarding our money.

CHAPTER THIRTEEN
BREE

To sit amongst the men who'd bought *and saved* my company was a humbling yet enlightening experience. I watched with disgust and heartbreak that it had come to this. Seeing the faces of those I trusted as they lied, stating that I'd approved their shady and unprofitable jobs to get my ass fired—or put on trial—was overwhelming.

I felt like I'd let my father down the most. My dad had built this company from the ground up with my mother's support, but she'd died before I was old enough to know her, so I wasn't sure what she would think of this entire situation. I'm pretty sure they were both looking down on me with the same pity I felt for myself.

I'd felt Alex's eyes on me more than once, and no matter how badly my tears wanted to surface, I wouldn't allow it. I could cry about it later. Was I emotional? Fuck yes, I was, and I wasn't ashamed about it. I was a human being who'd been through the wringer, and I also happened to be reasonably in touch with my emotions; fucking sue me. Unfortunately, women in my position didn't have the luxury of being emotional creatures, and God forbid it happened in the presence of a man lest we be branded as *difficult*.

In a business setting, an emotional woman was a handful of things:

hormonal, unstable, fragile, incapable, or a mess. It was such fucking bullshit, and for whatever reason, the universe had seen fit to make Alex a spectator to every last emotional bomb that was set to blow up in my face. I'd about had enough of that, too. I was an overly capable, well-educated woman. Hopefully, he'd get a glimpse of that side of his new partner at some point.

The lawyers were extremely clear that I wasn't at fault for any of Stone's wrongdoings after Mr. Monroe annihilated these thieves. Alex had uncovered the most critical pieces to their lying puzzles, thank God, and that information saved mine and Theo's asses—fraudulent paperwork that'd slipped right past us.

If only I were an extreme businesswoman who micromanaged everyone instead of trusting them not to screw me over. If I hadn't trusted them, perhaps I would have uncovered that they'd hijacked my finance department and paid them under the table to change the job bids so I would approve what I thought was profitable. The more Mr. Mitchell and Mr. Monroe spoke and pulled out the truth from these sons of bitches, the more shocked I was that it could've happened.

Thank God it ended with their confessions about how they manipulated things so Theo and I would never find out. It took Daniel Kyle trying to grow a set of balls by stealing Sphere to prove Alex's instincts were correct and catch the bleed in my finances. Stone was saved, but my personal life? Broke as a joke. So, I wasn't going to stand in that room and high-five the CEO badasses who shoveled the shit out of my company—no way in hell. We handled business, and now I had to move forward while being behind on all my bills.

Then there was Alex, a man who seemed to give a shit suddenly. I didn't expect to see *that expression* on his face, the sympathetic one. It was as if he saw how personal this was for me—it was my dad's company, and no matter how stiff a businesswoman I became to run it, I'd failed my father. Somehow, Alex seemed to care in one way or another. Feeling his empathy made me lose it, and I sobbed in the comfort of his arms as if he were Theo. That cryfest was not meant to happen around the man who seemed to only witness the worst in me; that was meant for the drive home.

The defenses I put up in his presence came down when he pulled me in his arms, and I felt the comfort of the powerful businessman holding me. Alex Grayson may have been flirty and somewhat playful, but there was a reason he wore that thousand-dollar, three-piece suit like he owned all of Southern California. He held himself with an air of power, unreadable in every way, and he was a man who seemed to ooze domination and business savviness. There was no explaining how attractive he was when he commanded the room as he spoke, his sharp features exploring every employee's face. His mannerisms were that of a man in charge, and he was incredibly gorgeous to complement it all. For all of that, there would be no way I could ever allow him to see I'd gone broke by having a soft heart. I knew he could never understand, even as he held me and spoke in a heartfelt way when he reassured me that we could move forward together now that it was *over*.

It was far from over for me. I had the personal fallout I had to deal with, and next up was the thing I'd pushed farthest from my mind today, which was selling my apartment. The thing would sell fast; I knew that. I also knew it would sell for a shit-ton of money so I could start over and get back to a place where I could financially breathe again.

My apartment—all three million dollars of it—was designed by Dad and me when I was a teenager. He had me help him design the entire building, and together, we brought our first joint vision to life there. I would never forget the day he gave me the keys to the penthouse as a college graduation gift. The apartment was more than a home to me; it was every happy memory of my adulthood wrapped inside four walls, and now, I had to sell it.

I had the real estate listing contract stuffed into the pile of papers Jacey was carrying when she ran into Alex. Thank God, Jacey could keep a secret, and she knew I didn't want Alex to know I was selling my home. Only three people knew about me listing the apartment: me, Jacey, and the broker. I didn't even go through Natalia to sell the place—I didn't want my wealthy friends to jump in and *save Breanne.*

It took time, meditation, and a lot of tears, but I knew what Dad would expect of me at this shitty stage of my life.

"Never live in the past, Breanne. You must learn from it, or you will never have the mindset to face life's relentless challenges."

I heard Dad's words in my head as if he'd whispered them from the grave and into my ear. Selling my home and starting all over again was what needed to be done to get my shit together. So, none of my friends would know about my place going up on the market until it was sold, and I got my finances corrected. Never again would I allow my *big heart* to put my employees' financial well-being before my own. At least that's what I told myself—I was still pissed off after four hours with thieves, interrogations, and lawyers.

"What the fuck?" I growled when the engine died on Natalia's BMW, and I had to coast the goddamn thing to the side of the road. "Come on!" I yelled at the car as I tried starting it again.

This wasn't happening. Not here, not on Beverly Drive.

"Jesus Christ! I just wanted a fucking chocolate cupcake from my favorite fucking bakery before I got home to watch old fucking movies!"

I hit the steering wheel on the car with enough frustration and force to make my hand tingle. Before I had time to study the check-engine light, a matte black, phantom-looking Mercedes AMG One pulled in front of me. In true, universe-punishing fashion, Alexander Grayson stepped out to see me in my twenty-seventh crisis of the month.

All power to the car was gone, much like my will to look Alex in the eye. I couldn't even roll a fucking window down. The car was as dead as my soul at this moment—not to mention my hopes and dreams.

"Un-fucking-believable," I said when Alex walked up to my door.

"Broke down?" he questioned. Although he chewed on the corner of his mouth in what appeared to be concern, I could sense the man's eyes were glittering with humor behind his square-framed Ray-Bans.

"I'm sight-seeing. Someone said Jack Nicholson lived around here, so I figured, you know, if not now, then when?" I said sarcastically, stepping out of the car that'd betrayed me. "When I imagined living in hell, I thought I'd burn, not live like this."

"You've had quite the day, or week, actually." He whipped out his cell. "I'll call for a tow and have it brought back to your place—or Jack Nicholson's if you prefer?"

"It's not my car." I covered my mouth when I admitted that.

Alex grinned. "I had a notion that was the case, especially since *your car* is in the shop still, correct?"

Right. That's the lie. "Exactly."

Alex went straight to business, called the tow company, and hung up. "Now, one of two things is happening here." He pulled me off to the safety of the shoulder of the road. "Either you have an incredible streak of horrendous luck following you everywhere, or this car was determined to breakdown whether you were behind the wheel or not."

He smirked, but I didn't smile in return after he walked around the car and sat in the driver's seat. The car wouldn't start, and all I could do was fold my arms and glance back at his. Mr. Moneybags seemed to flaunt his wealth like a peacock, driving a car that only sold at auction, and whoever bought it needed to be shitting gold bricks regularly to afford it.

Instead of being impressed by the man's wealth, I was officially put-off. Maybe I was just feeling bitter. I'd lost everything after being a shitty CEO, and the real reason Alexander Grayson could handpick his car was that he wasn't only the owner of Brooks Architectural. After doing some research, I found that he and James Mitchell had busted their asses *together* to make Mitchell and Associates a global empire. Alex was the man for the job when it came to acquisitions, and his resume spoke the reasons why it was most likely pocket change for him to buy the *fresh off the production line* Mercedes AMG-One.

Yeah, he wasn't going to understand my sad and pathetic story of losing everything because I had a *heart of gold*. He couldn't comprehend that if I brainwashed him.

"The alternator is most likely the problem. When's the last time this was serviced?"

"I have no idea. Obviously, my friend has been too busy selling real estate to take it to the shop."

Good God, Natalia. I thought you had someone servicing these goddamn things.

"Right," Alex chuckled. "Your friend probably hasn't even brought it in for its first oil change."

"That's a huge statement," I countered.

"She seems like she's a busy woman." He shrugged and eyed me over the rim of his sunglasses. "You know, being the fastest and most brilliant woman in real estate. It's why I hired her. A woman who puts business first." He reached in and grabbed my briefcase. "It doesn't matter. Let's get you something to eat and get you home, and then I'll loan you a car—that is if I can trust you not to blow up the poor thing."

"I don't need your charity," I remained firm. "This is a nice neighborhood. I was planning to head to my favorite bakery so I could buy a chocolate cupcake and then round out the day in a hot bath."

"If that's how you plan on ending this day, I insist I join you," he said.

"I don't share when it comes to chocolate."

He chewed on the corner of his mouth. "I wasn't talking about chocolate." He planted his hands on his hips. "After this week of bullshit being flung at you in every direction, and a long-ass day at Mitchell with Jim's lawyers, I'm talking about joining you in that hot bath and hand-feeding you that chocolate muffin myself."

I smiled at his flirtatious behavior. If only the man weren't known for being a player. "Well, your hands don't seem like they have the capabilities that my vibrator does."

Oh, fucking hell. I didn't say that. Yes, I did! I fucking said that, and Alex couldn't look more dangerously sexy and yet predatorial than he does at this moment.

"Vibrators, eh?"

"I meant my back massaging thingy," I tried to recover, but now I couldn't think.

"Thingy," he softly laughed. "I don't think I've ever—"

"Stop." I held a hand up and eyed his car. "Get back in your multi-million-dollar playboy toy and go mess around with some chick who's up for it. I'm not doing this with you, and since you mentioned my *incredible run of horrendous luck*, I'd like to add to that."

"Would—"

"I'm not finished," I interrupted him, seeing a shit-eating grin. I ignored the honks coming from the pissed-off drivers I'd forced into one lane and maintained my composure while begging for the tow truck to teleport itself here. "I have good reason to believe that *you*, Alex Grayson, are the very reason my life is going to hell at lightning speed. From the moment we've met, all I've come across are embarrassing situations, and it seems as though when I've encountered them all, I've been in your company."

He crossed his arms. "That's a profound statement."

"It's a fact."

It really was.

"Perhaps one day you'll see that in all of this bad shit you've encountered since being in my presence, I haven't once judged you for it. Instead, I've tried to help you."

"Shit, I'm sorry. Goddammit, don't be nice. It makes it harder to blame you for it."

"Perhaps that's because you know I'm not the reason for all of this. I'm just a guy who's remained firmly at your side while seeing you going through a rough patch."

"I want to believe you actually cared. I do," I said, now that our conversation went from Alex being a flirt to that compassionate man who held me while I cried on his shoulder earlier.

"Why can't you? Jesus, Bree. Why won't you at least allow me to help you?"

Because I might just fall for you, and then I'm royally fucked!

"I wasn't raised to have someone else fix my problems. If my dad had raised me like that, I'd be curled up in a ball, still crying in the dark, corner office I found at Mitchell after the lawyers were done."

"You seriously think that if I help you by offering you a ride home and loaning you one of the cars I never drive that I'm fixing your problems?"

"I don't know what I'm thinking," I said. "Please, just go. It's Monday, for Christ's sake. Maybe that's why it's a shitty day."

"You're a stubborn woman; you know that?"

I lifted my chin. "My dad said I got it from my mom." I tried to smile because the strange way Alex's voice changed while stating that fact reminded me of the many times Dad had said it to me.

Dad lectured me more than once on how to use my stubborn personality for good and not bad. The hard part was trying to decide whether or not refusing Alex's help was me being headstrong in a good way or a bad way. I couldn't allow the man to see me as a weak woman. I absolutely couldn't let that shit happen, or it would validate why my dad's company went under.

I smiled. "You're a great man to pull over and offer me a hand. You're also dead if you capitalize on this situation and use it against me."

"Why would I do that?"

"Because it seems like you'd be the type."

"You have a lot to learn about me, Breanne, and a lot to learn about my intentions with you as well. I don't plan on capitalizing on you going through shit, either." He smiled. "I have no idea where or how you formed such an opinion of me, but perhaps one day you'll trust my motives. From the moment you and I first spoke," he took his sunglasses off and locked eyes with mine, "that night you needed me to be your fake fiancé?"

"I...yeah..." Oh, God. I could hardly think with his beautiful eyes—all filled with concern—staring into the core of my entire being.

"I could've easily been my usual asshole self and made you feel like shit for it. I didn't. Instead, I gladly accepted the invitation to help you rid yourself of your ex and whatever else it was you felt you needed to prove to that man."

He turned to walk away, leaving me feeling like the asshole I expected him to be. I rubbed my forehead, and my brain pleaded with me to trust him and tell him my sad story, but I couldn't. I was swimming in confusion as the man offered me my briefcase, allowing me to handle this on my own as I'd insisted.

I felt the instinct to protect myself from him more than anything else, whether he offered help or not, and whether I felt like a weak businesswoman in front of him or not. All I knew was that a girl could easily trip and fall head over heels with the man's serious business expression, or his smile—or that way he chewed on the corner of his mouth—and I couldn't trust he wouldn't hurt me if I fell for the man like I knew I could.

Why did I have to have one of the world's most attractive men as my business partner? Why couldn't he be ugly or have horrible breath and rotten teeth? Why did he physically have to be a man that any girl would fall for and not regret it the next morning?

That's why I was stubborn. It's why he wouldn't get to me on a personal level. It's also the very same reason I could never let him in. I trusted a man with my heart once, only to find out he was fucking some whore the night before our wedding. So, why would I trust the world's most eligible bachelor? This man probably had a woman waiting for him to call if he needed *stress relief* after a bad day. Why wouldn't he? He was wealthy, gorgeous, and available.

Now, he was gentleman enough to give me what I'd insisted upon, and I needed to wait on the side of the road for a tow.

Real smart, Bree.

CHAPTER FOURTEEN
ALEX

*I*t had been a week from hell, trying to shake the last of the rotten apples from the Stone company's *family tree*, firing a handful of employees from Brooks who couldn't be trusted to do their jobs efficiently, and dealing with the fact that something was undeniably in Breanne's perfume because no matter what I did, I couldn't shake her delicious scent.

She was hypnotically beautiful and carried herself well as a businesswoman, especially since she'd been on fire all week after dealing with the last of her scandalous employees. If Breanne's no-nonsense demeanor were the only turn-on for me, I'd probably be safe from her charms. Unfortunately, that damn dimpled smile of hers was going to be my undoing if I wasn't careful.

She was entirely off-limits for a man who had no limits, cares, or concerns about a woman's feelings when it came to him achieving what he wanted. Instead of saying that Breanne Stone wasn't my type, it was the other way around—I was not *her* type. At all. I was a ruthless bastard who was always one step ahead of the hell hounds from my past that haunted me, and I wasn't wired to care for a woman, no matter their mental state.

Terminating Tish without caring about her excuses, tears, or pathetic expressions while she begged me to give her another chance was proof of the kind of hard-hearted man I was. The woman had been hired to make sure things were handled properly. She obviously didn't live up to the job description, and her lack of better judgment cost her in the end. Tish had cost this firm money by allowing her sales team to purchase that shitty property. It was negligent, and I didn't bend when it came to handling employees who didn't do their fucking jobs proficiently.

Regardless, Tish Dalton and her team were terminated for failing the company in their trusted positions. When they each cried their sad stories, I offered a tissue for their tears in response. That was a fragment of the son of a bitch boss I could be. In my opinion, they could cry on someone else's shoulder—especially Tish, who spilled her sob story to me as if I were her therapist or as if I fucking cared.

That was the man I was, and that was merely in business. My personal life with women was even worse. It had always been about me and never about them. No matter how hard I tried, I could never manage to care about a woman's feelings. Until Breanne, and that's why I was lost as fuck at the moment.

It was not like me to become enamored with any woman, except the one woman I knew I should never be attracted to, apparently. This was as baffling as something breaking the laws of physics. People like me didn't get the luxury of giving and receiving love. That'd been taken from me when I was a child, so what the fuck was happening?

All I could conclude was this: my olfactory senses had apparently sent a message to my brain stating that my punishment for being a heartless dick was to be enchanted by my new partner, who was all wrong for me.

It's because you keep smelling her goddamn fragrance, I thought, pissed I'd wasted five minutes of my time thinking like this. Easy fix. I took a tissue from the tissue box, and with my best effort, I blew my nose, hoping to clear my head of the lingering fresh scent of ocean breeze and lilac. To no avail. I was fucked.

Thank God the day was over. It was time I packed up my shit and prepped to head out and meet the guys. Brandt insisted we visit a new club so that Jim and Monroe could see the potential of his buddy's place. Maybe I'd get lucky, and it would smell like wings, booze, and other fragrances that were potent at a bar. Mainly strong perfume from single women who outdid themselves to meet dudes. Perhaps that's the way I'd rid myself of these sappy thoughts—pick up a chick, fuck her, send her on her way, and voila, problem solved.

Fat-fucking-chance! I thought to myself when Breanne sent me a text, telling me she was doing well after seeing off Theo and his husband at the airport today. I know for a fact she wouldn't have sent the message if I didn't text her two hours ago and ask, but part of me hoped that she would've. These were the unfamiliar, shitty emotions I was stuck dealing with. In my *former life*, I wouldn't have thought twice about her emotional state after her friend moved, but I texted her and asked because it'd been on my mind all damn day.

I chewed on my bottom lip, mentally willing myself to ignore her text and leave it at that. She was fucking fine, and that's what I was worried about, right? I studied her text, and because I was seemingly a man cursed by her perfume, I immediately texted her back.

Alex: *See you on Monday*

Like a schoolboy, I watched the message get marked as *read,* and she didn't respond. Instead of letting it go and getting my ass safely around the testosterone of my best friends, I texted again.

Alex: *Everything go okay?*

When my second message was also ignored, my brain shifted gears, and I got my ass out of the office and walked out to my car. It was nice to take the cover off this bitch, and let its horsepower shake off this woman from my mind. Even Zeus, my cat, was starting to eye me like the bitch I was acting like every night when I got home from work. My own cat was starting to judge me, and if I weren't careful, his butt would be running over the top of me next. That's how lame all this shit was. Me, of all the goddamn people, was the victim of that chubby little love cherub, and I had an arrow shot directly up my ass.

Breanne was likely having great difficulty saying goodbye to Theo. Still, after a week of flirty banter, stressful bullshit, trading in her car, and God knows what else she was up against after being robbed by her employees, I couldn't manage to get her to confide in me.

It was annoying as hell to be unexpectedly attracted to what I couldn't have, and that's what all of this boiled down to. I couldn't have her, so my predatorial instincts wanted her. It would be easily fixed with bourbon, and I couldn't get one fast enough.

I WALKED into Roux's after ensuring my name was on the list, and I sat next to the youngest man in our group, and the reason we were all meeting up at this place tonight.

"Cameron Brandt, this place is garbage," I teased, opening my menu. "Obviously, Jim and Spence seemed to have come and gone." I glanced over to the empty seats at the table.

"Too loud for your precious ears?" he smirked, sipping vodka on the rocks.

"You should know more than all of us that sensory overload can cause nervous breakdowns or something."

"He's a pediatric neurosurgeon, dip-shit," Jake, my good friend, and chief cardio surgeon at Saint John's, said as he took a seat next to me.

"You are a sight for sore eyes." I smiled at my best friend's younger brother, feeling like it'd been forever since I'd seen the guy.

"Well, since Jim made sure Collin and I make improvements on our hospital wards, you're lucky you see my ass at all." He opened his menu and wrinkled his nose. "Cam," he called out to the hot-shot playboy doc, who casually sat across from Jake and me. "What's up with this menu? Don't invite a cardiovascular surgeon to some deep-fried club unless you want to piss me off." He smirked.

"The menu for the health-conscious bitches such as yourself can be requested if you'd like. Everything's vegan on that one." Cameron laughed, always able to hold his own.

"You see," I took the bourbon I ordered before arriving at our reserved table, "that's the first thing I recommend your friend fixes— or whoever the fuck begged you to haul Jim and Spence down here to have Mitchell invest in them. Fix the fucking menu, doc," I advised with a laugh.

"Vegan menus added?"

"Yeah," I said, having been down the restaurant and club acquisitions road plenty of times. "This place needs to diversify if they want to stand out. Especially if I'm going to spend fifty bucks to end up going under Jakey's knife anyway because of all this goddamn grease."

"Good point," Cameron said. "You miss it, don't you? The acquisitions and being Jim's VP?"

"I guess I kind of do," I admitted. "However, I *don't* miss getting fucked over by a business that is trying to *charm* us into investing. Who knows, maybe I do miss working side-by-side with the big guy."

"That's bullshit. You *hardly* miss me," Jim announced as soon as he and Spencer joined us. "I saw the way you were looking at Breanne on Monday."

"The way I was looking at her? If I had *any* look on my face, it was because I knew you were thinking that I'm screwing my partner and going to end up sending her packing, Jimbo," I said as the men sat.

"Tell me you're not fucking her," Spencer said.

"No, *Spicy Spence*," I smirked. "I'm not. I wish I could say the same for you and your real estate agent, though."

"How did you hear about Natalia?" Spencer asked with a look of confusion.

"Oh, you know, through pillow talk. It's insane what you learn from a woman while you're fucking and not answering an incoming call while in the act."

"Hold the hell up right this instant," Cameron interrupted with a laugh. "Natalia Hoover is your real estate agent?"

"That he fucked." I sipped my bourbon. "How do *you* know her?" I questioned Cameron's amused expression.

The woman was hot, and she made it evident that she wasn't ashamed to explore her sexuality with men, so I shouldn't have been surprised that more than one man at this table may have something *in common* with Natalia.

I had to tame this conversation, knowing that Breanne would kill me if I allowed my friends to shame her friend.

"Natalia is Breanne's best friend, so let's keep the shit talk to a minimum, or my partner will bust my ass for bringing up Spence's sex name."

"How do you know her, Brandt?" Spence's voice was filled with annoyance.

"I met her at the hospital, Spicy Spence," Cameron said with a laugh. "Her sister's son was brought into my trauma unit after he got a concussion in a soccer game." He smirked at me. "That would be classic, though; Spence and me with the same woman."

Speaking of the devil, while Spence and Cam teased each other, I saw Natalia at the bar with another woman. I'd seen the other woman with Breanne the week before when I ran into them at the club. She was the one talking to Bree about trying on lingerie.

I couldn't help but smile at the fact that Spence was about to cross paths with Natalia again, the woman he'd made an ass out of himself in front of while fucking.

"Seriously?" I said to myself with a laugh that the woman was here on the same night we were. "Fucking hell," I continued as Collin, our neurosurgeon friend and last of our group to join us, sat at the table. "Of all the people…"

Collin laughed. "I've missed your sexy ass too, Alex. Thanks for the enthusiastic salutation, though."

"Natalia is here." I smiled at Spence's wide eyes, then scanned the room for the only woman who I actually gave a damn about seeing. "But where is Breanne?" I questioned too loudly.

"Wait," Collin held up a finger. "I know Jake and I have been out of the loop for a month or so, but you're actually asking about your business partner's whereabouts?"

"He's obviously fucking her," Jake chimed in.

Between Jake, Collin, and Cameron, any of the three witty doctors would cut to the chase and call a spade on my ass here and now. Jim and Spence would be a little more courteous, given their inherently more reserved nature, but then again, I'd just poked the hornet's nest with Spence.

I ignored the men when I noticed Breanne's ex, Max—the douche who'd burned Breanne somehow. Why couldn't I just interact with my friends like a normal human being? Instead, I was watching every-fucking-move this prick made since he decided to join Breanne's friends at the bar.

I watched as Breanne's friends became more and more upset. Natalia eyed Breanne's ex-fiancé while she covered her heart, and the once-smiling woman's face fell, and she glared at the dick as if he'd said something brutal. The looks on the two women's faces told me this dick-bag had likely said something about Breanne, and now my interest was piqued.

I was on the fence about looking like a complete jackass by walking over there, but watching the women becoming so deeply disturbed while I sipped my bourbon didn't seem cool either. This fucker had said something, and then he had the audacity to smile smugly at me after leaving Breanne's friends at the bar with their drinks.

"Isn't that Breanne Stone's ex-fiancé? Max, I think?" Cameron questioned, seeing her cocksucker of an ex taunting me with his slimy smile.

"How do you know that?" I asked Cameron.

"I was a guest at their *almost* wedding," he responded.

"Bride or groom's side?" Jim teased.

"My date was with the bride's family," Cameron sipped his drink.

"Bree mentioned that she fucked him over at their wedding. Is that true?" I asked, seeing Max walk over to the marketing executives for Jim's toughest competitor.

"At least we have the answer as to why the dick crashed the merge gala. He's here with the executives of Brakken. That little fucker is a spy for the competition, Mitch," Spencer said, using the nickname Jim gained while we were in college.

"It's about goddamn time our conversations move to office gossip and get off our backs for a change," Collin said to Jake and Cam. The hospital drama tended to dominate all of our conversations. Any time the subject changed to the business sector, Jake, Collin, and Cameron were usually delighted because it meant not having their balls busted as usual.

"What happened at the wedding?" I asked Cameron, knowing I was officially giving away my interest in Breanne, but I didn't give a shit what my friends thought at the moment.

His eyebrows shot up, and he smirked into his glass. "You wouldn't believe it. I almost can't believe it, and I witnessed it." He leaned forward as if he were about to drop the best story of all time. "Check this shit out. This wedding was stacked with upper elites. Super gorgeous venue, designed like the royal fucking wedding, right? You know the kind of wedding I'm talking about. The place looked like a wedding planner's wet dream, and it would've likely made it into a bridal magazine, too, were it not for the wreckage that took place when we all were prepped to stand for the bride to enter."

"What the fuck happened?" I asked impatiently, hearing the muffled laughs from the rest of the table.

"The lights dimmed, then the bridal march song came to a screeching halt. After that, a sex tape played—it was like, projected on the wall or whatever. It was of that dirty prick screwing some broad. Everyone was all indignant about it, but I thought the sex tape was the perfect solution for explaining why she wasn't marrying the cheating dick. Total humiliation."

"She played it for all of the guests? Oh, my God," I said with a laugh, oddly proud of her. "She started to bring up her wedding day and the way she ditched that prick at the gala once, but I had no idea the woman was that fucking bold."

"That's so fucking badass of her." Collin laughed, and then he raised the beer he'd ordered. "Cheers to your partner, man. That's how you get back at a cheating mother fucker."

"I'll drink to that." Jake followed his best friend's lead and held up his drink.

"I'd love to stick around and toast her bold behavior, but something's up with that asshole, and the looks on her friend's faces makes me think that *his* retaliation may have just come around."

"Not your business, Alex," Jim warned. "She's your partner, not your girl. This will only cause you problems unless she's worth it."

Unless she's worth it? Why were those words so eerily haunting?

"You know," Collin grinned at me, "just like when you asked if Elena was worth my trouble. The difference was, I knew what I wanted when I went after my little Cuban goddess."

"You don't," Spence confirmed. "That's written all over your face, my friend."

"Listen to the bloodhounds, sniffing shit out. I swear these two are goddamn mind readers," Jake added with a laugh.

"I'll see you guys in a few." I looked at Cameron. "First issue is the vegan menus; then, the bar lighting needs a little work. I'll try out the wings to see if they're worth the price, or if it's just a VIP price point."

"Got it. Spence is getting ready to add his two cents next," Cameron smirked. "Bottom line is that the chicks are talking about this place, and it's on fire with reservations. They're booking a year out unless you know someone personally."

"That's never enough when it comes to sparking my interest," I heard Jim say as I left the table and walked over to Breanne's friends.

"Natalia Hoover?" I smiled, seeing the woman was in tears, looking at her martini.

"Alex Grayson, right?" the other friend asked, roughness in her tone but set with a determination that I liked.

"Yes, I'm Breanne's new partner. It looks like the ex she despises has you both a little upset. I just wanted to make sure everything is okay, especially if that prick said something about Breanne."

"We both just found out that Breanne is selling the loft she designed with her dad. It was a huge deal when he gifted it to her after college graduation. First, she loses her car, and now we're finding out from *that* mother fucker about the apartment." She glared over to where Max stood, watching me talk to the upset ladies. "He put an offer on it. He's only buying it to rub it in her face, and he wants to insist on a short sale to get her out fast."

I smiled back at the man as soon as I gained this new information. "Natalia," I said, turning to her, "I'd like a non-disclosure agreement signed, and then I'm offering to buy Breanne's place, all cash."

There was no way in hell I would allow *that man* to buy her home —the home she loved and was being forced to sell. Fuck that noise. I was an investor anyway, and I knew if she and her father had designed that place, it was golden.

"*She's* selling it. I'm not listing it for her. I didn't even know she was doing this!" Natalia was still in shock. Apparently, Breanne had been keeping financial secrets from her friends too.

"And *she's* selling it to *me*."

"You can't buy it," Natalia said. "That would humiliate her."

"It's why I'm demanding an NDA. She will never know who bought her home until the timing is right." I pointed toward the dickhead ex, who was sitting with a group from Brakken, Mitchell and Associates' rival corporation. "That son of a bitch isn't buying her home. He's done enough to her. I'm offering fifteen million."

"Fifteen million cash?" she asked, her eyes wide with shock. "Max said he offered five million over her asking price."

"Which was?"

"He won't say. The house isn't an open listing, or I would've seen it."

"Well, it appears that Breanne doesn't want any of us to know she's in financial trouble," I spoke. "Where is she tonight?"

"Sick," Natalia said. "Really sick."

"That sounds like another line of bullshit," I said.

"No, it's not." The other woman held out her hand to mine. "My name is Cass. I'll give you her address, so you can go over there and see for yourself. Then you can nurse our best friend back to health."

"You just became my new best friend," I teased.

"We'll see about that, Mr. Grayson. Breanne has all but had a nervous breakdown since learning her employees have been stealing from her. Then there's the merge, Theo moving, the mortifying events that would lead you to cast some judgment on her as a shitty executive, and now we are finding out the girl has been paying her company's bills instead of her own. She's passed her limit, but she's a fool if she thinks I don't know what one plus one equals. She's trying to play the wrong people."

I was confused by what Cass was insinuating, but I knew she would tell me. I could quickly tell Cass was pissed about this, and Natalia was broken.

"And who is she trying to play?" I asked with a smile.

"She's trying to play us: the people who give a damn about her," Cass said.

"Do you think she's really sick?"

"I think she's ducking out and trying to hide her unfortunate situation from all of us so that she can fix things on her own. As I said, I know what adds up and what doesn't. I know her too well, and while she thinks she's trying to save us *the burden* of helping our best friend, what she's doing is isolating herself, and I won't fucking stand for that."

"Isolating herself only to bring in the wolves to prey on her—namely, Max the dick?"

"Exactly. Now, pull it together, Nat," Cass said as she looked at her upset friend. "Alex is going to help us out a little. Breanne didn't have you list the property because she's stubborn."

"I know. She's not letting us help her. I can't blame her, though. The goddamn car I loaned her blew up on her drive home."

"That was neglect on *your* part," Cass said as she rolled her eyes. "Listen, Alex. You're going to go to the store to buy whatever cold and flu remedies they have, just in case she really is sick. God knows the girl's immune system has to be shot after everything that's slammed down on her at once."

"Got it, cold and flu medicine." I reached into my pocket and pulled out my phone. "Here's my contact info. I'm airdropping it to you both so you can accept it. Text me her address."

"I'm not done yet," Cass said. I loved the woman's sass and willingness to put Breanne in her place for her pride and stubbornness and for hiding things from the people she knew would gladly help her. "Get stuff to make her a hot toddy and shut up about whatever old movie she may have paused on the television when you enter the room." She smiled knowingly at me. "You can be her prince and save her from Max's shit and from us, kicking her ass for this."

"Why me?" I asked. While I was more than onboard to do these things, part of me wondered why they were.

Nat had pulled it together by this point. "Because, Alex." She arched an eyebrow at me. "You're the hot piece of ass our friend needs to clear up her year-long dry spell."

"You're fucking kidding, Natalia," Cass said with a stare of death.

"Not even a little bit," she snapped back at her friend. "She needs a good, strong man in bed. Once she breaks that spell, this curse she keeps mentioning should be lifted."

"Ignore Natalia. Sex is her answer for everything." Cass shook her head and smiled at me. "This is why *you* won't be curing anything for Breanne with sex."

"After this devious little plan you've conjured up, it's safe to say I'll be dead before I know what hit me if you find out I hurt your friend."

"Oh, no. You would know *exactly* what hit you and what I hit you with." Cass smirked. "Once you and your gentlemen friends are finished with dinner, it would be nice to have you catch sneaky Bree—who's been avoiding us all week—in her little lie."

"So long as Natalia ensures that condo is sold to me and no one else."

What the fuck was driving me to do this? I was suddenly inclined to work with Breanne's friends to call her bluff and play these games to show Breanne we *cared about her,* and no one fucks with her. I was going to ride with the latter half of that. No one fucks with my partner.

Now, I needed to finish this meal so I could leave. I wanted to see

Breanne, and I knew I was at the mercy of whatever wrath was on the other side of her door when she opened it. I knew she was trying to do what she thought was right, but Breanne needed to lose the pride.

After hearing about how she put her ex on blast on her wedding day, it started to make sense to me as to why I was instinctively drawn to her. Something about Bree was alluring to me, and it was the woman I hadn't truly met yet. It was the woman who'd peeked out at me only a few times, and she held the dimpled smile I was falling for. It was *that woman* who I was drawn to—a woman who'd been freed from hell, and one who was, at her core, beautifully happy.

I was going all-in with her friends, risking her punching me in my balls, to dig up the real Breanne Stone. The woman I knew was hiding behind this beat-up version of herself, and if this girl's happier and less stressed personality matched that smile, I was fucking done.

I left dinner at around eight and went directly to the store to grab all the cold and flu products I could find, including a vaporizer and ingredients for the ultimate cold and flu remedy, the hot toddy. Breanne Stone would land safely in my arms tonight, and I would have a look at the place I was about to purchase—until, of course, Breanne repurchased it from me when she was financially able. In a perfect world, I'd have nailed this all down by the end of tonight.

CHAPTER FIFTEEN
BREE

I'd just dozed off, buried in mini-snickers wrappers and kettle corn kernels, when my doorbell rang. It had been a nightmare of a week, exacerbated by my lies and half-truths. Even I was finding it hard to keep up with my many deceptions, and now my friends were going to call my bluff. It was only a matter of time before it all caught up with me in one way or the other, I guess. I might as well face the music; I'd created this mess, and keeping secrets from my friends was turning me into the worst version of myself. It was time for them to let me have it.

I paused my third *comfort movie* and rose to get the door. Knowing that only Nat, Sammy, or Cass would show up at my place around nine in the evening, I opted to get the door in my pajamas, braless. I was years past caring if my friends saw my nipples through my shirt, and they didn't give a shit if my butt was hanging out of my shorts. After they saw me looking like this—my hair, thrown up in a knot with no makeup—they'd know that trying to convince me to go out with them was off the table even if I wasn't sick.

I walked up to the door and opened it, covering my eyes, hoping to play up the sick and sleepy act. "You guys woke me up."

"Jesus Christ, woman!" As soon as I heard his voice, I instinctively slammed the door shut in his face.

"What the fuck?" I said, shocked to hell by the face I saw when I uncovered my eyes. *This cannot be fucking happening. There's no fucking way Alexander is at my door.*

"Um, are you okay?" Alex asked as he knocked on my door again. I reluctantly reopened the door, feeling like the biggest idiot on the planet—and looking like it, too. "I have four bags for you. They're filled with all the remedies I could find for a cold or the flu." I could hear the humor in his voice.

"What are you doing here?" I eyed the paper bags he held by their handles, veins popping in his muscular arms. "And with all of this?"

"Well, I was invited to check out a club with my friends tonight," he casually stepped past me as if I'd invited him in, "and there was a rumor circulating the place that you're on your deathbed."

I turned and started to follow him down into my living room when I spied the brochures the real estate agent had set out on my entryway table. I quickly snatched them and dumped them into the coat closet before rushing to meet him in my living room. I tried to seek comfort from the lights of Downtown Los Angeles from my wall of windows behind where Alex stood, but nothing in this scenario could ever fix the fact that I answered the door half-naked, looking like I'd barely survived a tornado.

I tried to cough and sniff, leaning into my fake sickness, but that only made Alex's lips twist up in the sexiest way possible. Was I high on chocolate? This man shouldn't be here, looking *this sexy*, and I couldn't weasel my way out of the fake-illness lie if I tried.

"Well, well, Breanne Stone," he said in a sly voice. "It appears you are *quite* the sick woman."

"Seriously, Alex. Why are *you*, of all the goddamn people in my miserable life, in my home?"

"I heard my life-long partner is ill. How could I, in good conscience, have an enjoyable evening out with friends," his face scrunched up as if he were solving the world's largest mystery, "while you are home, your immune system positively wrecked by the stress you've been under all week?"

"Ah, so you're here out of the goodness of your heart?" I asked.

"That and…" he eyed my shirt. "Well, yes, that."

I crossed my arms, hiding my nipples from plain view, knowing he must've run into Cass and Nat at that club.

"You should go," I said. "Thanks for the—" I stepped forward and peered into one of the bags, "vaporizer, I guess. And thanks for what seems to be every cold and flu remedy known to man. I prefer to be sick and miserable alone."

"I prefer to take care of my business partner." He smiled. "What will I ever do without you and your eyes on the new blueprints my architects have been working on for Saint John's new pediatric wing?"

"You'll manage. I'm sure that after I ingest all of this," I waved my hand over the bags of cold and flu remedies, "I'll be dancing into the office on Monday morning, and this head cold will be a distant memory." I remembered to throw in a pathetic-sounding cough at the end of my statement for good measure.

"You are one horrible little liar; you know that?" He grinned at me knowingly.

Yeah, you have no idea the lies I've been feeding you since we first met, Buddy.

"I know," I admitted. "Listen, I wasn't in the mood to go clubbing tonight. I had a rougher day than I anticipated, sending off Theo and Stanton, and the club scene was not an appropriate cure for that."

"I can imagine," Alex seemed to egg me on. "They certainly didn't have Snickers candy bars, kettle corn, or," he pivoted back to my flat screen, where my television was paused, "The Wizard of Oz." He said the movie title dramatically and with a hint of surprise, and his eyes were wide and as adorable as a goddamn puppy's.

"That's why I lied about being sick," I said.

"You needed to stay home alone with the poor scarecrow who doesn't have a brain?"

"And now," I eyed him, "it appears the tin-man, who doesn't have a heart, won't leave even if I ask him nicely."

"Comparing me to a heartless man in a *tin* suit now?" he laughed. "Now, *that* is one that I haven't heard yet."

"Alex, please leave," I said. "Seriously, I have no idea why you're here."

As soon as I said the words, the power went out. *Jesus Fucking Christ in Heaven, now the electric company is selling me out.*

"Goddammit!" I seethed. "Well, I need to get to bed anyway." I grabbed his hand and dragged him to the front door. "The power is probably out in the entire building," I shoved him out the door. "It happens all the time. Thanks for the medicine. Good night."

I slammed the door behind him and found myself in utter shock that I forgot about the last luxury I was losing by not paying my fucking bills.

There was only one knock before my temper flared, and I reopened the door. "Go home, Alex."

Alex met me with an arched brow. "No. Not without you, anyway. Pack your stuff—the bras are optional—because you're coming with me," he said, using the flashlight on his phone to re-enter the condo. "Funny how the power is only out in the most expensive condo in this luxurious building."

"Alex—"

"Tick-tock, sweetheart," Alex snapped his fingers. "Time to grab your shit. Don't worry; I'll roleplay with you after we get you to a place where you can plug in this vaporizer for the nasty cold that's got you on your *fake* deathbed."

"Not in the mood to roleplay with you being my fiancé again," I said.

"Not your fiancé. This time, I'm your priest, and you're going to confess all your dirty little lies to me on the way to my place."

"Hell no," I said.

"You don't have a choice," he insisted. "You're coming with me to my beach house where you're going to cough up the last of your fake cold and all the details of what the fuck is going on with you financially."

"I don't have a choice? I can stay at a friend's house, you know."

The night sky that never fully darkened the city cast a glow on his cunning smile as he eyed me. "Either you come with me, or I allow Max, the cheating-ex dick—sex tape and all—to buy this place."

I felt my stomach tighten into a spasm. "How do you know any of that? Any of it?"

"Because Max was at the club tonight, and it just so happens that my good friend was at your wedding—well, what was supposed to be your wedding. Anyway, he informed me, in *explicit* detail, why he didn't question why you were a runaway bride."

"Fine," I said, more pissed off than my brain could comprehend. "Let's go to the goddamn beach, shall we?"

"Now we're getting somewhere. I'd take you to my place in the hills," he said from the other room while I went into my bedroom, "but I hear salty air is better for a head cold than that vaporizer."

"I think you already know I'm not fucking sick."

"True," he answered while I shoved clothes—that I could hardly see in my pitch-dark bedroom—into my overnight bag. "The beach *is* renowned for its therapeutic properties, though."

"I hate the beach."

"Another fucking lie to confess to your priest on the drive there," he said smugly.

"I'll drive myself."

"You'll ride with me," he said. "Or Natalia and Cass will find out all about Max wanting to buy this place that hasn't even hit the market yet."

I stumbled over my bed and landed headfirst into my dresser as I tried to flee my room, needing to get out to where Alex was.

"Jesus," I heard him say. "Don't you have a flashlight or something?"

I felt him at my side while I held my forehead, feeling a bump slowly rising to the surface. "No. I usually pay my electric bills, and…"

"And you aren't used to the power company teaching you the harsh lesson of what happens when you don't pay your bills on time?"

"That's why I'm not going with you."

"That is exactly why you're going with me," he said, flashing his phone light around my room. "Pack up the rest of your shit. We're out of here."

"What do you know about Max wanting to buy my place?" I softly asked, continuing to pack as Alex held up his phone's flashlight for me.

"I'm sorry to say it, but the jerk-off seems to have it out for you after finding out that you wanted to marry my sexy ass at our merge gala. He was there to spy on our company."

"He was spying?" I spoke. "I thought he was stalking me."

"Turns out, he works for Jim's enemy, Brakken," he continued. "I swear, that company has some majorly shady shit going on. This isn't the first time they've sent a spy of some sort to crash one of Jim's company merges."

I went with this conversation. Alex seemed to be more caught up with that, quickly forgetting that I was in the shittiest position of my life. Not only did Alex know I wasn't paying my bills, but he'd also made it clear he was done with my lies. Now, he knew I was selling my place, and that dickweasel, Max, was trying to buy it to get revenge on me. I was sure of that. Keeping Alex's mind occupied with business seemed to keep him from prying into my personal life, so all I could do was hope he'd rant until he was blue in the face.

I guess this is how it ends when you lie yourself into oblivion. The one person you don't want to know about your failures shows up while you're elbow-deep in candy wrappers, trying to eat away the shame of living a double life. Then, you take a header into a mahogany armoire and nearly give yourself a concussion, so you have a physical reminder that lying isn't good for you.

The irony was that all of these lies were started to save what little dignity I had left. If that wasn't the backfire of the decade, I didn't know what to call it.

By the time we'd reached Alex's car, I stopped in my tracks. "Are you serious with this?" I said, trying to turn the tables on him to get out of this situation.

"With what?" He took my duffle from my hand and tossed it in his trunk. "The car or the fact that you're about to cough up your lies *about everything* while we're driving in it?"

"The Ferrari," I said.

He flashed that sly smile that told me I should've let him continue talking about the last thoughts he'd had on his mind; the fact that my ex worked for Mr. Mitchell's competition.

"Aside from my cat, this car ranks at the top of things I love most." He stretched his arms over the top of the sleek, graphite-colored car and eyed me. "So, take it easy on your insults."

"A Ferrari 812?" I arched an eyebrow at him. "I didn't even think these were in America?"

"It's one of the first to sail the high seas to bring me the horsepower I desire. How do you know *anything* about the make or model of this vehicle?"

"Do you think that because I'm broke that I don't know anything about Ferraris?"

He smirked. "Get in the damn car." He opened his door. "And for the record, *you* said that shit about being broke, Breanne. Not me."

I stood there, listening to the low growl of the engine come to life, purring and idling while Alex sat patiently in the car.

"Fuck," I growled under my breath.

The window rolled down.

"Come on, dimples. Let's go."

"You have a cat?" I asked, climbing into the car.

Alex put the car in gear, and when the badass thing roared to life, I understood why my idiot ex had always drooled over this particular Ferrari. Max's stupid ass was the only reason I knew anything about the damn car in the first place.

"My cat's name is Zeus, named after the Greek god because he thinks he *is* a Greek god." Alex's voice changed into a more humorous tone, and it was incredibly charming despite how irritated I was by my current circumstances. "He's as black as the sin in your lying little heart, and he's the *only* living thing on earth who owns my ass." He pulled onto the street once the light turned green and allowed for us to merge into the cluster of Friday night party cars on this particular street. "Now, let's talk about more pressing issues."

I rubbed my forehead. "I'm—Jesus Christ. You're *not* the person I want to confide in about this."

I heard a ding, and my eyes widened when the car spoke to Alex in some British robot voice: *"Text from Natalia Hoover. Hey, did you get to Bree's..."*

Alex hit a button on his steering wheel to silence the car from announcing the rest of the text.

"What the fuck was that?" I asked, knowing exactly what that was —treachery.

"My car talks." Alex smiled. "It's like Night Rider. Pretty fucking awesome, right?"

"Now, who's the goddamn liar?" I said. "Unbelievable. How the hell does Nat have your number, and more importantly, *why the fuck* is she asking if you got to my place?"

"Listen, I can lie about the fact that I searched the database at the firm for your address, and after having small talk with your friends, I found you—"

"Or you can tell me what the fuck is going on," I interrupted, my limit for games rapidly approaching its end.

"Right." He pursed his lips, shifted gears, and flew onto the freeway and over into the fast lane of Interstate 405. "If we're going to get the truth out of you, then I'd better set the example, eh?"

"Yeah," I mocked. "And while we play this game of *truth or dare*, I want to know everything that happened at the bar."

"First of all, I'm thrilled you opted in for a game of truth or dare because I'm about to dare you to—"

"Answer the question," I ignored his attempt at flirtation or whatever the hell he was doing to distract me. "How did you find out about Max wanting to buy my place?"

"I thought I was doing the questioning. Interesting how you flipped that around so efficiently."

"Please, God, tell me!" I sounded whiney, but fuck, who wouldn't be? This was outright annoying.

"Your assclown of an ex taunted your friends tonight. He told them he made an offer on your place, and he's calling for a short sale. Nat was pretty distraught by the news, not only because you are selling your beloved home without confiding in her and your other friends," he glanced at me while I tried to swallow the lump in my throat, "but that Max was buying it to throw fuel on the fire. I would assume that not trusting her to be your real estate agent—someone who could help navigate these very personal and sticky deals—only adds insult to injury. I can't speak to her feelings, but you might want to have a conversation with her about that. Just my two cents."

"I had my reasons for keeping this to myself."

"Like me, your friend Cass seems more easily able to tune into your reasons for selling the place without telling your friends."

"And the reasons you've both seemed to realize are what?" I was suddenly feeling overly defensive, but that was because I knew I'd blown it with my friends, and Alex Grayson, of all the people in the fucking world, was the one I had to talk this out with.

"We believe that you're keeping everything on the down-low because you're stubborn, prideful, and, surprisingly, a pathological liar," he said with a smirk on his face.

"I don't need rescuing," I said, setting this record straight. "I knew that if they found out, they'd stop the sale and loan me the money to pull my ass out of the pit I fell into by trusting my employees."

"That's the prideful part I just mentioned," he said, shifting gears, navigating this car as if we were on a racetrack. "The stubborn part, well, that's why all the lying commenced; is it not?"

I frowned, willing myself not to cry. This was humiliating. I didn't want to admit any of this to myself, much less Alex. I fucking hated crying, and it seemed that's all I'd done since meeting this man.

"Listen," Alex's voice changed as he took an exit that led us into the hills, "we all get it. It's shit, and your friends give a fuck. That's a damn good thing, Bree."

He called me by my nickname—the one used by my family and friends—and it made me feel instantly at ease for some strange reason. Maybe it was because I needed some sort of comfort after being so vulnerable and exposed, or perhaps it was because the way he said it made me feel like Alex gave a damn.

"I appreciate it. I do. But I wasn't raised to have people bail my ass out of shitty situations that I brought on myself."

"That's because you had good parents," he said with a smile. "Did they also tell you never to stare a gift horse in the face? You have people who care about you, people who would never allow your ex to steal the home you and your dad designed together. I will hold your ass hostage at my place until you admit that this is a tremendous thing that we're all doing for you."

"That's the big question, though," I answered him. "What are you doing except taking me as your hostage?"

"We're helping." His face grew solemn as the car hung onto every turn it made, going through the shortcut everyone took when heading to Malibu from L.A. "I'm buying your place unless you pull that listing tonight."

"No, and no. No way in hell to both of those things."

"That's fine," Alex said. "I have plenty of wealthy friends who will ensure Max the wanker doesn't fuck you over because you made him look like the asshole he is."

"Please don't put me in this position," I said with a sigh.

"What position? A position to help you because you have a fucking heart of gold, and your employees fucked you for it?"

"Yes! That position."

The car slowed and veered off the road and into a vista point turnout. Alex shut off the engine and gripped the back of my seat.

"What the fuck is your problem with me?" he said, pinning me with his dark eyes.

"Excuse me?"

He did that sexy thing where his lips tightened, and he chewed on the corner of them. "No lies, remember?"

He seemed pissed, and so, who gave a shit what I said at this point? I might as well tell the truth since we were traveling down this fucking road together, literally.

"From the day I've met you—" Being in the car and too close to his sexy expression made me choke on my words, needing to fight for some breathing room.

I jumped out of the car, and Alex was hot on my heels behind me.

"From the day *I* met *you*, I've been nothing but supportive," he insisted.

"That's the thing," I said, letting the smell of the salty ocean air waft against my face. "I didn't want to look like a pathetic idiot who ran my dad's company. I didn't want the merge, either. I wanted to prove I could do it all on my own. Then you came along and found my employees stealing from me. You saw that my company was in the red and I was hiding down with the architects. Maybe I would've eventually been okay with all of that, but from the first second I'd met you, you led me to believe you were some *Logan* guy. It just feels like you're the one who's enjoying all of this shit going sideways on me."

"Really?" I snapped my head over to him at the sound of his lowered, upset tone. "Do you think that's also why I held you while you cried in my fucking arms? I'm an asshole, Breanne, but not *that* big of an asshole."

"Why, then?" I asked. "Why were you there for me? Why *are* you here for me now instead of allowing my friends to grill me and let me stay with them?"

We were officially in an awkward stare-off.

He chewed on the corner of his mouth while he looked away from me. "You're my partner."

"Not good enough," I countered. "None of it makes sense unless you're enjoying the fact that your new partner sucks and her company would've gone under without *you* saving it. Unless you enjoy watching me go through hell."

"I would naturally warn you right here," he turned to me, and I felt my heartrate react to the man's dark yet sincere expression, "but I won't because I don't..."

Suddenly I wasn't the one lost for words or lies; Alex was stumped about this shit too, and it's because he knew I was fucking right.

"You don't what?" I pressed. "Just admit it, since we're *not lying* to each other. The badass CEO and former VP of Mitchell and Associates, Alex Grayson, enjoys Breanne Stone's—"

"Companionship," he said in an exhale and then looked at me as if he'd just been given a sign from God. "Wow. That's not a word in my vocabulary that's used very often. Here's another one. I *love* being around you, even if it's all shitty. You intrigue me, and even though we're merely friends and business partners, I will admit that whether you want saving or not, I'm not going to walk away and pretend you don't need help. I'm here for you, and I enjoy that I feel enough compassion—for the first time in my fucking life for anyone other than my friends—that I'm not going to allow you to get crushed."

"Crushed?"

I didn't know how to respond to any of this, and the strange part was that I didn't think Alex knew how to respond to any of it either. It's like we were both up here, on top of the world, confused as hell about why we were here.

"I like you a lot, Breanne. I don't think I've ever taken an interest like this in *any woman*, much less a coworker. So, allow me to help and at least be here for you."

"All right," I oddly and too quickly conceded. "Let's get to your place because after you practically just admitted you're in love with me, I could use a beer or ten," I teased with a smile to kill this awkwardness.

Alex laughed loudly. "Jesus Christ, is this what loving someone would be like?"

He asked the question in a way that made me suddenly feel sad for him. It was as if he had no idea what that word meant.

"Love comes in many different fashions," I said, beginning to feel like Alex was even more lost than I was. I wanted to move this conversation to a lighter level, though, because I'd about had it with the revelations of tonight. "What you're saying is that you want to marry me and live in a house in the suburbs."

I smiled at his expressions as it turned more mischievous and returned to the Alex I was more comfortable with. This was undoubtedly an interesting interaction, though. I couldn't even begin to emotionally unpack everything that'd taken place within the last ten minutes, and I wasn't going to start now.

"Let's get to the beach house because if what you just said is true," Alex grinned, "I'm going to be needing a much stiffer drink than a beer. House in the fucking suburbs, my ass."

I chuckled at his statement, and I couldn't help but instantly wonder what kind of history he had to make him question what love was like—as if it were an emotion he'd never heard of before. A sadness crossed his features, and it was heartbreaking, to say the very least.

One thing I knew for sure was that if Alex was going to *be there* for me with my sad story, he was going to meet me in the middle, and I was going to find out why he acted like the word *love* was a foreign concept.

CHAPTER SIXTEEN

ALEX

I blame Breanne wearing next to nothing when she opened the door to her condo tonight for my brain misfiring when she called me out for helping her. The truth was, I had no good answer for why I suddenly felt more invested in her well-being than I should have been.

I tried answering her confusion about me wanting to help her, but I was perplexed by it as well. Beyond perplexed, actually. The brutal truth was that I didn't give a shit about anyone except for my close group of friends. So, I don't know when, where, or what the hell happened to make me give half a damn, let alone *this fucking much,* about Breanne's unfortunate situation.

None of that shit mattered at this point because trying to justify what I was doing would only give me a headache. All of it made perfect sense until she questioned my motivations.

"Listen," I finally spoke after we got back onto the highway and continued driving, "I'm probably as confused about why I'm..."

And there went my goddamn brain again. Blank. What the fuck was happening to me tonight?

"Why you're what? Suddenly switching up from Satan in a suit to my savior in a suit?"

I grinned. "Pretty much, yes," I answered, seeing that the tables had turned. "But you did mention that you believed I was doing this because I enjoyed watching you go through shit."

"There's no other better reason, is there?"

"I understand what you mean." I sighed and rubbed my forehead as I blew out a breath. Now her perfume was fogging up my brain. I needed to floor it and get to the house. "Since you and I are on the truth train," I found my bearings in the horsepower of my car, "I'll be honest when I say I think your perfume is fucking with my mind or something."

Breanne laughed in a way that made me think that maybe I was fucking right about the bewitching fragrance she wore.

"What the hell is that scent anyway?" I had to ask, given the woman's infectious laugh and the fact that I knew I'd solved the mystery of why I was acting entirely out of character with a woman I hardly knew on a personal level.

"It's called Sundazed," she laughed again. "Byredo is the one you should blame, I guess?"

"Makes sense." I glanced at her. "Seriously, I can't fucking think with that fragrance all up in—"

"Spare me." She rolled her eyes. "I *hardly* think my perfume is the reason you can't focus."

"Really?" I questioned. "Then explain to me why I'm suddenly at a loss for words for doing any of this. I *know* that I'm not reveling in your unfortunate situation. I also know for a damn fact that I wouldn't be bringing you to the one house that I've never brought a woman to, aside from my friends."

I pinched my lips, knowing I'd admitted to something I should have kept my mouth shut about. Could I make any of this more awkward for either of us?

"Well," Breanne finally said when I felt the heat of her gaze on me, "it looks like my perfume is going to have you and me well on our way to living in the suburbs together then, huh?" She chuckled. "I guess I should feel honored that you're bringing *me* to the one place you don't bring random women, eh?"

"I need a goddamn bourbon," I admitted. "Let's just get to the fucking house before I say another word."

"He's uncomfortable," she taunted. "Wow. I'm intrigued now."

"Intrigued or not," I answered, "I need to flush my sinuses and have a drink."

Fuck me. Okay. I gave more than just a damn about her. I loved her dimpled smile. I wanted her at my beach house tonight, and the power outage was a blessing from above to make that happen. Yes, I could've called her friends or allowed her to get out of this, but I didn't want that. I wanted her to myself. That was the truth-bomb. That was what I'd been too afraid to admit to her or myself—I wanted *her*.

How I went from being merely attracted to Breanne to *this* was the million-fucking-dollar question. I'd gone so far as convincing myself there was some love potion mixed into her perfume to rationalize all of this shit. This is why I needed a drink, this is why she should stay away from me, and this is every reason why I didn't want her to. For the first time in my impossible life, I was attracted to a woman beyond wishing to fuck her.

I wanted to see her smile *at me* in a humorous conversation. I desired to watch her green eyes dazzle when she flashed that dimpled smile—oh, sweet Jesus, I'd even called her *dimples* earlier! I was in so far over my head. Thank God she was so angry I was on this rescue mission that she'd missed that part.

"This is *your place*?" she asked when the overhead door opened, and we pulled into my immaculate garage. "Impressive."

I pulled in and parked next to my CJ7 Jeep, the vehicle that only left this garage on the rare occasion I strapped my board to it and met my friends to surf.

"Not really, considering the cars you've seen me drive." I smiled at her.

I opened my door faster than I should've, and I stepped out to inhale the masculine scent of my street bike, the opened top Jeep, and whatever else was manly in my garage, trying to shake off these unfamiliar emotions that'd sunk their teeth into me.

Was I really getting hung up on *love*? I wasn't in love with anything. I loved my cat, cars, and friends, but women? No. Hell no. I wasn't capable of *love* in a relationship, and every ex-girlfriend I'd ever had could testify to that. My thoughts had me flustered and confused, and my brain hurt, trying to reconcile everything. Regardless of what I told myself, this stunning woman who just stepped out of my car— messy bun on the top of her head and all—was about to follow my sorry ass into the place I'd never brought a woman before.

I glanced over at her, and she leveled me with that goddamn dimpled smile, an arch of her eyebrow, and a giggle to add to this chaos of emotional bullshit I had to deal with. If I was straight-up honest at this very moment, I was officially fucked.

"Alex." She had the upper hand on my ass, and she knew it. "I love your Jeep."

"Me too." I kept it cool. "Now, it's high time you and I get to talking about why you have such a loose relationship with the truth over a stiff drink," I said, leaving the woman to follow me into my house as if I were fleeing a demon. "Hop to it, dimples…"

Fuck my life.

"That's the second time you've called me that, and unless you're referring to the dimples on my ass, I assume you're calling me that because—"

Fucken-A. And now I'm thinking about her perfectly round ass and examining it for dimples? God help me.

"Your smile," I said, keeping it together after the salty breeze from the opened doors in my living area slapped some brain cells back into me. I'd have to tip my cleaners more than usual for leaving the doors open tonight. "Your cheeks have dimples when you smile. I find them quite appealing."

I scrambled to my outdoor bar, leaving no room for chit-chat. I rushed to the bar to down a quick shot, and once I'd set my glass down again and then gripped onto the bar counter, I found the woman watching me with a sassy smile.

"If you're *that* much of a chicken shit, perhaps I can call one of my girlfriends and leave you to have your house to yourself tonight."

I eyed her, the warmth of the bourbon chilling out my frazzled-ass nerves. "Nah," I smirked. "You're stuck with me."

"You're acting weird as hell." She laughed, then boldly walked to where I was and poured herself a finger of bourbon. I watched her down it and smile. "There, now we can talk."

I smiled, feeling like kind of a bitch. "What's your flavor? I have my outdoor bar prepped by my housekeepers when I know I'm coming down here to escape for the weekend."

Her smile was more mischievous than I'd ever seen it—or her. Hell, I didn't think Breanne had this side to her if I were honest about that too. Since I was getting hit right and left with these blasts of fucking honesty with *myself* tonight, let's add this one in there also. She looked sexier than fuck with this smile.

"Well, you seemed to enjoy me and that blow job..."

She paused and laughed while I choked on my bourbon.

"What, now?" I managed.

"God dang, man. You're a mess." She snickered pleasantly, watching me behave like an idiot. "This bourbon tastes quite delicious. I'll have what you're having."

"Good." I arched an eyebrow at her, taking advantage of me acting like a schoolboy who'd just caught his first glimpse of a pair of tits, and slid her a drink.

"Where can we sit to capture the best view on this fabulous patio?"

I watched her stroll around my lit-up pool, and her tanned skin appeared to glow under the party lights that were strung throughout the area. She was fascinating, and she was beautiful, so why fight any of this? I was attracted to her, so what?

While I watched her follow the path through the garden area that led out to the deck's second level, I was filled with compassion for her situation. My heart was bleeding for this woman and what she'd been through.

Her father, Brian, had liquidated his assets—which were many—to set up a trust fund for Breanne when he died. I knew that because he reached out to Mitchell and Associates as soon as he was diagnosed with early-onset Alzheimer's, and he did his best to set up the company for Bree. How could he know those rotten bastards would pillage everything? Her mother had died of breast cancer when Breanne was a little girl, so Brian knew his best chance at helping his daughter was to do what he did. I had the feeling his ghost was haunting the ungrateful mother fuckers who did Bree so dirty.

When talks of our merge began, and I saw Stone's financials, I knew something had gone dreadfully wrong with Brian's plans. To think that her vast inheritance was so swiftly depleted, to the point that she'd had her goddamn power cut tonight as a result of the betrayal she'd endured, made me feel angry and sad at the same time.

Strange that I could hardly give a fuck about it all back then, but now, all this knowledge I had about her father and her was hitting me directly in my heart at this very moment.

I sipped my bourbon and followed her to my lower deck. It was a well lit area with palms, a large spa, comfortable seating, and most of all, a railing that I leaned against more than once in thought when the things in my troubled past seeped in and tried to haunt me.

Strange how she seemed to find refuge and solitude in that railing herself. To hear the ocean, feel the breezes on a warm spring evening, and just altogether lose yourself in the waves below rolling into the wet sandy beach; it was quite a thing.

I had no idea why I was strumming up all of these emotional thoughts about Breanne's father on a night when all hell seemed to be breaking loose inside me. I might not have given two fucks about who Breanne Stone was when Mr. Stone spoke highly of his daughter back then, but now, I felt it more than ever. I cared deeply about this woman's happiness, and I wouldn't allow her to sell her condo. She'd been dealt a shitty hand, and she deserved a fair shake.

"All right," Breanne said as I stood next to her. "What's your story, Alex?"

"Nope," I responded as I stretched forward and rested my forearms on the top of the rail. "We're not doing *that*." I moved my snifter glass between my palms, studying the small ripples it made. "We're here to solve the riddles of why you've been lying—"

"No," Breanne answered me resolutely. "You don't get shit from me unless you *cough up* some facts about yourself too."

I looked at her cheeky grin and was lost in the dazzling eyes I wanted to see so desperately before. Now, these alluring eyes were working against me, not for me. I couldn't help but smile and nod in compliance.

"You know, you've got to be a witch, or maybe I had an ex-girlfriend start to dabble in the dark arts, and she's using *you* to break down a side of me that I don't talk about to anyone."

"No one?" Her eyes widened in humor. "Wow. It sounds like you are pretty screwed tonight because unless you get emotionally dirty with me, I'm not confiding jack shit into you. So, spill it."

I exhaled and narrowed my eyes at her. I wasn't a man who gave up details of his past to anyone. Hell, Jim was my best friend and closer than a brother to me, and he didn't know half of the shit in my past.

"What do you want to know?" I asked the question because I wasn't going to talk out of my ass for the hell of it.

She shrugged. "You seemed to spaz out back there after you questioned what *love* felt like. I'm curious why you were running efficiently on all cylinders, forcing me out of my powerless home, but ever since that word came up, and you've been acting strange."

I chewed on the corner of my mouth. This wasn't a question I was going to answer. Period. I was an excellent interrogator and negotiator; I was not the one who sat on the other side of *that* table. Turning things around is what *I* did, and I'd never fallen victim to someone flipping shit on me. I didn't plan on starting now, either.

"Spaz out?" She was nothing if not observant. She'd seen right through me earlier. "Truth be told, I was a bit surprised that you'd think I would enjoy watching you going through hell. I suppose we don't truly know each other, but you formed a hasty opinion of me, which caught me off-guard. So, with that said, I will clear the air."

"Please do because I have no other reason to believe you're not an asshole in a suit. I see the way your employees like to have you as their boss, but they are extra careful never to fuck up around you."

"I'm sorry, but shouldn't every employee behave that way with their boss? If they fuck up, I'll fire them," I answered truthfully. "That's no reason to believe I'd *enjoy* firing them, though."

"Fair answer, I guess." She took a sip of her bourbon.

"It's the truth," I returned. "If I allowed emotions to run my game, I'd be a goddamn wreck and would suck at my job."

"And your employees would possibly steal from you?"

I raised my eyebrows. "You're not fair with yourself about that. Jim and Spence have even ordered an audit at Mitchell and Associates because dirty employees come in all shapes and sizes. Jim's always being kept on his toes, and it appears that everyone *except you* thinks you should've easily known it was happening."

"You found it the first week in," she answered.

"That's because the thieves we busted got sloppy about a month before I started auditing shit myself. One confessed, and the other tried to steal your clients right in front of you and me and gave all the dirty secrets away."

"You're saying you got lucky, then?"

"Pretty much. They were sloppy, and I sniffed their asses out, and now they're gone. So, if that's what led you to believe I would enjoy you in the shitter financially, then you have a lot more to learn about me as your business partner."

"It's not just that, I suppose," she said

"What else do you *suppose* would make you form an opinion that I'm a twisted sociopath who would be happy to watch you lose everything?" I questioned.

"I've also heard rumors that when it comes to relationships, or whatever *you* might call them, you're an unsympathetic asshole."

I couldn't help but smile at this fucking truth and wonder who was talking shit about me these days—so much so that Breanne would already know my reputation with women.

"Yes, I'm an asshole in the romance department and a dick in every sense of the word when it comes to relationships," I admitted.

"Hence the reason you think you have a nasty witch on your ass?" She chuckled. "Perhaps with flying monkeys too?"

"Right." I smiled and nodded at her silly response. I'd let her have another pass on the Wizard of Oz jokes, given the fact that I'd ripped her out of her apartment while she was in the middle of watching the show. "I pissed off the Witch of the North, I assume."

The fact that she lightened up some with her interrogations— especially in the romance department—had me slightly relieved. I was cool to play along with fictional witches.

"That would be the good witch," she turned back to look out at the water. "You've likely upset the Witch of the West; that's the wicked one with the monkeys."

"Indeed. Now, about the condo." *And getting back on track.* "Why the hell are you getting rid of the last asset you have? Haven't you lost enough in all of this crap you've been wading through?"

"I have lost enough, and as I told you, I don't need rescuing," she said. "The sale of my home will pay off every debt I owe, get me into renting a new apartment until I'm financially stable enough to buy a new one, and I'll be able to afford a cheap car that can get me to and from work."

"You realize your next check—"

"I know exactly what my next paycheck will be. I've been donating most of it to help keep Stone alive. I also know what it feels like to liquidate funds and lose shit for things I think are good." She looked at me as I studied her. "But you already knew that, didn't you?"

"I've seen the millions that an anonymous person has donated over the years, and in all of the ledgers I've gone through, I had no idea who that charitable *giver* was." I pursed my lips. "That was, of course, until I learned you were in worse financial trouble than your company."

"I've learned my lessons; I think you know that. Now, back to you."

"You're not getting shit out of me," I said. "In fact, I feel like I've answered plenty of interrogating questions from you as it is."

"You walked into those by explaining to me why you're not the jerk I believed you were."

"The operative word here being *believed*. As in, you don't feel that way anymore?"

"For now. I still have no idea who the hell you are, though, and I'm not going to confide in you when I only know you as Alexander Grayson," she said with that stubborn streak I was finding oddly appealing about her.

"Good God," I sighed. "I'm not giving you details—"

"Then the truth train stops here, and I'm getting off of it," she said, cutting me off.

"You're stubborn, for sure," I said.

Even though it was frustrating as hell, I had to accept that I loved a woman with fire in her spirit. All the women I'd ever known had allowed me to walk all over them. Not Breanne, though. She would dropkick my ass right over this ledge and out to sea if I fucked around or even entertained the idea of walking all over her. This made her highly attractive to me, and as hard as I was trying not to, I was starting to fall for the woman.

"Oh, God. Let's make this easy, then. Your parents? Siblings? Do you have any?" she questioned, jerking me out of those thoughts.

"In a perfect world with a more *normal* person, I believe that would be an easy answer, but this is me, and it's not," I said.

I watched her frown. "Sorry. I lost both of my parents, and I'm over here acting like something as difficult couldn't have happened to you."

The concern I felt coming from her was written all over her face, and it softened me up the moment I'd somehow connected to her on this bizarre level. This *truth train* was about to turn into a runaway train that I may or may not be able to stop, and if there was one thing I didn't want to get to the core of in my life, it was the truth.

My lips twitched as my mind told me to shut the fuck up about everything, but the other half of me was feeling as though it wouldn't be a bad thing to open up—a little.

"Grayson is not my birth name," I admitted.

"Oh, so just like Logan, you made up that one too?"

Her smile and the way she teased me kept me steady on this course.

"It's my maternal grandfather's surname. I left home the summer after my freshman year in high school, and I moved in with him. My grandfather, Logan Grayson, adopted me, and I proudly changed my last name to his. The man was my hero and savior in many ways."

Her expression grew sincere. "Wow, well..." she stammered and looked away.

"Look who's perplexed with the questioning now," I smiled at her. "It's fine. My mother had a stroke a year or so ago. We had a complicated relationship. She made some pretty questionable decisions about keeping my father around."

"I'm sorry to hear that," she said.

I exhaled. "Whatever you say, don't apologize for anything I'm dumb enough to reveal about my fucked-up family."

"All right. Were you an only child?"

"Do we have to do the family tree shit?" I rolled my eyes when I saw her challenge me with her *quit acting like a little bitch* look. "I have two sisters. My younger one is married and lives in Arizona with my mom. The other, my oldest, went into the military to get the hell out as fast as she could and hasn't looked back since."

"The military?" she questioned.

"She's a badass fighter pilot."

"Top Gun?" she smiled thoughtfully.

I'd merely stated basic facts, and Breanne already had that concerned expression on her face that I despised people giving me. One question would lead to five more, which inevitably led to all the things that I would do anything to keep buried.

"Yep," I ignored the pity-gesture and continued. "Jane is the only thing I can say I'm proud of in my family. She's kicking ass on her aircraft carrier even as we speak."

"That's awesome. I didn't—"

"Listen," I interrupted before I took a sip of bourbon, "that's all you're getting out of my fucked-up past and family life. Your turn."

"I feel like I pissed you off," she said.

"No," I answered. "I just don't give this stuff airtime in my mind or conversation to anyone. In a nutshell, my family is like a goddamn Jackson Pollock painting."

She ran her hand along my arm, and I nearly jumped at the soothing gesture. "I can see that this is rubbing you the wrong way, and I'm sorry I brought it up. You're a strong man, though. I see it every day I work with you. It's half the reason I didn't want you to know about me fucking up my dad's company."

"Even the strongest person has a painful past," I said, repeating a quote that rang too true about me.

"Now that we got the headbutting out of the way," she smiled, and I could tell she was over my sudden shitty mood. "I have to say that I admire the way you think. The fact that you've had your feet held to the fire, and you're one badass mother-fucker in business is impressive," she said in some funny way that could only make me smile.

"Well, I'm happy you feel that way," I said. "Now, since I've confessed more than I should have, allow me to help you keep your condo and get you back on your feet again."

"I want you to explain why you care enough to help."

"I have my reasons, and those will stay with me. I've met your father, and I know it's the right thing to do."

Her face grew solemn, and she sighed. "I think we've both had our fair share of talking about things that are upsetting. Seriously, I think I'm done for the night."

"Hey," I touched her chin and brought her sad eyes to meet mine, "I brought you here to take care of you and help you out. Sending you off to bed *alone* wouldn't be my idea of helping you. Why don't we jump in the pool or something? I'll pour us some more drinks, and we can kick back and talk about dolphins or something."

She grinned. "Why don't we…"

I watched her tap her fingernail to her teeth, and the most daring smile reached her eyes. Whatever she was thinking, I wanted to be a part of it. *This* was the side of the woman I wanted to meet; the feisty, mischievous woman who seemed to be in there hiding behind the dimples I adored so much.

"Have sex?" Why not take a stab at that one?

"My girlfriends and I used to run into the surf late at night. It was exhilarating."

"I have wetsuits."

"Nah," she grinned. "You've got to do it in your clothes like a thrill seeker."

"You've lost your goddamn mind."

She chuckled. "Let's do it! If we're going to see if we're compatible with each—"

"Bull-fucking-shit, and I'm serious. I only go in that ocean at night when my friends have begged me to go night surfing or if I'm drunk."

"And here I thought we had a connection."

"From the flying fucking monkeys, or the fact that I'm not the dick you thought I was?"

"Both." She giggled. "You can be a chicken shit and stay here, but I'm taking a quick dip."

"Says the chick who *died* in Jaws," I smirked.

"And he doesn't like scary movies." She pulled off her top, revealing her perfect breasts displayed nicely in her white lace bra. "Another fun fact about my *kind* business partner."

"I never said any of that."

"Then get your ass in the water with me, and then we'll relax with a drink in your enticing spa. I need to cut loose, and that ice-cold ocean is calling my name."

"I think a goddamn great white shark is hunting the surf, and that thing is calling your name."

She grabbed a beach towel from the holder next to the gate that led out to the shoreline. Who the hell was I kidding? This was crazy as hell, yet I craved to be out doing something wild. I was done asking myself what the fuck was happening, and I was ready to start saying *why the fuck not?*

CHAPTER SEVENTEEN
BREE

*L*ast night with Alex was informative, to put it mildly. It took getting him out in the surf to finally see a different side of the man, a side that I felt entirely more comfortable around. The ice-cold water of the Pacific made both of us race out as quickly as we'd run in as if there really was a shark loose in the shallow water. It was crazy and fun, and if I was honest, I was shocked Alex had followed me out into the surf. I had to be careful with this man, though. I could tell that if I weren't careful, I would fall for the guy, and I wasn't about to have another man stab me in my heart again.

The weird part was that I stopped feeling like Alex was an asshole after spending last night with him and speaking candidly. It was quite lovely to be here, and Alex was the perfect gentleman after we were done for the night, showing me to a hot shower so I could clean up and get warm. When I got out, dressed for bed, and walked out to the balcony of the room I was staying in, I saw him standing out where we'd talked earlier, staring thoughtfully out at the surf. Maybe I conjured up some horrible stuff from his past, and that's why he was still outside and alone with his thoughts.

I'd gotten to know him a bit better, but I wasn't comfortable enough to walk out there and ask if he was okay. I felt a bit shitty that I might have brought up unpleasant memories, but I'd had no idea where to start when I asked the man about who he was outside of work. He was so damn attractive that part of the time it was challenging to think, but I knew I'd touched on a nerve when his features darkened and his voice lowered when it came to talking about his family.

I backed off at that point. Anyone could sense that the pain from his past was the reason he was intense, and it was also the reason he wouldn't talk about it. Being the person I was, I wanted to help him, and now I wanted to know more.

Goddamn it. I had to get off these thoughts, or I'd start in again, and the man would gladly throw me out of his house. It wasn't my business to ask him questions. I wasn't his girlfriend or his wife. I was his business partner, and as far as I could tell, whether he confided in me or not, he did just fine doing his job without my help. I was the one who sucked and had employees robbing her in broad daylight. I was also the one who was down here with Alex because I'd started down a path of lying to protect myself.

None of it mattered. Last night was a fun way to get to know Alex a little better, and because of his attempt to help me, I could happily say I wasn't a nervous wreck at the moment. I woke up feeling rested, and that was enough to make me feel grateful.

It took the smell of fresh bread coming from outside of my room to get my butt out of the most comfortable bed I could've asked to sleep in—while being on the verge of homelessness. I'd been awake for about an hour, but I was curled up under the soft, goose-down comforter, watching the ocean, so I was in no hurry to move until my stomach growled.

A chill filled the room. Unfortunately, because I was flustered by my unexpected power outage, all I'd thrown in my duffle was underwear, bras, leggings, and tank tops.

I walked downstairs, briskly rubbing my arms as I followed the scent of freshly baked bread to a display of chocolate muffins, croissants, and a large bowl of freshly cut fruit.

"Wow," I said with a smile, seeing Alex wearing jeans and another tight shirt—this one long-sleeved. "This smells delicious."

"Chocolate muffins are on the menu for the woman to nurse a hangover from her nightly confessions." He turned from his French press coffee carafe, and, my God, he was more beautiful than ever with his unstyled, wavy hair. "You cold?" he asked, the goosebumps on my arms giving me away.

"Would I look like an idiot if I said I was?" I laughed. "Especially after demanding to run into the ocean last night?"

"You couldn't look like an idiot if you tried." He winked and rubbed his hands on a kitchen towel. "Let me go grab you something. You obviously didn't have much light to pack at your house with last evening either," he teased, and his smile was radiantly sexy.

Great, now everything the man was doing was sending me into a hormonal frenzy. His dark blond hair with its sexy wave was beyond fuck-a-licious—as Nat would say. His ass was more pronounced, and with a firmness that only the distressed denim jeans he wore could outline *exceptionally well* for me.

I reached for a white square plate that Alex had set out next to the muffins and other baked goods. I smiled, recalling that Alex was keenly observant about my greatest weakness and most immense love —chocolate anything. The bite of the muffin I took melted in my mouth like butter.

Does the man bake too? I thought with a stupid smile on my face.

"Here you go," he said. "The hoodie might be old and raggedy, but it's warm."

I took the sweatshirt and smiled. "Varsity Football?" I arched an eyebrow at him. "Is this yours, or was it left with the house when you bought this place?"

"Believe it or not, I was the starting quarterback for our varsity team when I moved to Beverly Hills to live with my grandfather." He sipped his coffee while setting a small cup in front of my plate and pushing the cream and sugar closer. "It pissed off a lot of people, but eventually, I was screwing the cheer captain, so…" he laughed into his coffee when I rolled my eyes.

"So, he's a jock, and I saw that surfboard on your Jeep too. You surf a lot?"

"By the look on your face, I'm guessing you can't visualize it. Even after I ran out into the ocean with you last night too."

"I'm just trying to imagine you doing all of that in your three-piece suits," I smiled.

"Aren't we passed making the mistakes of Breanne's judgments of me?" He arched an eyebrow back at me. "I may be a little busier with work these days, but in the past, I got out and enjoyed good times."

"Hmm," I studied him, trying *not* to imagine this man as a quarterback or riding a surfboard because that would probably turn me on and lead to trouble.

"What's *that* look? It's like the judgy-Bree look or something."

I exhaled. "No *judgy-Bree* looks. It's just that you don't seem to be the athletic type, that's all."

His eyes narrowed. "That's because you haven't experienced me in bed."

"I've experienced enough of you in those tight shirts that you're trying to tempt me with to know that you at least work out."

He laughed. "And I don't typically bring baked goods into my house, either."

"So, you didn't bake for me. Shitty host."

"Hey, I got my ass out to the best bakery in Malibu to make sure you woke up to delicious baked goods. After seeing you drowning in candy last night, I took a wild guess that you like sweets."

"You get points for that," I laughed. "This is delicious, by the way, and thank you very much."

"Give me a sec," he said when his phone rang. "Hey, Laney." A curious smile crossed his face as he turned to look out the windows, giving me another treat while I ate my muffin. "Sure, no problem. Why the fuck isn't Collin on vacation yet? Aren't you like eighty-nine months pregnant by now?" He listened quietly and then nodded. "Sounds good, kid. I'll ask Breanne, but I already know the answer is yes."

I listened to him laugh and then turn back to me with the wide eyes and beaming smile I was quite attracted to. "You up for killing some time with the woman we need to get approval from for the Saint John's children's wing remodel?"

"We don't have the blueprints, do we?" I asked.

"She's down, Laney," Alex said, then hung up the phone.

"Seriously, don't we need the blueprints?" I asked, excited to start this project but concerned about not getting it right, never having been to the children's wing of the hospital or having met the parents of the unborn child the ward was going to be dedicated to.

The heartbreaking journey that Dr. Collin Brooks and Dr. Elena Alvarez—now Brooks—had been on together ended beautifully with their friends and the hospital board approving the remodel of the pediatric unit in the name of the baby they'd miscarried, Baby Jo Brooks.

It was an honor to be heading this up for Alex's friends, and that I was trusted to enhance it from what Brooks' architects had envisioned. At the moment, I was a bit concerned that not having the blueprints and the visual of the unit would ruin my attempt to create something so sacred.

"You don't need them," Alex said. "Jesus, you look like you've seen a damn ghost."

"I just don't want to screw this up. After hearing more about this project, it's quite an honor, but—"

"Relax," he smiled. "Elena's heading over, and I'm happy to introduce you two. She'll give you the rundown while we drive to the hospital."

"Oh," I said. "What a fun idea."

"I had plenty of other *fun ideas* for the day," he said, "but my very pregnant friend is pretty demanding these days, and I doubt she'll like to be kept waiting."

"Very pregnant?" I smiled. "I didn't hear this part of their story."

"Yep," Alex answered with a laugh. "I'm not sure what you've been made aware of in the few times you've talked to our architects about this, but after the dust settled and Collin got Elena to himself for a month, well, you can fill in the blanks."

"They made up for lost time?" I smiled.

"And the proof that their honeymoon was spent making babies is in her belly." He took a sip of coffee.

"Twins?" My eyes widened.

"No, just the one." He cocked his head to the side. "If you ask me, her doctor must be reading the ultrasounds wrong because Elena's tiny body looks like she's carrying triplets."

"Jesus Christ, man," I said. "I hope you don't talk like *that* around her?"

"She's a blue-blooded American, but her Cuban streak is always engaged; do I look like a fool?"

"One never knows with men," I eyed him. "You can be insensitive pricks sometimes."

"And your *mean* streak, it seems, can be just as harsh."

"When does Elena get here, or are we heading to her place?"

"Collin and Elena's beach house is right up the beach from here. She called while she was taking her morning walk, and she asked if I was up for heading to Saint John's. She wanted you there."

"She's got to be getting close. Is Collin with her?"

"The dipshit doesn't start his vacation until tomorrow," Alex rolled his eyes. "Elena had him bring her to their beach house for the weekend since she's getting uncomfortable lately."

"Well, let's keep her happy and busy today," I smiled. "I've wanted to see that unit anyway, and having Elena give us the tour is ideal."

"I feel the same," he said. "I'll call for the driver and the Rolls. It's comfortable, and it keeps me in the back seat so you both can't talk shit about me while I'm up front with the driver."

"Funny excuse for calling a driver."

"It's either that or head to Beverly Hills to get Elena's Land Rover. Another dumbass move on Collin's part was to bring her here in her favorite sports car. Now, we're all in Malibu with a bunch of two-door vehicles."

"Sounds like a supportive husband move on his part," I countered.

"Or a move the man made because his uncomfortably pregnant

wife would've probably beat the shit out of him for not complying with her crazy pregnancy cravings."

"You can be so damn charming one second and such a stupid dick the next."

"It's called having a personality," he winked. "If I were Mr. Perfect all of the time, how would I get you to date me?"

I choked as soon as he said it, and his eyes showed me that look of being serious, understanding, and empathetic from last night. Holy shit. Was he fucking with me or baiting me? Either way, I could only smile *bashfully* like a goof in response.

"And you know you want to date me after I behaved last night too," he said.

"I don't date men who have no sympathy for pregnant women."

His eyes narrowed. "When you're having my kid," his features were soft and playful again, "I'll take note of everything I'm doing wrong as a heartless bastard."

"Exactly, quit acting like the tin-man without a heart." I cringed at that one. *Why so goddamn nerdy, Bree?*

"Losing your witty banter already?" Alex smiled while he focused on his phone. "The Tinman was only funny last night when we were both caught in the middle of friendly fire from your *lies*." His eyes widened and his voice lowered, teasing me.

"I'm gonna take a quick shower, and then I'll be out in a few."

"Bath tonight, shower this morning," he smiled. "I'll get you a fresh towel. Follow me."

WHEN I FINISHED DRYING my hair, the door was damn-near busted down by banging on the other side of it.

"Fucken-A, Alex," I said, startled by his horror-movie knock. "I'm out!"

"Yeah, we're fucked," he said nervously.

"Fucked?"

The tone of his voice made me jerk open the door to see the man was in a complete panic.

"Elena's in labor," he said. "My driver busted ass to get here. Thank God I called him, and he was on his way before Elena got to the house. Jesus, we're so screwed." The guy was nearly panting.

"Do we need to call an ambulance?" I asked, rushing past him. "Is she in active labor?"

"I don't even know what the fuck that means?"

"Alexander!" I heard a wail from downstairs. "I'm leaving with Henry."

"The hell you are, Laney," Alex sighed in defeat. "We have to get her to the hospital now."

"Let's get some towels and warm up a heating pad, grab ice chips and anything else you can for the trip…just in case," I said.

"What? Why do we need all that?" Alex asked, looking at me like a three-year-old toddler being given instructions.

"Oh, my God!" I heard a tearful cry. "My water just broke. This isn't happening."

"That's why!" I snapped to Alex. "Get your ass downstairs and help her. I'm right behind you. Call a goddamn ambulance and Collin too."

I knew that if Alex and I didn't get our shit together, poor Elena wasn't going to make it to Saint John's. I heard her talking more steadily, and Alex kept her calm while I threw on my clothes as fast as I could. By the time I reached the lower floor, Alex had clean towels, ice chips, a heating pad, and Elena waiting for me as we rushed out together. Everything was perfect except the fact that we were gingerly helping Elena into a black Rolls Royce, not the ambulance that should've been here.

"Where's the ambulance?" I asked Alex while Elena clung to him, breathing through a contraction as he sat next to her.

"It's Southern California," he said as nicely as he could, his expression dark with panic and fear. "Ten bucks says there's an accident, and it's stuck in traffic."

"Oh noooooo!" Elena's cry started normally and ended in an octave that would've made Mariah Carey envious, sharing her panic and pain with both me and Alex.

Time to change the mood.

"Well, if any pregnant woman was going to head to the hospital in active labor," I smiled when Elena blew out a breath, and I reached up to wipe the tears from the corners of her eyes, "they'd all love the comfort of a luxurious Rolls. Let's get you to your husband. You're about to meet your sweet little one."

With that, we loaded up, and Alex and I looked at each other when Alex's fearful eyes realized that if Elena were to somehow deliver in this car, he was on the receiving end. He eyed me for help after the vehicle sped away from his house, and Elena went from sitting in between us to switching mid-contraction and laying her head in my lap.

Her contractions were getting close, and now it was all up to our side of the highway staying clear and the driver busting his balls to get Elena to delivery at Saint John's in record time. That's when the car slowed, and I reluctantly looked out the front window to see two lanes of highway lit up with brake lights that seemed to go on forever. We were officially jammed in traffic, most likely due to an accident. Holy shit. If there were ever a time that Alex and I needed to perform well as partners, it was right fucking now.

CHAPTER EIGHTEEN
ALEX

This is not fucking happening. That was the phrase that had been on repeat in my head from the moment Elena gripped her stomach and cried through the contraction that'd caught her off-guard. While Bree was in the shower, time seemed like it'd stopped—except for the time between Elena's contractions.

I called for the ambulance first, Collin second, then messaged everyone else in the group chat for any clever ideas to figure out what the fuck to do next. Elena was well put together and was calming me down instead of the other way around, but when the contractions became unbearable, I darted up the stairs to beat down the door and interrupt Bree's shower.

Collin was in surgery, no one was responding to my goddamn texts, so it was up to Breanne and me to safely get Elena to the hospital to deliver her baby. We had to focus, so staring at my phone, willing some-fucking-body on my side of the fence to get back to me, was the only thing I had left.

"I swear to God, Alex," Elena's voice reached a diabolical tone that was probably the only thing that could pull my eyes away from my phone. "I will shove that phone up your ass..." She paused and positioned her feet, pressing one into my ribs and the other, damn-near pinning my face against the car window. "Sideways..." she continued with agony in her voice.

"Alex, put the phone down," Bree said dangerously with some lunatic smile on her face to show that she *would kill me* if I didn't stop looking to the phone for help.

"Shit, that's right. Jim, Avery, and Ash are on the yacht. They're most likely in a dead—"

"You're going to be dead," Elena said through pants. "I'm serious as fuck when I say that."

"Laney, you're going to have to hold it in until we get to the hospital. The traffic will ease up or the ambulance—"

I was cut off when my face was pinned against the window again.

"Alex," Breanne said. "Shut up and give me your stupid phone before *I* shove it up your ass sideways. Right now, we're helping Elena, and we aren't worrying about anything but her. A phone conversation is certainly not going to ease the contractions and stop this baby if it wants to come." She looked at Henry, my driver. "Can you pull the car off the road as soon as a shoulder becomes available, please?"

"Yes, Ms. Stone," he said. "At the moment, we're not moving."

Elena wailed a sound that told me we could likely welcome Baby Brooks in the backseat of this car. Here I was, a man who fixed shitty situations, and there wasn't a damn thing I could do to fix this less-than-ideal way of giving birth.

"We're so fucked," I said without thinking how unsupportive *that* statement was. "Elena, you seriously have to wait and hold it in."

Did I just fucking say that to a woman in labor, for God's sake? I didn't know what I was thinking, much less speaking, in this situation.

"Elena can't *hold in* a baby," Breanne growled. "It's her uterus, not her bladder, you idiot."

"Oh, shit..." Elena sounded off like a siren, silencing my comeback to Breanne, trying to defend my stupid statement.

Breanne arched an eyebrow at me to make sure my lips remained sealed. "All right, Elena." She smiled sweetly at her, running a cloth over Elena's forehead while the woman's grip on Breanne's arms was turning white. "We're either going to make it to the hospital, or we're going to work as a team to bring this precious baby into the world." She looked down into Elena's wide eyes. "Breathe with me," she smiled. "I heard the *hee-hee, hoo-hoo* breathing method works. Let's try it when the next contraction comes."

"Okay," Elena agreed, tears streaming down her face.

"Elena, I'm here," I said, finally getting my head somewhat in the game. "Bree, she's cutting off the blood supply to your arms. Why don't we trade places?"

Elena's feet went back to my cheek and into my ribs again.

"Wait until after the contraction," Breanne advised, breathing with Elena. "Her contractions are getting closer, and we don't need you passing out at the sight of blood if Elena suddenly feels the urge to push."

We worked the first miracle of this backseat labor and delivery situation pretty damn good. Careful with her movements and with flawless ease, Bree set Elena's head on a folded towel that she'd placed on my lap.

"This works perfectly." I said the first words that came to my mind.

"Wonderful. As long as this is comfortable for you, Alex," Elena laughed as she collapsed back, enjoying the short break before another contraction hit. "Oh...God..." she wailed. "Where's Collin?"

"Elena," I said as I instinctively worked to move to the other side of the back seat without hurting her, finding a better position to hold my best friend's wife. "He's in surgery, and he's going to be one happy—" I was cut off when her fingernails dug into my forearms.

"Mother fuck," I winced.

"Breathe, Elena. Let's all breathe together," Breanne said as if she were a broke businesswoman by day and a delivery nurse by night.

The breathing seemed to work to get traffic moving outside of the car and inside the birth canal.

"Oh, Lord," Elena's eyes were fearful as she looked up into mine. "I think I have to push?"

"You think?" I questioned her. "Elena, I don't think...that you think...do you really think you want to do that right now? In the car?"

Goddamn it. I was a heartless, confused as hell son of a bitch at the moment, and I knew it with every foolish word that came out of my mouth. I couldn't think straight, though. I was a man who was geared to handle everything with a phone call or an HR rep. I was by *no means* the kind of guy who was down to deliver a child in a car. It was a Saturday, for fuck's sake. Why the hell was there traffic? Where the fuck were *any* of my friends?

Breanne's eyes were lit with fire when they met mine, obviously because I was making everything worse, and none of my medical professional friends were calling our sorry asses back. *"Grow a pair,"* she mouthed as she worked to bust ass and keep Elena calm.

I was falling apart too. Here I was, doing the breathing with Breanne and Elena as if it would help me as well.

Breanne rolled her eyes at my dramatics then looked back at a panting Elena. "Sweetie, the baby is coming whether Alex *thinks* it should or not." She smiled at Elena, who was nodding briskly with her as she gave Elena a serene look that even calmed *me* down. "So, let's breathe through the contractions, and when you feel like you need to push, we'll go nice and easy."

"I can't hurt our baby." Elena started crying.

I rubbed the cool washcloth we'd snagged from the house over her forehead, only to see her frightened expression. This was the look I needed to help me fall into place where I was needed. I was instantly reminded of the look on Collin's face when he found out Elena had miscarried Baby Jo, and now, I saw the look in Elena's eyes, needing me to be here for her when Collin couldn't. I wouldn't let my best friend's wife go through this alone. If he couldn't be here for her, then it was my responsibility to do it for him. Whether I knew what I was doing or not, I was damn sure going to bring this baby into the world safely.

"You're doing good, little mama," I managed with a smile. "If the little tyke comes before we get to the hospital, you have the best team players working with you to make sure it all goes smoothly."

I glanced up, and Breanne smiled at me—the dimpled one. Finally, I was doing something right while being thrown into the craziest situation of my fucking life.

Ring! Ring! Ring!

"That's Collin's ringtone," I said while Elena caught a break between contractions again.

"Dude Looks like a Lady?" Breanne eyed me as I answered with a smile.

"Where's Laney?" Collin demanded. "Your ass better be kidding—"

Elena screamed, moaned, and then scrunched her butt down in what I assumed was the fact she was ready to push.

"The baby is coming," Elena shouted to Breanne. "Oh God, this isn't happening!"

"It is happening, sweetie. It's all okay." Breanne reached for the towels she had me get before we left the house. "Alex, we're going to need some help to push through contractions, and we need to know what to do when this baby has been delivered. I need you to either..."

"No-no-no-no-noooo." Elena practically crossed her legs in protest.

"Hold on, Coll." I looked at Elena. "Collin's on the phone, so everything will be fine. If the baby is coming, neither hell nor high water is going to stop it."

"Breathe," Breanne said. "Loosen up. I need you to focus, or you will hurt the baby."

"Jesus Christ!" Collin said. "Laney."

"Yeah, she's in the middle of having your child right now. She can't talk," I said, then Collin rang my phone on Facetime. "Bree, can you take my phone for—"

"Shut the fuck up and listen to me, Alex," Collin said, stripping the surgical cap from his head. "Dr. Allen is in surgery, but I have been to every last Lamaze class *and* medical school for situations like this." He was rightfully in his medical professional frame of mind. "Laney, baby, listen to me, okay?"

"I hate you for this," she answered in a high-pitched squeal.

Breanne's lips pinched together while I shrugged at Collin, who was suddenly the asshole in this equation.

"I love you," Collin remained unaffected. "Now, when you feel the urge to push, I need you to bear down as we learned; remember that?"

"I remember not wanting to do this without pain meds…"

"That's not an option, baby," Collin said.

"Wrong choice of words, dick!" I said when Elena's hands went way too close to my own dick while riding out her next painful contraction.

In the process of Collin realizing he was as fucking stupid as I was for trying to coach his wife—who was about to pop out a baby in a car—Elena ripped the phone from being held in front of her face for Collin to see her. "I'm sorry. I love you. It hurts so bad."

"I'll breathe with you, baby," Collin said. "We've got this. Alex, is traffic moving at all? I heard the ambulance is stuck in it."

"We're moving some," Breanne said as Elena dropped the phone and dug her nails into the upholstery of the car. As Henry parked in a turnout area, it became painfully clear that we were delivering this baby now. No ambulance, no hospital, just us misfits in a Rolls Royce birthing wagon.

"That's it," Breanne said, pulling Elena's dress back and arranging towels across Elena's stomach as if she'd done this before. "On the next contraction, I need you to push. Okay? I see a dark head of hair, and that's a great sign that your baby is in the right position."

"Holy shit." I heard Collin's muffled voice coming from my phone which was lost somewhere between Elena delivering a baby and the seat she was lying on.

"You're doing great, kid," I said, trying to cheer Elena on while I felt around for the phone.

"There we are," Bree said with a beautiful smile as she stared at my friend's wife's vagina—not exactly a fantasy of mine, but here we were. "Okay, push with this next one. We're almost to baby."

A scream erupted from the car which should've shattered the windows.

"Just a little more," Breanne said. "Next one, and then push hard."

"Jesus, this baby doesn't want to be born," Elena collapsed back into my chest. "I don't give up, easily, but I think I'm done."

"The hell you are, champ," I said. "You're going to breathe and push out that baby. It's probably stuck because it's got its father's big head, that's all."

"You're right. It's stuck. Oh, shit! My baby is stuck."

"Elena Brooks!" I heard Collin's firm voice coming from the phone, which was either wedged between the crack of the seat or the crack of Elena's ass for all I knew. "Baby, you can do this."

"I think…"

"Elena, you're doing great. That's it," Breanne said in a cool, calm, and collected voice. "Keep pushing, sweetie."

Elena gripped the headrest of the seat, her other hand drawing blood from clenching my leg, and the next thing I knew, I heard a soft cry come from the other side of the back seat. I looked up to see Breanne was intently focused, and in the towel that she'd draped in her arms was the tiny baby that Elena had just busted her ass to bring into this world on the side of the Pacific Coast Highway.

"Here, momma," Breanne said, instantly laying the baby on Elena's stomach, and Elena laughed and cried while rubbing the newborn on its back. "Here's the warmer towel," Bree said as she draped it over the baby. "Thanks to that heating pad, little baby Brooks will be nice and toasty until we get to the hospital."

Breanne was fully attentive to everything while I collapsed against the car door. I watched in awe as two blue eyes peered up at Elena, her head leaning against my chest as she talked to the little man. While I witnessed Elena and her baby bonding for the first time, Breanne found the phone.

"Damn, I forgot about Collin," I said.

Without a word to my patiently waiting friend, Bree turned the phone for him to see the visual that had to be the most beautiful sight Collin had ever seen. Elena massaged their son's back, motherhood kicking right in as she kept their son breathing and healthy.

"Daddy, say hi to our baby boy." She looked at the phone as if she'd planned this all out herself.

"Boy?" Collin's eyes filled with tears as he covered his mouth and nearly brought the nurse who was waiting at his side into a chokehold. "Laney, he's beautiful."

I sat in awe, watching it all unfold. For the first time in my life, I could say with certainty that I'd witnessed a miracle.

"You're both so beautiful," Collin continued, and the baby's bright blue eyes moved from Elena while she continued to urge the baby to cry to help it clear out its lungs. "Alex, dispatch just said the freeway is open, and the ambulance is close to you guys. Breanne, I can't thank you enough. From the bottom of my heart, thank you," Collin said.

"You're thanking Breanne?" I countered, knowing we could joke now that no one's life was on the line. "I almost lost my balls in this fiasco, and you're thanking Breanne?"

"Who are you kidding? You didn't have balls to lose from the moment we got into the car," Bree teased.

I ignored her, Elena, and Collin laughing in unison. "You do realize you'll be naming your son after me for this, correct?"

Collin smiled. "If Breanne is right," I could hear the joy in Collin's voice as he continued to be enamored by his beautiful son, "we'll be naming him Alexandria," Collin teased.

"The ambulance is here, buddy." I opened my door as the paramedic approached and looked inside. "We just delivered—Shit. What time did we—"

"Eight thirty-three," Collin said through the phone. "We've got the time of birth on our end, Medic."

"Got it," the guy responded, taking my place, and then both paramedics worked to put Elena and little baby Brooks on a gurney so they could haul ass to the hospital.

I ran toward the back of the ambulance and jumped inside. "Hey, sweetheart," I said, smiling at Elena, "take the phone, or Collin will kick my ass. The paramedics can hang it up if he distracts them." I winked as she reached for my face.

"Marry Breanne, please."

"I think you're on a baby-high." I smiled. "We'll be behind you. Now, get your butt to the hospital before Collin loses his shit."

The ambulance hit its lights and sirens as it blasted down the highway, leaving me standing there in total shock that this had happened. I glanced at the open interstate and wondered why the fucking thing didn't open up *before* poor Elena went through the pain of laboring in the back seat of my stupid Rolls.

I looked over at the car, and because I was in my distracted, selfish bastard mode, I saw that I'd left Breanne and Henry to clean out whatever mess was in the backseat.

I met Henry at the trunk where he'd loaded the soiled towels, and the very last thing I expected was for Breanne to squeal, take my face in her hands, and kiss my lips. She was filled with utter excitement, and she'd instantly shifted my excitement about a precious baby boy to her planting an unexpected kiss on my lips. That came out of nowhere, and I planned to jump on the back of this immediately.

Then, my phone rang. Incoming call from Jim...*Fuck!*

CHAPTER NINETEEN
BREE

*B*y the time we reached the hospital, Alex had ended one of the many calls that came in after the ambulance took off with Elena and her newborn son. While I was texting my friends about the insane yet remarkable incident we'd been through, Alex discussed the details with his friends. Amid fielding phone calls, he received word that Elena and baby were healthy, fine, and in the hospital's care. Thank God.

I'd never been to Saint John's Hospital before, so to see this place in person for the first time was mind-blowing. It was everything I'd imagined and more since I'd learned that John Brooks himself had a lot to do with the architecture and lavish style of the place and seeing his work in this extravagant hospital put me in awe.

Alex was nearly dragging me through the hospital and into the elevators because this place overloaded my mind. Thank goodness he did, though, because if it weren't for that, I'd still be spinning about the fact that I helped deliver a baby in the backseat of a car.

The sudden *backseat midwife* I'd become was an easy pill to swallow compared to kissing Alex for no apparent reason at all. Thanks to a documentary I'd seen about a woman who delivered a baby in the back of a cab in New York City, I'd somehow managed to feel like I knew what I was doing in that situation. Crazy how adrenaline could spark up the subconscious mind to recollect things when least expected. I probably also had an angel or two whispering in my ear. Who the hell knew? At least Elena and her son were okay.

AFTER WE WALKED into the hospital's version of the Queen of Sheba's palace for a maternity ward, I stopped. "I'll wait here," I said to Alex. "Tell Elena—"

"You'll tell her yourself," Alex smirked and arched an eyebrow at me. "If she sees me after the support *I* lent, she might slap me."

I grinned at him. "Now that you bring all that up again," I followed him as the nurse told him which suite Elena, Collin, and their baby were in, "I might slap you if she doesn't."

He sighed. "Sorry. That was the first labor and delivery job I've been on. Sometimes people fuck up on their first day, unlike you. What the hell, by the way? That was some *Real Midwives of SoCal* action you busted out. How in God's name do you know how to deliver a baby?" He stopped and turned to me. "Do you have another career outside of being a CEO that I don't know about? Moonlighting midwives?"

"And the secret is out," I smiled at him.

Alex licked his lips, and he exhaled. "I should probably warn you that this smile of yours," he touched my cheek, igniting sparks beneath his fingers, "will either be the death of me or put you in the backseat of a car delivering *our child* if you're not careful."

"What?" I chuckled, touching my heated cheek. "Alex—"

"Don't Alex me with *that* smile," he winked. "I don't think I've ever seen you this beautiful."

Thank God I wasn't hooked up to one of the many heart monitors in this hospital, or I'd blow the thing up from the way Alex was talking to me. My heart was on rapid-fire, and I couldn't concentrate to save my life.

Think of something. Shit.

"Come on." He grinned, and now I was being humiliated by my sweaty palms as he took my hand into his. "You *will* tell me how you managed to deliver a baby at least, dimples."

"What can I say? I'm a jack of all trades."

"If that's the case, then I'm definitely having sex with you."

An awkward moment killed by Alex's nonsense. Thank God.

"Really?" I rolled my eyes after a nurse looked at him to check him out or to glare at the comment he'd made. Most likely the first. Alex was easier on the eye with this beaming smile plastered on his face. "Like that's ever going to happen."

Why are you encouraging this, Bree? I felt like I'd finally rid myself of looking like an idiot every time I was in front of Alex, only to egg him on like this?

"Trust me. It will." He smiled and held out his arm. "After you, *Doctor* Stone," he teased.

I peered in to see a tall man in dark scrubs and messy blond hair rise from a chair next to Elena's hospital bed. The man had bright, sky-blue eyes, a matching vibrant smile, and then the next thing I knew, I was swallowed up in his arms.

"I don't give a shit if you're not the hugging type," he said, stepped back and smiling over at Alex and then back to me. "I owe you my life for keeping my two loves safe until they got to me."

I smiled in return. This was the happiest man on the face of the earth, and with good reason too. I wouldn't go into the fact that he was drop-dead gorgeous—rumors ran all through Southern California that the doctors at Saint John's were not only exceptional in their professions, but they were also painfully good-looking. I could confirm that the rumors were true.

"You're welcome. DIY comes in handy sometimes, I guess."

"And you, dipshit," Collin said to Alex as I moved toward the beaming smile and warm, bronze eyes of Elena. "Elena said you were an absolute bitch in the car."

The men's laughter remained behind me as I walked to where

Elena held out her free arm for me to embrace her and see their beautiful, sleeping infant.

"He's so beautiful," I said, afraid to touch him. "You are officially my hero." I grinned at her.

Elena's arm squeezed me tighter. "I'm *your* hero? I don't think so. You are one-hundred-percent *mine.* What would I have done without you? I can't believe it all happened like this."

"I'm still shocked myself," I chuckled, taking the seat Alex had pushed next to the bed for me. "If you weren't as tough as you were, I'm sure—"

"No," she smiled so sweetly at me. I felt like this woman could've easily been my friend for life—or from another life. "You hung in there for me when I was losing it. I love you for that. Thank you."

"He's *actually* beautiful," Alex said as if he were shocked Elena didn't birth an alien. He ruffled Collin's hair and walked to the other side of the bed. "Shocking," he looked at Collin, sitting on the bed by Elena's feet. "I thought your ugly looks would have some pretty strong genetics, too."

"If that's the case," Collin answered, his hand running up and down Elena's leg casually, "then I pity your poor child."

"Good God, both of you can be too much sometimes." Elena shook her head and then smiled at me. "Have you been around these guys in the same room yet? Trust me when I tell you, if us gals don't stop them, they'll go on and on, and we're stuck listening to lame insults."

"Just Jim, Spencer, and Alex," I said. "I haven't had this particular pleasure yet."

"Oh, you will in time. I hear the gang is almost here, and once all the men get going, we'll be ready to kick them out of here. Would you like to hold him?" she asked.

"I'm afraid—"

"This one's turning out to be a pathological liar," Alex winked at me. "Don't believe a word she says. *Afraid.*" He scoffed at the word, obviously because my actions in the fear department spoke louder than words when I helped bring this baby into the world.

Elena chuckled then held her son toward where I was. "You *must* hold this little man," she scrunched her nose up adorably. "Especially since he's peacefully asleep."

"He's so itty-bitty. You both did good," I said. I smiled at Collin, who couldn't seem to keep his eyes off his wife or his son's face, and then I looked back to Elena. "You two should go into business, just making beautiful babies," I winked at Elena.

"He certainly looks like an Alexander to me," Alex stated. "A good, strong baby with a good, strong name.

"You mean, Alexandria James?" Collin said with some theatrics while waving his hand in the air. "We named him after *you*, happy?"

"You had your chance to back out of marrying him, Elena," Alex chuckled. "Now, it's too late since he's got you trapped with this little man."

I smiled, seeing the youthful and overly happy side of Alex that I'd never seen him wear before. He was, without a doubt, more handsome than ever before, and I was struggling to keep my cool and not gawk at the man in front of his friends. I'd look like a real winner, sitting here with googly-eyes on Alex while his friends teased him for wimping out in the car. I had to defend the guy, though. He did pull it together and at the perfect time too. When Elena needed her husband the most, Alex grew a pair and was there for her instead.

"So, Alexander James, eh?" Alex's deep, raspy voice took my eyes off of the baby and put them back on him. "Last I recall, *James* Mitchell wasn't answering any calls when your wife and child needed him most."

Collin laughed. "I knew you'd say something, and that's why we threw in James as his middle name." He looked at me and smiled. "I know we haven't been formally introduced, Breanne—"

"Forgive me," Alex said. "I think it's pretty well established who everyone is by now, but to be formal," he looked at Collin, "please allow me to introduce Breanne Stone, my new partner in labor and delivery."

"I heard a lot about your father growing up," Collin said. "He was quite the architect and a good man. Although my father was in fierce competition with yours, he admired your father's work greatly."

"My father was the same, competition-wise," I answered with a laugh. "It is lovely to meet the son of the great John Brooks. Your father's work deserves all of the praise it receives. It's always a pleasure for me to enjoy one of his projects, and this hospital is a testament to what a pioneer and visionary he was. Truly astounding."

"Well, what I think is astounding is the fact that, thanks to your contributions, Saint John's will now have the flavors of both our fathers' visions. I'd love to escort you down to the pediatric ward, but perhaps later when Elena is up for a walk and after Alek has eaten."

"Alek?" I looked at Alexander with a grin.

Alex rolled his eyes at his friend and reached over for the baby.

"It's Alexander," Alex insisted, holding the baby with ease. "*Alek* is a name I'm only called by people who hate me."

"And now you'll love it because that's as close as Laney as I are getting to naming our child after you, buddy," Collin countered with a grin.

"Elena, don't be impossible," Alex insisted. "You can't name him Alek. If you tack on the letter *s* to his name—like Alek's bath time or Alek's girlfriend—it's going to sound like you're talking about me. Alex and Alek's—it just can't work. See what I mean? Come on, now. Be serious."

"I hardly think anyone will think I'm talking about you when I mention bath time." Elena's laughter was infectious while Alex rolled his eyes.

"You think adding the letter *s* will confuse people into thinking we're talking about you, but your *actual name* won't be confusing at all?" Collin said with a laugh.

"Don't listen to your parents, little Alexander." He eyed both mom and dad's happy grins with a sly one of his own. "They were born with stupid names, so they're haters."

"We officially decided on Alexander John," Elena smiled at Alex then Collin.

"Goddammit, that's what I'm talking about, little man. The name of kings!" Alex said proudly, speaking to baby Alex in a silly voice as I stood. "Now, if anyone calls you *Alek,* your godfather, here, will kick their butts."

"Naming our first-born son wasn't enough for you; now you're insisting on being his godfather as well, Michael Corleone?" Collin teased.

Before the bantering went further, I decided to jump in and announce that I would head down to the children's wing. I knew the rest of Alex, Collin, and Elena's friends were due to arrive at any minute, and I wanted to give them room to visit.

"Would any of you mind if I went ahead and visited the pediatric ward we're going to be working on?"

"Not at all. I would love to know your thoughts," Elena said. "After I feed baby Alex, I'll have Collin take me on a walk to meet you down there. Dr. Cameron was going to meet us there until little man decided to make his appearance early."

"Dr. Cameron?" I questioned.

"Dr. Brandt—Cameron Brandt. He's a good friend," Collin said. "A hell of a lot better looking than Alex, too." Collin and Elena both had mischievous looks, but I had no idea what was going on. "So, tread lightly when you see him." He chuckled.

"Ask for Dr. Brandt when you get there," Alex said. "Cam runs the pediatric unit. He was planning to show us around when we got there earlier. I'll be there after Jim, Jake, Ash, and Avery show up if that's cool?"

"Perfect," I smiled at everyone. "Congratulations again."

The smiles and the positive energy in that room had elevated my mood, and I was ready to check out the pediatric ward. I could've easily spent my entire day just staring in awe at the geometric lines and shapes of this place. The trademark touch that set John Brooks apart from most architects was not only his skill but also his eye for adding the right touch of extravagance in all the right places.

"Hi, can I help you?" a receptionist with teddy bears on her scrubs asked when the automatic doors opened to admit me into the pediatric ward.

I glanced back at the doors. They were etched with critters from a forest that almost appeared three-dimensional, so much so that before the doors opened, it felt like I was walking into some enchanted realm. It was adorable and charming, and I was sure the kids loved it.

I smiled at the kind young woman. "Wow," I said. "This place is enchanting."

She chuckled. "I absolutely love it," she said, looking around at everything that resembled a children's ride at Disneyland. "Are you here to visit someone?"

"Yes. Dr. Brandt was going to show me around the area that is being dedicated in the name of Baby Jo Brooks?"

"Oh," she nodded. "Absolutely. Are you Ms. Stone?"

"Yes," I smiled.

"I've been to Blossom Hall." Her eyes widened like she'd met a celebrity, and it made me smile. Dad and I had designed Blossom Hall together, and it won us the award for the architect's guild that year. "My best friend was married there. It was so stunning. Everything was like a crystal palace, and I had to ask who built it."

"That's an enormous compliment," I answered. "Usually, people enjoy the beauty of the places we visit and never ask who built them," I laughed. "Unless you're an architect, I guess. So, thank you."

"I know what you mean. Normally, I wouldn't have cared to ask, but when the building outdoes the bride on her day," she laughed, "I had to ask." She rose and pointed a finger to her earpiece. "Give me just a second," she said quietly before responding to whoever had called her. "Okay, I'll show her in." She looked at me. "Follow me, Ms. Stone. Dr. Brandt is finishing up with a patient."

"It's Breanne and thank you."

I walked through the enchanting area and was in awe of the illusions everywhere. This place was its own little escape from the real world, and I felt like I was in fairyland or something extraordinary like that. The ceiling either sparkled with stars where lights were dimmed or in the brighter areas, this place had a fake sun that shimmered over the illusion of plant life. Just as I was expecting to have some unicorn show up or hop aboard a boat in Willy Wonka's chocolate factory, the most precious scene played out before my eyes.

"I won that one, and you know it, bud," a man wearing a white lab coat said, squatting down and tossing a nerf football in the miniature football stadium where I now stood.

"This is the indoor football field," the receptionist who led me into this open space said. "The kids get to dress up like football players if their parents allow it and play against holographic players."

I glanced around and noted numerous kids in their own spaces, rolling around in hospital garments or little jerseys and helmets with *Saint John's* printed on them. There was no way in hell I could live up to these standards. This was innovative and next-level, Tony-Stark genius type shit.

"John Brooks designed all of this? This is mind-blowing."

"And *this* is just the football area," she chuckled. "If you need anything else, I'm Elyssa. Dr. Brandt will be with you as soon as he's done with David."

She smiled at the endearing scene of the young doctor in a pretty good standoff with a little boy, and even though the child's head was wrapped in gauze, you'd never imagine that this kid must've gone through an accident or scarier—brain surgery.

"All right, David," said the peppy yet low voice of the doctor whose back was all I'd seen so far. "I've got to get back to work, and you've got to get to lunch."

I watched in humor as a nurse worked with the boy and Dr. Brandt. The boy was not quite finished with the doctor, but the game was over, and lunch was calling. The nurse and Dr. Brandt worked with the young man, and the doctor gave the nurse some last-minute information before he signed off on the charts she held, then he turned back to me.

I swallowed the sudden shock-lump in my throat when the stunning doctor, who matched the beautiful illusion of this ward, smiled brightly at me. He extended his hand, and his piercing blue eyes, which dazzled against his well-groomed facial hair, met mine.

"You must be Breanne Stone," he smiled. "I'm Cameron Brandt. It's a pleasure to meet you."

"You too." I looked around at the play arena we were in. "I'm starting to question why we need architects to come in and add *anything* to this place. If the gardens and this unit are being upgraded, there's no living up to—"

"Don't listen to her, Cam," I heard Alex say as he joined me. "She's got this, and she knows it." Alex eyed me. "I knew if I didn't get down here with you, you'd lie your way right out of this job."

"Very funny. You all realize this is super innovative stuff, right? Holographs?" I said, looking around at this futuristic children's area. "I feel like I'm on another planet. Any architect, unless they're John Brooks himself, would be lying to you if they said they could upgrade this."

"It's certainly next-level." Dr. Brandt chuckled. "It also helps the less fortunate children who live here with us."

"Remarkable. John Brooks thought of everything in his designs, didn't he?" I said, smiling at Alex.

Alex slid his hands in his pockets, still beaming from being with the baby, I'm sure. "John was a genius with everything he touched," Alex confirmed, "but you're only looking at what he dreamt up for children in a hospital. It was the engineers who made these concepts and illusions possible."

"And even at that," Dr. Brandt looked at Alex and then me, "Alex still can't throw a football to save his life on this field. I have patients kicking his butt all the time when he's down here screwing around."

Well, isn't that a charming and hidden secret I didn't know, I thought, eyeing Alex and trying to imagine him in the three-piece suit again, but this time with kids in the pediatric wing of the hospital.

"Right," Alex smirked and then looked at me. "Brandt was also an all-star quarterback. So, he gets a little competitive at times."

"I'm venturing to guess that the children love it," I said.

"They do," Alex grinned. "All right. Cameron is pressed for time, so let's get some expert eyes on the gardens, shall we?"

"Let's do it," Cameron answered as he led the way to the outdoor area of the children's wing. "So, out these doors are where the butterfly gardens are. It's stunning, yes, but in revamping it, Brooks' architects say that we should either go bigger or create more illusions."

"I swear this wing has every illusion under its fake sun," Alex said. "I'm not sure illusions are where we should go with this location."

"Agreed," Cameron answered Alex.

"What do you think, Breanne?"

I moved to an area that faced the gardens, and I ran my hand over the half-walls made out of white marble. I glanced at the plaques with names etched into them, seeing they were memorials, and even though it was quite beautiful, something wasn't sitting right.

I looked out at the plant life and botanical parts of these gardens, fashioned and groomed meticulously. It was stunning, and I couldn't tell if my hesitation was because I was in the midst of a John Brooks' design or because this was a project for Alex's friends.

"This is more or less a cemetery for the cremains of unborn or stillborn children at our hospital. We lay them to rest out here," Alex informed me. "The plants are meant to bring in butterflies, and the fountains are to attract birds. What do you see in that architect's mind of yours?"

"Well," I ran my hand over a marble column where more plaques were, "who visits this location? Is it only the families of the children who've been laid to rest?"

"We also have parents who come here to breathe in some fresh air and gather their senses while waiting for surgery, or perhaps a dreadful diagnosis was given, and they need some time," Dr. Brandt said thoughtfully.

I licked my lips and glanced around. "Conceivably, we can enhance this area under a glass dome that is etched to complement the butterfly garden. I know we don't have much rain, but it would be nice to cover this area, and if the glass dome is etched, and if each glass piece is shaped correctly, it would enhance the illusion of sparkling butterflies beaming through on a sunny day. While the sun moves, the illusions of butterflies will appear to dance around this place. Sometimes, and with the proper materials, you can get the sun to flow through glass etchings and create prisms. I'd have to work with it a little, but it can be done."

"I'm quite certain Elena would love that," Alex said.

I smiled and nodded. "Yes. Maybe run with a theme of dancing with the butterflies. We can use that dome to keep wrapping around the entire children's portion of the hospital. Maybe have a reflection area for parents to sit and get some fresh air after troublesome news. Yellow is a peaceful color. Maybe we create an illusion of a meadow and wildflowers. Daisies are a lovely flower," I kept on, the men quietly following me as I imagined stuff, and then I stopped when it was a bit too quiet behind me.

Alex's expression practically swallowed me up with that dark stare that was so attractive, most likely because his features were always sharp and fascinating with this tight-lipped expression.

"Did I say something wrong?" I looked between both men's solemn expressions.

"No," Alex cleared his throat. "In fact, you said a lot of things right." He ran a hand through his hair and eyed Cameron.

"Did Brooks' architects mention any of the personal reasons Elena drew the butterfly, the meadows?" Cameron asked me.

"No," I smiled. "Am I onto something, then?"

Alex's expression was beautifully sincere. "You were definitely in the wrong chair, wasting time playing executive. Good God. You captured Elena and Collin's story without even knowing it. You got everything but Baby Jo's angel wings."

My eyes widened at the beauty of that thought. "What if we brought more of an angelic and whimsical feel to the gardens? We can add stunning wings in the etchings that show up when the sun hits them at a certain time. Maybe the wings will display under a starry night sky, and we can use backlighting to enhance it with more of an effervescent feel."

"I think we're right where we want to be. What brought up the glass dome idea? The etchings in it?" Alex questioned.

"The receptionist mentioned she attended a wedding at one of the places my father and I designed together. We ran with a crystal palace-type feel, and I think that would be a beautiful and peaceful escape. We tame the illusions from the inside and transfer them into sparkles and things of beauty and hope."

"The meadow idea? Yellow being a peaceful color?" Alex smirked while Cameron answered a call on his phone.

"Well, daisies are a happy flower."

"You said yellow at first."

"I don't know. It just came out. I'm not even sure creating an illusion of a meadow will work. I'll have to think about it some more. It's either a meadow that seems to go on forever and put seating in that—or fountains."

"Why not both?" Cameron asked.

"Fountains won't work in a meadow." I chuckled. "Maybe a river with small bridges throughout? Yes, that's it. We can make it vibrant. We can backlight the crystal-like dome and allow for that to be manipulated too. The panels of glass can be run off of solar energy and can move sort of like animatronics."

"Either someone's been whispering in your ear, or you are a psychic genius. You just nailed the meadow that Elena remembered in her coma. The dancing with the butterflies is a term she said her dad told her when she was younger." Alex looked at Cameron. "Is this floor haunted?"

Cameron laughed. "You're haunted and a jackass." He looked at me. "It was very nice to meet you, and these ideas will be fantastic. Elena will cry when she hears about this, and that's to be sure. I have to go into surgery now, but where is Elena?"

"On the maternity floor, holding baby Alexander."

"Oh, God," Cameron rolled his eyes while I laughed.

"No shit, man. And Breanne delivered the handsome little man herself."

Cameron eyed me to see if Alex was bullshitting him or not. The expression on his face was as handsome as it was hilarious.

"Elena can tell you all about it," I smiled. "Thanks for your time, Dr. Brandt."

"It was nothing. I'm happy to finally meet a woman who can keep this guy on his toes." He popped Alex in the arm and then moved into the hospital after hearing a page come over the intercom.

"That's the friend who attended your *runaway bride* wedding."

"Jesus Christ," I cringed. "He's the one who saw the sex tape I played for our guests, huh?"

"Yep," Alex laughed. "And you're going to tell me all about the reasons behind that, more about this children's wing, and after we pack you up to stay with me—"

"I think it might be a better idea if I check-in and stay with the girls."

"Nah," Alex flashed me a smile I couldn't refuse. "I'm in a group text with your girlfriends. Natalia says if I don't have sex with you tonight, she's calling in for backup and replacing my ass."

"What the hell?"

We spoke softly and moved into another area, but I still felt like my response was a bit too loud.

"Exactly. Cass said that Natalia is right. You need to get laid by your hot partner, and Sammy, is it?"

"Yes," I hung onto the word, my expression probably looking like Cameron's, not knowing if Alex was bullshitting *me* or not.

"She had me send the group a dick pic—"

"Okay, shut up. That's all BS, and I know it." I sighed. "Let's get out of here. I'll see what the girls are up to and if they're heading out tonight, and you'd like to offer that room in your beach house for me again, I'd love to use it to escape another night from my crappy life."

"Crappy life," Alex scoffed, and then suddenly, he held my hand. "Your life just got kicked up a couple of notches because you're not being stubborn. We're going to enjoy some cocktails at the beach tonight." He pursed his lips handsomely and smiled. "Sound cool?"

"Sounds perfect."

It really did. I was looking forward to escaping to the coast and ducking out of another night of what I knew my friends probably expected from me: to go clubbing and face the guilt of listing my condo without them knowing.

Alex may have had a conversation with my friends, but that didn't mean he wasn't in contact with them, and this entire thing was all their idea. Who gave a damn? I needed a breather, and Alex was being cool. I wasn't quite so defensive against the man after today's events. We did exceptionally well as partners, and he was turning out to be a bit more charming than I imagined he could ever be. I suddenly felt a tiny bit bad that I'd prematurely judged the guy, but let's face it, I was heading down a pretty dark road before the guy with an angry witch up his ass came in and rescued me for the weekend.

CHAPTER TWENTY
ALEX

It was impulsive of me to take Breanne's hand in mine, but I didn't give a shit. If she didn't like the gesture, *or me*, she would've unquestionably pulled her hand from mine by the time we'd walked out to the Uber I'd called.

I was no longer going to pretend that I wasn't captivated by Breanne. So, what was the shame in any of this? There wasn't any. Unless, of course, she wasn't feeling it. I had to think she was because her hand was currently clutching mine in return—for the second time since arriving at this hospital—and it told me this was right.

Holding hands like we were in grade school was pretty standard for me, though. What was entirely out of my arena in the department of emotions was when jealousy struck after she left the room and went to meet Cameron. I wouldn't have given two shits about any other woman nearly tripping over their feet when they met him, but, in Breanne's case, this was more about Cameron being attracted to her.

Jealousy—what a fucked-up emotion, especially when you get all fucked in the head and consider your good friend a sudden enemy even though he'd done nothing to deserve the title.

It was apparent that I was twisted up with this foreign emotion when Jim, Avery, Ash, and the kids had shown up to meet baby Alex—giving me the excuse I needed to give everyone some space—and I couldn't get my ass down to Breanne fast enough.

I thought I'd made a casual exit until Jake came in, who was working on-call in the cardiac ward. As usual, he could sniff out bullshit from a mile away, and me telling everyone I needed to help Breanne, so she wouldn't be overwhelmed with work, was all he needed to hear to spread a massive smile across his smug face. There was no way in hell I wasn't going to be roasted relentlessly by everyone later. Again, who gave a damn?

I knew what I wanted, and that was Breanne Stone. This jealousy nonsense could kiss my ass, though. Because of it, I probably looked like an ass to Cam and Breanne for ditching my friends so I could walk through the unit I'd already said the architects could figure out on their own. Yet there I was...all fucking smiles while Cameron probably read me like an open book.

I would certainly have to kick this jealousy out of the way, and the easiest way to do that was to ensure Breanne was mine, off-limits to anyone who might find themselves feeling unexpected emotions toward her fun and snarky personality and those sultry, jade eyes.

"Nice, SUV," Breanne said as I finished sending a text to Elena to let her know that Breanne and I were leaving, and I told her the remarkable design features that Breanne had come up with on her own. I knew it would blow Elena away. "What happened to the Rolls?"

"I'm sorry. Give me a sec," I answered her after Elena texted me back immediately.

I glanced down at my phone to read Elena's text in response to mine.

Elena: *You're kidding, right? Did you tell her about my coma and what I told you about why I drew that butterfly for Baby Jo?*

Alex: *No. I wouldn't have sent a text the length of a novel to explain if she knew.*

Jake: *Dude. Chill the fuck out*

Alex: *Fuck. Did I just text Breanne's idea to the goddamn group text?*

Collin: *It was ducking beautiful. All 500 words of it.*

Jim: *I will kill you for starting this, Alex.*

I SMILED, realizing I'd accidentally texted on the group string that Elena had set up a while ago when she and Collin had announced her pregnancy.

With Collin and Jake on this string—both pranksters, knowing that Jim and I hated when these texts blew up our phones once the ladies got going with GIFs and emojis—I knew this would never end. Now, I was at the mercy of my friends, who were well aware that I was leaving with Breanne, and they knew something was up with me.

Alex: *No shit. Sorry, I didn't think I texted on this group string. Either way, now you all know. Breanne nailed it. You're going to love the concept she pulled out of her ass.*

Collin: *She pulled that shut out of her ass?*

Jake: *No shit? Or are we saying shut now?*

Ash: *I have chills reading it though.*

Avery: *Me too.*

Jake: *Me three.*

Collin: *Ducken-A! Me four.*

Elena: *You guys can be such idiots*

Alex: *Has Jim thrown his phone across the room?*

Avery: *Ha! No, he's holding the baby, and I muted the text string on his phone.*

Jake: *Too bad Alex doesn't know how to mute this shit on his phone. Is Breanne with you, fucker?*

Ash: *Hey, Av, you and Jim really should start trying for another baby Mitchell again.*

Elena: *100% YES!!!!!!*

Avery: LOL! And we'll use this string to announce when we start trying. LMAO

Jake: OMG! LOL! FTS!

Alex: *Okay. I'm out*

HOLY SHIT, what did I start? My phone would officially be blowing up until tomorrow.

Elena: *What does FTS mean, Jake*

Collin: *He's ducking with you*

Jake: *Ducking? Duck? Shut? Dude, fix the autocorrect on your whack-ass phone to spell out 'Fucking' and 'Shit.' Fucking shit!*

Collin: *I did. It resets itself. It's ducked up. Ducking shut!*

Jake: *Now you're just fucking with us.*

Collin: *Yep.*

Jake: *Dipfucker*

Collin: *Fipducker*

Alex: *Are you assholes all texting while sitting in the same room?*

Elena: *What does FTS mean? Seriously.*

Collin: *Yeah, we're in the same room, laughing as we blow your ass up too, bitch.*

Jake: *It means Fuck That Shit*

Avery: *LMFAO, yes, we're in the same room. You still with Breanne?*

Ash: *Yes. Ha! In the same room.*

Elena: *They're all still here, yes*

Ash: *Yes, are you still with her? I can't believe she delivered this baby in a car!*

Avery: *No shit, fucking unreal. Was she just as shocked as you were?*

Jake: *We heard you acted like a little bitch in the car, Lexi.*

Alex: *Okay. Breanne and I are leaving. We need to go over stuff.*

Jake: *Stuff? Like you're gonna fuck, stuff?*

Collin: *Alex might not be a cocksucker after all.*

Jake: *He's gonna hit that! Ten bucks says he does.*

Collin: *Doubling up on that wager to say she turns him down.*

Elena: *FTS*

Ash: *Idiots*

THREE DOTS WERE LOADING, and I turned my phone to silent. Collin and Jake would take this to a ridiculous level if the girls didn't rip the phones out of their husbands' hands. Jim's phone was muted, so he was the lucky one. Now, here I was on the ass-end of all the jokes, knowing these men had been long awaiting the day I'd put a woman before anything else—and goddammit, that's exactly what I'd done.

Holy fuck. I didn't think I was capable of giving a damn, yet here I was. Breanne was at my side, and my goddamn phone was buzzing like I'd shoved a vibrator up my fucking ass when I put my phone in my back pocket.

I could almost guarantee that the group chat had swiftly turned into an emoji fest: hearts and kissy faces from the girls, and eggplants, peaches, water drops, and middle finger emojis from the guys, and it wouldn't end until someone's battery died or my phone broke.

I loved my friends, but if Breanne were looking over my shoulder, I'd be fucked. She didn't know them as I did, and I could easily see her going into shock when she saw the other side of my personality. Out of all my friends, Jim and I were the two who were too busy to figure out how to mute these fucking group texts, and the rest of the gang knew it.

I glanced over to Breanne as she texted on her phone, knowing she could probably help mute the chat, but the last thing I needed was her eyes on my phone. For one, she'd already prematurely judged me. All I needed was her to believe that my two doctor friends who cussed like sailors *actually* talked this casually around patients or while in surgery. She'd likely believe their bedside manners were as foul as their mouths.

"Everything okay? Shit," Bree chuckled, and it was musical. It made me smile at the fact that I enjoyed her on a level I'd never experienced before with a woman. "It looks like you're dealing with work or something. You've been staring at that phone for five minutes."

"Yes," I smiled at her, my phone still buzzing and pissing me off, "and I already sent the address to our Uber driver to take us to a dealership to fix your car situation."

"No, I don't have—"

"I'd rather not discuss personal things in front of our driver," I smirked at her. "If Henry were here, that would be different." I sighed dramatically, trying to remain firm on the fact I was getting this woman into a car, and she wasn't going to argue.

"Is your car ruined from the delivery of the baby?"

I smiled. This would be a perfect way to get her to sign the pink slip, a new company vehicle. "The Rolls was actually the company car. Now, it's fucked with afterbirth and will be haunted with residual trauma, shit like that. So, Jim wants you and me to pick up another car to replace it."

"We're going to go *buy* another Rolls Royce?"

"I'm thinking graphite gray?"

"What's with you and that color, anyway? I've seen you drive two cars painted that same matte gray color."

I twisted my lips, acting like I was trying to think hard and long on that one. "Simple. I like the color."

She chuckled and rolled her eyes at me. "Do we need to buy a company car *right now?*"

"Yes. You need one to drive as an executive on Monday."

"I'll call for an Uber, thanks."

"An Uber?"

"Yes. That or I'll borrow a friend's car until I buy one myself."

Her cheeks flushed, and that was the first time I realized she was giving me her most important tell. I saw her cheeks turn this particular shade of red multiple times when she was caught lying to me. This was the lying Bree look.

"Uber, huh? Okay. And you remember what happened the last time you borrowed a friend's car?"

Cheeks red again.

"Oh…right."

"Now that we've established that I'm helping your ass," I stated, "you have to play by my rules."

Her head snapped over to me, and I arched my eyebrow at her. "What makes you think I'm playing by your rules? I never agreed to you helping me out."

"Yeah, you did," I said as the driver pulled into the Mercedes dealership.

Breanne's face was perfectly unreadable now, but I didn't give a shit. This woman got to me in ways I couldn't rationalize. She was the calmest human being on the planet when forced into a labor and delivery situation. Then she blew my fucking mind by visualizing that pediatric ward as if Elena were out there telling her everything Collin and she had gone through in losing the baby and the coma. Their relationship barely survived all of it.

Breanne and I hadn't had much time to develop any form of attachment for each other, but I loved the way she made me feel whenever I was close to her. I would gladly take the burden of a shitty situation from her and expect nothing in return. Seriously. This woman could ask me to give her the moon, and I knew I'd probably find a way to provide her with the damn thing. Explaining all of that to anyone or even myself was pointless because this shit made no sense. It just felt right and felt good.

"Why aren't we replacing the company car?" she questioned. "Last I checked, I didn't see any sort of model made by Rolls Royce on this Mercedes lot."

I grinned. "Last you checked? You mean when you were here last, turning in the keys to your lease?"

"How do you know about that? Damn it, you really are on a group text with my friends, and Nat probably started it."

I wasn't, but I'm thankful you fell for that line of shit from earlier.

"Quiet, sweetheart," I mocked, and this time when I took her hand, I weaved my fingers through hers. "Act a little bit bitchy. We can't allow this salesman to think—"

"May I help you?"

The man eyed Breanne and me like we must've been lost, so I put my arm around her and pulled her closer to my side. That's when I realized we both looked like we couldn't afford a goddamn used car that was totaled in the backlot of a salvage yard. I smiled with the knowledge that we'd rushed out of the house, not ready to go anywhere. I ran my hand through my hair to validate I hadn't even styled it. We probably had some placenta or something smeared on our shoes too.

Well, this should be funnier than shit. This man had better hope he's not an arrogant ass, or he'd be losing out on a hefty commission today.

"This is a new car dealership. If you tell me your budget, I might be able to make some calls and see if I can direct you to another car lot that can accommodate you."

I truly couldn't believe my ears. It didn't take a genius to know that, in a sales position, you should never underestimate your customer. We could've hit the lottery, and the first place we came was here, but he had the nerve to act as if we didn't belong. He obviously hadn't seen the movie Pretty Woman before, and even though I was positive the dealership's owner had trained their salespeople to know better, I was going to make this guy squirm.

Breanne's arm reached around my waist, and instead of being mortified, I watched fire light up her eyes. She was sexier than hell when she went to bitch-mode.

"I'm Bree, and this is my fiancé, Logan." Breanne smiled and extended her hand to shake the salesman's, forcing him to return the gesture.

"Nice to meet you, Bree. I'm Richard."

The dude was definitely taken by Breanne, so that was officially the *only* thing this idiot and I had in common. I smiled when Breanne gave a spicy look in return, and her eyes lit in humor while she brought her hand back around my waist.

"Richard," she hung onto the word, prompting me to wait and see if she was about to say what I wanted to. "May we call you Dick?"

She read my damn mind. I bit back a smile when Richard's eyes widened, and his cheeks flushed. He was obviously insulted that Breanne would make such a suggestion. It appeared that *Dick* didn't appreciate being called what he was—a fucking dick.

"You'd be the first to do so," he said, giving into Breanne's fake-Rolex smile.

"Well, sweetheart…" I sighed, and since all I'd done lately was smile, I gave *Dick* the best one I could.

"Excuse me," Richard glared at both of us. "I think you two should consider another dealership."

This guy was a straight-up fucking asshole.

"Bummer," she looked up at me and fake-pouted. "I really wanted that showroom car too."

I studied her fake smile and arched an eyebrow at her. The woman was pissed that the limp-dick salesman had insulted us. She was also seemingly thinking that picking out the hundred and twenty-thousand-dollar AMG sitting in the showroom would get us out of here.

I smirked at her while the moron snickered to himself. *This mother fucker is really treating us like we're trash.*

"You really want that one?" I asked Breanne. "I mean, it *does seem* like Dick could use a *long* and *stiff* commission."

I would've been the first to admit that Richard and Dick jokes were corny and probably only funny when I was a kid, but I couldn't resist clowning this idiot for as long as I could.

"Well, it's not like we can afford it anyway," she shrugged, "and poor Dick wouldn't get that *huge* commission."

"That's what I'm contemplating," I returned. "Do we pick a car that gives *Dick* a bit of softy, or help him out by picking up a car that will give him a big, thick one? It will depend on whether you want that showroom car or not."

Breanne's face flushed while I worked to pull as many limp-dick jokes from my ass as I could. These gags weren't my area of comedic expertise, but Bree and I were on the same wavelength, and there was no choice but to roll with it and amuse ourselves.

"We can't afford it." She shrugged. "Regardless, I don't think Dick wants a hard-on—Oh! I mean a hard *one*. A hard sale."

"For God's sake, woman," I smiled at her as she was beginning to unravel. "You mean Dick wants a big one? Because let's face it, the commission on that AMG will be ridiculous." I looked back at dick-face. "Dick's a *man*, and all men want a *big* one."

"I think I'd prefer to be called Richard."

Too late. You probably shouldn't have acted like a dick when you first greeted us.

"I understand that," she said, seemingly reverting to her business-self. "It's all too much. We can't afford what Dick probably needs. Hefty, soft, or firm." She eyed me with those beautiful, bashful eyes of hers. *"Let's go!"* she mouthed with a lethal glare.

I ignored her and looked at the pissed-off salesman, rubbing the red beard on his cheek. "Hold up. Is this true, Dick?" I asked. "Do you want a good, *stiff* bonus or no?"

"I don't know where you two came from, but your Uber driver left you." He looked at his watch as if we were suddenly wasting his time, and I was about to do just that after he sighed in annoyance.

All right, fucker. Let's play games, shall we?

"Tell me about these cars." I pointed toward the lot, releasing Breanne to be captured by the younger salesman who was eyeing us and watching her. He'd get our money if he could manage not to treat us like we had leprosy.

After close to an hour of me and this man, sweating it out, me dragging him car-to-car with some stupid reason to keep him out under the hot sun, Dick finally lost his shit.

Breanne was inside the air-conditioned showroom, having coffee with everyone in the dealership, or maybe she'd left—where was she?

"I have to take a piss," I told the flustered man. "Fire up this C-Class, cool it down inside, and we might take it for a test drive."

"Listen," Dick said, pissed off, "I don't have any more time to waste with you, sir. I'm not *firing up* this car. You and your lady friend should probably leave."

I narrowed my eyes at the man. "You suck as a salesman; you know that?"

"Whatever." He rolled his eyes and locked the last vehicle he'd shown me. "And call me Richard. Your crass insults for the name Dick prove why I knew you were a waste of my time since you walked onto my lot."

I know. That's why we acted like idiots and worked up every last tacky insult for the name Dick, dick!

I followed him into the dealership to see Bree's dimpled smile, three men obviously enjoying it as much as I did, and two young women were laughing. The man I'd pissed off snapped at the five younger, college-aged salespeople, prompting them to get their asses back to work.

Where was the fucking manager in this shithole? I wanted to give the young salesman who'd put that smile on Bree's face the commission, but fuck if I was going to help the dealership out if this prick was running the joint.

"Where's the manager?"

"The finance manager is in his office; our owner and manager take Saturday off. So, neither would be of use to you," the jerk-off answered.

I smiled when I walked over to a brochure and realized that this dealership was run and operated by a man I knew. What were the odds that James Faltino owned this one? I'd acquired his wife's boutique salon on Wilshire Boulevard when I worked at Mitchell and Associates, and the couple were two of the coolest people I'd met in a long time. Too bad that Richard the dick couldn't just do his fucking job. Then again, I would be doing James a favor by secretly shopping his business and cleaning house on his shitty employee. Breanne might even feel somewhat better, seeing for her own eyes that shady employees happened to the best of us CEOs. The fact I was blessed with luck and also the gift of sniffing this shit out was just a perk.

"This is James Faltino," James said when I dialed his number.

"Mr. Faltino, this is Alexander Grayson. I'm at your dealership, sir."

"Oh, Alex, I'm sorry. I don't pay attention to the caller ID. I'm too old." He chuckled that raspy sound I remembered from drinks and dinner the night we acquired his wife's business. "You're at the dealership?"

"Yes, sir. Fantastic place. However," I looked up to see all eyes on me, except for the dickhead who'd stormed off, "you and I might need to go over a few things that need tweaking."

"Now you have me nervous, Mr. Grayson," he laughed.

"Nothing to be nervous about, but I will need some help getting to your finance manager so I can have the money wired over to buy your showroom AMG. The white one?" I glanced around and chuckled. "The *only* one."

"Mr. Nodder should be there. He doesn't take lunch breaks on Saturday."

"Do you have a salesman named Richard?"

"Richard Langley?"

Langley? Fuck me to hell. If only I'd known Langley was Dick's last name an hour ago.

"Excuse me," I called out to Richard, who was staring at his phone across the showroom, ignoring me, "is your last name Langley?"

"Who exactly are you speaking to?" Richard snapped.

"You have got to be kidding me," I heard Faltino growl. "Does he know who you are? That man *did not* just speak to you that way. I'm mortified."

"Don't be, Mr. Faltino," I tried to be as reassuring as I possibly could. "He doesn't need to know who I am." I narrowed my eyes at the asshole who was marching over to me. "You can inform him on Monday, though, if you wish."

"Give me that phone. I don't believe you're talking to Mr. Faltino."

Richard's phone rang while Lucy Faltino greeted me on my end.

"Do you need to get that, *Dick*?" I taunted the man while Lucy told me to give her husband a minute to handle the employee who'd just got his own ass fired.

Richard took his phone out while I went back to Lucy. "Hey, Lucy," I smiled into the phone, "I just needed someone to get me up to financing, and past your little gatekeeper at this dealership so I can get my friend a car and get back to my place for cocktails on the beach."

She laughed, "Are you still with the one young beautiful lady? What was her name again, Autumn?"

"Summer," I said gravely. I narrowed my eyes at Breanne as if I saw Summer's face in hers. "And no, I'm not."

All the goofy nonsense left the building the second my ex's name was brought up. She was the biggest fuckup I'd made since leaving the nightmare of my family life in the past. How the hell could I forget who I was and what was I doing?

There was no fucking way in hell I wanted to go down this road again, and Breanne's smile had already told me that it was too late. Fuck. I'd dragged her in, and now, I would have to deal with it. The difference was that Summer was Jim's old secretary—Breanne was my goddamn partner.

CHAPTER TWENTY-ONE
BREE

I wasn't sure what'd happened to change Alex's mood from the time he called the owners of the dealership until now, but I could sense the shift from a mile away. He insisted that I drive the car off the lot, and I did so with the knowledge that I'd make sure to leave the keys with him when we got to where we were going.

We drove in silence for what felt like forever. He had been staring at his phone for the entire drive through the hills and until the ocean came into view, and I'd spent that time trying to remember whether or not I did or said something to offend him. We were having such an easy, goofy time, and the next thing I know, he looked like an old thundercloud.

"It drives nice," I finally spoke. "I'm guessing that your driver— Henry, is it?"

"Yes," he said distantly.

"I'm not sure if Henry's going to enjoy chauffeuring your butt around with you in the front seat so close to him."

I laughed at my silly joke—I was the only one laughing—and then I decided to drop it. It wasn't my business to pry, so I tightened my lips as the GPS in the car told me to turn right on Pacific Coast Highway.

"How do you mute a group text?" Alex said with some frustration.

I grinned. "You probably shouldn't have given my friends your number."

"Seriously," he said. "This is annoying as fuck. And it's my idiot friends, not yours."

I frowned. "Um, back out of the text," I said, trying not to crash while merging with the other cars that were flying up PCH. "Then swipe on the text towards the left. See that bell?"

"Yep," he said.

"Click on it, and it shuts them all up." I chuckled. "Wow, as genius as you proclaim to be, and after working over *Dick* at the dealership, I can honestly say I'm shocked you don't know how to mute a group chat."

"I never had the need to know until one of my friends thought it'd be cute to start one."

Alex's energy was off, and it sucked. I was thoroughly enjoying him up until now. If I was honest with myself, I could admit I might've been falling for the man a tiny bit. Especially seeing him dressed down and without his hair styled immaculately. He was simple, all smiles, and I loved being on the receiving end of him holding my hand as he did earlier. It was a simple gesture, but I loved the sparks that left his hand and went into mine when he held it.

Maybe Nat was right; if I was going to get laid for the first time in years, it might as well be with a man who—she'd learned through the gossip circle at her salon—was exceptional in bed. I guess that rumor flew around from an ex-girlfriend of his named Summer. She'd worked there for a time, and from what Nat said, Alex dropped her ass after he found out she was adding her name to his credit cards and shopping the shit out of them.

I still don't understand how *that* happened, but word gets around salons where everyone knows everyone, and there weren't too many who liked this Summer character. I felt bad for Alex, but at least in this gossip mill, the women weren't making out the man to be the asshole. They couldn't stand her.

Maybe one day he'd tell me about it all, but I wasn't going to be the one to bring it up. What if the guy liked her, and she buried him in debt or something? One thing was for sure, with the mood he seemed to be in now, I was sure I wasn't going to be hearing about it today.

"Just park it here," Alex said when I rolled up in front of his two-car garage. "No one messes with shit out here anyway."

"I could easily see that since we're in a gated community," I answered with a smile.

"Are you cool if I take a quick shower, call for dinner, and then we kick back with some cocktails later?"

I stared at his expression. The man looked like he'd been given the worst news of his life. I didn't want to press him, but I couldn't handle the tension anymore.

"Are you okay?" I finally asked.

"Yes," he ran a hand through his hair. "I'm just sticky from sweating in this long-sleeved shirt and delivering babies." He half-smiled. "I'm sure you want to get cleaned up too?"

"Yeah," I said. It was apparent that I would have to suck it up and hoped he perked up a bit. Maybe I was overthinking things. "Which shower do I use? The same—"

"Yep. The one in your room."

He skipped up the steps like I was some creep he was trying to escape from in his own home. All I knew was that I didn't do a goddamn thing that should've been offensive to him, so he could go kill someone else's vibes. If he wanted to act like a little bitch, then he could bitch it up all night long by himself while I enjoyed the view of the ocean from his terrace this evening.

AFTER DINNER and sharing nothing but awkward small talk, I opted out of having a cocktail when I watched Alex down his glass of bourbon like it was water.

I fake-yawned. "I'm gonna call it a night." His dark expression made me backtrack. Did he even want me here? His company tonight was worse than having dinner with a mannequin. Why was I putting myself in an awkward situation with some moody guy? I had no reason to stay here, no reason to apologize for whatever I did or didn't do—fuck this weirdness. "It's been a long day, and I think I should go. It's only eight, and I need to work out some financial stuff."

"Like what?"

"Like selling my condo. I think I'll pull the listing and give it to Nat."

"Why would you do that?"

Now I'm being interrogated? Does Mr. Brooding want to say more than two words at a time all of a sudden? "Because I haven't said anything to my friends about it. I know I hurt my best friend's feelings when I listed it behind her back, and I need to get back to reality before Monday."

"The keys to the car are on the counter if you feel like taking off."

His tone and voice were low, and I had no idea if he was being a dick or trying to convince me to stay. What I did know was that I wasn't taking that car.

"I'm calling an Uber. Text me the address to the house so I can send for one."

"The car I bought today is yours." He rolled his eyes. "Take the car."

"How about kiss my ass? I don't need you buying my way out of this mess. I don't *need* that particular car to begin with."

"Why the hell not?"

"Because whether I'm a goddamn executive or not, I don't need to drive *that* car. It's too much. If you're into shit like that, then fine. Here's one for you. I'm not."

"I don't get it," he said.

"You don't need to. Just text me your address. I really should leave."

I know I was rude in some way or the other, but he wasn't giving me very much to work with. He was a complete Richard-level dick.

I had my clothes shoved in my duffle, and I was heading out of the room when Alex's tall frame stood with that saddened look on his face again.

"What happened to you today?" I asked, needing to get to the bottom of this. "I don't mean to pry, but today has been really weird. It's like you flipped a switch or something, and to be honest, it's confusing."

"The truth?"

"No, please lie," I answered with sarcasm. "You know, since, in my recent experience, lying works out so well in the end."

He faintly smiled. "Something happened on that phone call I made to the dealership's owner that scared the shit out of me."

I studied this worn expression and became more serious again. "I could tell something was up. Even now, you look like you were given horrible news."

"I sort of was." He closed the gap between us. He ran his knuckles along my cheek, pausing all my thoughts and brainpower with the sensation. "I was given a reminder that I could hurt you. Fuck." He pulled his hand away as if my cheekbone electrocuted him. "I don't want to hurt you," he said, gripping the back of his neck.

He looked toward the opened doors of the bedroom's balcony as if the ocean would give him refuge from whatever trouble he'd conjured up in his mind about hurting me.

"How would you hurt me?" I asked, confused. "Seriously, hurting me would be doing something like forcing me to drive that car you bought today."

"How so?"

That somehow switched his gears, and his eyes met mine again.

I smiled at him. "Oh, I don't know, suddenly we merge with your architect firm, fire most of the assholes from mine, and now, I'm living the high life while we continue to do layoffs? Something tells me you and I probably have hits placed on our asses already."

Unexpectedly, he laughed, and his features softened. "What am I going to do with you?"

"Let me call an Uber and head back into the city." I rubbed his arm, and now I was the one practically jumping in shock, feeling his hard biceps. "My God, man. Lift weights much? Your arms are—"

My heated cheeks nearly combusted into flames when Alex placed his strong hands on my shoulders and pressed his lips on mine. I wanted to fight him off and do the right thing, knowing he was my business partner, but who was I kidding? I'd known my ex-fiancé since our Freshman year in college, and that started with a friendship then moved into a disaster of an ending with him cheating on my ass.

I deserved this. I wanted this. I was all in whether Alex thought he'd *hurt me* or not. The only *hurting* that had better be happening is him fulfilling the aching need deep in my stomach that was begging me to let this man inside me.

I moaned into his kiss, my fingers twisting and pulling each side of his shirt while I worked to step on my toes to get more from his lips as his tongue swept through my mouth and forcefully tackled mine. His kiss was the perfect mixture of the warm bourbon he'd downed from earlier, complemented by a soothing taste that could only be Alex. If this man looked as delicious as he tasted, chances were that I would hurt his ass and not the other way around.

Alex's groans escaped him through our bruising kiss and entered me, igniting energy that had been inactive between my legs for far too long. Alex's fingers molded against my lower back, bringing me to close the last of the inches we had between us. I welcomed this gesture by bringing my hands up to run along his soft cheeks. The aftershave he used to remove the small growth that defined his sharp features was filled with a rich, robust, and spicy scent that I would never want to leave my senses after this insanely hot kiss.

Breathing through my nose wasn't enough. Alex's kiss was proving he may have been starved of kissing a woman in quite some time too. There was no way on this planet a man this gorgeous—who could take down any woman as his own with just his flirty wink—wanted to kiss my sorry ass this desperately.

I pulled away, my head light and spinning as I panted through short breaths. Alex didn't let this deter him from moving his mouth along my cheeks and neck. His fingers gently maneuvered my face to offer him my neck while he massaged all along my jaw and chin to an area behind my ear that forced a jolt through my spine and made me gasp through soft moans of pleasure.

"Fuck, I'm going to…" I stopped myself. Lightheaded and swimming in ecstasy or not, I wasn't sure where Alex was.

The man was on a fiery pursuit with his perfect lips to conquer my neck while his hands instantly moved down to come up under my shirt the minute I'd stopped talking.

"I swear to God if you come..." he finished what I almost revealed after he pulled his lips away from me. Then he cradled my face in his hands and smiled the sexiest, greedy smile I'd seen him put on display for me. "From just kissing?" His lips pressed into my forehead. "Then I'm marrying your ass." He softly laughed.

"You think that's funny, eh?" I arched an eyebrow after he killed the moment.

His eyes were darker and so hypnotic that I could tell he was probably holding back on his own. He wasn't laughing, teasing, or implying that I was in desperate need to get laid. No, this was a look that a wild and starved man gave his lover right before he successfully quelled that appetite.

That's when I ignored all sense, reason, or idea of what was happening between us. I'd never felt sparks fly or energy charge up for a release of *anything* like this until this moment. Both our eyes locked in this interesting flash of silence before my hands took on a will of their own and went directly to unbuttoning his jeans while he removed his shirt. His tanned skin highlighted the grooves that were dipped and formed in all the perfect areas that required hefty workouts to achieve. I explored his warm pectoral muscles with moist lips, feeling his hands in my hair. He gripped me tightly when I reached into his boxer briefs for his hard cock.

"Jesus Christ," he said through clenched teeth, his fingers running through my hair. "Who's the one who's about to come now?" He breathlessly laughed in the sexiest tone, turning me into some daring and wild woman who smiled up at him in response.

Riding on this newfound and prominent personality, I walked backward toward the bed, each step helping encourage me to remove an article of clothing until I was completely undressed for the eyes of the most handsome man I'd ever known. From top to bottom, he was perfect and glorious. He was about to be all mine too. I was going to capitalize on this in any way I could, and Alex's wolf-grin told me shit was about to get real, and I was going to love every second of this.

One long glance at his long, hard cock made me wonder if I should've waited this long to have sex again. If I wasn't walking tomorrow—because I was gladly going to allow this man and his perfectly enormous cock to have their way with me—I was going to enjoy every last ounce of it.

"Yeah, apparently Alex Grayson won't even kiss a woman while he fucks her. Won't even look her in the eyes..."

MY EYES SNAPPED open when that gossip nugget about Alex's ex was brought to the front of my mind as if Natalia were whispering in my ear. Jesus Christ, what a way to curse a fine thing that was happening right about now.

All ghostly and unexpected intrusive thoughts from my friend, as well as the surroundings of this room, evaporated when Alex moved his body between my legs, opening them further to accept him. I ran my hands through his hair when his eyes roamed over my face. The rumor that had floated into my mind was gone with the gust of wind that brushed over our bodies as his lips returned to the arduous kiss that'd started all of this.

I clung to his back, feeling my heart pace rapidly with Alex's hands as they ran fluidly through my hair. His teeth gently captured my lips when I fought for air to calm down and enjoy these sensual feelings. I felt like I was a virgin again, but I was with the best man this time. I felt like I was floating out of my body in sheer bliss when I reached for Alex's cock, enjoying him devouring my body as if he was drinking his favorite bourbon from it. His lips grew rougher when I opened my legs wider and ran his tip over my slick entrance.

"I need you inside me," I panted, feeling a small orgasm ripple its way out. "I want you."

Alex's teeth seductively nipped at my bottom lip, and then he answered my desperate pleas for more. He gently moved his cock into my pulsating entrance, and a low groan escaped his chest while his nipping teeth bit down onto my lower lip.

The minor sting of his teeth clenching softly yet firmly onto my lip made me arch up and into his firm abs. He released my lower lip while he thrust further into me with sexy and growling curses under his breath. Once Alex was moving inside me, my breath hitching with each slow thrust, he took my hands into his, and I knew I was about to unravel every tightened nerve that had been longing to feel a man inside of me—not just any man, though. It was Alex I desperately wanted.

He gently swept his tongue over my lip that he'd accidentally softly bitten when his cock first entered me, and his kiss was so soft and passionate that I felt nothing but adored by this man. It was endearing to have him intertwine our fingers together and press the back of my hands into the soft pillows behind me.

"You feel so fucking good," he panted out. "Your lip," his lips came back over it with a soft kiss. "Shit, I told you..."

"Deeper." I gripped my fingers against his hands. "Harder," I challenged with a smile.

"I won't fucking last. I've wanted this and *you* for too long." He moved out a little then smiled that sexy grin again. "I'm holding back because I *will watch you come*, Dimples."

I sighed when his thrust was deeper, and his mouth went to my hard nipple, devouring it, and that's when any sensation of concern faded that I wasn't prepped to take his nine inches of erotic beauty. I let my legs fall into the bed so he could take me as I moved my hips to get him onto what my insides were hungry for—his cock to find my G-spot and ride that until I came hard and long.

"Arch your hips into me," he said in a breathless plea. "Come on. I'm bringing you all the way before I come."

I did, and his knees dug into the bed after he held my hips and body in place. Jesus Christ, he just hit the fucking spot.

"Holy shit, you're on it," I said, caught with shallow breaths and my hands, going over his flexed ass that was maneuvering his cock to manipulate my G-spot. "Did you just fucking read my mind?"

His lips captured mine while he worked diligently to bring me a hard orgasm—one I'd only ever felt one other time during a one-night stand with a man who proudly admitted he could take care of me like that. The difference between that man and Alex was that Alex was putting everything into this—locking eyes with me, watching and studying me to make sure he was nailing the right spot. His moist lips traced my parched ones, lending me to lick my lips and taste his kiss directly after.

"You're the most beautiful woman I've ever known. I need you to come, baby," he said. "Squeeze my cock."

I did, and Alex's lips crashed into mine, raising me to another level —one I'd never been on before. Every move, smile, lick of his lips, and crushing kiss let me know we were close and explosive.

Alex's hips thrust harder into that spot, and he caught my hands when I tried to grip his hips and control his movements.

"Ride my cock," he said. "Fuck, just like that. You're beyond tight. This is fucking unreal."

I worked my pussy to keep up with Alex's requests, allowing his cursing to confirm this shit was going down flawlessly. I felt my entire body tense, and I sucked in the first long breath as he forced his tip against my swollen spot, which was begging to release an orgasm that would possibly squeeze his dick off at this point. We moved, writhed, and kissed, and our eyes were both dazed. We were off in some other realm where our bodies had taken us to lose ourselves in each other.

When Alex grunted and bit down on his bottom lip, the energy boiling within my body clenched around his hard cock, and Alex sucked in a breath that sounded so fucking sexy. I whined and whimpered while I sprang into him, and Alex moved perfectly with me to stay on the spot that was delivering the freedom my pussy had waited for and deserved.

"That's fucking right," he smiled. "God, you feel so good. You're so wet that I'm going to pin you to this bed and fuck you hard. You want that?"

"Hell yes, I want that," I said, practically drunk on this man.

Alex gripped each side of my face and kissed me deeper than his cock was driving into me. Fuck, it was painful, but it felt so good to feel this man spreading my pussy open and filling it up. Once he found a rhythm deep inside me, his eyes rolled back in his head while another orgasm that hit from out of nowhere came roaring in to meet his cock as Alex pumped harder and deeper with each drive for more.

"Goddamn, your pussy is clenching the fuck out of me," he said.

I closed my eyes, losing myself in the raw and unrestrained power of the man who looked more handsome than I'd ever seen him up until this moment. I moved my hands over the rigid muscles of his back—everything was taut and tense—and that's when Alex groaned loudly, cussed, and with one last push, he rode himself into the orgasm I was so fortunate to feel twice.

As both of us steadied ourselves, I braced for the guilt that tended to follow when a person impulsively gave into hormones, the lack of sex, and the strong desire for it. I prayed to God this man didn't regret the one thing we fucked up about—no damn condom.

I was on the pill, which covered the pregnancy aspect of the situation—and having just delivered a baby in the backseat of a car, that was pressing on my mind the most. I only wondered what Alex thought of it.

The fact that he was gently kissing along my chest, over my softening nipples before bringing his mouth to mine again meant he was still on a euphoric high, or he was ready to go another round. One thing was sure—I'd never felt this connected during sex before. We didn't slam into walls. I didn't flip him onto his back and ride him —which I certainly planned on doing for the next round if we had one. There was nothing overly exotic about this, but I saw in his eyes that this was us, discovering something neither one of us wanted to lose.

"I'm in love with you, Bree," he softly said and laid his head against my chest. "I didn't fully realize that until now."

I played with the top of his silky soft hair as his fingertips ran goosebumps down my sides, and I contemplated what the man had revealed to me. We'd find out once he pulled out completely and this blanket of sexual appetites and cravings left us. I hoped to hell he meant it because I was starting to feel the exact words he'd just declared.

The hardest part would be getting over the fact that I didn't believe love could be like this—fast and hard. It was like we'd both opened the floodgates. I could only speak for myself when saying that I'd given up trying to control my feelings about him. Maybe the culmination of the challenges in my life had led me to this. I couldn't control my employees or finances, I couldn't control my ex-fiancé, and I certainly couldn't control my feelings for Alex.

I didn't want to try to control things anymore. I was exhausted, and I'd denied myself happiness for so long because of my need to be in control of it all. I wanted to *feel* my feelings, not control them. Letting go opened a new world for me, and it seemed like I wasn't the only one who was feeling this way.

I didn't give a damn how it might look to anyone else—except for our employees. Something told me to keep that shit tightlipped unless, of course, James Mitchell's lawyers were up for overtime with complaints.

I kissed the top of his head.

"I think I'm in love with you too," I finally spoke.

He looked up at me. "You *think*? After that?" He smiled and kissed the base of my throat. "All right, then. By the end of this night, you'll be screaming that you're in love with me after leaving nail tracks in my back. I promise you that." He rolled off of me, and I turned to my side, watching this model of a perfect male figure walk toward the exit of the room.

"Where are you going?" I asked with a laugh.

"I ordered chocolate for the cocktail hour you ditched me on earlier." He grinned that devilish smile. "You'll be having that with a fine glass of wine from my vineyard in a soothing bath."

"What?" I laughed but loved the idea.

"Like I said, screaming you love me and leaving nail tracks in my back."

He left with that flirty wink of his, and then I smiled, resting my head against the bed. The night was still young, and he seemed like he had a few tricks left for us to enjoy.

CHAPTER TWENTY-TWO
ALEX

I wasn't a careless fool. So, what the fuck happened to me being responsible while having sex? Never before in my adult life had anything taken complete control of my sense of reason, my body, and my actions until I impulsively kissed Bree's lips.

That's when I lost all self-control and my ability to function with a woman in my arms coherently. It felt beyond fucking incredible, but Jesus, how was this playing out in Bree's mind? She'd met a side of me that I didn't even know existed—a man controlled by wanting her more than he knew. A man who allowed his sexual drive to overrule his reason when it came to needing to be inside her, craving that more than anything when the possibility was made available to him.

A man who was growing hard while he thought about taking her body again, feeling her tight pussy again, and most of all, a man who'd decided to run a goddamn *bath*? This sure as hell wasn't a side of me I knew existed.

I smirked when I glanced at the silver fondue set that I'd placed near the bath, filled with warm chocolate next to a bowl of fresh strawberries and cherries. There was wine chilling in my silver ice bucket, and I'd even busted out the crystal wine glasses. I might as well fill this tub with red rose petals and call it a goddamn honeymoon. What the hell was wrong with me?

First, I was playing with fire by having sex without protection, and now I was running bubble baths? So much for thinking I couldn't be a romantic man when it came to having sex. Now, here I was daydreaming about being inside her again while looking out at the ocean on the other side of this window. I'd be a fool to shove these newfound emotions out of the way. As corny as it all seemed, the smile that I left Bree lying on the bed with—the dimpled and dazed smile that I was obsessed with—was the reason I was checking for the perfect temperature in the oversized tub I'd never used nor ever planned on using.

"Wow," I heard Bree say, and I turned back to find her concealing her beautiful body from my hungry eyes with a bathrobe. "I've seen those stone bathtubs in architect magazines. I love the rectangular design and the fact that you can fit three or ten people in them." She smiled, her lips still swollen from me kissing her like I'd fallen in love with the act. "I like the way it's centered in the middle of that long window. You can see the ocean glowing out there."

"Well, this will be its first use." I rose, still naked as the day I was born. "And if you want to enjoy all of those features you just mentioned, drop the damn robe, sexy." I arched an eyebrow at her.

I watched her blush when her eyes noted that I was hard and ready to fuck her in or out of this bath. I went to kiss her, then noticed her bottom lip. Now, I felt like an asshole. I knew I'd bitten her lip while holding back from exploding the minute I felt the warmth of being inside her and the sensations that sparked in me.

After I tried to kiss away the minor injury that my impulsive behavior had caused, I frowned when I brought my thumb and examined her lip further. "Dammit, I'm so fucking sorry I did this." I laughed at myself. "I swear to God that I didn't think I bit you so hard."

Her fingertips brushed over my stomach, around my lower back, and then her nails dug into my ass. "It's fine," she smiled. "It complemented the intense orgasm you were kind enough to give me."

I watched her eyes do that dazed look, and my cock nearly jumped with the idea of what it must've felt like for her and the fact that I could throw her ass up against the wall and replay it if she wanted it like *that* again.

Instead of acting like the desperate fool that I felt like, I opted for a more controlled route, and I kissed her bruised lip again.

"Get in the bath," I said. "I'll run some ice over this."

Unaffected, Bree reached for my cock, and surprisingly, I didn't jump. Hell, my dick acted like it knew her better than I did. I knew it certainly appreciated fucking her in all the right and tight spaces.

"Are you getting in with me?" she questioned as she slowly started pumping her hand around my cock.

"Only if you keep working my hard dick like you're doing," I said playfully.

I held her close to my body, pressed my lips softly yet firmly onto hers, and then glanced out at the welcoming view that made a bath sound like a splendid idea. Maybe it was the fact that I knew where this bath idea was heading, and that made it all the more enticing.

"Since I have no intention of leaving your side until I'm forced to," I smiled at her as she studied me in humor, "I guess it's time I soak in a bath for the first time since I was two."

She flashed my favorite smile at me and then left me to watch the beauty of her silhouette walk toward the enormous window and the tub after I dimmed the lights. *Fucking hell, what a damn fine sight,* I thought, watching her step into the tub and relax against the towel I'd placed as a cushion for her head. If only I could keep the perfection of this moment in my mind forever: Breanne, beautiful and fully relaxed in the oversized bath while the ocean sparkled under the moonlight from beyond the windows.

"Get your sexy ass in here with me," she said. "I'd like some fine wine from Mr. Grayson's vineyard handed to me, please."

I smiled at her newfound confidence with me. I would've wagered that I'd run off the woman by fucking her without a condom and biting and bruising her lip, but she was still here with me, both of us wanting more of each other.

I stepped into the bath, and the candle—yes, I lit goddamn candles too—highlighted what I thought was a shadow on her neck at first until I got a closer look.

"Holy shit," I said when she turned her head to the side to gaze out of the window, giving me a better view of the dark spot that I'd noticed. "Let me see your neck."

I brushed my fingers over two hickeys I'd given her on one side, and a darker one on her throat, leaving only the left side without a blemish. Fucking hell, could I just drown myself in this bath before I had to admit that I'd done this to her as well?

"What's wrong?"

"Trust me, you don't want to fucking know," I said, collapsing back on the other end of the bath. My recent hard-on was quickly gone, and my sense of pride that I was pretty damn good in bed was following right behind it.

"I might have kissed your neck a little too hard. You know, bruised it…" I stopped and cringed.

I couldn't say the fucking words. *'Sorry, but I gave you a hickey or three!'* What the fuck happened to me in that room?

"Do I have a hickey?" she said the word like a person who wanted to know if they had a spider crawling on them.

"I have to thank you, Breanne," I said, watching her, mortified that I'd done this. "You've taken my virginity, and now you have the battle-scars to show the world that I loved every second of fucking a woman for the first time in my life." I frowned. "It seems that's how I acted, anyway. A goddamn hickey—three of them, to be precise. I'm so fucking sorry about *that* now too."

She clutched her neck, and then she unexpectedly smiled. "I'll get you back for this." Her eyes met mine. "I'll admit that if I weren't gasping for air like *I* was the virgin tonight, I'd probably have sucked on your neck like I was a vampire too."

I rolled my eyes. "Good God, how will you cover that up?"

"I have scarves," she smiled. "It gives me a good excuse to pretend I'm a fashionable lady."

"Jesus, you must think I'm an absolute amateur in bed."

"Definitely not." She raised her eyebrows and reached for an empty crystal wine glass, and waved it. "But you are certainly an amateur when it comes to keeping your word in this bath."

"Right. The wine and strawberries."

"Chocolate dipped, right?"

"I'm going to dip them in chocolate." I poured wine into her glass, then wedged myself and hardening cock between her legs. "Then I'm going to lick chocolate off your nipples, your neck..." I paused and kissed her chin. "Maybe I should feed them to you like the queen I intend to treat you as from this day forward."

She laughed. "Good idea." She took a sip of wine, then eyed me with a look that made me hard and ready to fuck again. "In fact, with my love for all things chocolate," she reached for my cock while offering me a sip of her wine, "I've never actually had a chocolate-covered..."

I smiled at her, searching for words. "If you think I'm going to trust your perfectly white teeth around my chocolate-covered dick, tempting you to chomp down, you've lost your mind."

She squeezed my tip, and I sucked in a sharp breath. "I'm not you," she said. She took a sip of wine and offered me another drink. "I don't bite. How about I *suck* every last drop of warm chocolate off your cock." Her fingers ran from my balls and up my shaft. "I'll lick along here," she kissed my lips that thirsted to taste hers again.

"Sweet Jesus," I groaned in pleasure, then moved my mouth up her neck and under her chin.

She sighed as she pumped the tip of my cock, and I reached for her clit that was still swollen and ready for more.

"Maybe I'll drink your cum with the delicious taste of chocolate in my mouth. What do you think?" she questioned through that sexy panting she did that turned me on.

"Fuck."

That's all I could say before I fell under the sexual spell of Breanne Stone. She started working my cock with perfection between her tight hands, and I fell limp against the back of the tub. I opened my legs for her to do whatever she wanted with me. I gripped the hard sides of the tub, knowing my cock was undoubtedly harder than the stone bath we were in.

I couldn't just lay back like a bitch and let Bree do all the work, though. No way in hell. Not after feeling like a jack-hole from earlier. I was taking care of my girl, not the other way around.

She was so insanely beautiful, and that's precisely why I smoothly manipulated her to lay back against my chest while I dipped my fingers into her smooth pussy.

Her knuckles were white as she clung to the rim of the tub while I massaged the rough surface of her G-spot inside of her.

"I'm on your spot," I said, back on track in the pleasure and knowing how to fuck a woman department. "You want it fast or slow, dimples?"

Being back in control and bringing my woman the pleasure she deserved was my sole purpose. Her hands covered my knees while her back slid up and down where my cock was wedged between her and my stomach. I wanted so badly to be inside her tight pussy again.

That would come when I was out of this bath. Unless she was set on staying in here and swallowing me, anyway, because there was no way I was shooting my cum into this bathwater.

Thank God I was functioning like a normal man who knew how to fuck again because I was about to start questioning what I'd become after almost a month without sex. Jesus—hickeys? Fucking split lips because I gnawed on Breanne's luscious ones like she was a bone?

I twisted and manipulated my fingers to work with each sigh, moan, and gasp Bree gave me to direct me on how she wanted it.

"Faster," she gasped, her face twisting back to bring her lips to my chest as she sunk further down, her body helping my fingers find the exact point she desired.

My thumb flicked over her clit, and then I rolled that sensitive spot in circles after she whined out a moan and gripped my legs. I pushed my fingers deeper into her and pulled hard and fast against her G-spot.

Bree arched her ass into me, and I hung onto her G-spot, feeling the tight spasm of her orgasm clenching against my fingers. "Fuck, I'm coming," she announced my three favorite words to leave her mouth while getting her off.

"Sexy as fuck too," I said, smiling and watching the water splash around her, floundering through the energy of this orgasm I wished my cock was feeling.

Breanne turned, and the next thing I knew, her breathless smile was more daring. She pulled herself up as my fingers lost the one pulsating energy they could've hugged and massaged for the rest of the night.

"Get a condom," she said. "I want you inside me. Now."

In record-breaking time, I managed to half-dry both our asses off, grab a box out of my top drawer, and tear into the one thing that would bring me the sensation my dick was literally weeping for.

Before I could roll it on, Breanne's perfect and naked body knelt on the floor in front of me, and her mouth took me as deeply as she could. I gripped the back of her damp hair and mentally willed myself not to ram my cock down her throat. Not helping me with trying to steady my greedy habits of fucking, Bree grabbed each of my ass cheeks and hummed my cock into the back of her throat. My fucking ears started ringing as her tongue licked while she and I worked together in some style to allow me to fuck her mouth as deep as I could.

I had to go deeper and harder, and though this was close to making my knees buckle, I wanted to be buried inside her, to see the look in her eyes as she came while I hit the back of her pussy again. Her drunken and yet soft look of utter ecstasy was what drove me to pull her sexy lips from my dick and lay her on my bed.

She raked her fingers through my hair when I entered her hard, deep, and fast. I spied her expression to see if she was into this wild way of taking me, and her eyes, rolling back into her head as she licked her lips, confirmed that I was on the path to another hard orgasm for both of us. She was tight, wet, and her pussy was clenching against my dick as I went harder and deeper with each thrust.

"God, you feel so good," she said through a painful moan.

I slowed down until I felt her fingers clawing into my back as if the skin covering my tight muscles were equally as resilient as the stone tub she clung onto from before. I sucked in my bottom lip as I pumped hard and faster with each plea for more.

I never believed I could nail a woman this hard and deep, only to see her eyes stoned on the ultimate pleasure ride. This was sexier than anything I'd ever experienced. Her sounds, her nails buried into my flesh, and her legs, locking me in to continue hard and fast like we were both in a sex marathon of ecstasy and pleasure—all of it was driving me wild.

I felt everything on a higher level, and there were multiple times when I swore that I'd held off coming only to have the gift of a small, shooting orgasm. In all the sex I'd ever had, that's one thing that'd never fucking happened. I either lost it and came hard and strong, or I held onto that edge until I was ready to end it. Fighting back an orgasm was treating me with tremors of small pleasures right before the buildup of letting it go.

Bree wailed that she was coming hard, and I found her lips to validate we would ride this one together. It had me coming deeper and almost fully burying my nine to ten inches inside her throbbing entrance.

"Fucking hell," I gasped out through heavy breathing. "Tell me I didn't bruise your beautiful pussy this time."

"You did." I felt her laugh, and I winced with the fact that my cock was sensitive as fuck, and she was clenching hard around it with her laughter.

Bree's dimpled smile caught me like a deer in headlights while she grabbed my ass before I could pull out to save myself the embarrassment of breathing through her pussy contracting hard on my dick.

After her soft laughter ended, I chewed on my bottom lip when I felt every sensation of her still coming...again? Jesus Christ, this was my night.

"You want more?" I smiled at her. I kissed her lips, ran my tongue over her throat, and nibbled the soft flesh directly below her ear. "Like that, dimples?" I thrust myself deep into her again. My dick was softening and falling out of the game, but I still had enough to make her grip my back and nod, her beautiful eyes never leaving mine.

She reached down to where I slyly removed my cock from her pussy. "I'm bringing this guy back with that chocolate idea of mine."

"I'm not sure I'm down to turn my dick into your very own chocolate popsicle, babe."

She looked at me curiously. "I like when you call me that, which is strange because I hated it when my idiot ex did."

"Maybe because it's me and not his sorry ass." I smiled, laying on my back and allowing her to curl into my side. I draped my arm around her and used my other hand to run circles over her full nipples. "You're perfect in every way. I have no idea how or *why*," I said with a laugh, "you let me fuck you that goddamn hard."

"It felt fucking fantastic. Let's face it; I've never had sex with a *real man* before," she said in a deep, funny voice, laughing.

"Well, this was one way to feel what that's like," I teased.

Bree started to trace her fingers along my cock while I closed my eyes, pulling my hand away from her breast and resting it behind my head. "You have the most beautiful body I think I've ever seen."

"No, *babe*," I smiled, staking claim to the name she liked me calling her, "that would be yours, and if you keep tickling my cock and balls like you're doing, you're going to knock my ass out."

"I'll just wake you up with hot syrup or whatever the strawberries were supposed to be dipped in."

"Jesus Christ," I smiled. "I'll never sleep again with you in the room if you wanna play it that way."

She rubbed her hand over my abdomen and yawned while she nestled into my side. "I do love you," she said in a more serious voice.

"I know. I have those nail tracks on my back that you'll be applying Neosporin to after breaking flesh to prove my theory was right."

She laughed, and I sighed in absolute contentment. Whether we fell asleep wrapped in each other's arms like this or woke up through the night—my dick being turned into a hot fudge sundae or not—I'd never been *this* attached to a woman before...ever.

My eyes snapped open when I realized I'd let my fucking brain detach from my body again, and somewhere on my bedroom floor was an unused condom. Was I *trying* to join the baby-making club? I knew for sure that wasn't the case, so why was I acting like a reckless fool with this perfect woman at my side? They say that love is blind, but they failed to mention that love—coupled with desperation and passion—would lead to *me* becoming a fucking fool with Breanne after coming inside her twice tonight.

Regardless, I was keeping this woman around for the long haul. Something told me that if I didn't get the nerve to open up to her and talk like a school counselor about birth control, her idiot, selfish boyfriend, and sexually transmitted diseases, we weren't going to put a pin in this sexually impulsive problem I suddenly had.

Fucking unreal that I was always the most reasonable and responsible one out of my entire group of friends, and now I was acting worse than all the guys when they were single—combined.

I just hoped Breanne was truly feeling love for me and not just saying that after I'd acted so carelessly with her perfect body tonight. I sure as hell wasn't lying about it.

I wasn't planning on leaving her side any time soon, and all I could do now was hope she wasn't planning on leaving mine.

CHAPTER TWENTY-THREE
BREE

I'd never been in a position to crave sex in any manner until Alex. This was crazy, but I wasn't arguing. Having sex with him was off the charts, and any woman who'd experienced him on a sexual level as I had would be a fool not to desire sex after this night.

I was so lost in thought—running my fingertips over Alex's groomed balls, around his soft cock, and along the hard groove of his V-shaped muscles—that I hadn't realized I'd sent the sexy man off into a peaceful slumber. It was just as well after I couldn't seem to get enough of him fucking me as hard and deep as I could take him that I knew for sure I'd be sore in the morning.

I turned into him, draped my leg over his waist, and managed to fall asleep nestled into his side. The last thing I remembered was Alex's arm pulling me closer to him and his hand covering my ass.

I DIDN'T KNOW how long I'd been asleep when I woke up to Alex, readjusting himself to turn into me. The only shitty thing part about being woken up was that this intense craving for more sex was worse than it was when I first dozed off.

I was going to be screwed if I didn't knock this shit off. I'd had hard, good sex with Alex, and I'd fallen asleep at his side. But that wasn't enough since the dream I'd been woken up from was about Alex and me, and it was so arousing that I was hornier now than I was before I drifted off.

Good grief. I guess this is what happens when the sex is fantastic.

It wasn't helping that Alex's *hard cock* was up against my stomach, either. The aching sensations returned, and my lips were dry, imagining him forcefully kissing me as he'd done. Damn, I loved the way he kissed. The intensity of this man was sexier than hell, especially since I'd never felt a man show this sort of unhinged desire in bed before. I loved how rough he was, the way he groaned, and the deep, raspy sounds of pleasure he made. Who would've thought the force of him fucking me hard would be the biggest turn-on ever?

Ugh, why did I have to run my fingertips softly over his sensual body and send him off to dreamland?

Stop thinking about it and close your dumb eyes.

I turned to mold myself further into Alex, who now slept facing me, and draped my leg over his hips. His muscular leg moved between mine and rubbed against my clit. When I felt that Alex's cock was wet against my stomach, I smiled, thinking the man was hopefully going to wake up as horny as I had from whatever dream hardened his wet cock.

Hoping that he wasn't in a deep sleep and that he could easily be woken up, I slid my wet entrance over his upper leg. Nothing. I gripped his back and chewed my bottom lip when I moved my clit over Alex's muscular leg wedged between mine. My eyes rolled back, feeling my swollen clit getting off against Alex's leg.

Good God, Breanne. Humping the man's leg now? The fuck is wrong with you?

There was no way I was letting Alex sleep through this new addiction he'd given me. No way in hell. He was rock hard, I needed him in me, and I wanted him now. His wet tip told me the man was having a *fucking hot* dream, and it was time to make dreams come true with this sexy beast lying peacefully at my side.

I manipulated Alex to lay flat on his back, and with ease, he did. "You are perfect in every way," I said, softly trying to coax his eyes to open and wake up to quench my need for more.

If he was lost in this dream that his cock was proving he was having, I was happy to awaken him to finish it physically.

I crawled between his legs and started licking his shaved balls, then ran the tip of my tongue from the base of his now dripping cock to the tip. I slid my tongue in circles around it, tasting his salty precum and needing this man to wake his ass up.

"Alex," I whispered, kissing along his abdomen. "I need you."

Filled with a warmth sizzling deep inside me, now at a boiling point for wanting his cock buried inside me, I decided to wake him up in a different manner. I slid his tip over my entrance, and if I had one last ounce of decency in me, I would've stopped there. But now, I wasn't able to stop. Wait. Yes, I could. This was...

I sighed when my body felt jolts of blissful energy swarming again after Alex's hands came up to my waist. *Thank God he's waking up.* I smoothed my hands over his chest and watched as he chewed on his lip, eyes still closed, then he groaned while he thrust his cock into me fully.

"Yes," I whispered in a moan of gratitude.

I started moving up and down, rolling my hips and working his cock as I started rubbing my clit to enhance feeling him inside me again. He was huge and perfect and the best thing I'd had in far too long.

"Fuck yes," Alex answered in a low growl. Even though his tone was filled with ecstasy, his eyes were still closed. He moved gently in and out, licking his perfect lips while he molded his head further back into his pillow. "Goddamn, I love you." His voice was distant, and that's when I stopped my pursuit of fucking him like this.

I studied the sharp features of his face. Was he still sleeping? "Alex?" I said a little louder this time. "Are you awake?"

He mumbled in response, and I couldn't help but laugh softly. The guy could undoubtedly start in on a good fuck, even in his sleep.

"Dammit, we need a condom," I said, knowing I was the one awake and thinking clearly.

I went to pull off, but his strong hands kept me in place. "Don't move, baby. Keep riding me." I saw his eyes open after he groaned and bit down on his bottom lip. "You feel so fucking good."

I could see the desire in his eyes, and I could feel it cover me entirely. All I wanted was this sensation. I wanted him deep, and now I could control all of it from where I straddled him. I was about to ride him hard and deep.

And that's precisely what I did.

Alex thrust himself further into me as I rotated my hips in brisk circles, working my pussy up and down his shaft.

"Faster, baby. Tell me you're close too. Fuck," he moaned. His chin tilted up, and I could see that my brisk movements were as pleasurable for him as they were for me. "Oh, my God. You're so…"

His voice trailed off as his strong hands gripped my waist tighter. Alex captured my hand that rubbed my clit as fast as he moved his cock in and out of me.

His legs came up, and I leaned back against them and moaned when I felt his fingers taking my clit in a way that would make a vibrator jealous of his skills. My breath caught in my chest when his other hand rolled my nipple between his fingers, and he started pumping himself harder up into me.

I was the one spouting off the curse words of ecstasy while Alex worked me like he owned my body. "Fuck, I'm going to come."

"Rock those hips. I'm right there with you," he said in his low, raspy voice. "Come on, baby."

I could tell he was painfully holding back.

I looked at his face, and his eyes were moving from my pussy, where he was creating a massive buildup of an orgasm, then to my tits, and now his eyes were on mine.

"I'm so close."

"You're so fucking beautiful. Clamp that pussy hard around my cock."

I squeezed his fullness as tight as possible, knowing that the more I did that, the harder the orgasm was when I came.

"Harder," he said, rougher now.

"Oh, God," I breathed out.

"Come, baby," he begged.

What the hell was going on with me? I wanted this so fucking badly, and now my body wouldn't let go of the buildup that forced me to wake him up. I mean, he wasn't arguing, but I wanted this, and now my body wasn't letting go.

"Goddammit," I said in frustration, and that's when Alex had me beneath him.

"Hey," he kissed my lips. "Having trouble, love?"

The way he said the words so smoothly and low should have made me lose myself all over him.

"I'm so close. I…"

Alex silenced me with a devouring kiss, his tongue forcefully moving against mine, and I sucked in a breath when he started moving hard and deep into me.

"You want it hard and deep again? Tell me what you need, dimples," he said, his lips all over my neck and breasts.

I raked my fingers through his soft hair and braced myself for him by gripping his shoulders. "Deeper. Fuck me hard."

As soon as I said it, that consuming smile of his lit up the room more than the moonlight that peered through the windows. His lips went to work while he intertwined his fingers with mine. The man had me pinned hard against his bed, driving deep into me and pulling out the stubborn orgasm that was worth the trouble it gave me.

I nearly shouted after I ripped my hands away from his and gripped his hair while the orgasm shattered violently through me. Alex's eyes were swirling and beautiful when his mouth tightened, lips turned down, and then he moved briskly and hard.

"Fuck yes." He drove in harder. "I'm fucking there," he said with his face looking wildly stoned. "God, I love this…"

He groaned in pleasure, and I transfixed my eyes, watching him as he climaxed hard. The creased lines in his forehead, a frown on his tightened lips, and his eyes, trying to stay locked on mine confirmed that Alex was coming hard and enjoying the same intensity I'd just felt. This look and his damn sexy moans were partly the reason I think I was addicted to this man. He was sexy before, but he was even sexier now when he rode a hard orgasm.

He was my new drug, and I was unashamedly addicted to him.

He rolled onto his back and kept me on him. "Don't move. I'm keeping my dick inside you for as long as it takes to make up for being a total asshole and falling asleep on my lady."

"Your lady?"

"You heard me. My-fucking-woman." He smiled and shot up both of his eyebrows.

"Well, you certainly left me alone to dream about you fucking me." I traced my fingers on his chest. "Then I couldn't go back to sleep after *your* hard dick," I shifted my hips to acknowledge him still inside me, "woke me up."

"My dick woke you up?" His eyes lit in humor.

"Hard, dripping wet, *and* you even started fucking me in your sleep."

"Seriously?" he chuckled. "I'm a sleep-fucker too?"

"That you are, and because you're a sleep-fucker, I couldn't go back to sleep. So, here we are again."

Alex chuckled along with me. "Well, since I've done the unpardonable sin and left my woman wanting, I'm going to have to make this right to help your beautiful and sexy ass fall into a good, wholesome slumber. That or we give my sleep-fucking dick a few minutes, and I'll fuck you back to sleep that way."

"How about we opt-in for a warm glass of milk. I swear to God, I will be worthless to everything under the sun tomorrow if I don't get *any* sleep tonight."

"Hold the fuck up. Warm milk?" He looked at me as if I were his sudden enemy. "First of all, milk is the one drink I cannot stand. I hate that shit. So, I don't have any here."

"Whoa!" I smiled. "*First of all*, you say? Am I to assume you have a second point to make after your assault on milk?"

"And a fucking third point in the lesson of milk…" He arched his eyebrow at me. "*Warm* milk? The thought of that almost made me throw up in my mouth."

I pinched my lips together, trying not to laugh at the adorable look of disgust on Alex's face. "And the third point, Mr. Grayson?"

He kissed my nose. "If you want to go back to sleep, why don't we try chilling in the spa. I'll give you some bourbon to knock your sexy ass out. We don't do milk unless…" he paused, his eyes looking into mine attentively. "Jesus, I might have to break this whole thing off with you because you like milk. Fuck."

I laughed. "I never said I *liked* it, but it does help you sleep when it's warm."

"Bourbon is your new answer to falling asleep." He helped me off of him. "That and a nice soak in the spa outside."

"Now you're turning me into a sex addict *and* an alcoholic?"

"The sex addict part is easily cured. You can just move in with me, and I'll fulfill that desire any time of the day or night."

"Right." I rolled my eyes.

"What was the erotic dream about that made you wake up wanting me, anyway?"

I thought I'd torture his pompous ass with my dream after he'd insulted a harmless glass of warm dairy product. "It was more like a fantasy and not a dream."

"I'm listening." He eyed me.

"You were fucking me from behind on the edge of your deck, insisting I enjoy the ocean while you fucked me."

"That *fantasy* can easily come true."

"It was in broad daylight with people around."

Alex smiled. "Again, it can come true."

"The hell it can," I said firmly. "I'm getting my swimsuit, and let's hope this spa and bourbon idea will send me off to sleep."

"And if that doesn't work, I'll fuck you back to sleep, and apparently, since I *sleep-fuck*, I'll fuck you even while I'm out too. Sound good?"

I couldn't resist but to laugh at the man's arrogance and take his offered hand after he pulled on his boardshorts.

SITTING in the spa overlooking the ocean was not the cure for falling back to sleep, nor did I want it to be. After Alex confirmed it was around five in the morning, I was pretty shocked to realize I'd gotten more than a few minutes of sleep.

"Here, sexy." Alex smiled at me after handing me a glass of bourbon.

"Do you think we should start the morning drinking hard liquor?" I sipped it anyway and slid close to his side.

"Hard sex requires hard liquor." He chuckled and sipped the amber fluid from his glass. "Besides," he curled his lips after the warmth of the bourbon touched them, "it's all how you view it."

"How should I view it?" I smiled over at his eyes, reflecting the illuminating spa we were in. "Because the way I see it, this is the best bourbon I've had in my life, and I'll probably be drunk by sunrise and calling for an Uber to prevent—"

Alex's hand tipped my glass to my lips. "Take a sip, love." He smiled at me, saying that name smoother than the bourbon he held. "It's far too early to get into a fight and have angry sex."

"Angry sex?" I laughed at him.

He pressed his lips together and nodded, "Yes. You see, *our sex* consists of various types. Angry sex, which is hard and raw," he looked at me and did his sexy eyebrow arch, "and you pulling out my hair."

"Ah, I see. So, we have a particular way of having sex? When did this all make itself known to you?"

"Then there's make-up sex. Everyone has it—sometimes good, sometimes bad. Ours is different."

I rolled my eyes and couldn't refrain from smiling as if he were reading from a sex manual.

"How's our make-up sex? I'm lost on that since we haven't had make-up sex yet?"

"Simple. It's you, facing a wall while I hit the *Alex-spot,* previously known as your G-spot, and I'll make sure that is taken care of every time my dick is inside you." He laughed while I watched him going on and making up these silly lines. "Either way, I'm ensuring you know I'm sorry for whatever I did to cause an argument while fucking you up against the wall."

"And if I piss you off?"

He smirked and took another sip. "Same thing. Me fucking you hard from behind and having you climbing that wall in ecstasy."

"Let's change the subject," I said with a laugh. "Unless you're already drunk and have a list of various types of sex we'll be having."

"Office sex." He raised his glass to that one. "You might as well put that thought in your head now because it can and will be happening."

"Yeah, I don't think so."

"I do," he stated. "Because if I can fuck in my sleep, I can surely nail your ass anywhere in that building, and all the employees would be none the wiser." He looked at me as I studied him to see if he was as serious about this as he sounded. "Trust me, you won't make it past noon, and I'll barely survive until ten in the morning after seeing your sexy eyes looking at me with desire for more."

I sighed and enjoyed the fact that I loved being here at this moment, even if it did consist of Alex bullshitting while we stretched our legs out in his stone spa, allowing the crisp breeze of the salty air to keep us both awake.

"You're right. Change of subject," he said. "I'm getting ready to tear your ass up again. So, how will we handle this little relationship of ours?"

"So, this will be more than a friends with benefits situation, then?"

He eyed me with that dark business-stare of his. "I've never told a woman I loved her in my life. Hell, I've never felt this way about any woman."

He'd pretty much said what I'd hoped he'd meant from earlier, confirming how I was feeling too.

"Is it weird that we're just tossing the word *love* around? Do you think that's the sex talking?"

"It might be the sex talking for you, but in my case," he leaned down and kissed my lips softly, "I know these are strong emotions. I know I want you solely for myself, and I know for a fact that I'm never letting you leave me." His somber expression lightened up some. "You're sort of screwed if you don't return the sentiment, and I'm certainly going to look like a freak because I'm not sure I can blot out these emotions. Trust me when I say that I'm *not* an emotional individual."

"When did you *really* start having feelings for me? Was it before or after I made a jackass out of myself the first night I met you?"

He grinned, and his hand came up to rub my shoulder. "That night, I was certainly intrigued, but you were only a piece of *hot-ass* I wouldn't have minded fucking." He chuckled. "Honestly, I don't know where it all came from, but I'm not pushing it down. I was scared to death I would fuck this all up and hurt you." He grew distant as he looked out at the ocean the spa faced. "I don't know. I guess it was acting on kissing you, and then after we did have sex, that's when I fully knew I could never hurt the one woman who'd gotten through my coal-black heart somehow."

I rubbed his chest. "I can see it bothers you, though. You get this sad expression in your eyes," I said, seeing that look again. "I have no idea what the hell you're thinking or what's scaring you about me. As for this whole *hurting me* thing, well, you've heard the rumors about what happens to men who fuck me over..." I paused when he smiled.

"You play embarrassing sex tapes of them for everyone they know to see? Tell me," his eyebrows knit together, and he pulled me close, "did you love him?"

I rolled my eyes. "Honestly, no," I answered. "Maybe I'm not supposed to say that since we were going to be married, but in hindsight, I can say with certainty that it wasn't love. I thought it was back then, but I think he was just the closest person around when my dad was first diagnosed, and I needed someone. I was scared, and I needed something constant. My mother's side of the family went batshit crazy when Max proposed to me at a party they'd thrown for a bunch of wealthy friends."

"Jesus Christ," Alex said. "That asshole took away the way I was going to propose too?"

I chuckled. "Yep, and now my crazy aunts can't work up a greedy appetite to show off and *act* like they have as much money as their friends."

"So, you never wanted to marry the man?"

"Again, I think that's where me needing to feel something constant came in. I knew I was losing my dad, and my mother was already dead. I think I was subconsciously trying to root myself because losing my dad meant I was going to be an orphan, and I didn't know how to begin to handle that. Getting married and starting a family seemed like a good way to make roots, I suppose." I'd never admitted that to anyone and saying it out loud to Alex made me feel an odd sense of relief. "Max wasn't always horrible. He was funny in his own way, and he did things to keep my mind off losing Dad. I sort of clung to him through grief. Theo hated him, though, and the girls had their watchful eyes on him. That's how I got the video of him having sex with that bitch."

"Let me guess, Natalia was the friend who set him up?"

"I was so busy being thrown into having *the perfect wedding* by my aunts," I looked at him watching me, and I could tell he was definitely interested in this story. "They freaking flew me to fashion week in New York and to Paris to have my gown designed. It was so over-the-top, and I was looking for an excuse to get out of it. My first panic attack happened in the middle of all of that."

Alex frowned. "My God, was it all that bad? I thought young girls such as your beautiful self loved the idea of big, fashionable weddings?"

"No more than all young boys want to be the captain of the football team. I know plenty of women who want nothing to do with having a big wedding, so that's a stereotype, buddy. But anyway, yes. Nat's friend set Max up. That's why, Mr. Grayson, I should warn you now that if you think you can *hurt me*, you might want to think again. I have friends who will bury your ass."

I reached for his cock, which prompted him to lick his lips, swim around to face me, and bring his hands up to my cheeks.

He gently kissed my lips. "I know this is all new between us, and it's extremely fast. I say we enjoy each other and have fun with it all. I want to keep that dimpled smile on your face, and I will…" he paused, and his expression darkened again. "Bree, I will fucking work my ass off to accept all of these feelings and keep you smiling."

"Quit burdening yourself with everything between us." I ran my fingers over his cheek. "I like the idea of enjoying what we found in each other. If that moves in a direction that gets too heavy for you, you have to tell me. It feels like you're more afraid of failing me in a relationship, and we're not even in one yet."

"As I said, I don't throw the word love around lightly. I never have."

"I've also hoped that the rumors about you are true then."

His forehead creased in concern. "Oh, great. The angry witch must've sent her monkeys to fuck me without my knowledge in rumor-ville, then? What do you know, and how worried should I be?"

I kissed his forehead and smoothed back his wet hair. "Let's just say the woman who started the rumor would be pretty pissed to know you kissed me while fucking me, and you also made eye contact."

Unexpectedly he smiled. "Well, shit. How many witches are in The Wizard of Oz? Because if this is the case, it's all true, and it could be any fling or ex of mine who can't keep her mouth shut."

"So," I eyed him. "You seriously fuck women without so much as looking at them?"

"There's never been an intimate bone in my body while I've had a woman in bed with me…until you. I mean, running baths? That's all brand new too."

"What about drinking warm milk?"

I giggled when his hands came up to my sides, and his lips captured mine in a kiss hotter than the spa. Hell, this kiss warmed up my insides, and Alex's hand slid into my bikini and kicked on the sexual heat.

"I need to step out," I laughed through his kiss. "You're cranking up my internal temperature gauge, and I'm burning up."

"The sun's rising." He stepped out and grabbed a towel for me. "How about we enjoy it while wrapped up in this oversized towel and continue talking about how much we *love* each other."

I smiled at him and stepped out. "Sounds like a perfect way to start the day."

CHAPTER TWENTY-FOUR
ALEX

*H*aving a house on the Pacific Ocean didn't allow us to watch the sun rising over the ocean. Instead, the pastel hues replaced the darkened sky, and the sun's rays streamed out over the water, creating a glimmer that moved with the ocean currents.

Usually, after long weeks in the city, I would retreat to my beach house and spend a lot of time at the edge of my balcony, absorbing the serenity of sunrises with a cup of coffee. Today was different in every way. For starters, my stone-cold heart had thawed overnight, and I felt like an entirely different human being. It wasn't due to anything I'd done, either. Being with Breanne made me feel different—happier. My jaded outlook on life seemed somehow softer whenever I was near her. It was strange how a woman could change it all with just a look, the sound of her voice, and in Breanne's case, the alluring part of her stubborn yet golden personality. I was a man in love, and honestly, what a liberating feeling to *care* for someone so suddenly and intensely.

Knowing the man that I was and never being down this uncertain path before, I knew I could fuck this shit up as fast as it had started. I wouldn't go down that road, though. If I began to overthink this, I'd destroy the peace I'd found, given to me by the woman who put this goofy smile on my face—a smile I hadn't seen since I was sixteen.

As soon as the memories of my past started to bubble their way up in my mind, I knew I had to shut this train of thought down immediately and lock it away. Fuck. I felt suddenly nauseous at the idea of haunted memories resurfacing, knowing my first instinct was to close myself off and push Bree away for her and my own good.

As we'd said earlier, we would make this *fun* and see where it all went. There was no pressure, only me reacting to how happy I felt and the fear of darker times trying to ruin that. I lived all this time, shutting out the chaos, and I was perfectly fine. I could do it now too. I deserved a happy life with someone who made me laugh; why couldn't I have it with Bree? There was no good reason why not.

"It just got cold," Bree said, snapping me out of my thoughts.

"I have an oversized beach blanket." I brought it up and around me as I came up behind her and pulled her into my chest. "Better?" I asked, kissing her soft cheek.

"Perfect," she said, leaning her head back against my chest. "Aren't you the perfect man?"

"I don't believe I've earned that title yet, but if you're handing it out, I'll take it."

"This is so surreal," she said, looking at the sun's light as it changed the sky above the ocean into a variety of hues of purple and blue. "If only we could pause certain moments in time."

"And if you could?" I questioned as I nestled further into her body, kissing her hair.

"I would keep us like this for at least another hour." She laughed.

"Just an hour? Hell, I'd keep us here forever and un-pause the time so that I could fuck you and then hit pause again." I rolled my eyes at how lame that sounded, but I guess lame was all part of being the love-drunk fool I'd become since I'd accepted these emotions.

"Ah, and it seems he recalls the hot and sexy dream I had about us being out here?"

"He just fucking remembered?" I smiled, my dick perking up after Breanne reminded me about her horny dream. "And thank God for not pausing time because I need to make up for falling asleep on you like a teenage boy."

She lifted her lips to kiss my chin. "You were *hardly* a teenage boy."

"Well, I did make a promise that I'd fulfill that fantasy," I said, kissing the back of her neck. "How about you enjoy the sunrise while I fuck you into bliss?"

"Ha." She nipped at my bottom lip, turning my ass on even more. "I don't think so."

"You don't?" I smiled.

"Out here? Having sex? You don't have it in you." She reached back and clenched my hard dick, and her gasp gave away that she realized she was entirely wrong.

"Yeah, we're fucking." I stated with a laugh. "No one is around, and your hand clenching my dick at the moment isn't making my drive to fuck you here and now any less."

I slid a foot between her legs, gently maneuvering her so I could validate whether or not my idea of fucking her discreetly while she watched the sunrise was something she was down for. She'd released my cock while I slid my hands into her bikini to find her entrance was already wet, and that was all I needed.

Without hesitating, I pulled down my boardshorts, and my dick was throbbing to enter her from behind.

I took her neck into my lips with tender kisses and brought her back to feel my hard cock. Her soft moans and sexy short breaths told me I was heading in the right direction, and she wanted this as badly as I wanted to give it to her.

"I'm going to fuck you as you watch the sunrise, and you're going to come hard, dimples."

I heard her swallow. "God, I…"

I slid the crotch of her swimsuit to the side, and with a slight bend of my knees, I positioned myself to enter her with ease. Her gasp in response sounded more soothing to my rejuvenated soul than the waves rolling into the shoreline.

"You have no idea how perfect you feel," I told her as I moved slowly into her after sliding my hand through her bikini and pressing my fingers over the soft surface of her clit.

I found a slow and perfect rhythm to gently fuck her, moving my cock in and out and resisting the urge to drive harder into her greedily. I kissed along the back of her neck as she leaned forward and gripped the rail, tempting me to go deeper.

I loved that she enjoyed it deep and got off by me hitting her spot or going after what I loved the most, filling her and forcing my tip against the back of her pussy. Jesus Christ, the sounds this woman was making was going to make me fucking cum inside her before she came. This was about her, and I had to wonder what the hell I was doing in that dream of hers to make her wake up wanting me hard and deep, fucking her into that mattress as I'd done.

All motions, movements, and sounds stopped the second I spied two figures walking up the beach. Of course, *this* would happen as soon as I teased Bree with a deeper thrust. Bree saw them the same time I did, and she made pulling out that much more difficult when she snapped her legs together, rose, and locked my cock in place with a tightness that made me grip her stomach to hold onto my shit.

Fuck, that felt good.

"People are coming," she whispered through clenched teeth.

You have no idea how close I was to coming, I thought as I blew out a breath, forcing myself to adjust to how fucking tight her pussy was around my cock.

"I know," I whispered back, "and you're currently holding my dick hostage." I kissed her cheek. "Relax, dimples. Act chill, and they'll pass by. Everyone out here keeps to themselves and leaves the homeowners alone—"

"Alex?" I heard the voice of Mrs. Campbell, and instead of dropping my forehead to Bree's shoulder in irritation, I established my bearings to greet my friendly yet overly talkative neighbor from five doors down with a smile.

"Good morning, Mr. and Mrs. Campbell," I acknowledged them. At the same time, I steadied Bree where we froze in place—still erotically connected and trying to keep it together as if we were both bundled up enjoying a beautiful sunrise.

She walked away from the wet sand and toward the softer sand to engage in conversation. Jesus Christ, I'd only ever talked with this woman one time before after a long run on the beach when I was walking my heart rate back into a normal rhythm. She loved to talk, and it was a good conversation while I recovered from morning beach runs, but at the moment, I was sort of trying to fuck my woman, and this wasn't time for idle chit-fucking-chat.

"Herbert and I got up early today to enjoy the gorgeous sunrise," she said while her husband smiled up at us. "I love these colors."

"I see that. Nice to see you, both. Enjoy the sunrise. You know you can't pause them."

Bree sighed and eyed me while I looked at her with a stupid-as-fuck smile. I could pull this off. I knew I could. I just had to get Mr. and Mrs. Campbell on their merry little fucking way.

"It rained last night," she said. "So, Herbert and I were going to enjoy our walk a little earlier than usual."

"Sunrise might be behind me," I grinned, "but you're missing what you came out early to see."

"What's that, Alex?" she questioned while I exhaled.

"The colors, of course," I answered, and my dick could no longer sit parked in this hot and tight pussy.

I moved slightly just to feel what the fuck I was out here to enjoy, and also what my neighbors were on a fantastic mission to destroy unknowingly.

Bree softly moaned as I worked her tightness from behind.

"It's just so lovely to see you. I'm glad you came down to the house this weekend," Mrs. Campbell said, ignoring my polite way of moving her down the shoreline. "That way, you can enjoy the sunrise after the rain."

Fuck my life, lady. Keep walking. But nope...why would she? It was time for some wholesome small talk.

"It's why we're out here," I tried to act a bit more dismissive.

From out of nowhere, I couldn't resist but to inwardly laugh at this fucked-up scenario. I was steadfast in ensuring I fulfilled Breanne's fantasy. My dick wasn't letting up on her perfect pussy even if I jerked the damn thing out. We would have to enjoy each other while Bree met my neighbors in quite a unique predicament. Of all the mornings for my talkative friend to be nosier than usual too.

"Alex, I'm mortified," Bree finally spoke through a whisper while I tried not to laugh at Mrs. Campbell, who was in her pleasant little world, moving the sand around between her toes.

"Just keep the blanket closed, and they'll never have a clue." I moved my cock slowly into her. "You focus on my dick and the sunrise, and I'll deal with my neighbor.

"Can we...are we really doing this?" Bree's voice was lower than the sound of the waves crashing into the break just beyond the shoreline.

"Yes," I answered with certainty, eying Mrs. Campbell leaning over to gather a seashell. "We're going to fuck, talk, and greet that sun if it were our last sunrise together."

"It's *going* to be our last if she doesn't leave or finds out what you're back there doing." Bree tried to sound firm, but I heard the humor of this messed-up situation in her voice too.

I moved deeper into her. "That—" she gasped, and I kissed her cheek.

"What's that?" Mrs. Campbell said, all but setting out a blanket in front of my house to stare up and talk for the rest of the damn day.

"Sunrise is so beautiful," Bree answered nicely.

I licked my parched and hungry lips, hearing it in her voice that she was enjoying my cock as it worked its way around her pussy, slowly and subtly.

"So, who's your friend?" Mrs. Campbell asked.

"Oh, my God, this isn't happening," Bree whispered into her shoulder.

"Oh, it's certainly happening." I smiled down at Mrs. Campbell, whose husband was turning her attention to something in the sand near their feet. "It's going down like this. You're going to hold your composure while I fuck you and simultaneously move them down the beach."

"How can you fuck and talk?" she continued hiding her voice in her shoulder.

"You'd be surprised at how I can please my lady."

"Did you hear me?" Mrs. Campbell asked, looking up to us again, holding her hand like a visor over her squinting eyes.

I smiled, knowing the sun was saving our asses as it rose over the mountains behind my house. Thank God my boardshorts hadn't dropped to the ground as well.

"Yes. This is my girlfriend, Bree," I introduced her, hoping my probing neighbor would move on. Most people would've left already; I'd like to think so, at least.

I'd never been in a position like this, and somehow the dark, crazier side of it turned me on even more. Bree remaining wet told me she wasn't about to let my nosy neighbor ruin this in one way or another either.

"We're so fucked," Bree whispered back to me.

"Figuratively and literally," I chuckled and kissed her cheek. "Enjoy the literal aspect."

"Are you appreciating the sunrise from our beautiful Malibu shores, young lady?"

"I am," Bree said while I started moving to find her G-spot, forcing her to croak out the words.

"Act emotional or something. You have to cover that up," I said with a smile, bringing my cheek slyly next to hers as if I weren't on the verge of bursting into an orgasm sound with the slightest movement myself.

"Cover what shit up?" She clenched her throat. "Oh, my voice."

"Right, the fuck-sounds you just made when you spoke," I smirked. "Why don't you cough? Wait, don't cough!"

Bree faked a cough and squeezed the fuck out of my dick, forcing me to grip the deck in front of us and pull back the cum that almost burst from my goddamn loins with the tight clench of her pussy.

Bree softly laughed, knowing that I almost lost it, and she knew exactly why.

"Baby, loosen your legs. You're going to pull this right out of me. You're so goddamn tight."

"God," Bree said when I moved into her again.

"What was that?" Mrs. Campbell questioned.

"The rip currents are pretty bad this morning." Mr. Campbell, naturally stiff and silent, decided to join in on the fun. "Hope you don't plan on surfing."

"Bree seems to be awestruck by all of this beauty, Alex," Mrs. Campbell informed me.

Okay, I wasn't usually a complete asshole, and especially to my elderly neighbors. Still, things were about to swiftly change if they didn't figure out that I was trying to enjoy a sunrise alone with a lady. Wait, had they caught on to me?

I reexamined mine and Bree's current predicament and figured there was no way these two knew I was fucking my woman while they headed toward small talk. We looked like two sweet, cuddly kids, trying to enjoy a fucking sunrise, and my rude neighbors weren't allowing that.

I started to rub against Bree's clit, and now the games were on. She was delicious, even more so while trying to remain discreet and entertain my nosy and rude neighbors.

"Holy cow," Bree pointed out to the ocean. "Look at that!"

I grinned, hearing the rasp in her voice and her breathlessness as I went deeper and slower, pressing firmly against her clit and moving it in a variety of directions. My cock was soaking wet, and I realized that from this position, while Bree talked, her pussy put pressure on my cock in all the right areas.

"Fucking hell. Keep talking. Your pussy is massaging my dick," I said, kissing her temple.

"It's beautiful, all right," Mrs. Campbell said.

"Answer her, dimples," I ordered through an exhale of pleasure.

"You two walk out here a lot?" Bree asked.

"Jesus Christ." I closed my eyes. "Fuck, you feel amazing," I growled into her neck.

"Stop talking to me," Bree said under her breath, "or it's all going to get worse."

"There's no way *this* method of fucking gets worse," I answered.

"I'm killing you for this later," she laughed.

"I'll take death." I kissed the top of her head and worked her clit as hard as my dick wanted to come.

"Well, where's Zeus?" the neighbor I'd forgotten about asked.

"Fucking hell, is she trying to stay here until high noon?" I whispered into Bree's hair.

"She knows you're probably fucking me."

"No," I laughed. "She's more interested that I have a beautiful woman out here for the first time."

"Fuck, where *is* Zeus?" Bree practically sang my cat's name when I punched deeply into her, my eyes rolling back and her pussy clenching in gratitude.

"You know about my Alex's cat?" Mrs. Campbell asked while her husband went on looking for sand crabs or something. "Does Zeus like you around?"

My Alex? What the fuck with this line of questioning?

"Zeus adores Breanne," I said, feeling my hard dick soften at the newfound bitchiness of my neighbor.

"He sure is a sweet cat." Mrs. Campbell held her heart, but I wasn't amused.

"He certainly is," Bree said in place of me glaring down at my absurdly rude neighbor.

I let my dick slide out of Breanne. I was irritated, and this lady had finally killed it for me. My neighbor used a tone that was meant to put Bree in her place for being here with me, and she was lucky I didn't pull the blanket off both of us and show her I was in the middle of fucking my lady when she decided to interrupt the fuck out of us.

Bree cleared her throat and readjusted herself while I rose. "It's been lovely to see you, Mrs. Campbell. Enjoy your day. We're going to start ours with some breakfast."

I watched the woman eye Bree nastily, and it was confirmed that my neighbor seemed to disapprove of her.

"Well, if your lady-friend wants to make your breakfast, you can join me and Herbert on our walk."

I concealed my dick in my shorts and stepped out of the blanket, covering Bree fully and bringing her into my side. "Herbert seems to have ditched you, Mrs. Campbell," I answered curtly. "I feel sorry for him that our conversation seemed to ruin his morning walk."

"Herbert is just Herbert. Come on, Alex. Let's stroll the beach together."

"I'll pass," I said, feeling Bree's forgiving eyes on my dark ones. "As you can see, I quite obviously have a guest. Maybe where you come from, it's acceptable to leave them behind, but I would never dream of being so inconsiderate. I feel I've ignored her enough since you popped by to chat, so I'm hoping that if I make her breakfast, she'll stick around." I couldn't have cared less if the old bag wanted to burn my house down at this point. People like her drove me insane.

The woman frowned at Bree in some petty, bitchy way, knowing she must've come across like the pretentious hag she was being. This whole interaction caught me off guard. Mrs. Campbell had always seemed to be a very kind and easygoing lady. Where had this new side of her come from? I hadn't a clue. One thing I could be certain of, though, was that when it came to wealthy people, you could never take them at face value. Most of them could be the absolute worst, and Mrs. Campbell proved that.

"Good day, then," she snapped as she spun around and went after her husband.

I took Bree's hand, hoping that would be the last time I ran into my neighbor.

"Are you pissed because you couldn't get a piece out there?" Bree teased, softening me up some.

"I'm pissed because my neighbor is rude as fuck," I answered. "I'll have to have Collin blast his patio music loud piss her off after she acted like that. Fucking unreal."

We got into the house and then Bree ran her fingers down the center of my chest. "Wanna make up for it in the shower?"

I grinned. "A little aggressive sex is what will cure me from wanting to retaliate at my neighbor for ruining your sunrise by wondering where the fuck my goddamn cat is."

Bree laughed while I scooped her up into my arms, and that's when her phone went off.

"That's Nat," she said. "I have to get that."

"Where's your phone?"

"On the charger," she answered, hopping up the steps to her room.

"Not to pry, but do you think something went south?"

"Nat knows I'm with you." She smiled at me, walking to pick up her phone. "And because she hasn't heard from me since my texts yesterday afternoon, she knows we screwed."

"She's checking in?"

"No, dipshit," Bree laughed, unlocking her phone to dial out. "She would put the word out to all my friends to leave me alone until I got back to them. Something's up, or she wouldn't have called. Hey, Nat," I heard her say in the loveliest voice as I left her to talk to her friend.

I was in the kitchen for only a few minutes before I heard her tone change completely.

"Oh my God, this isn't happening!" I heard her say, and I instantly froze.

I didn't know if it was presumptuous of me to rush into the room and see if she was okay, but I also didn't care. If I seemed protective, then shoot me. I cared, and I wanted to make sure she was okay.

I went back down into her room as she hung up the phone and broke down crying into her hands.

"Jesus Christ," I said, rushing to her side. "Tell me what happened."

"It's nothing."

"The hell it isn't." I tilted her chin, and she collapsed into my chest, sobbing. I ran my hand over the top of her head, not knowing if her friend had gotten into an accident or what had gone wrong. "Talk to me, love."

"My aunts," she sniffed. "Between them and Max, I'm going to have a nervous breakdown."

"Not after the night we just had." I tried to smile through her pain. "Tell me what is going on."

"They're all in a bidding war to buy my condo. Max started this shit by telling them I was selling the place, and my aunts are jumping in. They told Nat I didn't deserve it anyway. I feel like they hate me because of what I did to Max. How could they even think to take his side over their own flesh and blood? Worse than that, I think they despise the fact that I outlived my parents, and they think I'm some spoiled little bitch."

I pinched my lips together and studied her tear-stained eyes. "They haven't met me yet, have they?"

"You're not buying that house. They have bid the fucking place so high that I won't allow you to waste your money. That isn't investing, and you and I both know it."

"What's the house at?"

"Ten million. Fucking stupid," she sighed.

"Pull the listing," I suggested.

"No. I need this place gone so I can pay off my shit and feel financially stable again."

"Then the bidding war will commence," I said, knowing she didn't want me buying the place.

"You're not buying it. As I said, it's no longer an investment."

That's when I frowned, seeing her bottom lip quiver. I traced it with my thumbs and brought her eyes to meet mine. "Pull the listing, baby," I said. "Allow me to help you get out of this nightmare. I know you don't *need* my help, but you don't deserve this shit either. Are these the aunts who were pissed about your wedding? The Paris, wedding-dress aunts?"

"Yep," she said stiffly.

"Interesting that they won't leave you to your business." I glanced at the view out of the windows. "Breanne, that place *is* an investment to me because of what it means to you. Either you pull the listing and get their grubby hands out of the pot, or I'm coming in." I ran my hands up her legs, letting my thumbs trail the insides of her thighs. "I *will* give you an offer they can't compete with, and you, my sweet, adorable, stubborn as hell love, will accept it."

"Or?" she became more playful.

"I'll dump your ass like we're in grade school," I winked. "Seriously, you can decide on whose offer you want to take. The most exceptional way to slap an asshole or two in their face is to take the lowest bid if you're going to concern yourself with real estate values."

Her lips tightened. "I don't know what to do."

"I told you what to do." I knelt in front of her. "If this is because it's *me*, and you're taking issue with the uncertainty of us, then Cam comes from old, oil money, and that man needs a place close to the hospital."

"Cam?"

"Cameron? Dr. Brandt?"

"Oh, Dr. Sexy." She leaned forward and kissed my suddenly frowning lips.

"That's what all the lovely ladies tend to believe he is," I smirked. "Sell Cam the place, and then you can live with me until this is fixed and you find another. Otherwise, I have Nat's number, and I'll play the bidding-war game all day long until your bitchy aunts and your asshole of an ex get beat. I mean, do you *really* need to sell it?"

"I can't even afford to turn the power back on," she rolled her eyes.

"Just look at what that condo's done for you and me in the last twenty-four hours? Hell, I'm purchasing the place, gifting the son of a bitch to *you*, and ending this shit here and now. That condo brought you to me, and what came of that was a way of saving me from my dark, tortured soul. I'm buying it, and your cute little ass isn't stopping me from it."

"It's not that I'm *trying* to be so stubborn. I just—"

I looked at her with sympathy and took her hands. "Baby, pull the listing and let me fix the rest of the hardship. I'll even throw the car you appear to hate up on the auction block, and you can use the proceeds of that to buy whatever car you want so you can start putting a dent in the debt you accrued by trying to save your dad's business."

"You have to know I love you."

"You *better* fucking know I love you." I smiled.

"Let me get out of here and go deal with this." She rose from the bed and kissed my forehead. "I'll let you know if I pull the listing or if I get greedy and say the price went up to fifty million." She chuckled.

"Okay. Take that damn car, please." I raised my eyebrows at her as she rolled her eyes at me. "Listen, it was my bad for not asking you if that was a car you would really want. If you hate the thing, I have a friend who'll sell it at auction. Then you can buy some beater, or whatever the fuck you want. I do need help getting it to the city, though, and you need a ride. So, it works out for the best."

"Fine. I'll drive the stupid car there."

"Would you look at us?" I grabbed her waist and brought her in close. "We're already acting like a good married couple that's learning to compromise."

"Shut the hell up. I am missing out on making up for sunrise sex because of this shit."

I patted her ass as she grabbed her duffle bag. "That's why we're going to have sunset sex."

"Yeah. The party's over, *baby*," she said adorably. "I'll text or call later. I'm going to handle this shit while these idiots are all in the same room. It's about time we clear the air on sex tapes and runaway brides, don't you think?"

"I think I'm a little offended that I'm not invited to this." I arched an eyebrow at her.

"I think you have an adorable infant nephew you need to go visit. Let's not pretend that none of our friends are talking shit behind our backs."

"I couldn't give two fucks about what my friends have to say."

"Right," she smiled. "I love you, and I'll call you later."

I would've naturally pressed, held my ground, and stormed out with her, but she held me back with those words in a way that was soothing to a tired soul. A heavenly sensation was finally replacing the hellish life I'd been gifted as a child, and I couldn't resist absorbing every last ounce of goodness.

This woman brought happiness into the troubled life I hid from everyone, and it was something I never knew I needed.

To hear the words *I love you* fall out of her mouth as if it were second nature was glorious. The last person to say those words to me was my mother, and I hadn't heard them since long before she had her stroke. She could no longer speak, and her mind was nearly gone, so feeling the warmth of those words again, being delivered in the most genuine way, was like basking in the sun.

After my father tried his hardest to fuck up my life, my mom begged and pleaded with me to find love, and she told me that one day, I would. She told me I should cling to that emotion because my evil, abusive father couldn't take that from me. I didn't believe her until Breanne found me.

If only Mom could comprehend things like she used to. If she were still mentally capable of understanding things as she used to, I'd tell her she was right about me and finding true happiness. I would cheerfully tell her that her prayers for her son had come true.

CHAPTER TWENTY-FIVE
BREE

I met Nat at our favorite restaurant in the city, where the outdoor patio made you feel like you were on a quaint street in Amsterdam. Flowers were always in full bloom no matter the season and changed in an array of colorful arrangements. I needed the escape to this place, and their delicious mango salad and strawberry iced tea sealed the deal.

"Hold up," Nat said before we walked to the hostess stand to be seated. She answered her phone and glared at me. "You're shitting me, right?" She narrowed her eyes and then ran her hand through her immaculately styled hair.

Shit, this can't be good. Nat would never screw with her hair like that, I thought, knowing Nat never stressed like *this,* or at least I'd never seen it, and I'd known the woman since forever.

"What?" I asked after she ended the call.

"It seems that *your* broker, a man whose name I will *never* say aloud for any reason..." she paused and sighed.

"So, now he's Beetlejuice?" I said with a smirk, hoping she was just acting dramatic, and this wasn't going to blow up in my face somehow. She wasn't amused. "Do I need to call him?"

"Yeah, call him, and pull that fucking penthouse off the market. This is getting out of hand."

"I thought we'd all be meeting in a conference room to fix this crap with my aunts and Max."

"Real estate doesn't work like that, Bree. We don't meet in conference rooms like executives. Agents call for their clients and give *your* listing agent an offer."

"How do you know about what's going on, then?" I stopped and cleared my throat. I hadn't officially listed the property with Nat, so technically, she shouldn't know most of the details.

"I've been in this business too long and have too many friends and contacts not to know what's going on. Everyone knows who you are to me," Nat said, sounding distracted or disturbed. Or both.

"I'm sorry I went behind your back, but I didn't want you or the girls worrying about my financial problems."

"And because of that, sister-dear," she said the words with oozing sarcasm, "Alex Grayson is involved."

"I think we both know that Alex is involved." I felt the heat in my cheeks when she smiled slyly at me.

"And because you two have obviously had mind-blowing sex since we sent him to do the dirty work for us, I'll forgive you. Good Lord, that shit must have been good."

"I'm not saying anything, no matter how hard you probe."

"You don't have to," she chuckled. "Your body is screaming that rich men can fuck good while they hang on for dear life with their lips on your neck." She arched an eyebrow at me. "Tell me the man was enjoying your perfect little lips so much that your love-bite is just that and not him trying to kick your ass."

"Jesus Christ!" I clenched my exposed neck, which had at least three hickeys on it.

My lips dried the second I recalled Alex devouring my neck, loving his firm lips and tongue as they pulled my soft flesh, not realizing I'd look like this in public.

"We need to get you a new *high-collared* outfit and get to your condo immediately. I'll buy you something from the couture shop three doors down. Don't argue. Let's go."

I picked out a flattering blue silk blouse with a neckline that concealed my hickeys, tucked it into my new high-waisted trousers, and slid on a pair of heels. I couldn't argue with Nat. I'd shown up in leggings and a tank, and all of my dress clothes were in my condo that my aunts, Max, and their agents were most likely viewing for whatever stupid reason.

I had no other option but to allow my best friend to buy me a new outfit while she gave me play-by-play details about this bizarre real estate situation. Nat was getting all of her news from her friend, Shelby Patton, who was the agent representing my two bitch-aunts. I'd met Shelby over drinks at a club after Max and I first broke it off. She was a sweet lady, and apparently, she liked me well enough to keep Nat in the loop about what was happening.

Ten missed calls and three voicemails from my broker told me that this morning had gone to hell and fast while Alex and I enjoyed his sunrise and neighbors. I hadn't called back my listing agent because I wanted to speak to Nat first, but I regretted waiting after listening to his voicemails. He'd arranged viewings, and when I didn't respond to him, he decided to open my house up and let the bidding war commence at my condo with all parties present.

I texted him immediately to hold him off, knowing Nat hated the man, and I told him I'd be there soon. What the hell had started all of this nonsense anyway?

After I was dressed, I wished I'd picked out my outfit and not let Nat do that for me. The blouse had an opening that accented my cleavage, and it seemed the opening started just below my high collar and ended at my belly button. I had no idea what would look trashier, my pronounced boobs or showing off the hickeys?

"You look fabulous. Stop fidgeting," Nat said after I stepped out of the car in the parking area of the condo. "What the serious fuck with this car? Is this on loan from Mr. Sexy-lips himself?"

"You don't want to know," I said.

"Oh, I want to know. I will know all about it too. You finally kicked that dreadful dry spell with a man who tore your hot little ass up." She laughed and smacked my butt.

"Well, you're in a pretty good mood, considering that we're about to walk into a hornet's nest. Do we need to be here?"

"Yes," she nodded. "Now, if I were your agent, I wouldn't have allowed for this showing, but you insisted on secrets, so your dick of an agent has. You *will* be here, and we're ending this once and for all."

"How are we ending this by being here?"

"Well," she said, hitting the elevator button to get us to the penthouse unit, "I figured that if they all saw you in person, they'd knock this shit off. I also know you," she raised her sharp eyebrow, "and when you get pushed to your limits, you start thinking smarter."

"Smarter?"

"Yeah, as in, pulling the fucking place off the market. I think you need to see them all swarming in your apartment like flies for you to end this."

"Oh shit!" I stopped before entering the elevators. "My power and water are shut off. I didn't tell the agent about that, and I can't have them knowing that was all shut off on Friday night."

"It's turned back on, sweet-Bree," she smirked. "Get your ass in here, and let's go face the music."

"Did something happen on our drive over that turned this into some fun game for you?"

"Yes," she grinned. "You look just as hot as you look sexy, and that puts me in a damn good mood." She looked at my hair and scrunched her face. "Do you have anything to pull up your hair? Good grief, you look like you..." she stopped and pinched her lips into a smile. "Damn, I can only imagine how glorious the sex was. This is *he fucked me senseless* hair." She became serious. "Either way, give me that..." She took the hairpins from my hand that I'd dug out of my purse. She ran her fingers through my hair, twisting it into a low knot and pinning it.

"Thanks for this. I feel like I'm getting steamrolled, and now I'm sick that I'm about to see them all again."

"Don't worry about their sorry asses," Nat said. "I've got this handled. I need you looking like you own the entire building and not just the penthouse."

She turned me to face her, and I felt tears surfacing. I hadn't seen my aunts since I left Max at the altar—the day they showed their true colors. Then there was seeing Max again. Why was this happening to me? I wanted to sell the damn place—as hard as it would be to let go—and start over again. It should've been a nice and easy transaction, but that shit wasn't in the cards for me somehow.

"Why?" I finally let a tear slip and hugged Nat. "I'm only in this position because I was trying to save my dad's company. Why do shitty things happen to good people?"

Nat withdrew from my embrace. "Look at me," she said, and surprisingly she had tears in her eyes too. "You're right. It sucks that assholes prey on good people. We both know life is fucked like that, but I'll be goddamned if you think I'm going to let you stand there and have a woe-is-me mentality. You're Breanne *fucking* Stone, and out of all of us, you are the strongest. *I* would be the one to crumble for losing my precious car or possessions, not you. Sammy and Cass wouldn't even know where to start if they had to sell their condos, but not you. Shit happens everywhere every single day, but these stupid fucks who are being horrible to you mean nothing in the grand scheme of things, and you know it. Don't let them turn you into someone you're not. You are loved and supported, and you don't have to go it alone. Tough times are why we have good friends, good *sex*, and hard liquor," she chuckled. "So, now that you have all of that in your court, let's end this. You'll know exactly what to do once we're in that condo." She glanced at her phone as it began to ring. "I need to get this. Hang on."

I waited as Nat talked to someone who sounded like a client for one of her listings, and I tried to pull it together. She was right. My hardships were not easy for me to deal with, but the world was an ugly place, and it was much uglier to many other people. I didn't like feeling sorry for myself, and I wasn't going to anymore. So, I nearly bankrupted myself; so fucking what? I was healthy, wasn't I? Better people than I had gone bankrupt and rebuilt their lives.

My pride had been in the driver's seat for too long, and it was time to shut down the pity party it seemed like I was constantly having. I hated being a victim so that shit was going to stop here and now. I was going to pull it together and handle everyone in that room. I didn't have to accept any of their offers if I didn't want to.

"Let's go. Time is of the essence with these creeps!" Nat said, ending her call.

I walked in, and my stomach twisted in knots when I saw my aunts.

"Breanne," Charlize said with her usual dismissive glare. "We didn't expect to see you here."

"Well, it is my place that has made you all go into some bidding frenzy," I answered as Nat and I moved briskly past five people and into my living area.

"You need to accept one of our bids," Max stated.

"I don't *need* to do anything, Max," I said, disgusted with him now more than ever.

What *did* I see in this guy that nearly led me to vow to spend the rest of my life with him? Thank God he was stupid enough to cheat on me and get caught.

"Ma'am," a man in a dark suit approached, "my client is willing to offer twenty percent over the highest offer on your home."

"I'm not sure if she'll love the place or not, but since it's an exclusive open house, I figured you'd want to see it." I'd just sat on my couch when I heard Alex's scratchy and overly humored voice say that to someone. I glanced up to see Dr. Cameron Brandt with a beautiful woman at his side.

When I looked up to see him, Cameron, and the woman—all who were dressed as if they owned the entire county—I saw that Alex's expression didn't match his humorous tone.

"Excuse us," Aunt Blaire snapped. "We were told that we could view this with our bidding partner and—"

"Bidding partner?" I said, standing up. "Just what the hell is going on between you three?"

"It doesn't matter, Ms. Stone," Cameron winked at me while the woman with brilliant blue eyes and black hair offered me a glowing smile. "My future bride and I would like to place an offer ourselves."

"What was it?" Alex smirked at the two, who must've been dragged into this game Alex was playing, and I had no idea what to do now. "Wait, let me guess. The two of you got nasty in the elevator on the ride up here, and that's why you demanded I go up in the other set of elevators."

"That certainly is the reason," the woman smiled at Alex's grin. "I don't know, honey," she patted Cameron's stomach, "after fucking in the elevator, I've been thinking that we might want to start considering a nursery too."

My eyes widened at the woman's language, and I couldn't help but love that my aunts nearly fainted when they heard what she'd said.

"Some women can be so—"

"Beautiful." Cameron stared into his lady's eyes. "Well, I'm thinking that making babies is going to be the best part of marrying you," he said excitedly.

"That and the hospital sex too."

"These two," Alex rolled his eyes and licked his enticing lips. "They're not even married, and I suddenly feel like we're watching a sex video at their wedding."

I shook my head and rolled my eyes. "Please don't," I mouthed when all eyes turned back to Alex, who was sporting a sharp three-piece suit.

"Please do," Nat grinned but was having a difficult time with the two overly handsome gods who'd entered the room. "There's nothing wrong with a good sex tape."

They're all going to be the death of me.

"This is stupid," Max said, glaring at Alex. "How are your and Breanne's wedding plans coming along? Is that why she's selling the place?" He looked over at my aunt. "I'm sure you two know Mr. Grayson. This is the man who demanded Brian sell his business to Mitchell and Associates."

"You're the snake who conned my poor brother?" Charlize snapped.

Alex leveled her instantly with his supreme, dark-business glare. "Aside from what a disgruntled ex-fiancé would have you believe," Alex slid his hands casually into his pockets, "Brian Stone approached *Mr. Mitchell and me.*"

"That's nonsense," Blaire said. "You're one of the wealthiest men in Southern California. I knew your grandfather well."

"Good." Alex's eyebrows shot up, and I could tell I was looking at the vice president of Mitchell and Associates now. "If you knew him well, then you'll understand I was raised by the most skilled investor you've ever had the privilege of knowing. If I make an offer on this place myself, you *will not* be able to touch it."

"You look like him." Blaire seemed to calm somewhat, and if I wasn't losing my mind, I could swear she was in awe of Alex. "I'm sorry to hear about your mother."

"A lovely yet unnecessary sentiment, ma'am," Alex stated firmly enough that it silenced the room. "What are your plans, Cameron?"

"Well, Juliet?" Cameron recovered his somber expression and looked at the woman, bringing her attention back to the handsome doctor. "Are we making babies here or not?"

"All we can afford is the asking price."

I heard snickering coming from my aunts, and Alex stood there, lividly pissed off, watching everyone in the room. I couldn't help but wonder what'd happened to his mother that my aunt knew about.

I looked around the room, seeing all of the people who were here to bid on the place, and my thoughts drifted to when my father and I first walked through this unit together.

"Breanne," I heard my father's voice inside my head as if he were standing in front of me again, *"look at this. It's our first completed vision. You and me, sweetheart. One day you'll sell it, of course..."*

"I'd never sell it. I can't even afford to buy it," I said.

"You know how proud I am of you. You've also proven that you've learned a lot from your hard work, volunteering your extraordinary talents at the company. I'm so proud that my girl focused hard and has graduated at the top of her class."

"I had to bust my ass if I wanted to work for the great Brian Stone, you know?"

I remembered how my dad's handsome face wrinkled in humor, and I missed him more than my heart could express. His beaming smile, white hair, and broad shoulders I loved finding refuge in when I hugged him. I wanted to burst into tears, thinking about that day and knowing that I was faced with the reality of letting this place go.

I didn't know what to do, sell it or not? Maybe I should? I was so confused. The pain of losing my dad felt raw in my heart, and I wanted to collapse into tears.

Alex must've seen the look on my face because he was at my side in an instant.

"Breanne," Nat said in a sympathetic tone as I clung to Alex's side for comfort, "pull the listing. Please."

I felt Alex's lips on my cheek and looked up into his concerned eyes. "Pull it, or I'll make the offer to put a pin in this once and for all."

"What if I rent it out?" I proposed the question as I looked at him.

"And move in with me?" he smirked and kissed my forehead. "I'm down for that. I'll offer you fifty million just to rid you of this nonsense."

"Fifty million?" I heard my aunt scoff.

"Make it seventy," Alex grinned. "Just because that woman annoys me."

"Well, I guess the lovely bride-to-be and I are out," I heard Cameron say, moving closer to where Alex and I sat on the couch.

"I'm pulling the listing." I smiled at Nat, then nodded as professionally as I could at the others in the room. "I can't let this place go, and I won't. This was mine and my dad's baby, the first place we designed together. I won't lose that. Sorry to ruin all of your horrible lives."

"You are an insufferable, spoiled brat. I can't even imagine what your mother would think of you," Charlize said.

"She'd say that her daughter was so beautiful and brilliant that even the harshest of men could be brought to their knees by her beautiful dimples," Alex rubbed my cheek as his eyes searched my face, "and that her daughter rescued a doomed man." He pulled me in tight and brought his lips to my ear. "And that's the fucking truth."

"The house is off the market, and you can all be on your way. Shelby, we'll talk later," Nat said as she moved everyone's unsteady footsteps out of the apartment and closed the door.

"Holy fuck," Nat said, waltzing back in. "Well, now that *that shit* is done and over with," she looked at Cameron and his woman, "I would like to say that it pains me to stand in a room with two beautiful men who are taken by such lovely women."

I heard a scratchy laugh come from Cameron's girl, then watched as she hugged him. "We *do* make a good couple," the woman laughed again. She looked at me. "Are you okay? I'm Avery, Jim Mitchell's wife. He said he knows you and hoped this would all work out."

My eyes widened as I looked at Alex's shit-eating grin. "What?" I stood to shake her hand. "It's very nice to meet you, Mrs. Mitchell."

"Call me Avery." She ruffled the hair on Alex's head. "And after witnessing *this* man do what he just did with you," she clicked her tongue, "I can't believe none of us believed you'd finally find the right woman."

"You can tell Jim I was right about all of this," Alex said, standing at my side. "And that I think you and Cam make a better couple."

"Now, you're asking for Jim to pummel my ass," Cameron laughed, then looked at me. "Are you sure you're okay?"

"Yeah, thanks," I said. "I just started thinking about my dad, and I'd had enough."

"If your father is haunting this place," Nat's eyes widened, "I suggest selling it to the bitchiest aunt in the war." She smiled at Cameron. "I'm Natalia. Please tell me you're hungry for dinner later?"

Cameron grinned. "Unfortunately, I'm going to have to pass on dinner, and I'm already kicking myself for turning down your offer too." He looked at Alex. "All right. Your ass owes me, and I'll see you later."

"I think the score is even, brother," Alex said. "I saved your ass with the board, remember?"

The two men exchanged humored looks, and it was apparent that the good doctor, who seemed just as taken by Nat as she was him at the moment, had some hidden details.

"I'll see you all at the next circus." He waved and then hopped up and out of the room.

"Damn, so close too." Nat smiled at the rest of the room. "Well, moving on past my rejection," she looked at me as we all laughed, "call your broker and pull this place off the market. We'll discuss where we're going with all of this next over coffee."

"He only turned you down because he knows you've met our friend, Mr. Monroe. Sexy Spence?" Alex poked, not letting the subject die.

"Oh, dammit. Mr. Cell phone fucked me over in more ways than one." She shrugged. "Well, it's their loss."

Alex walked over to her. "Isn't that the *damn* truth? Hey, thanks for involving us." He looked at me after giving Nat a half-hug. "Your stubborn butt almost missed out on meeting Jim's wife, seeing Cameron and me again, and of course, burying the bullshit as fast as it fired up."

"I didn't believe it would come to this," I said. "If you two are down, Nat and I are going to get some coffee."

Avery smiled. "We'd love to, but we're visiting Collin, Elena, and baby Alex today. It took a phone call from your friend," she smiled at Nat, "and a little convincing from Alex, and I was happy to come and play games with the jerks. God knows I've met my share of them and speak their language well."

"It's why she was the best for the role," Alex said to Avery. "Though, I still like my idea of Cameron walking in with three women on his arms—all future, hot wives—and ensuring we threw those aunts into a rage."

"You can be so ornery at times," she laughed.

"Okay, then. That's a wrap on drama for the day," I said and reached for Alex's face. "I hope you both came in one car because your AMG One is waiting for you."

"After what you just went through?" Alex laughed. "You earned that car, baby." He leaned down, kissed my lips. "Love you," he softly said, and then he and Avery left, leaving me staring at the beautiful man in awe.

"Did that all just happen?" I questioned.

"I'm asking myself the same thing, and I'm not talking about his friend, either. Alex just said he *loved you?*" she held her heart. "What the hell happened in Malibu?"

I smiled and took her hand in mine. "You know I don't kiss and tell."

"You will," she hugged me and sighed. "Goddammit, I want to know everything from the bruised neck and lips to the mother-fucking I love you."

I wasn't going to give in to Nat's probing, but I couldn't get past him rushing in and moving out the trash so quickly, and most of all, devising a plan with Cameron and Jim's wife.

He was as fun as he was sexy, but I didn't fail to see his expression when my bitch aunt brought up his mom. What did that woman know about Alex that I didn't, and why did it change her tone?

CHAPTER TWENTY-SIX
ALEX

*A*very had my back after I whipped out an *I love you* farewell to Bree as if we'd been together for months, and as to be expected, my best friend's wife peppered me with questions during the drive to Collin and Elena's equine estate in the hills.

My lame-ass smile was a dead giveaway. I don't even think the guys had ever seen me smile like *this* before. Either way, I played games with Avery for the entire ride. It was fun, and it kept my mind off of the lady who'd floored me by mentioning she knew my grandfather and, even stranger, knew what had happened to my mother.

I had no idea what circles Bree's aunt paraded in, but the connection of both my grandfather *and* mother made me wonder how she knew them. Mostly, it made me curious about what the woman knew about my family and me. If she knew about the Graysons, was the woman honoring my grandfather's wishes and leaving the scars of our tortured past where they belong—in the past?

My grandfather passed away many years before Mom's stroke, which was the *only* thing this woman should've known about my mother. My mom left Southern California before I was born and had lived in Arizona ever since. So, this lady should've had no connections to her, and she couldn't have known jack-shit about her stroke.

I started mentally running down lists of people in upper-class families that I knew, wondering if Mom still had ties to them. Instead of riding horses at Collin and Elena's house, I decided to find out what I could about this mystery-woman. My friends were fully engrossed with their kids, using Elena's therapy horses to entertain themselves, and I watched them riding cheerfully in the arena from where I sat at the picnic table.

I was in a fantastic mood, just perplexed as hell. If only my mom were still coherent, I could get the answers I wanted.

"Hey, lover," Jim said, walking over and sitting across from me at the picnic table where I pretended to watch everyone behind my sunglasses.

"Lover? Isn't that what Collin and Jake throw around when they get lost in each other's eyes like the dipshits they are?" I teased, stretching out my legs. I folded my arms and leaned forward on the table.

Jim looked over his shoulder at Collin, who held his newborn son, and at his younger brother, Jake, standing at Collin's side at the rail of the arena. Jake's son was not a fan of these horses, and he sat on his dad's shoulders unashamed about that fact, pointing at everyone else who was enjoying them.

"Yeah, but…" Jim paused and turned back to me. "I only say *lover* because Av alluded to the fact that something's up with you and Breanne." He held up a hand to stop me from saying anything. "Don't think for a second I'm *that* naïve to believe you didn't pack up everything and pull off one of your trademark stunts with Avery and Cameron just because Breanne Stone is your partner."

"That's exactly what I did," I said.

"I know you too well." Jim exhaled. "Spill the beans. You generally don't give a wild fuck about anyone, and after what you did with your partner today, I mean, come on."

I smiled at Jim's wife, knowing she likely couldn't stop herself from mentioning *something* to Jim about me saying I love you to Bree before we left. I couldn't blame her; it probably came as a shock to her as much as it did me when I said it like I'd been using that word forever.

"Fine. I wasn't going to allow Breanne to get buried by her dick of an ex and bitchy aunts."

"It's true, then," Jim said, my eyes not leaving his after he pulled off his sunglasses. "Good God, man. Do you know that if you fuck this up as you did with Summer—"

"Don't bring that woman into this," I sharply cut him off. "Summer and I are over, and you know that it was for a good reason too."

"Well, before you two were over," Jim said firmly, "you strung that woman along and made her believe you were *in love* with her."

"Summer believed what she wanted to fucking believe. If you want to take her dramatic side on this shit, fine. Know this, though: Breanne is unquestionably *nothing* like Summer. They are so opposite of one another that I would never have mentioned those two in the same sentence if it weren't for you comparing them."

"I wasn't comparing them," Jim countered, and then he shrugged his shoulders. "Perhaps I was. The comparison is that they're both women with whom you were involved. You've stated yourself that you are incapable of giving a woman the love she deserves—any woman."

"It all changed, I guess."

"You guess? Jesus Christ, man." He pinched the bridge of his nose in frustration. "Alex, Breanne is your goddamn *partner*. If you fuck this up because you wanted to get laid, I swear I'll kick your ass."

I shook my head. "It's different. Bree's different. I can't explain it, or I would."

"Your response is not convincing me that Monroe and I aren't going to be dealing with a fallout in the future from the co-owners of that firm after you piss off Ms. Stone like you did Summer."

I never aired out the dirty laundry of my messed-up relationship with Summer to anyone—unlike my ex, who told fucking everyone. I shrugged off the bad press the woman gave me, and I couldn't blame my friends for believing her sorry-as-fuck story. Part of it was true. I led her to think I could love her, but I certainly made it known there were no guarantees I could be *that man* in a loving relationship. She knew that and still tried to change me. It only pissed me off and made me more closed off to the woman in the end.

I might as well clear the air with Jim because until I accepted my feelings about Bree, I suspected I'd hurt her too.

"Since I never mentioned the real issues I had with Summer, I guess it's time to set the record straight once and for all. If I don't, you'll continue to believe what she's led everyone to think, and you won't know that my feelings are different with Breanne."

"What *really* went down between you and Summer? You're a closed book about anything personal, and you know I respect that, but I'm concerned that you're going down the same road with your partner of all the people in the world."

I gripped my forehead. I hated talking about personal shit. I was cool to hand out advice and listen to others, but when it came to flipping that coin, I wasn't the man to open up. The scary part about opening yourself up, in my opinion, was that it always led to more questions, and that's where I had to draw the line.

"Summer and I started as fuck-buddies, at least that's how I saw it. She was hot, fun, and a means to an end for a man who wanted to get laid," I started. "I thought she and I were on the same page after I referred to her as such, but she thought she'd captured my heart or whatever the fuck it is she's out there *still* telling everyone."

"I knew that. What I didn't understand is why you got back together with her after she pulled the *I love Alex* bullshit, and you treated her like shit to move her along. Then, you both split up, and I figured my predictions had come true. My best friend had run off a damn good secretary of mine." He laughed.

"Your predictions wouldn't have come true if she would've accepted what I told her when we first started fucking around. There would never be anything more than us fucking, going on the occasional trip, and going out to dinner, and stuff like that. She was good with it until I allowed her to run away with her fantasies about *our future*. It all went to shit when she decided she wanted us to get serious. When I mentioned that's not where I was allowing any of it to go, she rightfully broke things off with me and was *supposed* to move the fuck on."

"Then, she got pissed you were over her and had moved on with that masseuse, and..."

"And after she saw us together, she quit as your secretary."

"Why the hell *did* you get back together with her, then? *Love?*" he asked, taunting me with that word.

I knew what Jim was doing by this point. He was saving Bree the heartache he knew I could deliver. He was also making sure that I didn't make his and Spencer's lives a living hell if I fucked Bree over because I couldn't sink my teeth into a relationship like a normal person would. The man had seen me in my darkest and wildest days, trying to maintain a relationship with his former secretary and then back to selectively using women for my pleasure. I'd also mentioned multiple times I wasn't a man who was capable of loving women. I stood firmly on that and felt convinced about it until a switch had flipped with Breanne.

"Bottom line? I took Summer back, and as you know, she and I tried to make a run at the whole *relationship* thing. So much so, I trusted that bitch by putting her on two of my credit cards as an authorized user. It's when her whole fucking personality changed. She was using my cars, spending my money, and acting like she was one of the Rodeo Drive Housewives. It was beyond ridiculous, and I couldn't handle it anymore."

"When Elena ripped into your ass about you both being wrong for each other in Hawaii, that probably added to your doubts."

"That too. Although by that time, Summer and I were done. She was only there because I'd invited her when I was drunk."

Jim chuckled. "And spouting off that you love Ms. Stone? Still drunk?"

"Now you're just being a dick. I understand your concern. I fucked it all up with your secretary but trust me when I tell you that what I'm feeling for Breanne is as foreign to me as it is for you to try and accept. It's real, and it's fucking too fast, and yet, I don't give a shit what any of you dipshits think about it. She's a beautiful soul inside and out, and I'd be a fucking idiot to look the other direction and expect I'd screw it up with her too. I care about her too much to be the one who hurts her. I fucking love her, man."

Jim's expression was dark and calculating as we both sat in silence before he finally grinned.

"Did you just mutter the words *beautiful soul*? You? Alexander Grayson, my best friend, who doesn't have an emotional bone in his body when it comes to women?"

"I abso-fucking-lutely did," I softly laughed. "See, I can't explain this shit. She's nothing like the women I've dated before. While they've all been superficial, using me and my money for status, Bree is nothing like them. She's got a heart of gold, and her smile is the only thing that's ever put me at a loss for words."

"Well, slap the pig, and spit in the fire. Alex is in *love*," Jim repeated a saying we'd heard some drunk cowboys use at a bar.

The reason for Jim's ridiculous attempt at a Southern accent was that he finally understood I had developed feelings for a woman for the first time since he'd known me.

"It's slap the dog, dumbass. And I see we're back to the wealthy abusing animals again," I smiled at him, knowing responses like that got under his skin.

"Only vocally, friend. Well, shit." He laughed in what seemed to be utter shock. "You know I've asked it more than once, but seriously, what happened to bring all of us these amazing women that we don't deserve?" he asked, glancing at Avery, then back to me.

"Trust me, I know I don't deserve Bree or anything close to the happiness I feel by being around her. It's so fucking surreal, but for now," I pleaded, folding my hands together, "please, for the love of God, allow Breanne and me a week before telling everyone that *Alex is in love*."

"You're no fun," Jim said with a laugh. "Seriously, though, I hope this all works out for you. I really do. You deserve all the happiness in the world, buddy, and I don't say that lightly."

I blew out a breath. "Thanks. Now, let's pray to God that Bree doesn't transform into a snob, steal my money, and label herself as the future missus to everyone she knows." I smirked.

"Summer pulled that shit on you?"

"Yep," I said with disgust. "She told every last idiot she came across that I was going to propose. The worst part was that she dragged my damn cat into the middle of it with adoption shit."

Jim coughed out a laugh. "She definitely changed after she quit working as my secretary." He shook his head. "Fucking hell. Why didn't you tell me any of this shit?"

"Because it sounds enough like a goddamn soap opera as it is. I think she tried to use our engagement to get into the movie industry if I remember correctly."

"She most likely did," he teased. "That old money name of yours moves mountains."

My mind drifted back to Breanne's aunt, and I wondered if Jim knew the woman. It was a rare occasion if Jim knew someone I didn't, but it was worth a shot.

"Hey, I wonder if you know someone," I said. "You might not, and I was too thrown off my game to ask for a last name."

"Try me," he said.

"Two of Breanne's aunts were at her condo today."

"Yeah, Av said they looked and sounded every bit of the nasty crows you made them out to be when she went off to claim Cameron as her future husband."

"I'm curious as to who they are. Bree mentioned they play around in some exclusive circles, and one of them mentioned that she knew my grandfather, and she also said something about my mother."

Jim frowned. "Damn, you won't even speak your birth surname to me. How would I know Breanne's late father or mother's sister's last name? Maiden names for these women, no less."

"Right," I chewed on my lip. "I hate to bounce on everyone, but—"

"You're not bowing out with that fucked up death tone in your voice."

"I have to know how that woman knew my grandfather and how she knew my mom had a stroke."

"Well," Jim's eyes widened, "if you're *so in love* with Breanne Stone, text her and find out."

"I don't want her to question my past. You know I don't go there, and I won't."

"Has she questioned it yet? I mean, if you're in love with her, don't tell me something came up to have you push that shit down like you always do."

"She didn't press me for any additional information after she found out that Grayson is my adopted name."

"So, she's in the same mystery boat we all row in, then?"

"And you will all keep rowing," I smiled at Jim. "Trust me, if this shit surfaces, I'll probably go nuclear and get thrown into a mental institution when I'm confronted with it all again."

"Painful past, strong man?" Jim said, somewhat annoyed I wasn't giving up secrets of my shitty past. "That's how you pulled her off your ass, right? Your *go-to* quote?"

"It's not my go-to quote, fuckhead," I smiled. "It's the truth."

"You're probably in witness protection because when you were a child, you witnessed a mob hit, and you had to testify against the mafia boss, and you've been on the run ever since. Your real name is probably something like Pauly O'Russo, and you're originally from Brooklyn," Jim said, looking at me with prying eyes as if to confirm his ridiculous conspiracy theory.

"O'Russo, huh? I'm Irish and Italian at the same time?" I asked, rolling my eyes.

"You look like you could be either, so why not?" Jim said with a grin.

"Well, you caught me. Don't tell Tony Soprano where I am, or else," I teased.

"I knew it. If I get whacked because of you, I'm going to come back and haunt you," Jim said with a shrug.

I rolled my eyes and laughed as I texted Bree for her aunts' last names.

Dimples: *Charlize Foster and Blaire Gandy are their married names. Morris is the maiden name. Why?*

Alex: *Mother's sisters? Or married into the family? The one referred to your dad as her brother.*

Dimples: *She says that for the status, and she's a bitch. They're actually my mom's sisters. Why, though?*

Alex: *Ancestry stuff. You know, making sure we're not related.*

Dimples: *WTF?*

Alex: *Gotta get that shit out of the way if I'm in love with you today and proposing to you tomorrow.*

Dimples: *Oh God. Get over yourself. See you tomorrow.*

I SMILED at her response to the marriage joke. Shit like that would've had my clingy-ex texting back seven hundred heart emojis and happy-tear faces in response. I loved the fact that Bree saw through the nonsense. I also knew I'd gained her interest now, and I seriously didn't want to bring up the past. Maybe I should just fucking let it all ride. Who gave a shit about who knew my grandfather or knew that Mom had a stroke? But fuck me to hell, that woman had a look in her eye that made me more curious about her than I could imagine she was about me.

"All good?' Jim asked.

"Yeah. Blaire Foster and Charlize Gandy." I looked at Jim. "Not ringing any bells on my side of the table. How about you?"

"They have maiden names? Foster and Gandy aren't much to work with if the one knew your grandfather."

"Morris."

"That name isn't connecting any dots for me either," Jim answered.

"Fucking hell. How did that woman know who my grandfather

was, but we don't know who the fuck she is? That man hung in the same circles with your dad, Brandt's family, Monroe, Brooks...all of them."

"I haven't a clue. Gandy is familiar, but I think that's a client that you fucked over."

"Jesus Christ," I said. "Matthew Gandy. I saw right through his bullshit. There was no fucking way I'd let you invest in that company."

"No shit, and that's why the man left pissed, and his wife was held off by security in the lobby of Mitchell and Associates."

"What the hell was the wife's name?" I asked.

"At the time, I couldn't give a shit, but now, that's the million-fucking-dollar question," Jim said. "Text Bree back and ask her."

"You know that by doing this, I'm asking Breanne to peel me open like a fucking onion."

"If you love this woman as you say you do, trust her to answer you, and let her in just a fucking little, man. It's fine if you don't confide everything into me, but I'm not your future wife." He winked to soften the blow I knew he was about to give. "Bree needs to be aware of your past, or you might as well end it all now. Secrets suck and you know that."

"I won't keep *secrets* from her, but I know what I'm doing when it comes to delivering information about things that don't need to be reopened."

"Ask Breanne who the aunt's husband is," Jim grinned. "Stop running around with your excuses and get answers."

Alex: *Is Matthew Gandy your uncle?*

Dimples: *By marriage. I hate that man! Why the sudden family questions?*

Alex: *Curious as to why I struck a nerve with your aunt Blaire. It also looks like I'm the reason Charlize is pissed your wedding didn't work out with that fucker.*

Dimples: *???*

Alex: *I'm the reason she's fucking broke*

Dimples: *LMFAO! No shit? When you worked at Mitchell? You didn't buy into their business scheme, eh?*

Alex: *Nope. Had security take her ass out of there too.*

Dimples: *I think I'm more in love with you now.*

Alex: *Enjoy the night, Dimples. Love you*

"Well, if it isn't our sweet Alex who's in *love*," Elena said, sitting next to me and placing baby Alex in my arms. "Your Uncle Alex is in love with your godmother, little man." She rubbed my back briskly.

Jim shrugged and laughed. "You're the one who let it slip in front of Av."

"Of course, you'd defend her," I teased.

"Hey," Elena kissed my cheek. "I told you that one day you'd find love with *the right one*. Look at this softer, lighter Alex that you've become. You've lost your mind if you think we're all blind and can't see this *cheeky little grin*." She pinched my cheek. "I'm so happy for you. Now, take your little namesake, and let's bring this party inside. I'm starving, and he's waking up soon to eat too."

"Should we let Alex feed him?" Jim laughed after Addison, his oldest child, ran up to him.

"Let's not freak him out too soon," Elena said, then she gripped my shoulder. "It had to be baby Alex who brought you both together. See? I was right about that too. I told you to marry her, and you will." She gave me her usual wink and met Collin's tall frame with a tight hug.

"What is Alex all smiles about?" Collin asked, eyeing me.

"Dead giveaway, man. The always firm and unwavering one is now smiling like a little girl who just got a pony? You're fucked." Jim laughed and stood.

He wasn't wrong about that. I was going to hear shit about this too, but what the hell. If I were in love, I'd better face the music and own that shit like I felt it. If I didn't, I'd be sitting and getting questioned all night, and I just got done with my *interview with Jim*, so I wasn't about to do that shit again.

It was time for drinks anyway, and I could use a stiff one.

CHAPTER TWENTY-SEVEN
BREE

I'd arrived at work early, and while I was sifting through potential renters for my condo, the scent of Alex's cologne announced that he was on the top floor before seven in the morning as well. I tucked the papers away as soon as I heard him talking with our vice president Jacey, and their voices were getting closer to my office door.

"Good morning, Bree," Jacey said with a smile. "How's it going?"

As usual, our shared vice president seemed always to ask questions, and before you could answer her, she was out of sight. I smiled, and I noticed Alex was trailing her, head down and face in his phone. Before I started talking business with anyone this morning, I needed to call Nat about this list of renters she'd sent over.

"Nat," I whispered when my best friend picked up, "this is all we have? I don't want the place to go public. Not after what happened yesterday."

"You woke me up to ask me about renters? I sent that over last night. I'm sure I can ask around. I do not doubt that some corporate suit will need a temporary rental anyway."

"I woke you up because I know what you're trying to do."

"Oh. My. God," she grumbled. "Goodbye, Bree. Oh," she suddenly perked up, "and don't forget about tonight."

"How could I?" I smiled into the phone. "Do you think Robert proposed?"

"I know he did," Nat's voice was her usual tone of excitement. "And that's why you're living with me until your bills get caught up."

"I thought I was only living with you so that Alex could bring one of his friends over," I softly laughed.

"That too, and you're eventually going to give up the dirty details about you two in Malibu." She yawned. "Don't think that you going to bed prematurely last night went unnoticed. I'd bet good money that you were sexting Mr. Sexy-lips last night."

"Goodbye, Nat," I said.

I nearly threw the fifty pages of real estate off my desk when I saw Alex standing in my doorway in a nicely pressed white shirt, suspenders, and black slacks.

He folded his arms and eyed the papers floating slowly around me after I'd panicked for some stupid reason.

"And here I thought we worked all the secretive kinks out of your system." His closed lips pulled up on one side. "Which new lie is in the documents wafting around you?"

"No lies, just paperwork."

"Come on, Bree." He seemed more annoyed than anything as he walked into the room after closing the door behind him. "Who are these people?" he asked, looking at the list I'd been sifting through.

"It's a list of renters that I'm considering for my place."

He sat across from me and crossed a leg over his knee, thumbing through the papers. "Would you like my opinion on this?"

"No."

"Too bad. I'm giving it," he responded.

"I'm not moving in with you."

He grinned. "You will in time. For now, I have a better candidate for your place."

I folded my hands together and placed them on my desk. "Oh? Is Dr. Brandt interested in a short-term lease?"

"Brandt's not interested in short-term, so he's out."

"This is news."

"Not really," Alex said dismissively, then set the stack of papers he'd put back together neatly on my desk. "Out of all the people in that paperwork, the one who's in for the short-term lease has a smoking-hot boyfriend, who still has the battle scars to prove how much he wants her after he wasn't finished with her over the weekend."

I felt heat rush to my cheeks and saw Alex's grin in response to me, giving myself away.

"Oh, that's my renter?"

"Correct. She even had me write a check for her first and last month's rent. Let's just say the deposit should take care of everything for a year's rent, and that is if she doesn't get married and move out like she insisted she would."

I looked at the six zeros on the check and narrowed my eyes at Alex's unwavering expression. "Looks like she just broke it off with her boyfriend or her future fiancé."

"Her future fiancé is going to break it off with her if she wants to be stubborn and argue." He leaned his elbow on the armrest and rested his face against his chin.

"This is all very adorable, but come on," I said, done with speaking about myself in the third person.

"This isn't charity, nor is it me *helping* you out. It's me giving you a head start out of this financial strain and keeping you in your home because I'm simply in love with you."

I sighed. "Alex…"

"Knock that *Alex* shit off," he said, standing up. "You're keeping your place, and once we become more serious, and you finally trust how much I love you, that's when I'll pay the rest of it off—that's if you're still buried in debt. Until then, you have a year to keep the condo up and running. That check covers all your utilities, what a renter would pay you per month, and gas for that piece of shit car I bought you on Saturday."

"I love that car now. I might keep it too." I blushed. "Well, would you look at me?" I let out a breath with a laugh. "I admitted the truth to you."

"It's because you're admittedly in *love* with me," he winked. "All right. Now that's all settled; I have a meeting with HR in an hour. You want in on it, or do you want to wait and hear the highlights at lunch with me?"

"Damn it. I promised myself I wasn't going to dodge the BS part of the job." I tapped my fingers on my desk.

"Don't worry about it. Jacey will be sitting in on it anyway. I'd rather you share your vision for the pediatric wing with the architects on the Saint John's job. We already decided you've got what it takes to make this place stand out as it used to when John Brooks was running the show. I just wanted to inform you in case HR meetings were an easier way to give you the excuse to stare at me with lustful eyes."

"Hey," I said after he turned to leave, and the mask of *Alex, the businessman,* had replaced the man I'd fallen in love with. I was a bit uneasy that I didn't argue with him after his nonchalant proposal of offering me help. Still, I was done trying to act like I had any other options, and it was time to start being grateful and stop being bullheaded. Not everything needed to be so difficult, and after everything, I knew I needed to get out of my own way.

"What, dimples?" He smiled in response to my vibrant one. "I have to get my ass out of here, or people are going to *talk*," he dramatically mocked my request to keep our so-called relationship between us, "and we can't have them talking, especially after they notice that badass car that you're set on keeping. You know I couldn't give a damn if I tried about what people think, right?"

"Get your snarky and sexy butt over here," I said, coming around my desk only to be met with an overzealous kiss that pulsated throughout my body.

Alex gripped me, pinned me against the wall, and an array of delicious tastes thoroughly assaulted me. It was his hair styling products that reminded me of the expensive shampoo at his Malibu place, his robust yet woodsy cologne, and the delicious taste of his natural scent that could only be found in a heated kiss like this one.

His lips went below my chin, and then he stopped when laughter erupted from his chest. "I love the *guard* you've put up to prevent me from bruising your neck again." He pressed his lips against mine after his lips couldn't reach my neck because of the high-collared dress I wore to hide my hickeys. "I've been thinking about that and how to make it up to you since I enjoy devouring your body."

"Oh, yeah?" I said as I brushed my thumb over his moist lips. "What's your bright idea?"

"You'll find out tonight at *your home*. There, I plan to show you exactly where I'll be devouring your flesh, and that location won't bruise as easily."

I gulped, knowing what he was implying. It was too early for me to get worked up and wet over Alex, yet my body felt like we should be sharing a bourbon at his place and reliving sunrises in Malibu.

"Oh, no. I have plans after work," I said. "I have to go out with the girls tonight. We think my friend Sammy is announcing that her boyfriend proposed to her. Do you know Robert Kinder?"

Alex turned to open my door after Jacey knocked. He looked back at me. "Bobby Kinder? Is he Julietta and Thomas Kinder's son?"

"Please, God, tell me you don't have bad blood with him. He's like a big brother to me."

"No, not at all. He's a good guy. I didn't think he lived here anymore, though. The bastard didn't tell us he's back and dating my lady's girl."

"What?" Jacey croaked hoarsely, and she looked at me as if Alex had run over her cat.

"Do you know him?" I questioned the beautiful woman.

After what'd happened with Max getting caught before our wedding day, I'd inwardly hoped sweet Jacey wasn't going to be the wedding-wrecker in my best friend's worst-case scenario. It was apparent to all of us that an engagement announcement was happening tonight, especially after Sammy tried to hold us off from prying questions.

"No." She shook off her suddenly odd vibes when Alex looked at her questioningly.

"You sure about that?" Alex asked. "Because you're sure as hell acting like Breanne or I just said something that's about to make you lose your breakfast all over my expensive shoes."

"I thought she was talking about another Kinder. I mean, um..." She readjusted her glasses, cheeks red as she looked at Alex, then exhaled when she looked at me. "Listen, I'm getting everything ready for the meeting, but I'm not feeling very well. I'm probably going to go home unless you need me today."

For the first time since meeting Alex, I saw the man look as confused as I felt. "I swear to God, Jacey, if something's up, you'd better tell me," he said in a soft tone. "Jesus, you seriously look like you could use some water or something."

I walked over to her, eyeing Alex's shocked expression, and led her to my desk. "Your hands are clammy," I said, sitting her in my chair, "and you're as white as a ghost. This has to do with something we were just talking about, doesn't it?"

Her eyes filled with tears, then she smiled at me. "It's nothing. I sort of had this lame crush on Bobby Kinder. I met him when he waited on my table. I didn't realize he was in a relationship."

"Did he lead you to believe he could return your feelings for him? How long ago was this? He's lived here for at least a year, so I'm not sure why Alex hasn't been in touch with him if they're friends like that."

"As I said, it's nothing, and no, he's not cheating on your friend." She smiled at me. "Damn, I guess all the good ones are taken."

"I used to say that all the time." I eyed Alex standing with concern on his face behind her. "Trust me when I say that when the right one comes along, you'll be thankful the others were taken. Or, in my case, you'll be happy you got cheated on, and you broke it off before you ruined your life with the wrong one. You'll find your man. Nothing to get this upset over."

"I'm sure I will." She fanned herself. "I'm going to splash some water on my face or something and pull myself together. That was kind of weird."

She rushed out of the room, leaving Alex and me to stare at each other more confused than anything.

"Kind of weird?" Alex said. "Not to be harsh, but up until now, I didn't think that woman could be shaken."

"Oh, shit." I sighed and shook my head. "This wasn't about Bobby Kinder; it's about you—about *us*." I narrowed my eyes at Alex. "*This* is why we're not telling anyone about us. Good God, we almost killed Jacey with you saying *your lady's girl.*"

"You know what? This is precisely why they need to know," Alex became firm. "Fucken-A. Now, I have to deal with this shit, and I'm not in the mood for it."

"You think *I* am?"

"I didn't say you were, Breanne," Alex snapped.

"What happened to you mocking me and saying you couldn't give a damn what people think? Obviously, Jacey being upset made you worried."

"Not about us. If she wants to cry at a bar tonight because she magically believed I would entertain her as anything more than my vice president, then that ridiculous shit is on her."

"You can be such a prick; you know that?"

"It's not grade school, Breanne," Alex shot back. "How am I the bad guy in this?"

"You most likely led her on. Christ, how can you not see that she thought you probably felt the same way about her?"

"As I said," Alex's expression was dark and searing, "I did absolutely nothing to lead her on. Fuck me for being a nice owner and allowing a young woman to work as my next in line. Jesus, I'm *not* the bad guy here."

I could sense this was something more significant to Alex. It was about more than Jacey losing her shit about us being together. He was acting too dickish to make me think otherwise.

"Did something happen between the two of you before we merged the companies?" I asked, wondering if that could've been the reason Jacey was so easily triggered.

Alex's leveling glare made me swallow the lump it'd conjured in my throat. I wasn't backing down, though. What if he'd had a fling with her? He was known for dating Jim Mitchell's former secretary. I was trying my hardest not to judge him, but sometimes the past sneaks up and bites you in the ass when you least expect it.

"No, and though she was tempting to my callous and asshole self before I met you and found I wasn't a doomed-dick after all, I wouldn't allow that. She's like my fucking little sister, and that's why all of this is so goddamn disturbing. You judging me, yet again, doesn't help either."

"I'm not trying to, Alex," I said, crossing my arms, "but face it, you're an extremely attractive man. You must not have meant for this to happen, but it did. I'll try and talk to her. We can't lose her."

"I'll talk to her," he insisted.

"In *this* mood? You might as well have a detective grill her about being wrongfully attracted to you."

"Do what you have to do," he said. "I have a meeting to run and a job to go over. Lunch is still on unless you'd rather spend that time nursing Jacey's broken heart back to health."

"We'll see how the day goes. For now, get some coffee or something. Your attitude sucks."

"My attitude is reflecting the fact that Jacey has made me out to be some office man-whore, and that pisses me off. If she quits, she quits."

Alex was out of the room before I could respond to him. How the hell were we to manage this? I was officially in agreement that we should not keep the fact that we were together a secret, but I felt like shit for throwing Jacey's situation on Alex. What I'd asked him was presumptuous and shitty. He hadn't set out to hurt her, and I trusted that he knew nothing about the fact that it would crush her if she learned he was with me.

I desperately wanted to find a way to keep her around. Sadly, before noon, she'd sent her resignation letter, and even though I tried, I couldn't get her to stay. Now, I was pissed at her for storming out on an excellent job, whether her excuse of missing home in New York was valid or not. She admitted that she thought Alex and she had a thing, and finding out it was all in her imagination was enough for her to reach her limit. She was packed up and gone before I could even say good-bye.

"I need the sales and marketing teams in conference room B in five," Alex announced while I worked with the architects to start in on the 3D scale of the butterfly gardens at Saint John's.

"What's going on?" I asked, following Alex out of the room.

"The meeting is in five minutes if you're curious," he curtly said.

"Don't be a dick to me. I didn't know."

"You wouldn't, though, would you? We're back to judging me again, so that throws me back to *proving* myself. I don't have time for that. Our VP walked out in tears today, and I'm sure that after you saw her letter and watched her leave, you allowed her to cry on your shoulders about how it was my fault, yes?"

"I'm not dignifying that with a response."

"Of course, you're not. The meeting is in four minutes. I expect those teams in that room."

I watched him walk off, and Alex seemed to be more of an enemy now than ever. The worst part was that I felt like shit for accusing him. We'd have to talk later, and I would sit in on that meeting.

WITHIN FIVE MINUTES, we were all sitting in the room with Mr. Iron-Fist himself. His face was black with anger, and the mystery of what these teams did to put this expression on his face was about to be revealed.

"Who sold the Fittyship property?"

I eyed the room and saw that most people were sitting here as if they were waiting for Alex to fire them at a moment's notice.

"Am I sitting at this table talking to cardboard cutouts of my employees, or have you all lost your voices?" he questioned. "Who sold that property?"

"I did, Mr. Grayson," a young woman said. "It was a fantastic deal, and it works for the Fittyship family. They're having their home built in that location."

He pursed his lips and narrowed his eyes at her. "Did you visit the site? Who was the agent who offered such a fantastic deal?"

"Brendan Straight."

"I thought we were working with Natalia." Alex looked at me as if I were the reason that we'd bought a property that could never be developed without thousands of rocks being blasted out of the hillside in an area that was prone to mudslides. This was a washout. We'd never get the permits for this place.

"We are," I answered.

"Then why did you go outside of our exclusive agents and work with some random person I've never heard of before? He sold you a property that cannot be developed. Did you know that? Was Tish your manager before this?"

"No. David Hudson is," she answered, looking at the man sitting next to me.

"Why would you approve this?" I asked him. "This is a complete loss for our company, and good luck trying to sell the property to anyone."

"How much are we under with this, and was there an architect working with you?" Alex directed his question back to the woman who'd purchased the property, and from what I saw on the cut sheet, she was using the firm to buy it with the promise to build on it."

"I believed I could entice the Fittyship family to work with Brooks and Stone by purchasing the property in good faith," she responded.

"So, you didn't run this past any of us? Unless you knew about it, Mr. Hudson?"

"I told her to use it as leverage," David responded.

I sucked in a breath of anger while Alex's expression didn't change —but anyone would've been a damn fool to think he wasn't fuming.

"Do I look like a man who wears a clown suit to work?" Alex asked. "Do I appear to be handing out cotton candy like I work at the goddamn circus?"

"This is inexcusable," I said. "David, you will find a way to recover the losses."

"David, you will turn in your resignation letter, or you'll be fired for negligence, costing this firm 1.3 million dollars in useless land." Alex pulled out another piece of paper. "Why is it that we're suddenly trying to develop every last inch of real estate on Southern California's coast? Here's another piece of shit purchase from Rachelle Sanders. Again, rock blasting and mudslide land. Who was your agent? David," he stopped the man from leaving the room, "did you approve this as well?"

"I approved everything that you're firing me for, Mr. Grayson."

"Without looking at any of this?" Alex questioned him. "Why would you be so trusting of a sales agent we never approved?"

"I wanted to bring in profits before the quarter is out," the man answered.

Alex didn't falter with the man's broken response. "Well, your profits have thrown my margins in the red. Now, I'm up to 7.5 million in property that people get to stand on, or perhaps they can have a picnic lunch on the side of the road as the waves crash into the rocks below them that we can't blast. These are just two examples of our deficit in sales this month. Your negligence has taken this firm's profits by forty-five million dollars. Are you trying to bury us?"

"No, sir."

"Then how do we sell an ocean-front property without it being worth anything more than staking a claim on it?" He reached for his phone. "Call Natalia Hoover," he commanded his cellphone, saying Nat's name as if she were in trouble for this too. "Natalia, this is Alex Grayson, and I need you as our exclusive agent. No sales will occur by my team unless they go through you. I have no idea what happened to the man you recommended, but I need to know if you will sign an exclusive agreement to work with my sales teams."

Jesus Christ, Alex was on the warpath and not letting up anytime soon. He was handling shit, but this was the second time I'd seen the dark edge of the man that everyone feared—the guy I had previously referred to as Satan in a suit. I didn't think there was any rebounding from this, but what I did know was that Nat wasn't one to be shoved around, and if she felt Alex was too pushy, she wouldn't hesitate to hang up on his ass.

"All right. Well, if Monroe is here," it was the first time I'd seen Alex smile since the devil washed over his personality, "then you and I both know he's seeing what he's missing out on after hours. You too."

He set his phone down and eyed the room. "David, sit your ass back down," he said to the man he'd pretty much fired five seconds ago. "You have two options. You can walk out of here and hope you land a job to match what we *overpay* our employees for their work, or you can work with Natalia Hoover to dump these properties and replace them immediately with properties that your clients can build on. We don't do cheap. Ever. I am not impressed with cheap shit. I'm impressed with the best and nothing less than that. In everything, even in my personal life and preferences," he looked at me, his eyes darker than the night, "you will find that I *only* entertain the best whatever the cost. I'm an extremely picky man, so whatever I see in your purchases better be more impressive than the Taj Mahal. Am I clear on this? I swear I will lose my shit with the next faulty purchase any of you make. If you have one in mind, Natalia has agreed to work with us and will be in at three this afternoon. Speak with her and handle this trash. That's all."

Alex left the room in a rush as if he were taking his pissed-off mood to his next victim. I followed him out, annoyed that these people didn't seem to get it the first time we had a meeting like this.

I still felt like shit for calling Alex out for Jacey's broken heart. That was a low blow, and I knew it. I knew he wasn't happy about her leaving. He was as upset about it as I was—maybe even more.

"Alex?" I said, walking into his office to see him staring between the three monitors on his desk.

"Bree," he absently said. "What do you need?"

I sat across from him. "To apologize. I did it again, and I'm sorry."

"Don't apologize. You did nothing wrong."

"I made it seem like it was your fault for Jacey quitting. And I agree, we shouldn't hide our relationship."

Alex subtly smiled while he clicked around on the monitor he was looking at. "Thank God because I'm not the best liar," I finally heard humor in his voice. "I know you're an expert in the art of lying, but I'm not."

"I can see that. You were pretty clear in that room."

"I was just handling things as usual. David can thank *you* for still having a job," he said with a smile. "All I needed was to see your face, and it saved him from the fact that I know he doesn't deserve the job for being as careless as Tish was."

"My face."

"Yep, and the fact that we're exactly where I want us to be," he finally glanced at me and flashed a sexy smile.

"Where's that?"

"In love, and I think I'm going to take advantage of this apology you're giving me and use it as an opportunity to call for make-up sex."

"Ah," I grinned, feeling my tight nerves soften from being tense since Jacey wigged out on us today. "So, I guess we had our first fight, and make-up sex is the only natural progression."

"You recall what *our* make-up sex is, correct?"

"I recall what our *angry-sex* was. Maybe I'll keep you pissed off at me." I smiled at the softer expression he wore.

"I was never angry with you." He glanced back up from his computer monitors. "I was more upset with myself. I'm not guarded enough, and even though I pride myself in reading people, I got it all wrong with Jacey. Jim and Monroe are going to speak with her."

"You really think she's moving to New York?"

"I know she wanted this firm to advance her career, so who knows? Maybe she's headed back to Manhattan to make some miracles happen."

"Could be."

"Perhaps we try out angry sex?"

"Depends on who's mad?" I teased him. "Am I climbing the walls or just getting it good from behind?"

"If you keep talking like that, you're getting *that* here and now. Otherwise, when do you think you'll be done with dinner tonight?"

"I have no idea," I answered truthfully. "You're more than welcome to wait for me at the condo you've helped me keep, though."

He smiled at me. "Text me if you're up for it. Otherwise, tomorrow night, we're doubling up on angry sex, make-up sex, and you-made-me-wait, sex."

"You're just horny."

He chuckled, doing math or whatever on his computers. "As I said, I never got to finish what we started at sunrise." He looked at me. "The one who should be sorry is me. Let's just move on."

"I'll get you a key to my place. We both know you're paying to stay there anyway."

"I'll have a bath drawn, candles lit, and wine brought over."

"Make sure to warm the chocolate," I teased. "Because after all those various types of sex we're going to have, I'm going to have to lick chocolate off your sexy dick," I mouthed that word, now having Alex's full attention, "and ensure it gets a delicious massage while I curb my chocolate craving."

"I just might allow you to give me that unique massage," he grinned. "All right, I have to finish pulling more numbers, or I'll be working on this until tomorrow night."

"I'll text you when I'm heading home after dinner," I said as I turned to leave.

"I'll make sure your chocolate dessert doesn't let you down."

CHAPTER TWENTY-EIGHT
ALEX

I shot up in bed, drenched in sweat, hands trembling, and my heart practically pounding in my head. My breaths were short, and if I didn't calm the fuck down this instant, I was going to hyperventilate.

"Jesus Christ." My head fell back against my pillows as I worked to steady my breathing. "Fuck!" I growled, frustrated that this crippling and terrorizing sleep disorder had returned for the third time this week.

I couldn't lie here and stay in my drenched with sweat sheets for another second. I took a long shower, allowing the water to rain down over my tense muscles until they finally began to loosen. I hadn't had this *sleep phenomenon* occur so frequently in a long time, though they were never far away.

As a young kid, I had no idea what to make of them. All I knew was that that it felt like the hell hounds were coming for me to drag me to hell where my dad insisted that I belonged. The terrors hadn't changed for as long as I could remember. I would wake up terrified, not recalling my dream or whatever the fuck had happened while I slept to awaken me in this state.

I didn't want to succumb to the notion that this was happening because I was finally happy, and this was the universe's sick joke that I didn't deserve it—a quick reminder that I was never too far from the darkness that'd haunted me since I was a boy.

I'd spent many nights out of the last two weeks with Bree either at my place or hers, and luckily, these nightmares hadn't occurred when I was with her. At this rate, however, I was beginning to wonder when my luck would run out. The last thing I wanted was to stay away from her for the purpose of having my night terrors go unquestioned, but I'd found myself making small excuses to go home because I was afraid of this happening.

For the first time, I felt liberated from the belief that I wasn't capable of loving someone, and that was the most significant breakthrough of my life. I'd embraced every ounce of the meaning of the word. I was in love with the woman and finally *feeling* something aside from being a cold-hearted dick.

Maybe the thing that increased these episodes was the fact that I was going to be flying to San Diego to see my sister. It was the only other reason I could think of that would kick my subconscious into this gear, waking me up in this panicked, trembling state so frequently. It'd never been the case before, but I was desperate to blame these on anything else.

I'd prepped for a week to be in San Diego. Most of my time there was to be spent meeting with a team of our architects on a job that was close to missing a deadline and costing the firm money.

I wasn't expecting to see my sister on this trip, but she'd surprised me with a call yesterday, telling me she was home on leave with the Marines she flew with in Miramar.

So, I called Bree and asked her to hold down the fort for an extra day, so I could surprise my sister by standing with the families that waited for the jets to come in from the carrier.

I didn't see my sister often when she was on leave for two reasons: one was because I didn't live all that close to San Diego, and the other, more important reason was that we didn't have much to talk about aside from how fucked we both would've been if she didn't join the military, and I hadn't gone to live with our grandfather.

Bree gladly took over our business in L.A. for the week, and even though I desperately wanted her to meet my sister, it was probably best that she stayed home since we didn't have a VP to run things for an entire week. If there were any hang-ups because of contractors or bullshit regarding building permits, that was more in my wheelhouse to handle than Breanne's. One thing was for sure, though; I was going to miss the hell out of that woman.

AFTER THE CHOPPER RIDE DOWN, I jumped into the car that awaited me, and I wasted no time getting to the marine aviation base in Miramar. My crazy morning that'd started by trying to kick my ass mentally had changed entirely when I was let through the gates and funneled into where family members awaited the arrival of their loved ones. I had to admit that, surprisingly, I was excited to see my sister. Part of me thought that maybe opening myself up to Bree meant opening myself up to feeling everything, all of my emotions. I had to be honest; I liked it. There was a sense of freedom that I felt in my soul. The only thing that concerned me about that was that my night terror was a reminder that the darkness was never far away.

I saw all the families waiting for their loved ones, especially the baby girl who was about to meet her father for the first time since he was deployed before she was born. The energy was electric with nerves of excitement and anticipation, and that energy was radiating through the entire hangar as we waited for the jets to fly in. This was what it was like to be there for a family member who'd left home to serve their country, to greet them with gratefulness and welcome them back home where they belonged.

Part of me felt bad that I was the only one Jane had to welcome her home after a long deployment, doing God knows what in her fighter jet overseas. This was the only time I'd ever stood out here and watched her come home. She'd never had anyone wait for her before, and the thought of that made me feel oddly horrible—mainly because it'd never even occurred to me until now that she was always doing this alone.

The sound of jets flying in formation at high speeds silenced the group. I watched as older couples clutched each other's hands while their sons brought in their jets, and the reunion couldn't seem to come fast enough for them. As I studied the beauty of the families who were there for their children, I realized that my sister deserved to have a healthy mom and dad waiting alongside me as she touched down and brought the fighter jet to a stop.

I watched this private air show in awe, the jets landing one after the other until they were all taxing along their runway, and we were able to stand outside with the marines who worked at the base. The soldiers were in stiff and sound formation, hands behind their backs as they welcomed home their family of fighter pilots.

I was honored to be related to one of the first women Marine fighter pilots and the only woman fighter pilot from this base. My sister wouldn't settle for less when it came to getting what she wanted, though. She was an active-duty marine fighter pilot and Miramar's first woman to be stationed on this base. I couldn't have been prouder of her.

As the jets parked, you'd think I'd have been more fascinated with the super hornet she flew; instead, I was more thrilled that my sister was stepping out of that badass jet.

Jane walked in the center of the line of men as if she were their sister, and I smiled when I watched her cheerfully nudge an excited pilot at her side. She had no idea I was here, watching her with more pride than I could handle, and then our eyes locked.

I grinned when the other pilots took off to their loved ones, and Jane stopped with a look on her face that made me laugh in response. I knew my sister well enough to know that she was trying to figure out what had possessed me to show up to her homecoming.

Jane resumed her walk, and I met her with the same excitement and shock she carried that I was here. I was so damn proud, excited, and honored all at the same time, and that was expressed by meeting my laughing sister, hugging her, and spinning her in the air. She laughed harder at my dramatics, knowing I was most likely mimicking what was happening all around us.

"Put me down, you idiot!" she said and then raised her hand to my face and pinched my cheek. "Look at you, Alex Logan!"

"You know I hate when you talk to me like that. I'm about to leave you here."

"That would just make me think that this was some crazy dream, one where my little brother *actually* came to greet me on base."

I arched my eyebrow at her in her flight suit and gear, her curly blond hair pulled back tightly into a bun, looking every bit as badass as she was. "So, how was the flight in, Lieutenant O'Connor?"

She pulled her sunglasses back on and grinned. "The pilot sucked. I could've sworn that bitch was going to fuck up the landing and kill us all."

I wrapped an arm around her neck, and she gripped my side. Damn, it was good to be with my sister again. I'd never felt this way before when she would return from deployment either. Fuck, maybe I was the damn tin man, and Bree had managed to pull a Dorothy and get me a heart from the Wizard of Oz finally.

"Hey, Genius," she said to a man who'd just finished saluting a group of military men, "get your ass over here, and meet my baby brother."

The tall man walked over and tucked his sunglasses into his jumpsuit pocket. "Nice to meet the only family member we know about," he extended his hand and smirked at Jane. "Ace here thinks it's funny to fuck around and claim our sorry asses as her family. That's outside of you, of course. Alex, is it?"

"Ace?" I grinned at Jane. "Don't you guys have to do some crazy shit to get these names?"

"She flies with an ace up her sleeve." He grinned at Jane, and I could easily sense that he and Jane either had an intimate history or were in the middle of creating one. Unfortunately, Jane was a lot like me when it came to keeping people away emotionally. Well, like I was before Bree. Love was *not* a word that came out of our mouths, thanks to the fucked-up home life we both left behind. "We can't even lock her ass in drills."

"And Genius," Jane seemed to blush when she smiled up at him.

"Well, he's just a goddamn Genius. He's got the ultimate skill in everything."

"I'll bet," I said to see how the two would respond.

Just as I'd imagined, my sister was fucking a Genius. The fact that Jane was blushing was as shocking as me stating that I was in love. She wasn't giving me the man's full name, though, so that meant he wouldn't be in her bed for long, or this was as far as it went when it came to getting personal.

"I'm getting out of here and going for breakfast with my brother. I'll see you tonight," she said as she led me to walk away.

"Tonight? I gather Genius lives up to that name in bed, then?" I said, looking back at the guy while Jane elbowed me.

"None of your business, but because you stomached showing up out here amongst the family reunions, I'll give you just a little. He's a great companion in a world of living most of our lives deployed."

"That's all I needed." I smiled at her. "You and the Genius can hash out the rest tonight while you're banging in a hotel room."

"He has a place here too, dick," she laughed. "So, what brings my baby brother to Miramar?"

"I had to see it if I wanted to believe it finally. Shit, Jane, you're a real fucking pilot."

"Right?" She teased back. "It's been ten years now, and I still almost lose my lunch when I pull the G's."

"Quit bragging. In fact, why don't you retire from the military already and go join some fighter jet club like the Blue Angels so I can hitch a ride in one of those planes."

"I have a friend who's a Thunderbird, and he can take you for a joyride the next time they're in town."

"Finally, my sister is worth a damn to me."

"No shit."

ONCE JANE HAD CHANGED into civilian clothing, we took off and followed each other to a restaurant in San Diego. After we finished eating at a hole-in-the-wall cafe, we sat at our table, sipping on coffee, and Jane finally asked what I knew her questioning eyes wanted to know.

"Who is the girl in your life, little bro?" She smiled. "I've never seen you smile this much. Then, you meet me at the base, and that whole spinning, theatrical hug?"

I sipped my coffee and smiled. "You know, I was just adding to the homecoming stuff, right? I couldn't stand out there and look like we come from some basic family, could I?"

"Fair enough on that," she grinned. "Seriously, though," she cocked her head to the side, "you are different. What made you show up at the base? And don't tell me it's because the timing worked out either."

"Fine," I answered, knowing Jane wouldn't leave it alone if I didn't. "Her name is Breanne. And before *you* say anything, the answer is no. She's not right for me."

"Another gold digger, eh? Who was it last time? Ainsley? Halsey?"

"Haley," I rolled my eyes. "Goddamn, that was a long time ago."

"Why isn't this one right for you? Still letting Paul's words fuck up your way of thinking?"

My stomach clenched into a knot at the sound of my father's name. "You know I only tolerate our surname when I see it written on your jumpsuit and because I respect your position in the military. I still think you should take it off the side of your plane and your respectable military clothing."

"I know you do," she smiled. "Answer the question about this woman who put a goofy grin on my brother's face."

"She's my business partner. I have no idea why, but she's got this way about her that..." I paused, not knowing how to explain.

"That," Jane dragged out the word, "makes you think she's not like any other chick you've dated, one who wants your money and status?"

"Seriously, Jane."

"Hey, you chose *that* life by following our grandfather's strict, silver-spoon ways and hanging around Howard Mitchell's sons—all of those men only hang around the upper echelons of the wealthiest people. I know who rides in those circles, and Jim Mitchell being your best friend in college proved how you'd associate yourself once you got there too." She took another sip of coffee. "I can't blame you, though. I joined the military and left you and our little sister." She frowned. "You know what? I'm being a bitch, and I'm sorry."

"Don't apologize," I said. "I think our reunions tend to bring it all back up again, no matter how hard we try to dodge the subject."

"I want you happy, Alex," she said. "I can see that happiness on your face, but I don't want you hurt either."

"I'm a grown-ass man. I ran a global empire with Jim for years and am doing a damn fine job of running my best friend's late father's architectural firm as well. I think I can handle a woman."

"You've always thrown them away, though. I've never seen you happy because of one—as I said, you've changed. How long have you been with her?"

"Two weeks," I announced the truth that widened Jane's eyes.

"Are you in love?" she asked.

"That's not a word *you* use. I guess I should send that question back to you and Genius-boy."

"No, I haven't changed. I'm not in-fucking-love, and I asked a serious question."

"I guess I am," I responded. I felt my defenses going up against my sister because she was calling me out on something she knew was ridiculous about me.

"Do you even know what the goddamn word means?" she said incredulously. I went to retaliate, but she stopped me. "Listen to me, Alex. Paul nearly destroyed you. The abuse, the mental attacks, the fucked-up way he handled everything about what happened that day. You were his punching bag, and he didn't let up even an inch."

"You don't think I know that? I have the scars to prove it."

"I know you know it, but have you moved past it?" she said. "You can't love anyone unless you can forgive and move forward. Drinking yourself to blackout drunk, nearly beating dad's ass to death after he went after mom that night, and grandfather taking you on from there? How did you rebound from that and fucking find love after two weeks of knowing someone?"

I swallowed the lump in my throat. Jane was striking me where she knew I could fucking crack, but she was a marine, and she'd walked through the fire to become the hardcore woman she was today.

"Are you trying to ruin this for me or save her?" I asked.

"Save her from you," she answered, her eyes locked severely on mine. "How *does* this woman feel about you being in love with her? Does she know about your fucked-up past? Does she know *everything*, Alex?"

"No," I seethed. "And why would I resurrect it to tell her? I don't plan on bringing that to the surface again. Ever, goddamnit!" I was breaking, feeling my heart pounding in my head, and a severe headache was coming on while thinking about this shit. "Listen, she's the best thing to happen to me, and I've allowed myself to *feel* for the first time in too goddamn long. So, shoot me for being fucking happy."

Her harrowing expression softened. "I don't mean to dig up shit from the past, but whenever I used to bring up a woman making you happy one day, you always told me that nothing would change what Paul ruined in you. I want you to find that happiness. My God, out of all the people in this world who deserve it, you do."

"Then why are you trying to bring up everything I worked so hard to bury? Yes, at one point, I did fully believe myself to be capable of only basic emotions. The only people I cared about were my friends because I saw them as family. Even Jim only knows the bare minimum about my past, and I've been close with that man as if he were my brother for years. Nothing has threatened our friendship, though; in fact, my group of friends has become closer over the years. What I'm saying is that through it all, I've forged relationships and maintained them. Maybe I'm just getting old and sentimental, but for better or worse, I feel what I feel."

"Maybe you have found the love you deserve."

"A peaceful life, and a woman who makes me enjoy living it?"

"It can get a little exhausting," she smirked, "just fucking and being vacant while you're with someone. I get that."

"It is," I answered her. "And you deserve happiness too, Jane. It seems we lost Jenny in all of this, and even though you weren't subjected to that man's wrath, you seem to—"

"From the time you were five up until you left to live with grandfather, I had to watch you suffer the horrific and disgusting abuse from Paul, and that was enough to fuck with me. I was powerless to stop him or help you. All I could do was scream at our bitch of a mother, who allowed us to remain with him after he lost his shit and went off the rails. She should've taken all of us and left."

"There's a reason she stayed."

"She's a fucking bitch. What kind of mom allows her kids to endure that? What kind of mom watches her drunk as fuck husband brutally assault her boy, and then allow that little boy to believe it's *his fault?*" Jane's face was red with rage. "Fuck, why do we always come back to this conversation?" she sighed. "I love you, Alex Logan *Grayson*, and don't you ever forget that."

"Mom's not doing well," I told her.

Jane had already stood and grabbed the tab—as she always did when our conversations became too heavy, and we seemed to go round and round.

"Sarah O'Connor can suffer like she allowed us to suffer." She bent to hug me. "I'm happy that you're happy. I hope with all my heart that this works out for you. I just worry that if you let anyone close, they'll pry into our family life, and they won't like what they find. The Graysons hid this shit, and grandfather ensured the truth of what happened would stay hidden. Was that for your good or Grandfather Grayson's good name?"

I stood with her. "I lived a life of hell since I was in kindergarten. My father hated me. I'm confused as fuck about it to this day, and Grandfather wouldn't allow the conversation to take place."

"I don't know why he wouldn't talk about it, even to ease your conscience. I don't know what happened, Alex. I wasn't fucking there."

"Why can't I remember what happened?"

"Grandfather left you most of his inheritance, cutting Sarah out of the will entirely, and that resulted in Paul hating you even more. You'd think with all that money, you'd be able to get someone to do a miracle on your brain so you can figure out all that shit on your own."

"Money doesn't work that way," I answered her. "You can't just *buy* your way out of a nightmare."

"Really? Some people think money is the solution to everything."

"You think the reason I busted my ass to sober up and make it to *Oxford*, graduating at the top of my class, was to snag an inheritance and have money be my solution to this fucked-up problem?" I asked, walking out of the diner with her.

She ran her hands through her thick, curly hair before she finally pulled it out of her face and into a ponytail. "Isn't it? Isn't that what dear Grandfather baited you with after he covered up everything with Paul and Sarah?"

"You know," I said, standing next to her car, "I used to have these night terrors daily until our grandfather helped me close the book on our family drama and bust my ass in everything I did. I used sports as the first part of that, then my pursuit to be the best in college—which is how I met Jim and why we became close friends—and then in business."

"It's called burying your head in the sand."

"You are a product of that too. You just found your way out of this mental fuck-show in a goddamn jet that can assist in getting the aggression out. But it seems when you're on land, in my presence especially, you can't cope either. And here I thought you were a badass marine."

"You know what they teach us in those multi-million-dollar jets when we're running combat drills?" she held me off and grew serious. "When there's a lock on your ass, and you can't shake it, it can all end as quickly as it started. In under a minute, I've had to get my enemy off my tail. I had no time to think, just work to shake the lock on me— thirty seconds to maneuver my way out of a life-threatening situation. I wasn't *thinking* about how I'd save my ass; I was saving it. So, yeah, if you want to think less of me because I hate our family for what they did to you and the fact that I hate seeing you happy because I know it won't fucking last, then whatever. I slammed the door shut on all of it,

and I work my ass off to serve my country. My real family is the
Marines. I love them, and I love how I'm constantly pushing myself to
be better and do better by every one of them. I hope the way you
throw yourself into rigorous work is enough, that's all."

For the first time in my life, after having yet another shitty
conversation with my sister, I felt sad for both of us. We couldn't
speak to each other because we'd never been given a chance to have a
relationship as brother and sister outside of our messed-up family. We
didn't know each other outside of that nightmare, and when we tried
to reunite, knowing that we both loved each other, the only thing the
two of us could talk about was our trauma

Her true family was with her brothers and sisters on that base and
that aircraft carrier. I was just blood relation, as she was to me. I had
to let this go because I hated the pain it suddenly caused me. I wasn't
about to destroy what I'd felt about Bree because my sister and I
couldn't hold a civilized conversation if we tried. Fuck. I hated this,
but I was also inwardly thankful she had her military family, and I had
a family with my friends. Jane and I didn't need each other. We just
put on a brave face every time we met.

"I love you, Alex. I hope it all works out for you."

"I'm glad you got yourself out of a deadly scenario," I answered.
"Well, this went the way it always does."

"I know," she patted my cheek. "Now, go do what you do best. You
were down here for work, right?"

"Right," I said. "I guess we'll see if we get another chance to meet
up again on another time."

"We always do." She grinned and then got in the car and drove out
of the parking lot.

I had to hold onto the happiness I had with Breanne, the feelings
of love and being loved for the first time. I wouldn't allow any of it to
go to waste—no way in hell. I was moving forward whether or not
Jane believed I could hang onto this like she could hang onto her
plane.

All I wanted now was to be in Bree's arms, but I knew I had to
detox from this conversation first, or I'd be spilling my guts to her.

Just when I thought the thought, my phone buzzed.

Bree: *Surprise! I finally met your friends, and we had a pretty fantastic flight to San Diego.*

What the fuck? Bree texted the hotel where they were headed and where to meet them for Elena's tuna sandwich picnic, and I knew they were all here. All here, and there was no shoving down the confusion, anger, and sadness I felt after my conversation had gone to hell with my sister.

I needed to switch gears, or Bree would see right through me the second she saw my face.

I'd never been in a relationship where a man adored me. I loved spending every night with Alex, and though we couldn't make it five minutes in the door after work without giving in to our desire for one another, it was heavenly to experience a man who adored me with or without flaws.

I loved how he made me feel—empowered, in love, and more than anything else, appreciated. Alex had made it clear that being with me had changed him for the better, and somehow, I believed him. I could finally say that I knew what love truly felt like, to be someone's treasure while treasuring them yourself.

The ultimate asshole had already played me, and I almost married him. Thinking about the nightmare that could've been if I'd married Max made me sick to my stomach. Even though Max and I had started as good friends—we laughed, we lived, and I thought we loved —I'd spent years with that fool, and yet it paled in comparison to how Alex made me feel within the span of two weeks.

Jim had mentioned this morning that my dad was to be honored at a masquerade event in San Diego, and I was to accept an award on his behalf for his work. I'd never been to San Diego before, so I hadn't a clue about what to expect. I didn't even know what my dad had done to receive an award, making me attend a full-blown charity event thrown by socialites from all over the country. Thank God Avery and Jim were going, and if Alex could break away in three more days, I hoped he'd be an arm I could cling to if it became overwhelming.

Jim had assured me that Mr. Monroe would be in L.A., bouncing back and forth between his business and the firm to ensure no one tried to slide anything behind mine and Alex's back while we were away. So, I gave in and welcomed the help that was offered to get me into a fancy gown and prepped for the event.

While on the flight to San Diego, I was introduced to Alex's friends and couldn't help but smile at the scene onboard the luxury flight: the guys were joking, the children were playing, and the wives were excited to get out of town. On top of being reunited with Elena, Collin, and their newborn son, the flight was the perfect way to bond with everyone over getting to surprise Alex.

I'd finally met Jim's younger brother, the heart surgeon, Jake. Between him and his best friend, Collin, the jokes never ended. Together with Avery and Ash, Jim and Jake's wives, and Elena, I had a blast goofing around with the men, who were relentlessly teasing each other. It was a great way to get to know the gang, and I could see why Alex loved them all so much.

Now, we sat and waited for Alex to show up after he'd texted to say that he was twenty minutes away and was looking forward to seeing everyone. The sun was bright, the weather ideal, and the ocean just steps away from the perfect park where the kids now played while Elena fed baby Alex.

I was entirely caught off guard when Alex answered my yearning thoughts about him, and he kissed me on my cheek. Then, as if his friends weren't at the table with us, Alex and I were wrapped in each other's arms, laughing and kissing, until the comment I'd anticipated finally came.

"Jesus Christ, get a fucking room," Jake's humored voice said.

"I had one, but I had to change that venue when I learned all of you decided to come to San Diego," Alex said, sitting at my side and bringing his arm around my lower back. "Turns out, unless Bree has a nice room waiting here, we're going to have to get arrested while we make up for missing out on each other last night."

"I'm glad I didn't place bets against your sorry ass," Collin said. "If I had, I'd have lost a lot of money."

"Isn't that what Alex is, anyway?" Jim said with a smile.

"The joker's wild. The unpredictable mystery man, to be sure," Collin said.

"Oh, he's predictable," I teased, rubbing his back and offering him a sandwich. He declined and stole a few grapes out of my fruit bowl instead.

"I'll bet," Jake snickered. "Let's change the subject. I'm already gagging down this tuna fish sandwich, and I don't need the details of why Alex has had this cheesy-as-fuck grin plastered on his face for two weeks solid now."

"Jacob!" Ash snapped at her husband.

"Listen," he held his hands up, "I love you to death, Laney, but God dang. What's with the raw onions, olives, fucking celery, and whatever else bullshit is in this goddamn sandwich? You don't fuck a fish over like this."

"It's cilantro, jerk," she said with a laugh.

"Oh, God. All together? Sometimes less is more, you know. Regardless, it certainly isn't a Cuban sandwich, something you promised me quite a while ago," Jake said with a playful arch of his eyebrow, most likely to ensure I was hanging onto the way all of these friends bantered with each other.

"You'll never get one after insulting my grandmother's tuna salad recipe either," Elena shot back.

"Don't tell me this is the shit Collin ate to impress you."

"No, it was her egg salad sandwich," Collin chuckled. "And it complemented our picnic at the lake perfectly."

"No shit?" Jim interjected. "What was in that recipe?"

"Probably grass or tree bark to *complement* their picnic at a lake," Jake laughed.

"Bark is great for your heart. You know that, fucker?" Collin said.

"And the neurosurgeon figured this out how? Because his heart found love?" Jake said. "Egg salad, tuna salad. Why so many salads? Aren't these concoctions supposed to be saved for potlucks?"

"Oh, shut up and eat it. Or don't!" Elena said with a laugh.

I suddenly felt like we were all back on the plane, the guys debating the Sea World versus the San Diego Zoo experience, and the children were pulled in to learn about the marine life and zoo animals. Everyone ended up being compared to either a monkey or a meerkat.

"Goddamn," Avery said, coming back from the walk she'd taken with her kids. "You guys just can't get enough of the jokes today, huh?"

"No kidding," I laughed. I rubbed Alex's leg, who was quieter than I imagined, given the jokes floating around. I didn't fail to notice Jim's expression, which was more solemn than it had been all day, and I saw him looking over at his best friend multiple times.

"Where's your sister? I hope we didn't pull you away from her?" Jim questioned before I could.

"Seems she's got her own man to please," he grinned, but it looked forced. "We had a nice breakfast, and as usual, it's the same old shit whenever I see her. Breakfast, some catching up, and then we go our separate ways."

"Was she happy that you surprised her at the hangar?" I asked.

"She certainly wasn't expecting it, but I'm sure she appreciated the sentiment," Alex said.

Alex suddenly grew robotic in his answers, and my lips tightened when I noticed the entire group at the table felt the awkwardness of it too. Everyone was silent, trying not to make it evident that something was off. I guess asking about Alex's sister wasn't the best topic to bring up.

"So, what brings two surgeons, the owner of a global company, and the co-owner of a badass firm all the way to San Diego?" He looked at Ash, Avery, then Elena. "I'm sure you all had to close up shop too?"

"We have people covering for us. You know what they're referred to as, right? Employees?" Ash winked at Alex, who was forcing yet another smile on his face.

What the hell went weird for him today? Did we interrupt his visit with his sister? Here I was so proud to be in love with the man, but I had no idea what to think, say, or do when it came to him being in *this* mentality.

I eyed Jim, seeing the man more as Alex's best friend now than the intimidating owner of the company that'd bought mine. When you got Jim away from the workplace, he was entirely different, just like the two surgeons I sat in the midst of.

When I questioned Jake and Collin's explosive cursing and pranking, they quickly made it known that they never spoke or behaved this casually around their patients. It made me chuckle to wonder how many other doctors behaved like *real humans* outside of work. I, personally, liked that they had such fun personalities, given some of the sad things they must've witnessed regularly. It displayed a certain resilience that I found endearing.

We spent the rest of the afternoon at the beach. Alex ran up to the hotel to change after encouraging us to head down to the shore and set up things for the kids to play in the water. I watched as I played with Jim and Jake's adorable daughters and Jake's little son, John. We built pitiful sandcastles, and I laughed as Addison informed us that our work was certainly not making it into a sandcastle competition anytime soon.

I watched Alex go out with the guys when John forced them to get wet and enjoy the warm water, which was as beautiful as any resort in Mexico. I could've easily lived in San Diego if I was freed up to do so.

Once the men were fully engrossed, Addison joining them and Ash and Avery bringing out the little ones as well, I laid on a lounge chair next to where Elena was shielding baby Alex from the bright sun.

"I told Alex that I predicted he'd marry you," Elena chuckled as I stretched out on my stomach, feeling the gentle ocean breeze brush over my back.

"I'm sure he didn't argue," I teased with a smile.

"I'm always right," Elena said. "You're good for him."

She said that in a way that made me lean on my side to face her. "He seemed pretty off when we brought up his sister. It makes me wonder why he says things like *I've saved him* when the truth is the opposite."

She grinned at me. I had to admit that Elena's smile was as contagious as her personality. "When I watched him with his ex—I hardly knew him then, of course—it didn't take long to see how miserable he was. He has always been firm, but he's friendly and understanding, selfless, and all of the stuff that makes him a beautiful human being. However, he never seemed truly happy until you."

"I've done nothing special, trust me." That was a fact.

"You don't have to, you know. When the heart is joined with the one it knows it wants, it's all over except for the screaming babies that wake you up at night." She laughed.

"I'm happy that he's happy. I love being around him. Even when he does ruin the old movies that I like to watch to unwind after work."

She giggled. "Collin was the same way. Sex, right?"

I laughed in return. "They all must somehow be related."

"They're cut from the same cloth; that's for sure."

"Whenever a kissing scene pops up, he uses that as an excuse to prove how he can outplay those actors." I rolled my eyes in humor behind my sunglasses.

"I positively love hearing this," she looked out at where the men were playing with the kids, "it proves that two souls have found each other. Now, I just want to know how long we'll have to wait to watch you get to finally walk down the aisle like the beautiful bride you must've been the day you had to play a sex tape."

"The only thing special about *that* day was when I mortified all of the wealthy people my aunts invited and my ex's ability to lie his way out of the affair. You know, all the stuff that goes along with playing sex tapes at weddings."

She relaxed further into her lounge chair with a grin. "You've got the same feisty spirit that I have; although, I would've cut the bastard's dick off."

"Holy fuck," I heard Alex state as he walked up to us. "Please don't give Breanne any ideas about how you and Collin like to get kinky, Laney."

I shivered when his dripping wet hair ran down my spine as he kissed my cheek. "You all good?" he asked. "I heard that something came up with the Julip project. What was that about?"

I turned onto my back as Alex took the lounge chair to my left. "Nothing that Sexy Spence and Natalia can't fix with the sales team and architects involved."

Alex pulled his square aviator sunglasses down. He wasn't even trying to be flirty or unforgivably gorgeous, but he nailed both in one simple move. "Please, God, tell me that's a joke."

"What?" I grinned.

"Well, I'm walk up to hear Elena, advising you about cutting off dicks, and now you're putting your poor friend in a shitty work situation?"

"Are you kidding?" I laughed. "Natalia will wear her most classy yet tempting outfit and make Spencer drool and wish he'd never answered his phone while in bed with her. Besides, she's the agent on the job, and she doesn't let shit slide. So, matters and issues will get handled. If it makes you feel better, Jim warned Spence about her being involved and mentioned something along the lines of *this is what happens when you fuck the wrong one!*" I laughed, repeating what I heard Jim tell Spencer Monroe when he asked him to help Natalia and the firm in our absence.

"You okay, though, Alex?" Elena pried. After learning more about her personality, she was the type to concern herself more with her friend's well-being than what the friend thought about her asking.

"I'm fine, Laney," he answered, lying flat on his back now. "I know you mean well, but there's a reason my holidays are spent with all of you. You're all my real family."

"You can check out all you want," she became firmer. "We all know you don't need the tan you're pretending to soak up, Mr. Olive-toned skin."

"I know I don't." He smiled. "Thank you for bringing my girl with you, though. Seriously, I'm good, just tired from being up at the ass-crack of dawn."

I studied him as he pointedly avoided us, ignoring Elena's kind concern. "Well, I'm going to go cool off in that enticing water," I said as I stood and then brought my lips to Alex's. "Then I'll be sure to come back, kiss you, and drip all over your body."

His lips pulled up on one side. "If you wake me out of a dead sleep out here, I might just ruin everyone's day and take you here and now under a beach towel."

"Good God, there's a baby who's named after you that shouldn't be allowed to listen to this come out of your mouth," I said.

"It's been too long," he chuckled. "Now, get out there, and give me a show so tonight will be as amazing as you dreamt it would be all day."

"Arrogant ass!" I said.

"Don't talk like that in front of baby Alex," he teased back, and then I was pulled over his stomach, and his lips were on my ear. "Tonight is ours. I'm addicted to every last part of you, and I plan to prove that later. Now, go run in slow motion on that beach like you're on Baywatch."

"You're sleep-deprived." I looked at Elena's smile as she pretended to ignore us two. "If he starts snoring, just shove him off the lounge."

"Violence in front of my godson?"

Elena giggled. "Go enjoy the water. I'm about to trade with Collin, so I can too. Why don't you ask him if he'll do a Baywatch slow-motion jog up to me from that water, will you?"

"Super slow-mo or just slow?"

Elena and Alex laughed at my lame joke together. "Make it super slow," Alex said.

I went out to the shoreline and informed Collin what awaited him up the beach between his wife and Alex.

"Is Alex cool?" Jim asked.

"He says he's fine, given his sister seemed to have blown him off."

"Yeah, it usually takes him a day or two to get his head right after he sees her. I don't know why he tortures himself with it all. I get that they're family, but without Alex ever explaining anything, I never know where he'll end up whenever he sees her."

"So, you're in the same boat as me?"

"As Alex likes to say, we're in a rowboat," he smirked as he swung his youngest daughter's feet over the water. "And we'll just keep on rowing."

"The man has a past that he doesn't want to be dug up," Jake added. "Might as well leave it all there. He's a badass, and he's doing okay. I'm certainly one for allowing him to keep it buried."

"I almost lost Avery over burying stuff," Jim said.

"Your stuff was different," Jake countered his brother. "Besides, we all have something shady that we hate bringing up and reliving. Who doesn't?"

"That's the damn truth," I said.

"That's too bad because you know that we all want that sex tape so we can sneak it into Jim's rival company and embarrass that piece of shit ex once again."

"Well, if that company is anything like the guests at my wedding, you'll look like the asshole in the end."

Jim smirked. "And here I thought my brother was on track to take down our stiff competition."

"So close." Jake shrugged his shoulders.

We spent the rest of the day letting the kids enjoy the warm water and mild surf. It was a beautiful day to unwind at the beach, and Alex's brighter smile by the afternoon and his teasing demeanor with the kids told me it was a better day for him.

I did worry after Jim told me he was also in the dark about Alex's past. It wasn't just that, though. He'd met his sister on what seemed like it would be a killer reunion trip, and either the man didn't give a damn about fighter jets and his sister flying them, or they didn't have that tight of a relationship. I wouldn't know unless I peeled the guy's brain open and dug deep into his past—something I never intended to do. If Alex needed to talk about something that upset him, then he would.

CHAPTER THIRTY
ALEX

A long day in the sun, watching Bree smiling more than I'd seen her smile since the day I'd met her, was exactly what I needed to push past seeing Jane and the reminder of our nonexistent relationship. We sure as hell tried to keep *something* going outside of our nightmares, and even though I was happier than I'd ever been, that didn't change the pathetic situation with my sister.

Jim and I sat next to a gas-lit, fiery waterfall and enjoyed a bourbon, but the relaxing ambiance wasn't what made me steal glances of the woman I loved. Bree's dimpled smile was more alluring than whatever this resort had set in place to make one believe they were thousands of miles overseas at a tropical resort.

Jake, Ash, Collin, and Elena opted to join family night at the hotel, watching a movie outdoors that the resort had set up for families to enjoy with their kids. Jim and I watched in humor as Jake and Collin took a few shots and acted as if they were heading down the *long road to hell* to do a family night with all the kids. The best part was when Jim and Avery's daughters tagged along, and Jim raised his bourbon glass to the two doctors as they were on their way to be devoted husbands.

Before Bree, I would've been happy to have everyone show up in

San Diego randomly, and then I would've returned my focus to what I was down here for in the first place: handling business. If the group didn't insist on me sticking around, I would've gone back to L.A. Yet, here I was, shaking off mine and Jane's short reunion and more thrilled than ever to have a wonderful woman in my life to enjoy these brief trips with my friends.

Sitting next to Jim with a sense of joy that Breanne was down here —and her electrifying laugh that was heard from where we sat— completed the happiness I was feeling. It felt so fucking amazing to have someone to make me feel alive inside for the first time. I suddenly understood why my three closest friends were grateful that they'd found the right woman to blot out the mundane bachelor lives we all once lived.

"Is it me, or is this bourbon smoother than the usual drinks we have at these resorts?" I asked Jim.

Jim took another sip of his drink after handling a phone call from Spencer. "It's you." He eyed me with that cheeky grin he held since I admitted I was a fool in love. "It's also her." He lifted his glass toward where Bree and his wife were fully relaxed in a world of their own. "It is good to see my best friend like this, though."

"It's good to have some emotional freedom finally, I guess."

"Emotional freedom?" Jim laughed while I continued to sip on my drink. "What exactly is that? You know it's easier to say that you're just in love, and the woman who made that happen has also made it possible for you to enjoy life a little more. It's a hell of a thing, but emotional freedom? What makes you say that?"

"Because I seriously have no other way of describing it," I answered honestly. "I'd usually chill with you guys on a random visit while I'm on a business trip and not feel anywhere near as excited as I'm feeling now."

"It's called being in love, buddy. Enjoy it." Jim laughed and leaned on the armrest of the cushioned chairs where we'd found refuge away from the party animals in the pool. "Listen, I need to bring up this event we're going to that's honoring Brian Stone. The money raised at it will be given to the company."

"Yeah," I sighed. "Thank God, Breanne's here. I hate these masquerade events, and I know you do as well."

"That's an understatement, but it's in honor of your lady's late father. I wouldn't miss out on my best friend watching his *love* with profound pride whether the masks stay on or come off."

"What does Breanne know about the award? This one sounds unusual. They're donating the funds that are raised in Brian Stone's name to our parent company?"

"It's not that unusual to offer the check to the one who receives the award. I've already spoken with the chairman and requested they give the money to the late Brian Stone's daughter. Unfortunately, since we own Brian Stone's company, they're entrusting us to offer her the money to donate to a cause of her choosing or to use it to advance the architectural firm in his name."

"Why do the chairmen of masquerade events act as ambiguous as the masquerade itself? They should give her the funds raised on his behalf and allow her to invest in the company if that's what she desires." I sighed. "It all has to be fucking difficult, and she is still the CEO of the fucking place."

"I'll cut the shit about the award, the group, and why Brian Stone is being honored and celebrated," Jim said, seeing my frustration rise because shit like this annoyed the hell out of both of us.

This was particularly annoying because these things were always staged for the wealthiest to attend, act like they gave a fuck about the recipient of the award, and then use the evening to prove who was the richest in the room by *accidentally* saying how much they'd donated. It always depended on the group hosting the party, but the donations would easily start at hundreds of thousands of dollars.

"Please do," I answered.

"The Marin project," he said. "Do you remember that?"

"Yeah," I frowned in thought. "Brian Stone was the architect who built that place to help those in need. Doctors, nurses, teachers, and every last good Samaritan was part of helping the less fortunate get back on their feet with that project. A lot of people are alive and well today because of that place."

"Exactly, it's sort of like Avery's center that helps women who suffered abuse and so on. Although we both know that the building *and* the land was worth more than we believed the cause was worth. Hell, how many people have you and I fired at Mitchell due to a failed drug test? Because of Marin, we had a place to send them to get sober, and they came back to the company better than ever."

I nodded. "Too many employees to count. We could've lost some great people at Mitchell and Associates if we didn't send them to Marin to get help."

"Yes. Well," Jim's lips tightened as he looked at Breanne, "Brian Stone was the original donor to that place."

"Shut the hell up," I answered in surprise. "He's the anonymous donor that we were all questioning at the time it was being built?"

"Yes," Jim grinned. "Remember that other stupid-ass *masquerade ball* we had to go to? The first event we attended after John Brooks told us to."

"I remember Brooks insisting that we get into the executive life and fast," I said. "You know he was testing our asses to see if we could handle ourselves while taking over Mitchell straight out of college."

"Brooks always had a method to his madness. He's partly the reason we hate these things."

"Well, it appears the masked man was Brian, the one to pour money into that thing. Jesus, the apple doesn't fall far from the selfless tree, I guess," I said as I smiled at Bree. "Does she know her father is the reason countless individuals were able to go to Marin? Because her father donated the money to get that place built faster than any of us anticipated?"

"She doesn't. You'll tell her."

"Well, I'll be happy too," I said, but I didn't fail to notice Jim's perplexed expression and meet it with one of my own. "What's the catch?"

"She's going to ask why Mr. Stone was so charitable to that cause so many years ago. She's not aware of it from what Javier told me. Brian almost took his own life after he lost his wife." Jim stopped and shook his head. "I can't imagine the grief and sorrow he must've gone through when he lost Brianne's mom. It took someone speaking to him from a small place like Marin that helped him refocus and see that his wife may have been gone, but she didn't depart this life without giving him the gift of their daughter. Through counseling, I'm sure, Brian settled himself to continue, and of course, this is why he came to you and me and begged us to keep his illness from his daughter."

"Jesus Christ, man." I suddenly felt torn for Breanne. I could never tell her that her dad almost ended it all while he was lost in grief. "I remember humoring the man, wanting that business under Mitchell for our greedy interests and thankful he came to us."

"Sort of makes you feel like shit, doesn't it?"

"Not anymore," I answered him truthfully. "I'm honored he trusted us with his firm and his daughter's well-being. It's a shame that she almost lost the place after trying to run it with a bunch of thieves."

"And because she's quite the gifted liar," Jim chuckled. "We hadn't a clue that she was the *anonymous* donor in the numbers to keep Stone looking okay in reports."

"Yeah, and her little donations cost her everything. She's broke as fuck now because of that. I've never jumped her ass about hiding it from us, but she should have mentioned something when all her jobs turned out to be losses."

"Pride," Jim said. "That's why Mitchell and Associates is matching the collected funds from this event, and *you* will be giving them all to her in the name of her late father."

"Jim," I tried to level the man, "you realize the woman *only* took that outlandish car I bought her because she had a few fun days in it, and of course, a few fun days with yours truly. The penthouse she nearly sold? She wouldn't even allow me to buy the damn thing so she could continue to live there and pay all the debt back that was drained by those fuckers since Brian passed away."

"That's why you're giving her the check. It's going back to what we promised Brian. We'd take care of her, and we're finally doing that. Before, she was floundering, and we saw that in the numbers. We should've known better."

"We let the man down on our word."

"Something we always prided ourselves in. Our promises and our word, and now we have a duty to do what's right." Jim was resolute, and he was right.

I shook my head and smiled at the woman I was in love with. "She won't accept that money, even if we do come up with a crazy-ass story."

"True. We obviously can't lie as well as she can." Jim shrugged his shoulders and laughed.

"So, we tell the truth?"

"In this case, the truth may sting a little, but isn't that why you're with her? Isn't that what will get you both through this? Love, correct?" Jim said.

"Jesus, I'm just getting my feet wet in the love department. Now, you want me to dive headfirst in all of this?" I asked, knowing that his request shouldn't have felt as heavy to me as it did.

"Does she deserve to know the truth?"

"Fuck yes, but shit, she might lose it," I said, knowing how she'd reacted every other time she was offered something she thought was charity.

"That's why you lift weights and workout every morning," Jim chuckled. "Nice biceps to hold your lovely woman with."

"Hilarious." I rolled my eyes and studied Bree. "Shit, okay. Well, this thing isn't for three days, correct?"

"And she's been advised that she and Avery will be dressed to impress by Clay and Joe too."

"Well, I have to be on that job this week. I need to figure out why we're stuck with the city and what we need to fix, or we're back to losing money and missing deadlines."

"Already done. Breanne is going with you tomorrow. She showed me the issues with the site she found. She mentioned that she believes she could alter the dimensions of the project, and with your asshole self riding up everyone's butts, you'll get it all pushed through by the end of the day."

"We'll see," I answered, knowing this project was held up over bullshit, and I had no idea how we'd get it moving again. "So, what else is on the agenda? And please explain why it feels like we're all down here for a wedding or something? How'd Jake manage to take off time to come down?"

"Chief surgeons put in for vacation time months in advance like the rest of the hospital staff."

"And he chose to come here for what, an award? To stay at a resort that, if we're honest, feels less like a tropical resort than his beach house?"

Jim laughed. "Well, first of all, it was a perfect way for us to impose on your sappy ass and meet Breanne, and Jake used it as an excuse not to go to Disneyland for the hundredth time this year."

"I'm not going to Sea World." I eyed him. "You all may think I'm a true sap with my feelings about Bree, but I'm not a theme park kind of guy."

"Wait until you have your own kids, and then tell me that nonsense," Jim said. "And you will go because Collin and Jake plan to use the Dolphin Experience to shed light on the mammals that like to ride the surf with them."

I shook my head. "Shed light?" I asked, rolling my tongue under my upper lip. "What the hell do a neurosurgeon and a heart surgeon need a dolphin to shed light on?"

"Collin read that they can bring the kids into the water, and the trainers teach them how to communicate with dolphins through sign language."

"*The kids* being the two nine-month-olds, and John and Addy, correct?" I chuckled.

"Do you think those two jackasses would let the opportunity to speak to a dolphin in sign language pass them by?"

"No, but I'm curious as to what their excuses are for it now."

"Trying to impress the Tahitians they try to compete with while surfing," Jim said.

"I wish I could say you were joking, but part of me believes that shit."

"And the best part is," Jim laughed again, "those idiots are proud that you're *in love* because they think we'll start surfing with them again."

"If it's confirmed, and I see Collin and Jake in that arena trying to learn dolphin sign language, then you can't keep me away. I'll be the first one on a surfboard just to see the look on Flex and the other Tahitians' faces when those two idiots try that in the wild."

"That's why I knew you'd join us at Sea World and take time to surf with the guys."

"Well, Collin only has two weeks of this maternity or paternity leave left, whatever you call it. He'd better hope he's a fast learner, too. I'll be pissed if I go to Sea World and no human to animal communication happens."

"What are you two going on about?" Avery asked as she and Bree walked over wrapped in towels with their wet hair in buns.

"Alex wants to learn dolphin," Jim lied, and Bree quickly caught on. She must've been given a crash course in my friends' ridiculousness on the flight to San Diego.

"More than anything in the world," I answered.

"Why would a man who is fluent in three languages want to learn dolphin?" Bree teased me.

"So, I can ask them to help me while I ride a surfboard. I'll tell them to get my back while I take a wave," I teased.

"Such bullshit," Avery added. "And are they going to use your sign language to scare off the sharks?"

"I suppose so. Even our science-geek doctors recommended it for safe surfing."

"I'll bet," Avery added. "Speaking of which, I need to run inside, shower, and save those doctors from our kids."

"I'll sit with our kids. See you down at the beach where this theater is set up," Jim answered Avery. He looked at us, "See you both tomorrow night."

After Jim had taken off, and Bree and I went up to our room, I felt my dick aching to feel her again. When we got inside the room, I decided a hot shower was the perfect way to loosen up both of us. I had my girl facing the wall, and her beautiful hands stretched out over it while I answered her as she begged for it hard and fast. I'd never get enough of this woman.

Three rounds of fucking later, I'd switched it up entirely. We were both situated on the bed, her face more beautiful than ever, and my heart was so full of pride and love for her that I'd managed to slow it down in a way I didn't even know I was capable of doing.

Bree's groans were smooth and unwavering as I moved in deep and out in a way that made her grip my biceps. I nipped and tugged at her hard nipples, relishing in her full and large breasts as I'd always done, and then used my tongue to caress her neck.

"You feel so amazing. Right there." She moaned when I brushed my cock up against her deep spot. "I'm close," she whined, and I loved this slower way of watching her orgasm build.

The way her voice changed, her whines, whimpers, moans, and her legs fully open and allowing me to fill her deep was intoxicating. I was coming undone in my own way with her erotic sounds, the goosebumps covering her body, and her fingers, which were now digging into my forearms.

She went to turn her head the second I felt her pussy tighten against my last thrust, and there was no way I was losing out on the expression I was waiting to see. I cradled her face to keep her dazed eyes staring into mine. I was holding back but ready to feel this bliss the second I allowed my dick to have its way.

She closed her eyes when she licked her parted lips. "Fuck, I feel so high right now," she said, confirming the exact numbing sensation that was occurring within me. "I love you fucking me." That's when I felt her pussy clenching all around me in a fiery orgasm that nearly went into me.

"Fuck yes," I seethed, my eyes becoming heavy as they always did right before I came hard inside my woman.

While Bree's fingers firmly dug into my ass, I kept myself from exploding into her. Instead, somehow, I throttled down the explosive sensations of my own orgasm and was so fucking stoned on Breanne's faded eyes that my lips were as dry as hers. I pushed in deep, feeling myself release more cum into her, only able to close my eyes while she ran her fingers through my hair and kissed along my chin.

"That's it, baby," she coaxed. "You look so sexy."

Bree's lips went to my jaw while I held my mouth open, my lips softly moving down the side of her cheek.

"Shit," I whispered, still coming. "Jesus."

"I love you," she said, adding to this slow way of taking her.

My forehead was in the pillow next to the top of her head while I felt a full-body shiver of completion to this hotter than hell way of fucking.

When I nearly collapsed on Bree, she went back to our usual pattern of riding out the last of an orgasm. I kept still and let my muscles loosen as her fingertips tingled over my back.

"Well, I'm hoping we at least can say that's enough for one night," she said as I rolled off of her and collapsed on the bed. "But I'm sure it's not."

I kept my eyes closed, still feeling my dick pulse in and out of my heartbeats as the blood returned to my head. "Most likely not," I smiled.

CHAPTER THIRTY-ONE
BREE

Call it whatever you want, but even a nice resort and great sex right before drifting off to sleep couldn't keep me asleep through the entire night. This incredible hotel suite and the handsome man I was excited to be reunited with should have made me kick my habit of not sleeping well unless I was in my own bed—or Alex's bed. Unfortunately, that was not the case.

I went to curl around him, seeing that it was still dark outside our balcony windows, but when I moved closer, I found a drenched spot instead of him.

"What the hell?" I questioned quietly, shifting to turn on the light and check the time. "It's two in the morning. Why is he in the shower?"

As soon as I asked the question, I heard the shower shut off. I eyed the soaked sheets where he'd been sleeping, and I was confused as hell.

Did the poor guy have a fever or a nightmare? I had to wonder because the room wasn't hot, the doors to our balcony suite were open to let in the crisp ocean air, and yet unless Alex had gone for a swim and taken a quick nap while soaking wet, I had no other conclusions as to what'd happened.

"Hey, dimples," he said, the natural scratch to his voice was lower, and his face appeared as if he'd been given the worst news of his life.

"Hey." I got out of bed and walked to where he had a towel neatly wrapped around his waist. "Are we meeting at the job site six hours earlier than I was told?"

He frowned and rubbed his forehead. "No," he stated with a heavy sigh.

I took his hand and grabbed a hotel robe from the closet. "Tell me what happened."

There was no getting around the fact that this man was disturbed about something, and I had a weird feeling it had to do with reuniting with his sister. I walked with him to the other room in our suite—a room that I thought was utterly unnecessary until now.

Before I could pull him to sit on the bed, he took me into his arms and pulled me into his chest. Instead of Alex's usual way resting his chin on the top of my head, he leaned his forehead on my shoulder.

"Baby," I softly said, "talk to me. What happened? Did you have a nightmare or something?"

I was completely lost. I'd never seen this man show any weakness, and now, here I was, holding him—something I never imagined myself doing with the outwardly *and* inwardly strong man I knew. This was a completely broken version of Alex, and it was so heart-rending that it brought tears to my eyes to hold him.

"I want to say it's nothing," he pulled back and rose, and his mouth twitched in humor, "but I'm not the pathological liar in this relationship."

I eyed him and gave him a nudge. "I thought we were past the days of you catching me lying about finances."

"I know, but you did it so flawlessly." He climbed onto the bed, reclined against the fifty-seven or so pillows on it, and held his arm out to invite me to lay next to him. "I can't explain why I woke up sweating like I did, but it seems I had a night terror."

"Were you or *are you* concerned about your sister?" I peered up from where I leaned against his shoulder and saw him staring blankly at the wall opposite our bed. "You didn't seem particularly thrilled at first when you joined us at lunch. I mean, everyone was screwing off with their jokes, but you seemed distant. Jim seemed to see it too."

"I suppose it's all coming back because I saw Jane again. I have no clue," he said as I sat up to face him.

"All I know of your past is that it was shitty, and your grandfather adopted you. I never pried, but I'm not stupid either. Something had to have happened for your grandfather to move away from your parents, and your reaction to seeing your sister makes me think that maybe there are some things you haven't processed entirely. I don't know."

He chewed on his frowning and tight lips, and it was almost as if I could see a certain darkness wash over his expression. It was as if he were seeing right through me and staring at something else.

"Alex, baby," I said, him blinking a few times and looking at me again. "You know you can tell me anything, right?"

He let out a breath that was almost a laugh of disgust or that there was something I didn't understand. "I know that, yes."

"What happened to give you night terrors?"

His hand rubbed along where my leg was exposed. "My father was a horrible man," he finally said. "He hated me with every fiber of his being. He was a physically abusive drunk, and…" he stopped himself and closed his eyes.

"I'm so sorry. Did he beat you?"

"As often as he could," Alex sighed. "And in every way he could manage. Mentally and physically."

"Oh, my God." A million thoughts were flooding my brain, and I couldn't form any of them into a sentence that could've been construed as an appropriate response.

"My grandfather took me out of my abusive home on the night I'd had enough. I was a troubled teen at that point anyway. I may have been an all-star freshman quarterback, but I was stealing booze from my drunk dad's liquor cabinet and getting wasted just to numb the abuse."

"When did he start doing this to you? Was he abusive to your sister?"

"Just me," he answered flatly. "If I was gone, he'd drag around my mom. I came home from a game one night—sober, for once—and found the old man slapping around my mom, and I just snapped. I pulled my dad off of her, and I beat the shit out of him. My mom had to throw herself on me to get me to stop. I wanted to kill him, and I almost had my chance." The look on his face was distant as if he were reliving that night, and I could almost feel the hatred for his father bubbling inside him as he told me the story. He shook his head, and part of me felt like the defenses he'd laid down to start sharing with me were quickly put back in place. "Ultimately, my grandfather did the one thing my mother wouldn't—protect me."

I felt my heart racing, and perhaps it was because I'd heard many stories of horrific abuse, and it never failed to hurt my heart. I could imagine him as a helpless child, being beaten by the person that he should've been able to trust most, and it crushed me.

Alex reached up and smiled when a tear slipped out of my eye. "Don't you *dare* cry over that, Bree. It's in the past. I'll move past this like I always fucking do. I've managed to attract a lot of success in my life, and my grandfather did everything in his power to make sure I would survive my traumatic past."

"Still," I said, "I can't imagine how you could move on without therapy. Why didn't anyone call the cops on that bastard?"

"What seems like an easy solution is not so easy to the people living with an abuser. We were all terrified of him." He was right. I had no idea what it must've been like, and part of me was beginning to think it was much worse than he was letting on. "My youngest sister finally called our grandfather, and that was only because that night, it was obvious that one of us was going to die. My mother's father offered to take her and all of us children—to get us all out of there and into safety—but she chose my dad instead. I guess she thought that she could help him. I have no idea why she stayed, but she insisted that I was the problem and that he wouldn't hurt any of them. So long as I left, they'd all be safe."

"What the living fuck?" I said, not knowing if that was what Alex needed to hear or not. I wasn't a mother, but the thought of a mother saying that to her child—letting him feel that he was the one to blame —made me feel instant rage and disbelief.

"That's why Jane hates her. Maybe it's too forgiving of me, but I just think my mom was in a position that she wasn't emotionally capable of handling. I think it was the only way she knew to survive."

"Emotionally capable? Fuck me. She made it seem like *you* were the problem. I don't even know what to say to that." My gut reaction was to tell him what I really thought of his spineless, wretched mother, but I also didn't want to shut him down either, not when he barely started to open up. "Alex, she chose an abusive alcoholic, who hated his son for God knows why, over you. What kind of parent does that?"

"One who's terrified he'll find her?" Alex shrugged. "Jane left for the military soon after I went off with Grandfather Grayson. My grandfather insisted I keep the Grayson name clean and do right by it."

"Fucking bullshit," I added, getting pissed at that man too. There were a lot of things in life I was ambivalent about, but victim-blaming and shaming were not one of them. How dare these people pile all of this on the child? What the fuck was wrong with them?

Alex smirked. "Jane would love you if she and I could get past the fact that all we ever talk about—no matter what is going on in our lives—is our fucked-up family." He exhaled. "My grandfather was set on sobering me up and teaching me a better way to cope and overcome a painful life and being stronger because of it. And I did that. He was a strict, no-nonsense man for sure, but he was at every one of my games, and he made sure I did what I needed to attend Oxford, and he insisted that I go into therapy." He shrugged. "I guess therapy has a shelf life because these dreams make me wake up feeling like I'm in a horror show are back with a vengeance. I haven't felt this way in a long time."

"If it keeps up, at least you can talk to Elena. Having a best friend who's married to a therapist can be lovely."

He relaxed some with a lazy smile. "If it keeps up, I'll be sure to make an appointment with Dr. Elena Brooks, ride a horse or two, and get back on my feet again."

"Does Jim know about this?"

"Jim knows that my father was an abusive alcoholic, and my grandfather saved me from that bastard, just as his father saved him from his drug addict mother."

"Oh, wow," I said. "And is he okay? Jesus Christ."

"In the end, Jim's story played out nicely," he grinned. "He's happily married with two beautiful daughters."

"And your story? How does Alex's story end?"

He grinned at me. "He learns to love hard and become fearless in doing so." He pulled me to lay on his body. "You say I saved you. Well, that was merely in business." His hands ran over my back. "Because of you, I've learned how to do what my family said I was never capable of doing."

"And that is?"

"Loving. I'm in love with a beautiful woman. That's my happy ending, baby," he grinned. "And one I never believed I deserved until recently."

"You probably felt that way because your dad impressed that in your brain a long time ago."

"Possibly. Either way, now you know the dark secret of Alexander Logan Grayson."

I chuckled. "You seem a little lighter now that you talked some of it out."

He touched my nose. "I can promise you this right here and now that you're the woman for me, and since I gave you more information than even Jim knows, you have to marry me now."

I laughed. "Nice try, buddy," I smiled. "You think I'm going—"

"I'm serious." His eyes widened as if he'd seen the light, and the heavens opened up with some revelation. He sat up and framed my face with his hands. "I know that I'm decided on loving you and only you until I die. I know that I've never felt this way about anyone, and I know I never will. If you don't feel it, then please tell me."

"Well, it happened quickly, but I've never felt this way either," I answered him truthfully.

"If I fuck it up, I'll personally record some humiliating tape you can play on our wedding day," he chuckled.

"If we keep forgetting a damn condom, we might end up with a baby, and *then* what?"

He smiled. "I'm in love with you. When the time is right *for you*, I will secure your hand in marriage. You're having that big ass wedding, and I'm inviting those bitchy aunts of yours to sit next to Max so they can all see you finally marry a man who loves your sexy little ass more than anything in the world."

"A big wedding, huh?"

"I'm turning Ash's best friends loose and rolling out the damn red carpet for my bride," he grinned. "You're going to get the wedding you deserve—a day where everyone honors the bride and adores her dimples and beauty just as I do."

"I never pinned you as a man who'd want a huge wedding."

"I never pinned myself as a man who'd want to get married." He laughed.

"You're serious. Really serious?"

"I'll lock it in with a ring if I have to. After you meet Clay and Joe when they dress you up for the award ceremony, you'll understand why I'll likely be their favorite as everyone else took the easy routes on the small wedding venues."

I straddled him, and this time I held his beautiful face in my hands. "You know I'll marry you, my handsome stud," she said with a funny expression. "Let's give us some more time, though."

"I can claim you with a ring, though, right?"

"Shit," I said, recalling when I saw Sammy's engagement ring. "There's no way I can get engaged right after Sammy. Sorry, buddy. Now you definitely have to wait."

"Why?" He looked at me, questioning me with a smile. "Is it an old wives' tale that two best friends will curse the other if they're both engaged at the same time?"

I twisted my lips in thought that only made Alex laugh. "There's no rush. I'm not going anywhere, so let's wait. We do great at the fake fiancé stuff anyway."

"You never cease to amaze me; you know that?"

"How? I just turned you down, and now you have the *I'm gonna tear you up* look on your face."

Just as I suspected, I was quickly pinned beneath Alex. "Because every chick I've ever been with, especially my last girlfriend, would've never turned me down. They would've jumped at the chance to make my money theirs, and they'd be shattered if I insisted on a prenup."

"Well, all I'm concerned about is the prenup stuff." I giggled in response to him moving in between my legs. "I've got to pay off my debt somehow."

"I already offered to do that, but you won't allow it. So, nice *lie*." He arched an eyebrow at me. "Anything else before I do the one thing that has you screaming the word yes?"

"No," I traced my fingers over his lips. "I'm ready to become your *yes girl*."

After Alex and I shared a glorious round, wrapped and tangled in unimaginable ways, I had to wonder if he was just coming off of having frazzled nerves from his night terrors or if he genuinely wanted to marry me. Either way, we needed time. There was no doubt in my mind about that, but it was also fun to talk about these things with him and know that we were both on the same page.

CHAPTER THIRTY-TWO
ALEX

The masquerade charity ball was the first time I found myself enjoying an event of this sort. Being groomed and raised around these sorts of affairs since my grandfather adopted me, I always found them mundane and used them as an excuse to possibly get laid. But even at times, that was a stretch for me.

This time, instead of bullshitting with everyone and drinking booze to help pass the time, I was lost admiring Breanne. Even wearing her dazzling mask, she was welcomed and appreciated by all in attendance. Instead of jealousy creeping up on me, I felt a swelling sense of pride that the auburn-haired beauty was mine.

I watched as Avery and Bree moved through the room with style and grace, and I was rendered speechless on more than one occasion. I knew words were being flung around the room about us, and whispers were made behind masks—a blatant excuse to gossip if you pulled off your attire well at one of these occasions. Regardless, my eyes were only on the gorgeous woman in her shimmering onyx dress, white gloves, and diamond-rimmed mask, and that gave the crowd a reason to gossip.

When the evening drew to an end, and the award was accepted on Brian Stone's behalf, I finally had my girl to myself. I knew the time was at hand for me to be honest with Bree about why she needed to accept this money and donate whatever she wanted after fixing her finances. It was not a conversation I wanted to have, but it had to take place.

"Bree, as I mentioned earlier," Jim said, "there couldn't have been a better recipient for the award. Congratulations to you and your father for the achievements of making a remarkable contribution to society."

Bree smiled. "My father was a very generous man. I plan on making sure this award, and the outrageous amount of money that was raised in his name tonight, go to an excellent cause as well."

"Make sure it's something your father would have wanted," Avery added with a wink. "Love you both. Good night."

With that, my cloaked best friend, his stunning wife, myself, and Bree split, quickly disappearing to our rooms to get out of the penguin suits and ball gowns. I couldn't shed the damn tuxedo fast enough, but I paused when I saw Bree standing in front of the floor-length mirror Clay and Joe had brought to the room for Bree and Avery to see how they looked before we left for the event.

I walked to her and ran my fingertips over her bare shoulders. "I've thought of nothing all night but removing this gown from your sexy body, and now you've destroyed that," I smirked at her as she smiled at me through the mirror, bringing my lips to caress the goosebumps on her skin.

"I'm sorry I ruined your crazy fantasy," she teased. "Do mysterious and creepy masquerade balls turn you on?"

"No," I smiled. "I'm only turned on by the one who received the money that was donated to them."

"I knew there was something scandalous about you, sir," she taunted. "My fiancé wouldn't approve, you know?"

I smirked at her, using the sultry tone she teased me with while playing along at the event tonight. Once her mask was on, Bree had transformed into a more flirty and humorous date. I could easily sense she thought the masquerade was just as bizarre as I did, and I welcomed her fun way of engaging in all of it. Another enjoyable side of the evening was that I had experienced a different side of the woman I'd fallen for, and I staked a hard claim on loving her and being in her presence that much more.

"Your fiancé was a fool not to put a ring on this finger," I said, sliding my hand up her arm and pulling her left ring finger to my lips.

She turned to face me and tugged on the bowtie I had hanging from my neck. She casually started finishing where I began to unbutton my shirt before I spied her standing in front of the mirror.

"Did you enjoy the night?" Her eyes lifted to mine, filled with passion and desire. "Or do I need to make up for hiding behind this mask, as you mentioned more than once while we danced?"

I wanted so desperately to take her right here and now, to do precisely what she'd reminded me of whenever I had a moment with her, and I stole her away for a dance or two. My cock was begging me to ignore my sense of reason about doing the responsible thing. Overruling my sexual appetite and craving that seemed to be endless with her should have been the hardest thing I'd ever attempted, but strangely, it wasn't. I needed to fill her in on this charity money, and I wanted to do it correctly.

I wanted to say that I hadn't had the opportunity to tell Breanne about her father until now, but it was more accurate to say that I hadn't conjured the nerve to do so. Seeing her sparkling personality all night and that she seemed to enjoy the evening up until now, I was certain no one had mentioned why Brian Stone received the honor. The announcement was made that his benevolence was the reason for it—being selfless with his money, time, and architectural skills. It was obvious enough that they wouldn't mention the man had become suicidal after losing his wife. Still, I suppose that was another reason my eyes were constantly on her throughout the night—watching for some miserable fuck to come at her sideways and tell her the painful truth.

I wanted to duck out of this with everything that I was. Historically, I wasn't the most empathetic person when it came to delivering such news—and that is putting it mildly. I was scared shitless that I would relay this vital information to the woman I loved, sounding like a cold-hearted bastard.

That was the man I really was when it came to handling situations like these. Even when I had to help Collin through the worst possible time of his life, I was strictly business with him, even though my heart broke for him and the uncertainty of Elena.

Fuck. I knew I could do this. I understood that Bree needed to know, but could I be the man she needed if this news was received horribly? I was throwing that damn word *love* around like I understood what it entirely meant. Hell, I pulled a marriage proposal out of my ass, and why? Because I trusted and cared enough about her to let her in a little bit on my fucked-up past?

"Alex?" Bree questioned, her hand brushing along the stubble on my face. "You look like you're going to tie me up and have your way with me or something?" She smiled as I let out a breath. "Why the dark expression so suddenly?"

I chewed on the inside of my tightened bottom lip. "How's a walk on the beach sound?"

She cocked her head to the side curiously. "I'd rather take my sexy lover to bed," she grinned. "I'm down for a walk, but we missed the sunset by four hours or so."

"San Diego beaches are beautiful with or without sunsets," I smiled. "Go and change into something that will keep you warm. There's something—" I stopped myself, knowing I was about to fuck it all up if I kept talking.

"What's up with you? You better not be worried about the job. We fixed everything, and the permits are in the process of being approved."

"I know," I smiled. "You and I seem to have a grand way of fixing things and saving the Titanic while doing so."

"The Titanic?" She looked at me as if I were the silly one to bring that idea into play the way she did when we saved the Sphere job.

"You don't recall comparing the Sphere project to the sinking of the Titanic?"

"Oh, damn!" She laughed and ran her hand down the center of my chest. "Back when you were the asshole in a suit."

"And now, what do you see me as?" I asked with a dry tone and an arch of my eyebrow.

"Sex in a suit?" She leaned up and kissed the hollow of my throat. "You're really up for a walk on the beach?"

"You're making it quite difficult..." I swallowed when her hand roamed over my cock. "Extremely difficult, I might add. Get dressed, dimples. If we truly believe we've both been shot in the ass by the cupid's arrow, then tonight we'll test that theory."

"You're acting stranger than that masquerade event."

"Just get dressed," I smacked her flirty ass. "Trust me, with the way you're turned on at this point, I'm letting you tie my ass up and do whatever you want with it when we get back."

"Shouldn't tempt me," she said, and then she disappeared into her closet while I put on a pair of jeans and a long-sleeved shirt.

BREE'S LAUGH was contagious as we passed our friends, who were chilling with drinks in the lounge area of the pool. The guys had cocktails, and the ladies were in the jacuzzi, enjoying the freedom that came with having Jake and Ash's nanny watch the kids.

"We're being romantic," Bree teased after Jake questioned where we were going as we headed to the pathway that led to the private beach.

"Can't wait to report that two grown-ass adults are having sex on the beach," Jake countered back.

"I'm sure we'll be joining the club of doctors who do crazy-ass shit on the SoCal beaches, correct?" I asked with a grin.

Collin raised his gin. "Get it done, man." He smirked.

Jim was the one to make eye contact with me, knowing that I was on my way to tell Bree the truth about her father. Part of me wanted to withhold this information, knowing that what she didn't know couldn't hurt her, but there was no way in hell that my best friend and I could have this information and not tell her. I was holding back enough secrets from the woman, and I was certainly not going to add this one to the list.

. . .

"So, what is with this romantic walk, anyway?" Bree questioned once we reached the beach, took off our shoes, and allowed the soft, warm sand to massage our feet as we walked.

I brought my arm around her and held her close.

Please, Alex. Don't fuck this up.

"I should have mentioned this the night Jim made me aware, but I wanted to make sure that I delivered this news in the best way I knew how."

That stopped all forward progress, and now the only sounds were the waves as they softly crashed into the shore. "What news?" she questioned in a voice that was the most serious she'd used since she was busting balls on the job we had to fix yesterday.

"It's about the award and why your father received it and all of the proceeds of the event tonight."

"It's because he donated his money. A lot of the work he did was charity," she said.

The full moon lit the beach, and I saw her perplexed expression. I instantly wanted to leave our conversation at that.

"Correct," I said as I reached for her face. "It appears that you're a lot like him, being charitable and selfless."

She sighed. "Alex, if you're out here trying to use the ocean and a beach walk to get me to keep that money for myself, you've not learned anything about the person I am."

I took her hand and led her over to an area to sit in the sand. "This isn't easy at all for me to tell you, but I believe you have every right to know. I need you to understand that Jim learned more about the reasons that your dad helped create that center and why they're giving back after all these years."

"Go on," she said, her hands defensively crossed in front of her.

"Well, first of all, when your father approached me to ask if Mitchell and Associates would invest and acquire his business, I was a ruthless asshole at the time. Since getting to know you better, I have changed my opinion about taking his business."

"I was so angry with him for not telling me. The whole merge pissed me off too. It's like my dad didn't trust me, but in the end," she laughed, "I couldn't run that company right. I fucked it all up. I've moved on, though, and I am grateful for you and Jim's company taking on my dad's. I'm thankful to you for uncovering everything." She brushed her hand on my arm.

"I am too. Your dad wanted to ensure you were taken care of. He demanded that we not mention anything to you and insisted that we keep the company going and allow *you* to keep his vision alive. I don't believe he wanted you to run the company, and that's only because he mentioned that your heart was in design, not the corporate affairs."

"That sounds like something he'd say. I guess he was right," she said with sadness in her voice.

"Were you happy running that business, or are you happier designing and keeping that part of his vision alive?"

"I just feel like I failed him."

I took her hand. "Jim and I feel as though we failed him in his requests. You've seen me work, and I'm sure you understand that I'm all numbers, profits, and business. At the time, we were more focused on the fact that Brian Stone was handing his business to us, and we weren't so concerned about *keeping his daughter* happy. I am now, of course. Jim and I failed him, letting it come down to the fact that we let you have too much freedom at Stone Company. I should've insisted you and I meet back then and that I audit the company to see why it needed regular *donations*." I arched an eyebrow at her. "We should've been more involved, but we were assholes, and I'm sorry to you and your father for that."

"Don't you even think about taking on that burden," she insisted. "I hid the real numbers, trying to prove a point to myself and trying my best not to fail. It bit me in the ass in the end, but I did what my prideful mind thought was best."

"With that said, Jim is matching the donations from the event tonight. He and I both want you to take the money you need—even if it's just the match from Mitchell and Associates—and use that money to recoup what was stolen from you. I'm not sure about the numbers, but I know that an anonymous person made millions in donations. That was you. That was the inheritance your dad left you. You had no idea the underhanded shit that Jim and I allowed by not being more involved as the parent company. We were looking at profits, and that was fucking it. We should've been helping you."

"You trusted the company you owned was delivering the numbers you needed to see. Alex, I did this to myself."

"Please, don't fight me on this. Take the donations Jim is matching and fix things. Replenish the funds—it's everything your father left behind to keep you financially stable."

"Why are you so worried about this? More than that, why is Jim?"

I gripped the back of my neck. "Babe," I said, using a word that was becoming more common when I spoke to her in more of an emotional way. "Your father had reasons for donating so much to the cause down here for those who needed help to solve problems they deemed unsolvable. To help those who sought counseling through stages of grief, and he did all of that because he faced horrific battles after losing your mom."

Fuck. There, I said it.

"My dad never said anything to me about struggles or things like that when we lost my mom. He said he was thankful he had me, and because of that, my dad and I were extremely close."

"Yes," I said. "However, Jim has learned your father was not well after your mother passed. He knew that if he didn't seek counseling through a place such as the one he funded, he might not have continued on. He knew that your mother may have left him too soon but that she gave him the best gift a wife could give the man she loved."

Goddammit, Alex, you're not making any sense.

Bree was quiet, and I watched her body language as she pulled her legs into her chest and leaned her chin on them.

"Breanne?" I ran my hand over her back, wanting to kick myself for what probably sounded like incoherent rambling to Bree. "Am I fucking this all up?"

"He was going to kill himself?" she asked through a cracked and broken voice. "I—I can't—Holy shit. I would've never believed that my dad could fall into a depression and end it all even though he still had a little daughter who depended on him—who was suffering too. What was he thinking? What would've happened to me then? I would've been forced to live with my aunts?" she said, anger dripping from her voice. As quickly as she flared up, she deflated again, hanging her head. "I want to hate him for considering that. It's such a selfish fucking thing to do."

"Grief is an unpredictable emotion, and depression can cloud even the clearest of minds. Sometimes people see no other way, and I can't pretend to know how low you have to feel to think about ending things, but I imagine it's the most difficult thing anyone can ever face." I may not have been overly in touch with my feelings, but I knew the darkness, and I knew what it was like to do almost anything to stop feeling like you were drowning. I wasn't world-renowned for my empathy, but I knew about struggling with the darkness inside that made you feel like the worst person who ever lived. I knew that all too well. "Some people don't realize they're struggling with depression until it's too late. That's why that center is such a blessing, and you heard tonight how many lives were changed and are now better because of it because that building was funded and went up so quickly."

"Why are you telling me this?"

Her voice was riddled with anger, which was precisely where I expected this whole damn thing to go. My heart ached for her, and she was right; why the fuck did I have to tell her this?

"Bree, even though the event was a beautiful thing for your father, people talk. When donations are involved to honor someone, people like to dig up dirt. There was no way in hell Jim and I would allow you to find this out from anyone but us. I'm sorry to be the one to tell you this, but your father was a brave man. He sought out help instead of giving up. After he did, he didn't take the rest for granted. He used his experience, knowing it could happen to even the strongest of people. It took therapy to help him realize he would find that healthy life and light, and it was through you. That's why he didn't want to leave unless you were financially cared for."

"He was a beautiful soul," Bree said with a sniff. "A beautiful man."

She looked at me. "Thank you for telling me this."

"Come here," I said, pulling her rigid body into my arms. "I'm here for anything. I know this isn't easy to hear, and God help me, I wish I never knew it so I wouldn't have to tell you. But I will say that Brian Stone was brave beyond words, and I can look back on that day with him in my office and remember the humility it took for him to ensure you were cared for. The man loved you, and I only hope I can love you as well as he did."

She leaned into me and kissed my chin. "I love hearing you say that."

I held Bree on the shoreline, both of us quiet and watching the surf without speaking a word. I was running everything through my head and hoping to God that I'd said it right, not twisting up the memory of Brian Stone for his daughter. I had to believe I'd delivered the news the right way, the compassionate way, and that she understood I was here for her.

After we got back to the hotel room, Bree seemed numb in thought, and that's when I knew for sure that love was more than sex and more than admiring a woman from across the room, or while she worked, or hearing her call out my name. All of that was a fantastic addition to being attached to a woman, but what love was proving itself to mean to me was entirely different. It was allowing this beautiful soul to curl up around me and let me hold her as her broken heart shed tears until she fell asleep peacefully at my side.

I didn't interrogate her. I didn't try to fix her sadness. I didn't do all the shit I always did when I delivered shitty news. I just held her and loved her with every ounce of my being. I knew now that Breanne Stone was mine to love, care for, and adore until she either pushed me away or I left this life.

There was no other woman for me but her. No other woman I could ever hold and give a damn about. When you were with her, you saw sincerity and love that went deeper than anything on the surface.

Now, it was a matter of getting her to accept that we were meant to be together. To accept that even though it had only been a couple of weeks, when this strong emotion swarmed you, you felt it, and you knew it. I knew it now. If this were all surface romance, I know I wouldn't have pulled her tightly into me and kept her in my arms as I drifted off to sleep, knowing that I would protect this woman with my own life.

What a beautiful feeling. This love beat all of the horrible things I was told growing up—that I was too damaged ever to understand this emotion, rendering me useless and unable to love or feel compassion.

Fuck everyone who tried to tell me that. Fuck all of them. I was capable of being more than an iron-fist bastard who ran businesses like a ruthless son of a bitch. I could do all of that, and I could still hold the woman who was sent to prove everyone wrong about who I *really* was.

CHAPTER THIRTY-THREE
BREE

*T*ime gained wings and flew after San Diego. Learning the news about Dad was a bit too much to swallow at first, but now I understood why he'd never remarried or tried to find happiness with another woman. My mother was his one true love, and I imagine losing her brought about an unimaginable amount of grief for him.

I was grateful my dad had sought help, and I knew that allowing Mitchell and Associates to buy his company took a lot for him, but I knew exactly why—he was the most selfless and loving man anyone could meet. That giant of a man may have held himself boldly in my presence, but he had a weakness, as all humans do. My dad seemed to be a superhero—in some ways, he still was in my mind—but his heart broke when he lost Mom, and I can't imagine the pain my father felt.

It'd been nine months since Alex told me about this in San Diego, but it still weighed on my mind. On days like yesterday, when Sammy was married and had the privilege of her father walking her down the aisle, it peeled open memories of my dad.

I took Alex's advice and used the money from Jim's company matching the donation to fix my finances. I was officially debt-free with too much money in the bank. After talking to Avery, knowing that she worked with women who came from abusive situations, I used her contacts and learned that we could donate to a facility in Downtown Los Angeles.

With my love for Saint John's, after seeing the pediatric wing fall perfectly into place with my designs, I knew that was where I wanted our own treatment center. It was easily done since the cardiac wing of the hospital had been moved to the newest building at the hospital.

Through concentrated mockups, staying up late, and Alex strangely not coming over to my place or vice versa as often, I could use my evenings to nail down a beautiful renovation of Saint John's former cardiac wing that consisted of the left tower of the place. Renovations had started two months ago, and I was thrilled that with the help of my money, it would go up quickly.

Soon, residents from this location would no longer have to travel to San Diego to live in the center, and their loved ones wouldn't have to drive all that way to visit them. We did have centers in Los Angeles and surrounding areas, but they were nothing like the one Dad had donated all of his skill and money to. This one would be just as nice and welcoming, and it would mainly serve as a way for people to attend meetings or seek counseling shamelessly.

Even after throwing money toward that, I wanted to do more, and Alex laughed at me becoming *little miss charity*. With the obvious help of planners and approval from Jim and the board at Mitchell and Associates, I started the process of raising more money for another place of refuge like this to be opened in Orange County. *Helping Hearts* was well on its way to showing everyone that there was help for the dark and sad periods in our lives.

With my charitable heart, my debts all cleared, and finances back to where they once were, I found it a perfect opportunity to auction off the AMG-One I'd played around in. I always knew it wasn't my style of car anyway, and we raised a shit load of money auctioning it at another event, this time in the name of Brooks and Stone Architects.

As excited as I was for Sammy and her handsome husband's wedding day, that was the day we were to cut the ceremonial ribbon on the new facility in Orange County. Alex took my place at the event because being a bridesmaid kept my ass super busy, and if I so much as thought about leaving the city on Sammy's big day, who knew what the beautiful bride would've done?

All in all, everything was moving so smoothly. I had to wonder what the hell happened to force a one-eighty shift in my life. I mean, down to the fact that Brooks and Stone had fully merged, and it ran like a well-oiled machine. A lot of that credit went to Alex, though. He was undoubtedly no bullshit in the office, and when mandatory meetings were called, the man carried himself as someone you didn't cross with a lame-ass remark.

So, here I was, enjoying nine months of sheer bliss with a man I deeply loved, my best friend was getting married off, and now, all of this charity stuff was rolling out beautifully. I couldn't help but have a smile plastered on my face everywhere I went. The only thing that was missing lately was the amount of time I got to see Alex. We were constantly missing each other.

Even when he invited me to dinner with all of his friends, Alex got held up at a job site, and his friends got to enjoy my company without him. It all worked, though. The men always had their conversations, and Avery, Ash, Elena, and I sat there, making silly jokes about weddings and babies in a world of our own.

The best gatherings were when we all somehow met up for a day at the beach, and Nat and Cass joined us. How strange that we blended as if we'd grown up together as tight friends. Nat, of course, kept the ladies humored, but she always had to be tamed when Addy or John were digging sandcastles around us. As fun as all of the times we'd had in the last nine months had been, I'd been missing Alex like crazy lately.

"Hey," I said, dialing Alex from my car phone, "will you be in the office later?"

"I'm on my way out, or else I'd probably be violating your *no sex at work* rule the moment you stepped into my office."

I listened to him laugh and loved the way it made my insides feel. "Jesus, how long has it been?"

"Nine fucking months," Alex snickered. "At least that's what it feels like to me. You went all charity on my ass, and I haven't been alone with my woman in too fucking long."

"You're the one insisting on going home, saying that it would be *best* if I worked on my stuff at my place."

The phone line grew quiet, and I ignored the insecure thoughts that moments like these tended to evoke when I mentioned that we were hardly at one another's house anymore.

"What about tonight? You busy?" I asked Alex.

"Did you forget what tonight is, dimples?"

"I guess so."

"Well, if you're at the office, get shit handled quick. The plane takes off at seven tonight. That project you and I are pitching in Florida is at eight in the morning at Bells Place."

"Shit," I rubbed my forehead. "Can't you go without me? Bring Lisa. She's practically been my shadow while designing. She'll have—"

"You're fucking kidding, right?" Alex answered. "I'm not bringing Lisa. I'm bringing *you*. We finally have a VP running the company for us who's more of a tight ass than even I could've been. Pack your shit, and I'll pick you up at five. We're fucking on the plane too."

"I like the sound of that."

"I like it even more," he said with a smile in his voice. "All right, I'm at the site, and if Cullen fucks me on this, I'm firing his ass."

"You say that about everyone."

"So long as they know that, they don't fuck up."

"See you tonight. I'll wear some sexy lingerie on the plane."

"Might as well wear it to the airport. I plan to fuck you in the limousine I'm using as transportation. It's the only reason I chose that particular shuttle to LAX."

"I need to walk tomorrow."

"I'll rent a wheelchair."

"Bye."

.   .   .

AFTER ENDING THE CALL, I rushed through last-minute pressing issues and quickly left the office. I wasn't sure what I was most excited about, finally having more than two hours alone with Alex, or that we were heading to Florida to check on this job and spending the week together to catch up.

From the second Alex picked me up until we landed in Florida, we quickly made up for lost time in each other's arms. It felt so good to slow it all down and feel the raw power of Alex's body, making mine feel alive inside and out again. The groans of pleasure that seemed way too long overdue were enough to send me off into my multiple-orgasm runs that reminded me why I loved this man fucking me hard and deep. Now, if only we could get our busy schedules to slow down and find more time like this when we got home.

"Fuck, baby," Alex groaned after he pulled his face from massaging and sucking on my clit. "I love this so much."

Alex and I had just walked in from our final meeting with the Bells Place job, and the man went primal the second we walked in the door. I was up on the table in the dining area of our suite, and before I could blink, Alex had my panties off and thrown somewhere in the hotel room. His face was instantly buried between my legs, and his mouth and tongue worked me over as they always did when he devoured my pussy like it was his favorite meal in the world.

I crossed my ankles around his back, feeling his tight muscles and knowing that when he entered me, I was getting it hard and rough—just like I wanted it. Right now, the man was working on my orgasm high while his tongue and teeth devoured my opening in ways that made me wonder how he knew what perfect pleasure was for me. Goddamn, he was good in every way.

My nails clawed into his hair as I felt my orgasm plunging to where his tongue lapped at my opening, probing in and out and then back to my swollen clit.

"Come on my fucking face, baby," he growled. "I'm drinking your cum. It's been way too long."

I worked on the new technique of being able to ejaculate while I came and was still shocked that Alex loved it. Then again, I was always up for swallowing him, so it had to be the same turn-on to take your lover and swallow the orgasm physically while they came hard on you.

These orgasms, though—the ones that consisted of me forcing it down while it was already on its own electrical surge? The sensations were un-fucking-real. Just as it was happening, I followed my new way of sending my cum into Alex's mouth and practically screamed out the orgasm when the dam of pleasure burst loose.

My hands went from nearly tearing out his always perfectly styled hair from his head to massaging it while I rode out the pleasure. My favorite part of all of this was when Alex brought his mouth to cover all of my opening, his tongue massaging my orgasm as it gushed into his mouth. His whimpers and soft moans as if he were devouring a savory steak was what created the constant ripple effect of a throbbing sensation that surged through my clit and inside of me while I came in him.

Alex kissed and licked at the inside of my thighs before I was in his arms, and we wound up using the bedroom to continue through the night. Thank God tomorrow was a beach day because I was all about laying out and dreaming up our next rounds. The addictions and cravings were back, and I seriously wondered how we managed only to have sex once a week after this perfect reunion.

I was on my stomach, ass in the air, and Alex was working over my pussy with his length when his phone alerted that Alex never put the stupid thing on silent. Over and over again, the fucking thing rang.

"Fuck me to hell," Alex snapped.

I chuckled. "If you answer it, then Nat and I will have something in common."

Alex flipped my ass over and buried himself deeper in me, his smile greedy. "I won't answer the fucking phone. I'm shooting all of my cum in this pussy. You got that?"

"Now he's ordering me around?"

"I'm about to tie your sexy body—"

Ring! Ring! Ring! Ring! Ring!

I laughed when the phone now seemed to echo from the kitchen area of the suite, and Alex's head dropped onto my chest. He tried to move in and out, but with one reach of my hand, I felt he was growing soft, and it was pretty much a lost cause at this point.

"Baby, answer the phone unless it normally does this when it's on silent."

"Never," he said, kissing each of my hard nipples, the center of my chest, and then rising up. "Thank God we survived a nine-month relationship just in time for me to have sex interrupted by a goddamn call."

"This is why I'm not marrying you. I can't be married to a man who'd rather answer a phone than have hot sex with me. I feel so cheated," I said with a dramatic tease and pout.

Alex pulled out of me, rolled off the bed, and smiled down at me. "Keep your legs open and that pussy wet. I'm not even close to finished with you."

Alex left the room to get his phone, and it didn't take long before I heard Alex's loud and exasperated words. It seemed as though something was wrong with him and whoever he was talking to.

"The bastard didn't have insurance to cover this?" Alex said. "Fine, fuck him. Give me the name of the funeral home. I'll take care of all the arrangements." Another pause. "Listen, Jen. He doesn't have to know. I don't *want* the son of a bitch to know. Give me the number to the place, and I'll handle everything. The money will be wired over. Say it was donated in her name by someone who knew her father. Make sure everything is as she would've wanted it."

I could practically hear Alex breathing heavily from here. After hearing what little I did, I knew this was all bad, and I had to be prepared to help in any way I could.

"Is that what mom wanted or what Paul wanted?" he snapped. "Then I'll send over more than enough so that everything is secured, and Paul can ride behind the horse-drawn fucking hearse. I'll see you at the wake."

By this time, I was out of bed, wearing a robe, and walking out to Alex and watching him zipping up the slacks that he'd peeled off in our crazy sex attack when we first walked into the room.

"Jesus, Jen, is that how you feel? She was my mother as well. I want this to be as it should be regardless of what you and Paul want. This is mom's parting wish, so this is what she gets. I'll see you in a day or so. Fuck!"

Alex ended the call, and then his eyes were on me. "I need to go to my hometown. I'll be gone for a few days until I ensure my mother's funeral arrangements and burial goes as she had apparently wished they would."

"My God, Alex," I said, taking his hand in mine. "Your mother passed away?"

"Yeah, and now I have to deal with my goddamn family. I already dealt with this shit after her stroke, and I knew the day would come when I had to face them all again. I'm just not in the mood to deal with it."

"Alex Grayson," I said, more shocked by his reaction than anything. "I'm coming with you."

"The hell you are," he looked at me and shrugged my hand off his arm as if I were this Paul of a dad he hated. "You're going home or enjoying the rest of Florida. I'll see you when I get home."

"Bullshit," I snapped at his hardened expression. "Sure, you have a past that you want to keep buried. I get that, but I'll be damned if you think you're going into what seems to be a freaking lion's den alone."

His eyes brimmed with tears. "This is so fucked up. Please, God, stay away from this and allow me to make sure my mother is buried properly. I beg you to stay the fuck out of this."

"How am I to ever marry a man who pushes me away when I can see on your face this is the time you may need me most?"

"Because I don't want you to witness this side of me. I'm only going to make sure my mom is buried and say a final farewell so I can finally put that family in my past for good now that she's gone."

"Alex, I love you," I said to break the ice wall he'd instantly forced between us. "Let me be there for you. If it were me, you would insist on it."

"Would I?" he challenged.

"Yes. I think I've witnessed that you have that heart the *Wizard of Oz* gave you, and you would."

That pulled a half-smile out of the dangerous expression Alex wore. "I'll even play the role of your fiancé when I'm there."

"You *should* be my legitimate fiancé by now," he raised an eyebrow at me. "My bet is on the fact that Max fucked all of that shit up for me."

"What? Where the hell would you come up with something like that?"

"Explain to me why you've turned me down twice now."

I had no answer. "Time's flown in the last nine months. We've hardly seen each other, and the two times you've proposed to me were not situations where you were thinking clearly."

"Whatever." He shrugged me off. "If you want to go, then go with me. This won't be pretty. Perhaps we'll both discover together why it's probably a good idea for you not to marry me." He brushed past me. "Trust me, my father will give you plenty of reasons to stay far away from me."

"Alex!" I stormed into the room after him. "Look at me."

He glanced back, and that's when I saw tears slip out of his eyes. "What?" he choked out.

"I'm here for you, and I plan to always be here for you. I love you, and I guess this is the point when I do accept your proposal because I'm not leaving your side ever." I took my hands and brushed his tears from his wet cheeks. "You're officially stuck with me. Are you okay with that?"

He sniffed. "I don't want to lose you."

"Then don't try to push me away again like you just attempted to. If you want to play *let's get married*, then I suggest you allow the one you want to marry to stand at your side during this time."

"You have a point."

"I have a good point, and that's why I made it." I smiled at him. "Damn, your muscles are tense as hell," I said after he pulled me in to embrace me, and I hugged him. "Let's go jump in the shower, clean up, and order in food. We'll talk about the funeral arrangements, and maybe I can help advise on things. I did have to bury my father."

He brushed his finger over my nose. "Please don't judge the man I am today after meeting these insane people. I wasn't raised in that family for a reason."

"I can see that your grandfather got you out just in time to make the perfect husband for the woman who finally said yes."

"You're serious?" His face finally lightened.

"Don't ever think that Max ruined anything for you with me. There's no comparison, and I won't allow that dick to ride anywhere near you and me. I'm only sorry I've been pushing it all off. I never once thought you'd imagine it was because I had issues after my last failed marriage attempt. I can honestly say that I don't have any hang-ups or issues revolving around that relationship."

His face grew somber again. "Perhaps it was my insecurities, knowing I could still hurt you in the end."

"Well, if those are your insecurities, then lose them," I insisted. "Now, come get in the shower so I can help rub these knots out of your shoulders."

I had no idea what to expect with Alex's family, and I hated funerals, but there was no way I would let Alex run off and deal with this on his own. His father had started a fundraising account for his mother's funeral, and Alex was going to cover all the expenses as an anonymous donor so no one would know? His youngest sister begged him to stay away, yet she called him for money and announced that his mother had died? What kind of lowlife would call the one family member they knew could pay for the funeral, then tell them they couldn't attend?

I knew this might reach a heavy boiling point, but I also knew that I wasn't allowing Alex to face this alone. This would be proof that I was going to be by his side no matter what. Why not embrace it all—good and bad—before you tie the knot, right? All I knew was that Alex seemed instantly distant, and I couldn't blame him. I could only be there for him.

CHAPTER THIRTY-FOUR
ALEX

*T*he plane was descending when I ended my call with Jen, my youngest sister. I would lose my mind if I didn't make it to the upcoming shit-show as soon as possible, and the fact that I had Bree in tow weighed as heavily on my mind as the rest of this fuckery.

For the last nine months, after being with Bree had opened what I now referred to as my own personal Pandora's box of emotions, I'd been struggling to sleep through the night without having night terrors. They were constant and I'd made more excuses than ever not to stay the night with Bree, leaving me to sleep in my bed alone. I missed the fucking hell out of her, but it was my only fix. It was the only thing I knew to do to deal with all of these horrors of my former life as they surfaced.

Being a man who fixed everything, I knew I could handle this shit on my own, and once these terrors ended, I could resume the relationship that I longed for with Bree. I wanted her to fall asleep in my arms every night. I longed to have her wake up in my arms every morning. Instead, I had a black, purring cat who seemed to judge me with his green eyes every morning. Zeus most likely hated me for pulling Bree in and out of his world, but like all felines, he got over it and moved on. Even my goddamn cat was a reminder that what I had with Bree was the best thing to ever happen to me. She was the only woman the picky guy seemed to adore.

I hadn't realized until receiving news of my mom's passing that I was stuck in such a clusterfuck of emotions. Emotions I never felt before Breanne, like accepting that I was capable of giving and receiving love. Who was the cursed one now? But didn't I deserve this curse? I know that my father would surely remind me I did.

I told myself that I didn't give a fuck about what my old man said or who he said it to while I was here paying my final respects to my mom, but here I was, unable to sleep—afraid to sleep—worried that Bree was about to discover the truth of who I really was.

She would see the man behind the illusion I put on for the world. Although, it never felt like an illusion until these damn emotions took control of me. My grandfather busted his ass to give me the second chance I deserved. Even though my mom had sent me away, and Jane hated her for that, my mother never treated me like the evil human my father did.

"So long as everyone is fucking aware, the past is in the past, Jen," I whispered from where I hid in my usual office on Mitchell and Associates' luxury jet.

"Alex, we all swore not to say one word about you or any of it. This is why I don't understand why you showed up after her stroke and why you're coming here now."

"I have my reasons. Regardless of what everyone believes, I'm not the monster that bastard led you to believe," I said.

"Is that what grandfather put in your mind? Maybe that's what you had to believe to get the inheritance that wasn't yours to begin with," Jen said with a tone that made my blood boil.

"You sound just like him, you know?"

"Mother begged me not to hate you and not to judge you, but I'm sorry. I know the truth."

"You know the truth? You were a baby when all of it happened, so you don't know a goddamn thing," I seethed. "Just keep your fucking mouth shut around Breanne, and I will be gone as soon as that casket lowers into the ground."

"You're a selfish man, Alex. Sometimes I wonder how you're even my brother. I've got to go."

I felt a lump in my throat when Jen hung up the phone. My youngest sister was raised to see only the darkness in me, and it never bothered me until now. Fuck these goddamn emotions. It was so much easier to live my life with my feelings buried, and I gave all that shit up when I allowed myself to feel more with Bree. When I experienced how wonderful it was to *feel* again, I embraced that solace with everything I was. Now, I was fighting not to resent the beautiful woman.

"Is Jane going to be here?" Bree asked as the plane smoothly landed.

"No," I answered, my head killing me as if I'd had ten bottles of bourbon the previous night. "She didn't care for my mother and thinks I'm not only a complete idiot for showing up here, but for bringing you along too."

"It's nothing I can't handle, Alex. You met both my aunts, correct?"

When I looked into her soft jade eyes, I couldn't hold anything against her like I wanted to. Not spending the night with her because of my fucking night terrors was so stupid, and why? I hadn't had one terrifying dream since being back with her and in Florida. I was prepped for them to happen because if I wanted this woman to spend her life with me, I had to embrace it all—even the questions my night terrors would conjure. Maybe the hell hounds that'd been chasing my ass for the last nine months had lost my scent and were gone altogether. I could only hope.

I rose, unable to resist her touch. "I saw the way you appeared in that room with your aunts, and they had an effect, dimples." I smiled while I accepted her tight embrace.

She lifted her chin to meet my eyes. "You never came to bed. I thought that's what red-eye flights were good for."

"Couldn't sleep." I ran my hand through her soft hair. "You look beautiful, as always." I kissed her nose. "I just want to get this over with."

"We're in Flagstaff, correct?"

"Flagstaff in January," I smirked. "You're going to feel the wintry sting until I can supplement our wardrobe with some warmer, non-Floridian clothing."

"Where are we staying?"

"You'd feel more welcome on this plane, comfortable too," I smirked. "I reserved a nice bed and breakfast and worked it out so that we'll be their only guests. It's in town, and it should be nice enough."

I kissed her lips when I was met with her no-bullshit expression.

"Then let's go get some sweaters and handle all of this." She pulled on my arm as I turned to exit the plane. "Alex," she spoke with authority. "I love you."

I forced a smile. "Please don't allow that to be your famous last words to me after this trip."

"You should relax. I'm here for you. Besides," she arched her eyebrow at me, "haven't we passed the days of me judging you?"

"I sure as hell hope so."

IT'D BEEN TWO DAYS, and today was the day that my mom would be laid to rest. After I'd manipulated ways of being at the funeral home to make arrangements without having to see anyone I may have known, my mom was officially going to be buried as if she were the town mayor.

Word came to me that my father knew I was here to make sure my money was spent solely on Mom—which was not an inaccurate assessment. He despised the fact there was nothing he could do to pull my mother's body from the astounding mahogany casket that was flown in just for her.

Everything was beautiful and as my mother had requested, and this was probably the most ostentatious show of wealth this town had ever seen. I did what I felt was right by her, though. The horse-drawn hearse that Jen had insisted my mother wanted seemed a bit excessive, but I wasn't surprised. Mother used to speak of horses when we were children, and I saw the show-jumping awards she'd earned in my grandfather's library. Either way, it was time to view her for the first time since I'd been here and the last time ever.

This beautiful city, filled with stunning pine trees and blanketed with fresh snow, didn't have the usual brisk chill that a winter morning brings. Instead, it felt heavy and dank and colder than a dungeon.

The hair on the back of my neck bristled with nerves as I stepped out of the home Bree and I had been using as a hideout. I wore my long black overcoat, a dark three-piece suit, and leather gloves I had flown in along with some of Bree's more comfortable clothes. The cool air blowing on the back of my neck offered me more of an uneasy feeling, prompting me to instinctively pull the white scarf I had draped around the nape of my long coat and bring it up to cover my exposed skin.

I probably should've waited for Bree so we could arrive together, but I wanted to see my mother alone. Bree accepted my reasons for going ahead, but I could tell she wasn't thrilled by it even though she didn't say as much. She told me she'd meet me there once she was dressed and ready, and I didn't stick around for her to change her mind and insist on joining me early. Was it a dick move on my part? Probably. Was I pushing her away from me subconsciously because I was terrified of her being here in the first place? Definitely.

"Alexander O'Conner?" I heard a young woman say, prompting me to halt my easy walk into town from the bed and breakfast.

I turned back, praying to God this wasn't going to be an awkward conversation. The woman was dressed nicely and was familiar, but I could hardly remember my life in this town.

"I'm sorry, but you have me at a disadvantage," I said, forcing the fake smile I'd been using even with Breanne since the call about my mom came in.

"It's Emma..." she paused and gave me a kind yet flirty smile. "Emma Porter? We dated freshman year. We won homecoming prince and princess together."

My smile turned into that of humor. This was the chick I'd worked my ass off to get into bed, but she always insisted we wait until marriage to have sex. She'd hardly aged a day and still had bouncing blonde, natural curls, beaming blue eyes, and a stunning smile. "Wow. That was a long time ago," I said. "You look fantastic."

"And you certainly look nothing like that jock I remember dating," she teased. "Look at you." She reached for my tie and tugged on it. "You're all grown up. Let me guess; you're a stockbroker or some wealthy, dapper man now?"

I half smiled, not particularly comfortable with any woman aside from Breanne, friendly or not, touching me. "Investor, owner," I said.

"I'm sorry to hear about your mom." She squinted as the bright sun beamed off the brilliant white snow.

I readjusted my sunglasses. "Thank you. Even though I'm sure gossip to the contrary circulated around school in one way or the other, I did love her. I'm only here to say my final farewells."

"No one knew why you left town," she chuckled, obviously a lighter conversation for her than me. I was guarded, walls up all around me in some bizarre self-preservation mode that was leading me to be cold, stiff, and unapproachable. Obviously not to Emma, though. "We missed you when you left. Can I ask why? It's always been a mystery, and your mom..." she smiled, and her eyes went to what I assumed was a memory of my mother. "Being her hairdresser, I can say that she seemed happy all of the time, even after the stroke. The only time she ever seemed upset was when I'd ask about you."

"I was a troubled kid," I admitted that truth, even if her tactlessness didn't warrant a response. "If it weren't for my grandfather, I suppose I would be serving a life sentence in jail or something of that nature."

"I doubt that," she chuckled. "Well, it looks like it's my loss. I should've chased you down, ignored you *cheating on me* with the captain of my cheer team, and kept you. You age like a fine wine; you know that?"

Very original, I thought, ready to get the fuck to the funeral home and end this reunion that meant nothing to me.

"I'm sure your husband wouldn't have approved," I offered in a colder tone, seeing her wedding ring.

"I married Thomas Foster. Do you remember him?"

"Not really. Listen, as fun as these types of reunions seem to be, I am trying to get to the funeral home before the visitation begins. It was a pleasure to see you again."

"Perhaps we'll catch up another time? After the funeral, maybe?"

"Sounds great," I said curtly. "Another time, then."

I briskly strode off and hopped up the cleared steps of the funeral chapel. After announcing myself, the funeral director led me into the largest hall, where the overwhelming scent of floral arrangements blasted me harder than the image of my mother inside that casket. I eyed everything in the room, seeing it was all perfect and set for a queen. Paul would undoubtedly hate me for this extravagance—why waste all this perfectly good booze-buying, card game money on a dead lady, right?

I was a grown-ass man now, and Paul would have to deal with someone who didn't tolerate bullshit from even the greatest of assholes. I'd met worse men in business. I knew I could handle a drunk who hated me with everything he was.

I quietly walked up to where my mother lay peacefully at rest, her hands gently folded, and I couldn't resist but to cover them with mine. "You look like the angel you always were," I whispered, seeing where her former stroke was still recognizable on the side of her face. "I forgive you." I focused on her closed eyes. Why was I suddenly speaking like this and to someone who wasn't here to hear it? "I forgive you for everything. Rest in peace now…" I felt tears swell in my eyes, and I had to choke this shit down.

I had no idea where any of this was coming from and why those words came out of my mouth. Why would I forgive someone I don't recall blaming? I felt bad that the woman couldn't stand up to her nightmare of a husband that she feared, and I was saddened that I fucked it up enough that it made her ask her father to finish raising me, but never this. I never felt like she'd wronged me in a way that I'd stand quietly at her casket and tell her I *forgave her.*

I heard a rustling at the doorway, letting me know I'd stood here for too long, and when I turned back, I saw the evil bastard. The fucker looked broken, older than he should have, and every ounce as revolting as I remembered him. His red hair was now all white, his face was ruddy and swollen, and the rest of him looked leathery and worn. Thank God I got my mother's genes from the Sicilian side of the family because that's what allowed me to inwardly smile at the fact that I looked nothing like this wicked mother fucker.

"I see you've put on quite the show for her," he spoke as I locked eyes with him. He stood shorter and stockier than I did, so making eye contact had to be a brutally charged moment for him—the day when he had to look up and meet my eyes. "Not surprised," he said, then eyed the group filing in behind him. "You can go now. I guess I'll be forced to see you again."

"Until she's in the ground," I said firmly, then brushed past him, eyeing my sister Jen and her greasy-haired husband on my way out of the chapel hall.

Fuck if I didn't hate that man more with every stride that I took out of that room. Son of a bitch. I suddenly felt like that little boy who didn't understand why his father despised him. I felt weak with emotion, and I hated it.

I had to go to the grave. I had to see it for myself and try to finally make sense of it all. The grave was the reason the old man hated me with every bone in his body.

I marched through the brisk streets, seeing the entrance to the cemetery and the plot that was dug up across the tree-covered, snow-filled lawns—Mom's final resting place. I kept walking, and I chewed on my bottom lip when I stopped and stood in front of the headstone that read my twin brother's name.

"Albert," I softly said, not remembering him well. We were only six years old when it happened.

I couldn't say another word. I couldn't do anything but stare at the grave of the six-year-old boy who'd died so tragically. This was the reason my old man hated me and became a raging alcoholic, the reason my mother finally kicked me out of the house, and the reason why I stood at her coffin and told her I forgave her. She hated me for this too—for Albert's grave and the fact I could stand in front of it with a life ahead of me. This grave was the reason I was told I would never find love. It was the very reason I didn't deserve to be happy.

Fuck. Why was I standing here?

"Alex?" Bree questioned from behind me.

I quickly turned and walked away from my twin brother's grave, praying to God the woman didn't ask who was in that plot.

"What are you doing here?" I asked her, treating her as if she were suddenly my enemy, just like everyone else in this town.

"I came looking for you. My God, you look awful," she said carefully with grief-stricken eyes. "Are you okay?"

"I'm burying my mother in a fucking hell hole today. Why would you possibly fucking think I am anything close to resembling okay?"

She stepped back, and her face was as stern as mine was. "I know this isn't easy, but I won't stand here and listen to you talk like that to me."

"Why did you follow me?" I insisted, feeling like those goddamn hell hounds were on my ass again. "Answer me, Breanne. You can't leave me alone for two seconds, can you?"

"Hang on a second," she confronted my diabolical-sounding voice with a menacing one of her own. "I wasn't following you. I saw you cross the street and walk here from the funeral home. I was coming to check on you. Jesus Christ, what the hell has gotten into you?"

I moved out of the cemetery, feeling as though it was that place that was provoking my mental ass.

"Sorry," I responded coldly. I was irritated that I had to worry about her on top of processing everything else. I knew it was irrational, but it was also the reason I didn't want her to fucking come on this trip in the first place. It was hard to process shit that you couldn't even bring yourself to share with someone else. I was forced into this situation, and I wasn't handling it well. "I saw my old man, and things are just fucking with my mind. I didn't expect that they would."

"The last thing I want to do is cause you any more strife today than you're already feeling, but you can't talk to me that way. I'm not some weird-ass stalker. I'm only trying to help."

"I get it. Sorry." The last thing I wanted to do was fight with Bree, especially when there were so many other people I wanted to lash out at, but I was barely holding myself together at this point. It was unfair of me to expect her to know she was crossing some invisible boundaries within my fucked-up psyche.

"Let's just get through this and go home. That's what you want, right?" she said, looking at me with confusion.

"It is."

"I noticed you didn't sleep again last night. That and you're treating me like I'm some alien who's following you around. Don't you dare shut down on me, Alex Grayson."

"I don't plan to. You're the only one in my corner here."

"Then if you want me to stay there, don't act like some psychopath in the cemetery," she half-grinned. "You look like death yourself. You probably should eat before all of this starts. Maybe take a nap unless you have somewhere else you need to be that consists of me stalking you in this freezing-ass weather. Please tell me you're at least hungry."

"I could eat," I said.

"Then let's make up for you going on twenty-four hours or more now without sleep by fueling you up with food."

I licked my lips and glared over at the group of people standing outside of the funeral home. In just four short hours, we'd sit in that room together, and then I would excuse Bree and myself after mom went into the ground.

Something strange told me that I wasn't leaving directly afterward, though. An odd feeling slammed into my chest, telling me I wasn't getting out of this hell without everything finally coming full circle. The past was rushing back to haunt me. No matter how I tried to push it down, it was bubbling and about to boil over. The dark side of my life would finally end this slight reprieve of happiness I'd had since I gave myself to Breanne Stone. I knew that more than anything at this moment, and I should've tried harder to get her home instead of allowing her to come along.

This would end it all. It was only a matter of how.

CHAPTER THIRTY-FIVE
BREE

The funeral services were beyond lovely. Kind words were spoken about Alex's mother, and I felt nothing but sorrow for the man sitting stiffly at my side. He was undeniably an outsider here even though this was his mother, and he'd funded the entire thing.

It was bullshit that he had to grieve her death on top of people eyeing him weirdly for whatever reason. I simply ignored the staring. Alex was dressed like the billion-dollar man he was, and it was evident that it was making him a target. He presented himself intimidatingly, his dark gaze set solely on the casket throughout the entire service, and he looked like the most important, influential person in the room.

I lifted my chin, held onto his forearm while he clasped his hands together in his lap, and I wondered where it would go from here. When Alex's knuckles grew white, and his forearm tightened, that's when I deduced who his father was—the short, white-haired man with the flushed face walking to the front of the room in a dark suit was Paul O'Connor.

Apparently, O'Connor was Alex's surname at birth, and it only took me insisting I join him at his mother's funeral to get that tiny bit of info. There was so much information from his past that he kept from me, and yet he wanted me to do a backflip of love into marriage.

His actions at the cemetery earlier today didn't make me feel better about how things had been going since he found out about his mother either. I knew he was going through something beyond grief. I knew grief all too well, and this was much more than that. Whatever was bothering him was much bigger than he was saying, and that bothered me most. I didn't know what he was dealing with, and the fact that he still wouldn't open up to me at such a time concerned me because there was no way I could support him if he were entirely closed off.

Maybe I was wrong about everything. It sure as hell didn't look like we were in friendly territory, so I figured it would be best to wait and see how everything played out.

Younger people our age in attendance expressed their sympathies to a cold and indifferent Alex, and I could sense they were pretty shocked to see him in town again. One woman couldn't remove her eyes from him, but we were in his hometown, so it was probably an ex-girlfriend or something. I didn't blame her for being captivated by the guy and studying me skeptically. Even at a funeral, he was the hottest guy in the place.

"Thank you all for attending, those of you who were invited, and those who deemed it necessary to pay their final respects. My wife was a beautiful woman, and the only sweetheart out there who has the ability to bring even the darkest of individuals to see her onto the next life," he chuckled, but his words seemed to be directed at Alex. "She was with me while I wasn't a pleasant man. Our children were young, and things were difficult, to say the least, but she remained loyal to her husband over all things—even her children. I felt that from my sweetheart, and I'll cherish her until I meet her again in heaven."

"Pack flip-flops, mother fucker. It's scorching where you're headed," Alex seethed under his breath.

"I didn't expect the donations you all so kindly offered on this day we celebrate her life, but my family thanks you for that. To those who took it upon themselves to prove something to the entire town—

arranging this elaborate casket, the thousands of flowers that are here, and of course, the horse-drawn hearse that awaits to carry her to her final resting place—well, none of that mattered to her. She wasn't a woman who flaunted herself to anyone, and almost everyone in this room knows that. Then again, when you have those who feel guilty," he sneered and waved his hand over the beautiful casket and floral arrangement lying over the top of it, "well, this is a perfect example of guilt from our greatest donor of all."

"Please tell me he's not speaking about *you*," I said under my breath so that only Alex could hear.

Alex nodded with a look of death directed at his father, who was making it blatantly obvious that Alex was unwelcome. I tuned out that vile man's words after that. I completely understood why Alex didn't want me to see this side of his life now. After witnessing this small portion of the funeral, my heart broke for Alex, and by this point, I knew why the man never spoke of his past.

Alex's dad was a singularly miserable piece of shit. What kind of person would do something like this to their child, especially at their wife's funeral? This man couldn't shut up about how much he *loved* his wife, and in the same breath, he was hateful beyond belief to his son. All that love sentiment seemed like a crock of shit to me.

I held tightly to Alex's arm, hoping that the gesture would ease any anger or hurt his dad may have conjured during his speech—or whatever the hell anyone would want to call that disgrace.

After the graveside service, more people than not asked Alex to join them at the luncheon at a local hall in town. I could hear the resistance in Alex's voice, but he finally conceded.

"We're here for fifteen minutes tops. I can't believe any of these people want a reunion," Alex stated as we walked into an area decorated with tablecloths, centerpieces, and a cafeteria-like buffet.

"Maybe they're happy to see you again, unlike your mother's husband." I was careful not to refer to that man as his father.

"I can hardly remember anyone here," Alex said, pulling out my chair for me. "That's the most annoying part. Anyone who I might've remembered or considered a friend," he sat next to me, "have grown up, gotten careers, and moved away. I don't know why I agreed to this."

"From what I witnessed, they seem to remember you well. They knew your mother, and they seem to be happy you came for her funeral." I patted his leg, trying to get his posture to loosen some. "Let's just play it by ear and see how it goes."

Alex glanced around at the people filling the room. "The question that can't be answered is who exactly *was* my mother to all these people after I left to live with my grandfather? Was she a counselor for every fucking kid I went to school with? It seems those are the only ones who asked me to stay behind for this reception or whatever you call it."

"If she was a helpful and kind woman in her town, that's never a bad thing," I said. "Aside from your dad's underhanded BS at the funeral, her services were lovely. I understand why you wanted to say your goodbyes."

"Do me a favor," Alex turned to me, still solemn and grave, "just stay away from my family. What my father said up there today were only jabs compared to what I know the man *really* wanted to reveal to the room."

"And that is?"

"Things I have buried for a reason," he answered curtly. "And will keep buried."

Alex's hand was sweating as it held onto mine under the table. He didn't want to be here, and that was obvious, but something inside him had broken somewhere between him not sleeping since he learned about his mother's death and now. For Alex to be convinced to show up at this—or do *anything* he didn't want to do aside from closing a business deal—that surprised me. I'd never seen him cave to anything in all the time I'd known him.

Alex called the shots in everything he did, and not even his friends could convince the man to do things he wasn't down for. It was something I loved about him. He was unwavering, set in his ways, and never one to be spoken down to or persuaded to do something he didn't want to do.

"Alexander O'Connor," a young woman said, walking up with her young son, sucking on his fingers. "It's damn good to see you again."

Alex's lips tightened. "I'm having to ask a lot of forgiveness for forgetting people today, it seems," he said, his hand clenching tightly onto mine like it was a stress ball.

She took one of the six empty seats at our table. "Well, how should you remember me?" She winked at him, friendly and indeed the friendliest face out of the bunch so far. "Look at you," she smiled at him adoringly. "You grew up, and you look a hell of a lot like Mr. Johnny Depp himself. I would think you moved to California to either be that man's stunt double, or maybe you are the real—"

"Not to be rude," Alex said with a pretty damn rude tone in his voice, "but that comparison drives me mad. So, please, if we were friends, I'd rather discuss *that* instead of movie star comparisons."

"Well, aren't you the lucky one?" She looked at me. "Even if Alex wants to ignore the fact that he looks like him, he needs to accept the lucky genes he got that make him comparable to him. I'm assuming you both are an item?"

"This is Breanne," he offered, and I could tell he was done with the woman.

"Nice to meet you. I don't think you offered your name, though?" I smiled at her.

"I'm Shannon Dwight." She looked at Alex, then me. "So, you're the lucky woman to get this Johnny Depp look-a-like I spent a fun summer with?"

Alex remained highly annoyed, looking away now. I decided I'd answer the poor girl who hadn't a clue that Alex was rarely in the mood to be compared to the handsome actor, much less while being in *this* particular situation.

"Unfortunately, I never crushed on that actor," I tried to lighten Alex's mood in any way I knew how. This woman was harmless, and he was being a dick. Alex looked at me. "I wish he looked more like..." *Fuck, think of a hot actor, Bree.* Great, I was stuck. "Burt Reynolds," I finally said.

Alex unexpectedly grinned and looked over at me. "Burt Reynolds?" He chuckled for the first time in three whole days.

"Smokey and the Bandit?" Shannon said with a fun laugh.

"Yes. There's something about that mustache."

Alex looked at me with the funniest expression, and thank God that my random Hollywood hunk name saved the mood. Maybe Alex could have a decent conversation now.

"Well, you're screwed," she said to me.

"She's only turned down my marriage proposal twice now," Alex smiled at me and draped his arm over the back of my chair. "So, I need a mustache and a shitload of chest hair to get you to marry me finally?"

"You proposed?" the woman interrupted.

"I did. Twice." He smiled. I could see some relief in his face and over such a silly save too. "Turned down by this beauty, but I now know I'll be working my ass off to transform my looks into resembling another actor."

"Is California filled with actors?" she asked.

I eyed her. "You're kidding, right?"

"She's not," Alex said, colder again. "A lot of people assume actors are everywhere in California. Sorry, but I've yet to run into the man I'm forever compared to."

"Changing the subject," Shannon said. "Why don't you both join a bunch of us tonight back at my place? You know, I live in the same house where I grew up. The same room even. You might remember me then?"

What the fuck? I thought when Alex frowned.

"We'll be flying home from here. Thanks for the offer, though." Alex stood. "I'm going to head across the way, handle the final bill for all of this, and call for the chauffeur to transport our luggage to the plane." Alex stopped and turned back to me.

"I'm going to grab some hot coffee, and then I'll wait for you here."

Alex's eyes scanned the room while Shannon took Alex's obvious clues and left. He'd made it clear that he might've been a cool guy back when she knew him, but he was not the same.

I walked over to a refreshment table to get coffee for Alex and me to drink in the car on the way to the airport.

"Breanne Stone," a woman said, shocking me that she knew my first and last name. I turned to recognize Alex's sister, Jen. All I knew about her was that she was the one who hated Alex after being brainwashed to feel that way by their father.

"Jen? Is that correct?"

"Jennifer Malley," she said. "I'm Alex's youngest sister."

"Very nice to meet you. I'm sorry for your loss."

"Don't be sorry for me," she said in a bitchy-tone I wasn't expecting. "You should watch your back with Alexander, though."

"Really?" I said, knowing better than to let gossip about Alex poison my mind. "How so?"

"Of course, he hasn't told you why our family will not accept him anymore."

"I've heard enough stories," I said.

Her soft red hair looked frazzled under the fluorescent lighting, but her eyes were as beautiful and green as Alex's, and she stared at me as if she were about to drop the biggest hammer of all time just to fuck with Alex on behalf of her dad. "I'm sure you've heard that *we're* the horrible people in his life."

"He doesn't speak much of any of you. I know about his grandfather, the amazing man who raised him."

"That man was the devil himself. The only reason he'd take a murderer on like Alex—"

I felt a lump in my throat. "Murderer?" I croaked out.

She smiled, and I could smell the liquor on her breath when she let out a laugh. "Oops. My bad," she said. "That's something I suppose he wouldn't want anyone to know since that would be reason enough to ruin the Grayson family name."

I could hear the slur in her words, and I didn't want to give this woman more than I already had.

"Well, let me tell you about Alex," she continued. "He killed his brother. That's a hidden gem that no one wants to talk about. But call my father the bad guy, right? Call Paul O'Connor the horrible man who became an alcoholic because one of his sons murdered the other in a jealous rage." She giggled, and my eyes went to her travel mug that must've been filled with hard liquor. "Mother tried to forgive him," she said with tears in her eyes, "but how do you forgive your rotten son who murdered his twin—the same son who forced your husband to become an alcoholic? Alex was every problem this family didn't need. And now he's here to spit on all of us with the wealth he stole from my grandfather after moving in with that old man."

"I think you've said enough. The smell of liquor tells me you're a bit on the drunk side," I responded, not knowing what to believe.

"Watch your back, Breanne Stone," she said, stumbling backward, caught by her father. "You're with a wealthy man, but he murdered—"

"That's enough, Jen. You'll have to excuse my daughter. She's a little drunk," Paul said in a mysterious tone. His glossy eyes roamed from my heels to my eyes. "But she is right about one thing. It might be wise of you to keep your distance from Alexander."

"I'm picking up on that, thanks," I said, willing Alex to walk back into this room.

"Don't say we didn't warn you. That boy has demons and the ones that will come alive when you least expect them. He all but ruined this family," he said in a deep growl. "But that's for a better day. A better conversation, I think?"

"Yeah, I think so too," I said, completely caught off guard and not knowing whether to defend Alex or just shut my mouth at this point.

"Word is already floating around that you plan to marry him?" Paul asked.

"Let's get out of here, Bree," Alex said as he rapidly approached me, his tone lethal.

"Why so soon, Alex?" Paul taunted him.

"Because I have no desire to eat food while my mother's casket is being lowered into that boneyard across town. I'm out. It'll be the last you ever see or hear from me. I only came to say my farewells to my mother. The arrangements were made courtesy of her father as well. He made me swear on his deathbed that *you* wouldn't be the one to put her in the ground. I was here to make sure she was laid to rest with the honor and grace he raised his daughter to carry. Sadly, you tarnished all of that."

"Funny, isn't it, Alexander? And why would your Grandfather Grayson want you to be the one to put another of my family members in the ground? You ever think about that while that twisted son of a bitch raised you?"

"Because he knew you would eventually kill her, fucker," Alex snapped.

"Me, or you?" Paul slurred, obviously as drunk if not more so than his daughter. "Ah, ah, ah." He waved a finger in front of Alex's chest. "Old man Grayson knew exactly what he was doing by insisting *you* were the one to bury my bride."

"We're leaving," Alex grabbed my hand, then turned back. "Keep on drinking, though. That's always worked out marvelously for you as I remember vividly."

"Drinking was the only way that took my pain away, you murderer!"

Alex looked at me. "We seriously need to go."

"I think you're right. Day drinking at a funeral and screaming murderer to silence a room isn't my sort of funeral reception."

"It's to be expected," Alex said as we rushed to the exit. "That fucking asshole ruins everything, and he even found a way to spit on my mother's grave by being drunk at this."

"Your sister seems like she might be sharing his bottle," I mentioned once we loaded into the black SUV that Alex had waiting for us out front.

"He ruined Jen's life a long time ago. Jane would lose her fucking shit if she were part of all of that."

"Is it true?" I finally asked Alex.

"What?" Alex looked at me as if I were his sister and dad.

"That you murdered your brother?" I said softly.

Alex pulled on his sunglasses. "You're welcome to go back to your ways of judging me as you did when we first met," he said.

"I'm not judging you. I'm asking a question."

"A question put into your mind by two drunks at my mother's

funeral. People who single-handedly picked the only person who put a smile on my face back there even for a moment, and they told her I was a murderer."

I noted the driver was listening to us, and I had to play this down. "Being drunk at three in the afternoon following the lowering of a casket makes you say the craziest shit, right?"

Alex didn't smile or move a muscle. He continued to stare straight ahead even though I could hear his phone buzzing and blowing up in his hands. I had no idea what the fuck had just happened. Was he standing at his brother's gravesite in the cemetery when he acted like I'd *caught* him doing something he didn't want me to see?

He wasn't giving this information up, but I'd be damned if I was going to sit back and let people call him a murderer if it wasn't true. What was I supposed to think if he wouldn't talk to me? Hell, I was going to judge his ass if he didn't start clearing the air.

He was utterly unapproachable. I'd expected him to chill some once we boarded the aircraft, not disappear on the thing, leaving me alone until we landed. At this point, I was left to imagine the worst as I rode the elevator up to my apartment...and Alex was headed home alone.

CHAPTER THIRTY-SIX
ALEX

*T*here was a very special place in hell for people like Paul O'Connor. There had to be. If I thought that he wouldn't burn for what he did to me, from the abuse to making me believe I was the monster that killed his son, I'd lose my mind.

I woke up drenched in sweat for a solid month since getting back from making the most significant mistake of my adult life—going to my mother's funeral. Not only attending it but also bringing a woman I felt I loved around that family.

Now, my mind was fucked into a million pieces. I'd been *recalling* the goddamn nightmarish memories of my past. I couldn't help but wonder if my recollections were all the things Paul had put into my head since my brother died, or if they were what actually happened when I was a little boy?

Who the hell knew? If all of this shit were true, that would mean that when I was six years old, I murdered my brother. The nightmares that I couldn't discuss with anyone told me I was the one who killed my twin brother on that fishing trip.

Fuck me to hell. Why would I be allowed to live another day on this earth if that were the case? The dreams revealed the sickening visual of seeing Albert drown in that massive lake, and I was the one to tell him to jump in the water while Paul wasn't around. My latest night terror showed a dock, and in the dream, I convinced Albert to go to the edge before I pushed him off of it and watched him go under. The other dreams revealed that I insisted Albert get in a boat with me, and then I pushed him over the side and watched him go under. In every instance, I watched him drowning, and it was because I'd done something sinister.

Jesus Christ, I couldn't do this anymore. I hated myself more each day. These night terrors made me wake up like this every morning, and today was the worst morning yet. These dreams seemed to chip away at my psyche slowly, and it crushed my soul to realize that maybe I had done this wretched thing. It didn't seem possible, but the memories were there, and I didn't know how to explain it away.

I felt tears streaming down my cheeks. I hated my fucking life, and that going to my mother's funeral had caused these memories to come back. The real problem was that I'd allowed myself to feel something more with Breanne, and that was what opened me up to this in the first place.

How could I live another day not knowing the truth? Why couldn't I just fucking remember what happened instead of having these dreams? The only reason I hadn't checked myself into some mental institution was that I was a man known for fixing shit. Now, I needed to fix myself.

By the time I showered, I'd shaken off these terrible feelings. I may not have remembered the day my brother died, but I did remember one fact about myself growing up: Paul O'Connor was a lying, abusive drunk who hated me. He'd always blamed me for something I felt he was responsible for. Those were solid feelings.

I also knew for a fact that my grandfather hated my father. More than once, my grandfather said he was thankful he got me out of there. He only wished he could've saved my mom and younger sister too. He was helpless to save them from my dad, but he thanked God that Paul hated me enough for my grandfather to take me away and work relentlessly to heal my trauma from Paul's abuse—what trauma he *could* help to heal, it would seem.

My grandfather eventually resented my mother for ignoring his help and choosing Paul O'Connor over the ones who loved her. When he signed nearly everything over to me before he died, he remarked that his daughter wasn't to receive anything from his estate. Still, he set aside enough to give her a proper burial—the preparations to be handled by me—because he knew that Paul would spend all of the money. Hell, Paul probably would've thrown my mother in a shallow grave after he pulled the gold out of her fillings if he thought he could've bought more booze.

I eventually became the son my grandfather had always wanted, and my mother became an estranged daughter. My grandfather was an exceedingly wealthy man, and he wasn't a fool. He was strict and inflexible with my upbringing, and that structure was what I craved, whether or not I knew it at the time. All I could think of now were the many times my grandfather had expressed how proud he was of me, so how could I believe these dreams were true? My grandfather would've had nothing to do with me if I was some psychopath who killed my brother.

All I wanted to do now was erase the dream, forget the fact I'd pushed Bree away for the sake of being able to fucking breathe normally since this shit started happening, and start my day. Fuck my feelings.

I still don't know how she hadn't chewed my ass out for dropping her as if being together for almost a year didn't mean anything to me. I even gave her my fucking cat—of all the stupid goddamn things a heartless bastard would do. I knew I'd cracked and was fucked in the head, but I needed space from everything, and the only place I could function was at work after I made sure Bree wasn't around. Thank God she was busier than hell. She had four projects that kept her out of my life and allowed me to work, go home, and fall asleep, only to wake up like this every damn day since that funeral.

Imagining Bree's smile from yesterday when she walked up to me when I was talking to an HR rep was enough to torment me and add to my miserable life. This day had to have been the worst of them all because I longed to hold her again, and it was painful knowing that may never happen again.

My chest was heavier than fuck, my respirations shallow, and I knew if I didn't calm the fuck down, I'd probably end up in the emergency room. I was so all over the place emotionally that I didn't know which way was up or down anymore. Usually, this shit would've passed by now, especially after taking a hot shower to snap me out of this guilty-as-hell mind-fuck.

I closed my eyes and tried to breathe it all out—the pain that stabbed like a fucking knife in my chest, the fact that after all these years, the hell hounds had finally ripped the flesh from my skin and left me in this state, and that opened me up to finally become Paul O'Connor's victim. There. I admitted it. I was a goddamn victim even though all my life I'd been told I was the victimizer who'd ruined my family.

"Son of a bitch!" I wailed, unable to suck in a breath and pissed as fuck that I was stuck in some madhouse of emotions.

It felt like my chest was being crushed, and I knew something was wrong. I needed to get help. I slipped on a hoodie and sweats and called for my neighbor to drive my ass to the hospital.

My eyes were closed the entire ride, and I couldn't tolerate Shirley's voice for another second. I should've just fucking collapsed at home and let my father finally have his day in the sun where he was able to spit on my grave. At long last, the son he hated would be off the face of the earth like he intended with every punch to my face, kick to my stomach, and the rest of the torture he subjected me to when I was a kid.

"We're here, honey," she said, running her hand over my sweaty forehead. "I'm running in ahead of you. I'll kill you if you die on me, Alexander."

AFTER BEING RUSHED into the ER and having to call in Jim as my next of kin, I was given a heavy dose of medication for a panic attack, and I knew I was a solid case of fucked-up now.

"I've got him," I heard Jake. "What time did he come in, and what did his EKG's show?"

"He suffered a pretty severe panic attack," Dr. Sanchez told him. "And don't give him hell for this, either."

"Oh, don't worry. My brother will be more than happy to give him hell. I don't need to do a thing," Jake said with a laugh.

I felt calmer than I had in months, and I could probably catch up on ten or eleven months of sleep about now. The last thing I needed was my chief cardiothoracic surgeon friend walking in and grilling my ass. Jake wouldn't allow me to get up and leave this place as if nothing happened. Jake would go on a mission to uncover what'd caused my sorry ass to end up at Saint John's ER if I didn't start talking.

"Hey, handsome," he said, walking in with his white doctor's lab coat over his suit. "I was just making my evening rounds when my boyfriend, who stopped talking to me a month ago, had a panic attack because he knew losing me was the stupidest fucking thing to ever happen to him."

"You're lucky I'm loaded up on drugs," I said, half-smiling.

"What happened, man? Is Jim putting you and Bree under so much pressure at that firm that you stopped sleeping with her, making you —the last person on this earth I'd ever expect this from—have a panic attack? What will everyone say?"

"You think I give a fuck?"

Jake grinned. "I need to run more tests on you." He sat on the side of my bed. "It would take you having a heart attack for you not to give a damn about what we'd say about all of this bullshit."

I frowned. "What are you talking about?"

"Bree and her friends happen to be pretty tight with Ash and the girls." His eyes rose in humor. "Chicks talk, man, and especially when they feel that one of their own is getting shit from a dickbag of a boyfriend..." he paused. "Or was it *fiancé*? What the fuck are you, or *were* you two, anyway?"

"I'm not talking about relationships with you," I said.

"I knew I waited too long to get down to you. Now, all the meds have worn off, and you're an asshole again."

"Seriously, Jacob," I said. "It's all a goddamn nightmare. I'm not taking more drugs. I want to get the fuck out of here, and I'm not talking about any of this."

"The hell you're not, fucker," Collin said, entering the room. "Jake hit up the group text saying you were in for a heart attack?"

"It's what it fucking felt like," I added, my brain foggy from the medication, not knowing how to shut the hell up. "It doesn't matter. I had a panic attack. Big damn deal. Dr. Sanchez was supposedly sending me home, but apparently, he decided to let dipshit here know he helped me."

Jake eyed his neurosurgeon best friend. "That's because I was paged that a friend of mine was coming in with heart attack read-outs. Do you remember insisting only *Dr. Mitchell* cut you open?" Jake asked me.

"I remember I was scared as fuck," I raised my eyebrows at the two men who were trying to remain stern with me. "Then I still didn't believe Sanchez knew what he was talking about when he said it was merely a panic attack and not a heart attack."

"Next time, I'll ensure that medical science separates the two that can mirror each other," Jake said. "Perhaps a brain aneurism is occurring as well because something caused this, and I know you're not under pressure at work."

"I could peel his skull open and check for any damage," Collin smirked and patted my leg. "Listen, I just got paged. Scans aren't looking good for this trauma patient, so get some rest, and get back in the game, buddy."

"I don't want Breanne knowing about this," I told Jake.

"Then you probably shouldn't have gotten on the hospital intercom and called for her and me while vocalizing your last will and testament for all to hear." He sighed while I closed my eyes and pinched the bridge of my nose. "You're giving her Zeus? We all know that Collin got first dibs on your cat. That's straight-up fucked."

"Jake, is he okay?" I heard Jim say.

"Panic attack," Jake said. I wasn't daring to open my eyes at this point. "He'll be fine."

"Sign him out of here," Jim said. "Alex, your ass is coming home with me."

That's when my eyes reopened. "I have a panic attack, and now I'm being treated like a helpless child?" I said. "No thanks. I'm heading home and thankful I'm alive." I swung my legs over the side of my bed. "How about that? People in business have panic attacks all the damn time. This is nothing new. I'm leaving."

"In what car?" Jim asked.

"I'll hitchhike before I sit here and have to listen to anyone tell me where I'm going. I'm not talking shit out. I'm not doing therapy, and I swear to God that if Bree finds out I was here and not on some job site, I'll lose my shit."

"Too late. You've already lost your shit," Jim said as he eyed my hospital gown. "I'm not just talking about the hospital either. All of it. I thought you and Bree broke up, so why would I tell her you came to the hospital?"

"Ah," I grinned. "It looks like Av doesn't like to talk as much as Ash does."

"What the fuck is going on?" Jim flashed Jake and me his dick-head look.

Jake pointed his thumb back toward me. "Ash mentioned something about this one acting out of character since getting back from the funeral he didn't tell us about."

"It's just child psychology coming full circle," I looked at Jim. "Nothing I can't deal with on my own."

"All while you're losing the *only girl* you've ever loved and checking yourself into a hospital? Your full-circle idea sounds like a circle of bullshit to me."

"No kidding. When did we ever imagine Alex would come in here, begging me to cut him open and fix his ticker?" Jake added.

"Yeah, that's enough to make me believe something else is up," Jim said. "Now, grab your shit. I'll take you home," he turned back to me as he and Jake went to leave the room, "and you're going to come clean on whatever caused you to think you were having a coronary, Mr. O'Connor. I fucking knew you were Irish."

As Jim and Jake talked in softer voices, leaving me to grab my stuff and get the hell out of this ER room, I pulled on my clothes and tried my best to figure out how I'd deal with Jim. This wasn't going to be an easy blow-off, but Jesus, I didn't even know what the truth of my past was.

"START TALKING," Jim ordered when we reached my house, and he followed me in. "I allowed you plenty of time to think in silence on the ride here, and now it's time to talk. What is going on with you?"

"You know what's going on," I said, walking to my fridge and grabbing a bottle of water. "I opened myself up to feeling all these emotions, and it all backfired on my ass. Now I'm a walking, talking, emotional horror-show."

"Bullshit," Jim said, sitting in the chair next to the couch I slumped onto. "I'm not buying it, Alex. Try again."

"What do you want to know?" I looked over at him. "That my dad got to me? That *falling in fucking love* opened me up to emotions that are responsible for me having a goddamn panic attack?"

"Start at the top," Jim crossed an ankle over his knee. "You're my best friend. We both have fucked-up pasts that we never liked to talk about. I know that fucker beat the hell out of you. I also know that it was fucked-up that your grandfather didn't report that abusive asshole too. I just have one *stupid* question." He knit his eyebrows together. "Why was it all covered up?"

"You know that answer." I tipped back the water to moisten my parched lips. "The Grayson name was to remain untarnished. I was groomed in that manner, and I was also removed from the other fucking family so things would end there, and mom would be safe?" I posed that mainly as a question to myself I'd never asked before. I'd never talked about any of this to anyone, even Jim.

"Your mom would be safe?" Jim instantly caught on to what I'd said. "What the fuck was going on that your grandfather would bury this? He had the money to pay off your father and get him completely out of *all* your lives if he needed to. Still, your mom just let him take you out of there and remained behind?"

"I don't fucking know why anything went down the way it did, Jim. I seriously can't remember anything but that son of a bitch hating me and me being pulled out of the family to save the rest of them." I pinched the bridge of my nose and sighed.

"What prompted the panic attack? I'm your best friend, and you *will* talk. We're practically brothers, Alex, and you have to know I'm here for you in any way I can be. You cut Breanne off, and you won't talk to her, but I'll be damned if I let you take the easy way out and not talk out whatever it is you're dealing with. Something is up, and it's not just that your father hated you."

"Fine. Since coming back from that funeral, I've had dreams that scare the shit out of me, all right?" I looked at him. "I've had night terrors since I was a kid, but they've intensified since I started to loosen up *emotionally* with Breanne."

"Night terrors?" Jim questioned.

"You heard me. When I got home from that goddamn funeral— something I was too stupid to insist Bree *not* attend—that's the first time I was able to recall the dreams that went along with them after I woke up. Who am I kidding? They're not just *dreams*. They're fucking terrorizing nightmares. They point to me murdering my twin brother."

Jim stared at me in disbelief, which was the way I suspected he would—the way he probably should. I'd just admitted what I was always told as a child—I was a murderer.

"Night terrors, dreams, visions, or whatever you claim this to be, I don't buy what you just told me," Jim said firmly. "Last I checked, Alex Grayson didn't pop up in the databases as a murderer, and I know for a fact Oxford wouldn't have admitted you if that shit were true. Let's back up just a fucking second, though. You had a twin brother who died?" Jim's eyes were filled with shock and sadness after hearing about Albert for the first time.

"Yes, and that fucker of a dad always told me I killed him. Now, these dreams are so vivid, and they're making me think that he could be right."

"There's no fucking way you killed your brother. How old were you both when this happened?"

"We were six. The date on Albert's grave confirms that much, anyway."

"And do you remember him? I mean, do you remember anything about his death?"

I shook my head. "No. I only remember being told I killed my brother and ruined my family. My dad tortured me any way he could—beat the hell out of me, choked me, burned me, and starved me, whatever he could get away with—but it wasn't until I caught him beating the shit out of mom that I nearly killed the mother fucker myself," I sighed. "That's when my grandfather took me away."

"If you *murdered* your brother, the law would know. Court and custody battles with the State would have ensued, Alex. There's no way in hell you can cover something like that up, not even your wealthy grandfather with all the money he had."

"What if my grandfather paid everyone off? Judges or congress members or senators? You know the influence he had. What if I killed Albert?"

"You believe that shit?" Jim questioned. "There's more to this, and I know that without question. If your old man put something into your brain to make you believe that you murdered your brother, well, goddamn. That's the worst thing I think I've ever heard in my life. That's fucked-up beyond all else."

"Why would Paul let me stay in that house with my sisters until I was a teenager? Or with his wife?" I pulled my feet off the coffee table and rested my elbows on my knees. "If this is true, this makes me the monster he's always said I am."

"Fuck that," Jim's voice was lethal. "I'm serious. You're going to lose these irrational thoughts. Get some goddamn counseling and fix yourself. I'm not even falling for your line of bullshit, saying that this is all started because you were finally in a relationship where you opened yourself up. I don't believe that's the reason you're having a full-blown emotional breakdown."

"Regardless of your opinion, I was a shallow asshole before her. I'd been raised to believe that I was incapable of giving or receiving love. I believed that until I met Breanne. Once I allowed myself to open up, that's when the night terrors began coming on more frequently, and now they're unbearable. I can't live like this. If it means shutting it down and moving on without her, then I'll do that. I have to, or I'll go insane."

"That's the most selfish thing I've ever heard you say," Jim said. "With Summer, at least you had a good reason to break things off. This reasoning you're giving me about Breanne sounds as if you're blaming her for finding something good in life."

"Finding something good?" I said with disgust. "Tell me how anything could be *good* when all I have is night terrors? I'm haunted for life because my twin brother is six feet underground, and it's my fault? I don't deserve it. Knowing my fucking father and how much he hated me, I wouldn't be surprised if he put some blood-magic curse on me to make sure this would happen if I ever found happiness."

"You need to speak to a professional, and I'm serious as fuck about that."

"I'm not sharing this with Elena or anyone. I can't. It could ruin a lot of lives if it were true."

"How the fuck did you *murder* your brother at six years old?" Jim asked. "Seriously, I want to know why my best friend's dark, cursed past is now coming to light, and I'm learning Alex is a fucking murderer."

"Million-fucking-dollar question." I stood up. "I'll look into some form of therapy because I want answers myself. I want to know if what these night terrors are revealing is true and if I did it all intently. If it's true, the authorities need to know. They need to—"

"Slow the fuck down," Jim rose to meet me. "Let's get you some good therapy, and we'll deal with the rest as it comes. I'll have Bree and your new VP cover for you, and you go wherever the best therapy is for people in your condition." He exhaled and walked over to grip my shoulder and look me in the eyes. "You've got to fix yourself before you can think about anything else. Bree will understand." He stopped when I went to speak but halted me with his sympathetic grin. "She doesn't need to know anything if that will keep you from self-sabotaging."

I frowned. "I wouldn't even know where to start. Part of me thinks I need to call up a witch or something."

"You and Breanne relate the Wizard of Oz to yourselves too fucking much." He smirked. "She probably feels like Dorothy on some yellow brick road, trying to find answers for you."

"Oh, God," I finally laughed. "Let her know I'm out for the month. She'll know if I'm not in London, so that's exactly where I need to go to get the fucking treatment that might help. I'll call Elena and see if she can recommend someone who deals with adults who have issues like mine."

"It's called childhood trauma and abuse," Jim said. "And yes, it haunts more people than just you. My bet is on the fact that your old man had a lot to do with this, and there was a reason your mother allowed her father to raise you. You might want to think about hypnosis therapy or something to tap into your subconscious."

"I just wish I could block it all again, be fucking happy, and move on."

"Well, it's obvious that you can't. I mean, you gave away your goddamn cat, for Christ's sake. We should've known something was fucking with you after Bree said you felt like you were developing allergies." He rolled his eyes. "We were all stuck in a fucking world of our own, ignoring all the red flags that you needed some help."

"But isn't that how I prefer things to be? Even now, Jimmy," I pleaded. "I don't want anyone knowing this shit. Just hearing Bree question whether or not I murdered my brother after my brainwashed sister told her—"

Jim eyed me. "Hold up. Jane told her this?"

"Jennifer," I said. "Sorry, she's one I never told you about. She's the youngest. She was hardly a year old when it happened. She grew up hearing my father call me a monster, seeing him locking me in closets or beating the shit out of me whenever the wind blew the wrong way. After I moved, Jen was given a little more insight into her murderous brother."

"This sounds like a fucking horror film," Jim said. "All right. Get this shit out of your mind. Get your ass to London. Find a reason to be there since Bree's best friend is your London VP and will mention you're in town." He stopped and sighed. "Do you *really* think it's wise to lie to her? Why not just come fucking clean, and if she bails, she bails?"

"Because I don't want rumors flying. I shut it down as best I could after Jen decided to make me out to be a murderer to her, and she's not brought up that trip since. Let's not get her involved on this topic again. If it turns out that I did this—"

"Then we deal with those issues properly, and I'm quite confident your therapist, or whoever you seek help from, will guide you in the right direction. Though," Jim's eyebrow arched at me, "I would probably warn Paul he might have cops on his doorstep soon. And fuck the Grayson name too. Your grandfather is gone, and it's only you who is left. If the name goes to hell, so be it. I'm here for you, and I think you're going to find a different truth. Now, pack your shit, and I'll handle things on my end."

CHAPTER THIRTY-SEVEN

BREE

*A*fter a long-ass month of allowing Alex to pull back and pretty much determine I was out of the picture, I'd had enough of this dysfunctional relationship. If his response to what happened at that asinine funeral was to push away the one person who he claimed to *love*, well, I had a problem with that. I wasn't raised to be treated like shit or brushed off by anyone, especially a man who believed it was okay to string me along with excuses.

Now, here I was with *his* cat—which I gladly adopted because Alex seemed like he was in a pretty dark place, and no animal deserved to be around someone who was spun out and behaving like the biggest dick I'd ever met. Even at the office, Alex Grayson was a bonified shithead in a suit all over again, and I dealt with the fallout of him going off on everyone who made even the slightest error. It was all bullshit.

Throughout the month of him blowing me off, I only saw him in passing at work. The honeymoon was officially over, and so were we, I guess. He never smiled. He never showed any emotion at all unless it was some menacing way of making people look incompetent, and I seemed to be constantly disgusted by his newfound persona.

Now, I'd learned this morning that the prick was heading to

London. The whispers that continually buzzed in our firm these days were always about Alex. This time, everyone's general feeling was overwhelming relief that he was leaving for an entire month.

"Can we talk?" I asked, opening the door to the angry miser's office.

"Talk," Alex returned flatly, his eyes dark and studying me as if I were about to go down as his next victim. A shiver ran up my spine, and instead of being attracted to this look like I used to be, it reminded me of him being called a murderer by his family. That, of course, was something he refused to speak about with me. A *minor issue*, he called it. His last words to me on the topic were these: *"I'm sure you'll judge me either way..."* I had no idea what to think about it anymore, but as I stood in this office, I couldn't help but wonder what was in this mystery man's past.

"I hear you'll be giving us all a break from your shitty mood and spending some time with my former VP in London?"

"Theo is still our vice president, Breanne." Alex rolled his eyes, then looked back at his computer monitors. "Anything else?"

"I'd like to go," I simply stated. "I'm uncertain about him being *my* vice president at all since I'm not on my way as co-owner to see whatever it is you need to see in person at our London offices."

Alex's expression tightened. "I'll send him your regards." He looked at me. "You're needed here to finalize Saint John's. I'm not sure why you'd be willing to walk away from a project that you're heading up."

"Are you questioning my way of running the business?"

"I shouldn't have to be, but I guess I am. Why would you go to London to deal with something I already have under my control? I believe the Saint John's project finalization would be more important. The three other projects you're spearheading should be too. It sounds like this is an excuse for a reunion with a friend."

"Sounds like you're a complete asshole, and I have no idea what makes you feel like you can talk to me like this."

I was fuming, but this had just broken the record for the most extended conversation he and I had since getting home from his mother's funeral.

"I'm not trying to be an asshole. I just need to handle this trip on my own." His expression seemed tortured. "Fuck. I warned you I could hurt you, and I see that shit written all over your face. I've seen it since we got back, and I can't do this anymore. I need a break."

"A break from seeing that you've been fucking with my mind since your mother's funeral? You have given me your cat for some reason— a consolation prize, maybe? I don't know. What I do know is that you seem to be blowing everyone off these days. I'm so fucking confused by everything that you have me right where you want me."

"And where's that?" He hardened up again.

"Not giving a damn about us or wanting to question why you flipped some switch and turned into the evil bastard you…" I stopped when I watched his expression turn ominous. "I'm sorry," I said, flustered. "So, we're done, then?"

"With this conversation? Yes."

"No, with *us*, Alex," I snapped, feeling tears trying to bubble up and forcing them away. "We're done. You know, the two people who were talking about marriage after a month of dating?"

He exhaled. "I think it's better for you if you moved on, yes." He rose and turned his back to me, staring out of his office windows. "I think it's obvious I didn't know what the fuck I was doing when I spouted off words of love, relationships, and fucking marriage proposals. Jesus Christ, unless you were desperate, most women would call me out on that and would have smartly ditched my ass a long time ago."

I felt my blood burning in my veins with each thundering beat of my heart. This man was colder than I'd ever seen in a human being, and it all happened after that godforsaken funeral.

"You may say all of that shit, but I felt love from you," I called him out for the truth of what I knew between Alex and me. "It was fast, completely crazy, and fun, but you proved you loved me."

"How so?" Alex scoffed.

He asked the question as if he didn't believe me, but he was curious. This was the most bizarre conversation in the world, aside from the conversations I'd had with myself about whether or not I fell in love with a murderer. Alex, a murderer? I highly doubted that. I knew there was more to his story, and I wasn't foolish enough to fall for the lines that came out of two disgruntled drunken family members at a funeral. There was no way in hell I would fall for that.

"I knew you truly loved me the night I saw the difficulty in your eyes when you had to tell me about my dad. That night, when I felt so alone, you held me. I don't know how to explain it, but something deepened between us. I felt it, and I know you felt it."

"I'm glad I could be there for you during a hard time, but it's over, Bree. Accept it and move on. I'm going to London. I need to address issues there, and if you want to meet up with Theo again, do it when I'm not there."

"What the fuck happened, Alex? Jesus Christ, please fucking tell me. You mentally checked out after that funeral."

"Goddammit, I'm not reliving that day and especially with you," he said. "Move the fuck on. How hard is that to understand? I'm not the man you want or need." He turned back to me. "They refer to relationships like this—where people like *you* try to fix a man like *me* —as toxic."

"No shit?" I mocked him. "But I was never trying to fix you." I rose, pissed and heartbroken. "I was trying to be there for you."

"I don't need *anyone* in this hellish world of mine to *be there* for me," he said. "I'm sorry I pulled you in like this. I'm sorry I wasn't smart enough to end it before it began, but maybe that's the bastard in me I tried to warn you about. I selfishly let us run on for almost a year in a pointless relationship."

"You're not him, you know? If that's what this is about—childhood memories of a hateful father, and a mother who sent you away. You're not that man's creation. I saw the good in you, and you have a huge heart. It's what I fell for when you used your crazy ways to try and help fix my financial burdens."

"Speaking of which," Alex said, "I made a promise to your father, and I believe I kept my end of that deal. Your finances are fixed, and the business is growing nicely with you, running our creative departments."

"You failed to mention that I would remain happy," I said in anger.

"I don't believe he requested that Jim and I *keep* you happy."

"All right," I practically shouted. "I get it. It's over. You're right. A month apart could do both of us some good. Hopefully, the morale in this place can be restored as well since you've turned into a miserable dick."

"Just don't let the place go to hell while I'm gone."

I looked at him in disbelief, and then suddenly, through this mask of anger he hid behind, I saw his eyes showing an intense amount of fear and sadness. His stern expression faded that second, and I saw how worn and exhausted Alex looked.

I had to leave. I couldn't stand here and look at a man who was fighting battles outside of what we *had* in a relationship and on his own. I couldn't help him. He wouldn't let me, and I would only become exhausted by trying.

"Bree," he said with an exhale. It was the first time he'd said *Bree* in far too long.

"What?" I turned back, my hand already on the door, ready to leave.

"I'm sorry it came to this. I don't know any other way of preventing..." he paused and ran his hands over his face. He dropped his hands and slid them into his pockets. "You made me feel love again," he said, cocking his head to the side, "and made me believe that the emotion was not just a word but an essence and the core to being happy. I only wish I could've cared for you as I wanted. Fuck, I don't even know what I'm saying, but I did feel love with you, and I'm sorry that I couldn't hold up on my end in this relationship."

"I have no idea what went wrong with you," I said softly. "Obviously, something cracked, and it was after you had to face your family. That's when you changed, and we've hardly talked or have seen each other since. You're right. Being in a relationship with you in *this state* is not healthy for either of us. If you're struggling with something deeper that you don't trust telling me, then maybe it's time you lose the pride instead of me." I recalled when Alex busted his ass to involve himself in my financial problems, and he called me out for being too prideful. He was right. I was prideful, and I'd learned a harsh lesson from that.

"The tables have turned in such a bizarre way," he half-smiled. "I miss you."

"Talk to Elena, Alex," I offered, knowing his best friend's wife was a psychiatrist. "I'm sure she could direct you somewhere to get some help. I guess you have to want the help, though, and I don't know how you feel anymore. You've not given me much after hearing what your family had to say."

"Do you believe them? Or did you?"

"Would it matter at this point?"

"I think it would."

"Well, I would've believed *you* if you answered me in the first place. Now, I'm only left to wonder while looking at a man I don't recognize anymore."

"Right." He nodded. "I'll be gone for a month," he reminded me. "Try not to let the *Titanic* sink while I'm gone, eh?"

Titanic jokes again? I had no idea how he could attempt to be cute at this point. I'd opened the door for him to defend himself against his drunken family's accusations, and nothing. Maybe he was what they called him. If he wasn't, why wouldn't he put up a fight? Instead, he made it seem like it would be easier to push away and go on living separate lives. This would be so much easier if I didn't love the man.

IT TOOK me remaining friends with the wives of Alex's best friends to learn that he'd talked to Elena, and he was headed off to London. He wasn't going to check on that office, though. He was going to get help. No one knew what was truly up with him, but Jim. From what Jim had said, Alex had some severe childhood trauma, and he was getting help for it.

None of us wanted to gossip about him, but no one knew what was going on either. I'd finally accepted that Alex and I were over and that if he could at least get some therapy for whatever happened in that household, maybe he'd find peace.

Elena said Alex was pretty vague with her, saying that he didn't know the truth of why his father hated him, nor why his grandfather took him in. He was overflowing with horrible emotions, and I was hoping that in the two weeks he'd been gone out of the month he was scheduled to be away, he would get help and maybe find peace.

I didn't know what to think anymore. I was just happy that it was girls' night at my place, and the only male in the room—Zeus, the cat—wasn't concerned about anything but napping on the foot of my bed.

Knock! Knock! Knock!

"Who knocks these days?" Nat asked with a laugh. "Seriously. We're at *your* place, Bree."

"It's most likely Jake or Collin," Cass said while she swiped polish over her toenail. "I swear, I don't know how you girls deal with your husbands' pranks."

I left the girls with their margaritas and bounded up the steps to answer my door. I also figured that Ash and Elena's husbands most likely came over to give us grief because they rarely missed an opportunity to do so.

To my utter shock, when I swung open my front door, I saw my Aunt Blaire. I had to take a step back, wondering if Max were standing behind her, showing up to laugh in my face about my newly failed relationship.

"Blaire?" I questioned as the laughter of the girls died down behind me.

"You used to call me aunt," she said with an arch of her perfectly shaped eyebrow. "I still haven't figured out why you stopped."

"Family members are referred to by family names. Family members don't take the side of the man who cheated on you, so if you ask me, you lost the familial title all on your own."

"May I come in?" she responded.

"Why are you here?" I questioned her. "Max has already laughed in my face after he found out I split with Alex. Let me guess; you're here to do the same?"

"Why would I do something so childish?" she eyed me.

"Because Alex made sure that you or that dick didn't get this place from me."

"Breanne," she said more sternly, "I understand that we have some rocky ground in our past since you embarrassed yourself on your wedding day, but that's in the past. I need to tell you that Alex is the main reason that I'm here. I just returned from my former friend's grave—Alex's mother's. I found out that Sarah passed, and I've been worried about Alex since I ran into that son of a bitch, Paul O'Connor. I listened to what he had to say about you and Alex being at her funeral."

"What?" I said in a tone of disbelief. "If you're here—wait, you were *friends* with his mother?" My brain was scrambling to make heads or tails of why this woman was here in the first place, and now, I *think* she just said she was friends with Alex's mother.

Why the fuck would she be worried about him? Did she want his money? Who knew, but I had a psychiatrist sitting in my living room, and if my aunt were here for anything other than what she said, Elena would see right through her.

"Come in," I said, shaking my head and not sure if I wanted to hear this woman speak about Alex without him present to defend himself.

"I'd rather we speak in private," she said as more of an order than a request.

"Whatever you have to say about Alex, you can say here. You're surrounded by people who love him. If you're here to talk shit behind his back, then you might as well leave now."

She looked at me. "Has Alex said anything about his life as a child to you? About Albert?"

"No," I said, wanting her to talk to see if anything would add up. "All I know is that his father and sister told me to stay away from him."

She sighed. "Paul O'Connor is a dangerous and extremely vile human being," she stated. "I hated him from the second my beautiful friend started to date him, and then married him because he got her pregnant." She had the same sadness on her face that I remembered her having at my father's funeral. "I thought that drunken abuser would kill her. I begged her not to marry simply because he got her pregnant."

"Jesus Christ," Avery said. "You're serious?"

My heart was racing in my chest. "If you knew Alex's mom, did my mother know her too?"

"Your mother married your father when I was in college, and that's where I met Sarah. Sarah and I were close, and that's when she got pregnant. She dropped out soon after, and then she got married to Paul. I was always worried about her well-being, and I was extremely grateful that she worked so hard to stay in contact with me. I didn't trust Paul at all. He was a violent, raging drunk even then, and I watched my best friend marry him because she thought it was the right thing to do. I need to make sure your Alex is okay," she insisted, looking around the room.

"He's not mine anymore," I said. "We ended things."

"A shame. I knew that bastard would ruin the boy's happiness somehow, and after everything that Sarah's father did to protect Alex too. He seemed to be doing rather well when I saw him here. He's very handsome—he gets his genetics from his mother. She was such a rare beauty, and she fell for that scumbag's charms. All he wanted was her family money, you know?"

Sort of like you with every man you've ever met? I thought.

"Alex is grieving his mother's death," I said, not knowing if I should mention his father and sister's bullshit and what made him snap at the funeral.

"Does young Alex remember his past in that home and why his grandfather and mother insisted on him leaving?"

"*Young Alex* is a grown-ass man now who's determined not to speak a word of his past," I said.

"That makes sense," she nodded. "Mr. Grayson *and* Sarah knew he was going to end up damaged and as horrible of a man as his father was if they didn't rescue him from that home."

"What happened, Aunt Blaire?"

"His drunken father came back from a fishing trip." She closed her eyes and held her chest. "Alex was alive, and a search and rescue team was scouring the lake for his twin brother's body."

"What?" I said, and I could've sworn the other women in the room said the same thing at the same time.

"Paul blamed Alex for the death of Albert, but we knew Alex did not kill his brother," she said. "We kept tight-lipped about it, and it was filed away as a drowning accident. But as time went on and Alex grew older, I would meet Sarah for clandestine lunches and beg her to leave that man. I pleaded with her to take her kids away before he ruined all of them. It seemed as though Paul only had it out for Alex, you know?" she said as if I could answer any of this with the current shock I was in at the moment. "Paul blamed that boy for everything, but there was no way that happy child would kill his twin. Those boys adored each other."

She remained serious, and then she smiled, her eyes looking at the carpet while I trembled, listening to what she was saying. "Before Albert drowned, Sarah and I would meet. My God, did Paul ever hate that she had friends. He was insanely jealous, but the man was drunk morning, noon, and night. She was pregnant the last time we met. I saw her oldest daughter and the twins—she would have to sneak out the children, of course. Alex and Albert were feisty, and I found it so adorable how Alex would grab Albert and kiss him, giggling when Albert became annoyed. So happy," she said as a tear slipped from her eye. She sniffed and looked at me. "When I saw him with you, the way he came so protectively and lovingly to your side validated that Mr. Grayson did the right thing. He got that boy the help he needed, and Alex never turned into Paul O'Connor's victim. Your father would've certainly approved."

"I honestly don't know what to do with any of this information," I said, looking back at the stoic expressions on my friend's faces. "Alex should probably find out about this from you. Maybe it's something he'll need to hear when he gets home."

I looked at Elena, who was studying my aunt. "You're sure that Alex was *blamed* for his brother's death?" Elena asked, most likely because I was looking at only her for help.

"I know Sarah didn't believe it, but Sarah was stuck in that abuse and so contaminated by Paul that I don't think she could leave him. All she could do was remove Alexander before any more damage could be done. He was a troubled child for many years, and even I didn't believe Mr. Grayson had enough money to save him from his ways, especially after hearing from Sarah that Alex nearly killed his father after he caught him beating her."

"Alex was raised to believe that he murdered his twin brother," Elena repeated. "He mentioned something about terrifying dreams," she looked at me with apologetic eyes, "and he believed he didn't deserve the happiness he felt with Breanne. He couldn't accept that he was anything more than the monster his father always said he was."

"I'm sorry, young lady, but who are you?"

"It doesn't matter," Elena said, looking at me. "This is a classic case of childhood trauma and thoughts being stirred because of association. Was it in the presence of his father that Alex mentally shut down on you?"

"It was after the funeral. I mean, before that and after he saw his sister, he was distant."

"Jake said Alex came into the ER thinking he was having a heart attack," Ash added. "He had that panic attack soon after they got back from the funeral that he didn't tell anyone about."

"Why all the secrets?" I asked.

"It was most likely because of the threats Paul made," Aunt Blaire answered. "Mr. Grayson was a tough man, but if he feared for his daughter's life, he would silence all of it."

"All while Alex repressed the truth of the traumatic situation," Elena said, standing up. "Holy shit, I need to call him. He needs to do another type of therapy, or he'll never uncover what his cognitive brain buried when his brother passed away." Elena began to pace. "It would make sense." She spoke as we watched her tick her fingernail to her lips. "Alex was made to believe *by an abuser* that he was a monster. He ruined the family, and it was all his fault. In our brains," she looked at us, "there's a defense mechanism that will bury a traumatic situation that is too hard for us to process. It's why Alex is struggling to remember any of it. His terrors seem to be memories to him, but they're based on what his father has told him about what happened with his brother. I don't believe for a second Alex had anything to do with it." She looked at me and sighed. "He said feeling *love* started all of this. It would've had to be a love that he felt was associated with Albert—the one taken from him tragically. Unconditional love. Those sorts of things combined can suddenly start jarring buried emotions. Alex said he buried all this in the past. Jim didn't even know his birth surname before. He never brought any of it up, most likely because he may have believed he was a monster but was somehow redeemed. Who knows?"

"He said he'd moved on from it all. He always said he never wanted to hurt me," I said. "I don't think this was what he was talking about, though?"

This was like solving some murder mystery, cold case that just became hot right here in my living room.

"That poor young man," my aunt added. "I can't imagine what was said to have him disturbed. I'm sorry for him."

"He's getting help," I told her. "If only his mother were more reassuring back then."

"She was terrified of Paul," Aunt Blaire defended Sarah.

"Makes sense as to why his oldest sister hated Sarah and Paul," I said, trying to dig more out of my aunt. "What kind of mother abandons her son?"

"One who wants to protect him," my aunt snapped at me. "You have no idea about that family's tragic history, and Alex was brainwashed to keep his mouth shut. All to keep Sarah safe, the girl's safe, and Alex safe."

"Do you think Paul killed Alex's twin and blamed him for it?"

"I wouldn't put it past that sick, evil man," she said. "I hope I didn't make all of it worse. I just wanted to see him, hug him, and tell him she always loved him whether he believed that or not."

"Let's hope he comes through all of this, then," I said, feeling my heart racing. "Let's hope he gets the right care. My heart is broken for him."

"We'll get him through this," Elena smiled at me. "This was an excellent bit of information. I've heard of things happening to trigger a traumatic past, and it seems in Alex's case, he recalls what his dad led him to believe. He doesn't remember what really happened. He started to feel love again, he said, and that was when?"

"He said the night terrors started coming more frequently the week before he met his sister, and after we started getting a little more serious. It got worse, I think, after we got more connected in San Diego."

"That's it. Damn it, Alex," Elena said, her eyes deep in thought as if she were putting together a puzzle. "He has to undergo regression therapy. He needs hypnosis, and I need to speak with some doctors in London, or he's doing this with our staff at Saint John's. He does not remember the truth; I know that much."

"I agree. London wakes up soon, so can you call him? I mean, how would you tell him?"

She looked at my aunt. "Secrets are out, and the only way we heal my friend is by telling him everything that happened when you came over tonight. I need him to want to get this hypnotherapy. I need him to remember, and then the doctor treating him will help him cope. He does need to remember what his young mind went through when they were with their father."

"Don't you think that will go a bit nuclear?" I questioned Elena. "I mean, seriously. Can't he seek therapy in acceptance and moving forward?"

"No," Elena said. "These are deeply buried emotions. He'll never find peace or happiness unless he knows what happened beyond what his wretched father led him to believe. His reality is based on a lie, rooted in him being worthless and unworthy of love."

My lips were suddenly dry. I had to trust Elena. I was scared to death for Alex because this was heavy shit. Though, knowing what she dealt with daily with brain injuries and traumas, we had to know that if Elena made this call, it was the right one. It would help the torn and terrorized Alex Grayson find the truth he needed to end his misery once and for all.

"Let's get him the help he needs," I said.

"I'm heading home. Coll and the guys are at our place tonight, and the men need to know about this. Jim needs to confirm some stuff too."

I looked at my aunt. "I have to thank you for telling us this. I know we look like a bunch of girls just drinking margaritas and being irresponsible, but you came on a night when we tend to separate the guys from the girls, and the husbands get to babysit."

She unexpectedly smiled. "It's always a fun night when it's just the ladies." She looked around the room. "I hope you can help him. I only wish that Jane and Jenny had the same support, but the torture that Alex endured was unbearable in comparison." She walked over and hugged me. "You know what?" She stepped back and smiled at me for the first time in forever. "I think it was pretty nasty, but you were so much like your mother to play that video at your wedding. I was just mortified for your guests and their opinions of you after you played that."

"I didn't give two fucks about what they thought of me," I half-smiled.

"And your mother would've felt the same way." She chuckled and reached for my face. "If Alex wants more information, and you think he'll want to speak to me when all of this is hopefully over, and he is well, please let him know I will tell him everything I know. He can also rest assured that you ladies are the only ones I've spoken these truths to. I did it out of concern for Sarah's son, and I knew my niece was in a relationship with him. There is no malice, and no one else will know about this. I trust you ladies will respect your friend and keep this to yourselves as well."

"I'm relieved to hear you say that instead of me having to beg you to stay quiet out of respect for Alex having already gone through enough shit," I spoke.

"I love you, sweet niece." She grabbed my hand and squeezed it. "I hope you'll forgive my absence after all this time."

"I'm just glad it was Alex who somehow made it possible for us to have a conversation again."

"Me too, dear."

The room filtered out, leaving me with Cass, Sammy, and Nat. I hugged Ash, Avery, and Elena goodbye, and now, all we could hope was that Elena could work this out because I had a feeling it would be Alex's best friends who would convince him to go along with this.

The worse part now was waiting and hoping that, with any luck, he'd come back to me.

CHAPTER THIRTY-EIGHT
ALEX

*O*f all the crazy shit I'd done in my life, this was going to top them all. Out of sheer frustration, exhaustion, and wanting to feel fucking normal again, I'd decided to take Elena's advice and try a specialized form of therapy. Regression therapy.

I had no idea what to think and no reason to believe it would help me, but I was at a loss for how to help myself at this point. I'd gone through therapy after my grandfather moved me in with him, but this was different. This was hypnosis and regressing into my past, something that would've ordinarily scared the shit out of me. The truth was that I didn't think whatever this was would work for me. This type of shit was for damaged people who were in desperate need of resolution—people who were willing to believe anything just to make themselves feel better. I couldn't have been any farther from that.

If this hypnotist could crack open my walnut and uncover whatever childhood traumas were hidden there, more power to her. I was skeptical as fuck, but I was willing to try.

"I need you to let it all go," the woman's soothing voice advised me. "You're not relaxing enough."

Sorry, lady. After seven weeks of nightmares, no sleep, and knowing that Bree's aunt filled her in on enough dirty details to make Elena beg me to do this, good luck getting me to relax, I thought since that's all I did these days. Fucking think to myself and rarely speak a word to anyone.

Fuck. Relax, Alex.

I didn't know how long it took or what the fuck this woman's monotonous voice did to me, but suddenly, I was a robot and hearing myself answer this woman without trying to think. It was strange how I was aware of my surroundings and even stranger when I heard myself admit that I was in love with Breanne Stone.

"Tell me what made you love a woman who you say you shouldn't have loved," the woman asked.

"She amused me and intrigued me. She made me feel lighter somehow. I love her smile. The way she tried to hide things from me." I laughed out loud, seeing Breanne in that apartment again, knowing she was broke and still taken by her in ways not even this therapist could pull out of me. "I was there to help her, and I wanted to. By that point, I wanted to take care of her. I wanted to love her, but I was afraid of that."

"You say you were afraid. Why would you be afraid of loving her?"

"I would hurt her. I didn't know how to love anything. I wanted to help her and never hurt her."

Suddenly, I saw the younger version of my father flash in my mind's eye.

"You are a piece of shit. You know that, boy? I hope you know you're an evil little spawn. You think you love your baby sister? Answer me, fucker!"

My stomach tightened, and I almost threw up when I felt him land a punch to my gut.

I suddenly thought about my sister. I saw her now; she was just a baby. I saw her button nose and mom crying as she held her, but baby Jen slept while my dad ran around with a beer can in his hand, hollering about how much he hated me.

"I can't love. I couldn't love my newborn sister," I said, confused and stuck in this weird memory—one foot in the memory and one foot out to where I could hear this therapy lady talking.

"Do you feel like you can't love her? Are you angry your newborn sister is in your life?"

"I love her," I answered without a second thought. "My dad says I can't. My dad hates for me to be around her."

"Do you know why?" the lady questioned. "I need you to relax more, Alex. I need you to go back. You do love your sister. Your dad hates that you're around her. Your mind knows this answer. Search."

Fucking searching, I thought in frustration, nauseated I was seeing the scene replay in my mind. Poor Jen. She never had a chance to know I loved her, and that bastard made sure of it.

Oh, my fucking God. Albert.

I saw my brother. I felt lighter and so unbelievably happy, running with him while we held our kites and they chased us. His hair was darker than mine, but his green eyes, his nose, and everything else was a mirror image. Albert and I were identical in everything. We laughed the same, and we both fell at the same time when we ran too fast for our kites to stay in the air.

Albert was crying, but I wasn't. I wasn't hurt, but I felt so bad that Albert was. I got to my feet fast. I didn't care about my kite crashing. I cared about Albert holding his knee. It was bleeding, and his elbow was bruised the same way. He'd tripped into a fallen tree, and I had to help my brother.

"Albert, it's okay," I said out loud what'd I'd said in my memory. *"I love you."* I thought the words would help him stop hurting. I held him and kissed the top of my brother's head, praying my dad wouldn't find out my brother was hurt or he would hurt us both worse.

We drove him wildly mad, two wild boys who were too rambunctious.

"Don't tell dad," Albert told me. *"He'll hit us both. We broke our kites."* I spoke our dialog aloud for some reason, and I didn't know if it was because of the hypnosis or not, but I couldn't stop myself. *"I hate him, Alex. He hurts all of us."*

I rubbed his head and smiled at my scared twin brother. *"I'll protect you from him,"* I said, and Albert smiled. This felt as real to me now as the moment it happened—like it was happening all over again. I'd forgotten about this. *"Albert, don't be afraid. I'll protect all of us from him. I'm tough, ya know?"*

"What did Albert say when you said you would protect all of your family from him?"

The therapist's voice was more distant the deeper I became entrenched in this memory.

"Albert hugged me," I answered her. "He trusted me, I think."

My thoughts changed when the therapist spouted off some verbal command that my mind seemed to be controlled by.

"Where are you now?" she asked.

"I'm camping. Albert and I are in an old rowboat, and Albert is afraid. I don't know why he's scared, but my dad is with us," I answered her.

The memory jarred me so hard that I felt as ill as I was when I felt my father punch me in the stomach in the other memory.

"Albert," my dad said, *"you're gonna learn how to swim."* The words were slurred, and Albert was terrified when he looked at me. *"We're not fishin' unless you jump out of this boat and learn how to swim."*

I stood between my dad and Albert, defending my brother from Paul's drunken threats. He took his hand and shoved me so hard that I staggered back, tripping over the bench seat and into my brother. My dad stumbled and fell against the beer cooler, passing out immediately. I thought he was dead. In fear, I panicked and jumped up. I didn't know what to do. I turned back to tell Albert we would have to try and get the boat to shore, but Albert was in the water, splashing and screaming. My dad had shoved me so hard that it knocked Albert overboard. It'd all happened almost simultaneously.

I reached for Albert, but I was too late. Albert was screaming, water was splashing, and all I saw were his frightened eyes, and then he disappeared deep into the water.

"Albert! Albert! Dad," I turned to the passed-out man, *"wake up! Albert fell in the water!"* I slapped my dad hard on the face to get his attention. Why wasn't he waking up? How could he have lost consciousness so fast? Why couldn't he hear Albert's screams?

"Where are you, Alex? I need you to talk to me," the lady's voice came into my panicked thoughts.

"I have to save Albert. I think I accidentally bumped into him, and he fell out of the boat. I can't save him. I can't find him in the water. I'm in the water now. I was never afraid to swim. I knew how but Albert didn't. My dad hated that Albert was weak. I tipped the boat back and forth and finally thought to start splashing water on my dad after I was too tired to swim and couldn't get into the boat to wake him up. I don't know how long Albert was in the water."

"What happened next?"

"My dad finally wakes up, and he pulls me into the boat. I'd been holding onto the side the whole time. He shouted and asked where Albert was. I tell him everything, and he says he has to call the cops. They will find Albert. I'm relieved when he says that they'll find Albert because that means he'll be okay."

"Did they find Albert?"

"Dad said that when we get home, I'm not to tell anyone that he fell asleep. Albert won't be coming home because I killed him and pushed him out of the boat."

"Did that make sense to you?"

"It still doesn't. Why did they believe it?"

"What else did your dad tell you? What did your mom say?"

"My mom cried uncontrollably. She cried so hard I thought she stopped breathing, but then she told me she loved me. My dad dragged me out of her arms then and told her she could never touch or hug me again. I'd killed her son, and there was nothing he could do to stop her wild boys from eventually killing each other. The cops would come to the house, and even though I'd killed Albert, we had to say that Albert fell off the dock when Dad and I were fishing. That he drowned by accident."

"Did the cops talk to you?"

"Yes. I told them it was an accident. I said everything my dad told me to tell them because I knew he would kill me if I didn't."

"And did the officer get mad at you?"

"The cop hugged me and said he was sorry but to be strong for my family," I answered her. "The cop was sad and hugged me again. After he left, my dad pulled us into the room and told my sister Jane and my mom that I'd killed my brother because I was a monster. He said the only reason he wouldn't let the cops take me was that he knew that would make mom sad to lose both of her sons."

"What did your mother say?"

"She just cried. For days and days, she cried. It felt like forever."

"Did they find Albert?"

"They did. I went to see him in a white casket. He was asleep, and he didn't have to worry about Dad waking him to hurt him because people were in the room. Dad wouldn't smack his face to wake him up because he didn't do that when people were around."

"Did you know Albert was dead?"

"I didn't want him in the ground," I answered. "I begged my mom to keep him safe in the casket. We could take him home in the box, and I could still be with him. He might look like he was sleeping, but I could see him whenever I wanted. I just wanted to take him home with me. I couldn't live without him." My mind shifted and snapped out of this lucid memory. I was thrust into the present, lying on this couch drenched in sweat, panting as if I'd run a mile. "Fuck! Oh, my God. That drunk mother fucker did it." I sat up, pulling myself out of the trance, and rubbed my face as if I'd just woken up from another night terror. "He blamed me so he wouldn't go to fucking jail?"

"Alex, I need you to try and calm down some," the lady said. "Please, you've broken out of your hypnosis, and I need to pull you from it safely. While we go back under, we're going to help you cope with Albert's death and deal with your emotions about your father."

"I hope to hell this works because if it doesn't, I might lose my mind."

"That's why we must have you come out in a healthy way, and we'll remove any emotional feelings you may have about your father."

"He made me believe all these years that I killed Albert, but I saw it, and I remember it all so damn vividly that I know that wasn't true. What kind of evil bastard does that to a son who loved his brother like I loved mine?"

"We need to get you to cope with Albert. Accept his death, and we'll continue to work from there," she said. "Lay back and let us work on these issues, or your psyche can be further damaged after these memories have surfaced."

I focused on her words, let them relax my mind, and now, we were on the path of moving forward past all of this, most of all, carrying no more emotions for my father. That man would mean nothing to me when all of this was over, but I would know the truth, and I would find peace. My father wouldn't even rot in jail for this. It was all brought about by hypnotherapy, and whatever I would say about that fucker wouldn't be admissible in a court of law, but the longer my hypnosis session went, the less I cared.

The love I felt for Albert was overwhelming. I hadn't felt *that* type of love since I'd lost my brother, but I felt that with Breanne. I felt it so sincerely that it was bizarre to accept at times. I could never lose her like I lost Albert. That wouldn't be fair to me. I deserved to have her and to have that unconditional love.

I knew Albert was at peace, and I needed Bree in my arms. I wanted the love I felt with her, and I craved it—I craved her and missed her so damn much that it was almost like a knife stabbing me in my heart. I couldn't go another second without calling for the plane and getting her back in my life.

Thank God, Jim was here, having flown out after Elena spoke to all of us about what Breanne's aunt found. If I couldn't have Bree right now, I would take the next best thing—a best friend. A brother who was there for me no matter what happened with all of this therapeutic shit.

I had one more session, and then I would get back to the states and find a way to make everything right with Bree. Today was break-through day, and I felt like a burden was lifted. The hell hounds were gone, and my tortured life was in the past where it all belonged and would remain.

Sadly, my mother never got this chance. She was too afraid to leave with Jen. She thought they would be safe, and she begged my grandfather to make sure I grew up right and became the man she always knew I could be. How fucked up was it that an abuser could hold people hostage just like that miserable prick did to everyone in my family?

I broke the chains on that bastard's mental control and manipulations, and I was ready to finish it and get my mind healthy again.

I'D BEEN BACK in the states for close to two days now, and I had to slow my roll on getting Bree back. I wanted to do this right because I knew it was total bullshit on my end—fighting demons of the past or not—with how I left her hanging.

Strange that the final piece to the *heal Alex therapy puzzle* was for me to find love with the woman who my mind, body, and soul craved. Breanne and I had started peculiarly. Who knew I had already fallen for her the night we first met when she begged me to be her fake fiancé? As time rolled forward, I found myself captivated with her as she tried her hardest to fix that Sphere job. I was taken by her. She had such a creative personality, and she was a woman who powered through situations, not giving a damn what people thought of her.

Then the physical aspects of her quickly charmed my hungry eyes, but I'd been down the road before of being fortunate enough to have my way effortlessly with beautiful women. So, I steadied my course on *falling* for Breanne Stone, believing at the time it was all shallow. Though, my heart knew more than my mind could've comprehended, and that's why I allowed her in. Although we didn't have time to allow for a relationship to fully mature, we found a way to accept our deeper feelings and hang onto *us.*

If it weren't for my internal battles, constantly trying to reassure myself it was *normal* to feel something like this for a woman—even though it was the first time I'd felt more between myself and someone else—I could have seen us on a much better path. That's what I planned on now, starting over and taking the only woman I'd ever loved the right way—finding the proper way to get her back. Thank God Elena had told me that Bree felt nothing but sorrow for my situation after her aunt downloaded my past onto her. There was still hope that I could get her back, and this time, she would be loved without reservation on my end.

Buzz! Buzz! Buzz!

My phone was blowing up in my pocket while we hung at Jim's house for the night. Tonight, I mostly talked about my plans for getting Bree back, and I was thankful my friends could pull off a quick weekend trip with me. All I needed now was to pray Bree's friends would work with me in joining all of us as well.

Buzz! Buzz! Buzz!

"Are you going to answer that, or are you some sick fuck who gets off with his vibrating phone while having a beer with his friends?" Cameron asked, hanging back with me while the guys were in the pool, having a night game of water polo against the girls.

The older kids slept in the theater room, which was transformed to make sleepovers much more enticing. The babies, of course, were sound asleep upstairs in the playroom that Jim and Avery had Breanne design, which looked like some Chuck E. Cheese version of a nursery.

I finally pulled my phone out of my pocket to see who had been blowing me up at ten in the evening. "What the fuck does my sister Jenny want?" I asked, looking over at Brandt as if he had the answer to that dumbass question.

"Who knows? Maybe she found out the truth that her brother's more of a lover than a hater?" Cameron rose. "I'm out of here." He looked at the pool. "Some of us doctors work for a fucking living." He took a ball that he'd brought out of the pool after he smoked everyone in the last game of water polo when it was just the guys, and then he threw it directly at Collin's head.

Collin's reflexes were as stealthy as Brandt's, and he managed to snatch the ball. "Hey, I have to be in at six in the morning, and I guess I'm not a little bitch like you are. I can stay up late and still get up in the morning," Collin said.

"Funny, asshole. Do you have surgery first thing?" he laughed while pulling on his shirt. "Because I do."

"You win. Go home and rest up," Collin said, then took a ball to the head sent from Jake across the net.

While my friends fucked around, I studied Jen's name on my phone and her eight missed calls. Strange how I didn't feel high or low about my younger sister. I felt that if she wanted a relationship with me and could accept the truth of the good man I was, I'd be happily open to that. If she were still stuck in Paul O'Connor's horror show, that would be the end of that. We were blood, yes, but that was the only thing we had in common for now.

"See ya, Brandt," I said as I tapped on Jen's name and dialed her back.

"Alexander?" she answered in a sad, breathless voice. "Alex?"

"I'm here. What's going on?" I spoke. "You've tried eight times to call me, and unless mom—"

"Please, just shut up," she snapped.

"Listen, you blew my phone up, *not* the other way around. What can I help you with?"

"They found dad tonight. He's dead, Alex. Gone," she sniffed and cried out a painful moan. "I know he was hateful to you, but he was your father."

"Biologically, yes," I answered her, noting that she was much sadder on this call than she was when she called to tell me our mother had died. She wasn't even sad when she told me about Mom, but now, she sounded like her world had crashed in on her with Paul gone. "That's all he was and ever will be to me."

It was unbelievably liberating not to care whether the man was alive or dead. I'd resolved to let the man go during hypnotherapy, and it was the healthiest thing I could do in moving forward. The man who deserved my respect as a father was my grandfather, and that's how it would remain.

"I know you hated him," she sniffed, "but..."

I could hear that she was drunk. Paul had ruined her. I would gladly help pull her out of the pit he'd thrown all of his kids into, but that would require her wanting to be helped. If there was one thing I knew, it was that you couldn't help people who didn't want it. It pained me to know she was his victim, and it reminded me of so many people out there who were messed up because of men like Paul O'Connor. Thank God the woman I loved had gone on a wild mission to create centers for victims—a center that I would've gone to if the help I'd gotten in London didn't work.

"Jen, you're drunk. Call me when your mind is clear."

"We need money for his funeral. You want to know why he took his own life?"

"No, but I'm sure you'll tell me," I answered.

"Because of you. *You* ruined everything. You were the reason mom died too."

"I'd love to sit here and take the heat for these accusations, but I won't. If you're calling to blame me for one of the many horrible and selfish things Paul O'Connor has done in his life, then you dialed the wrong person."

"Selfish?" Her voice sobered up some. "How is what he did selfish?"

"I'm not talking about anyone but Paul in this scenario. I can say that very few things Paul has ever done were unselfish, and this is no exception. He was a miserable, horrible man."

"It's your fault."

"Think whatever you want. Is this why you called me, to blame me for that man killing himself? It seems to me that mom was an anchor for him, and he lost that. He was a man who somehow managed to keep her through all of that abuse. He lost control when she died, and I'm sure it's pretty lonely for an abuser when they have no one left to hurt."

"You're a…" she paused. "Forget it. Listen, you owe this family. So, I'm calling for money to bury my daddy."

I pinched my lips together and studied the gang getting out of the pool, my elbows on my knees while I leaned forward, trying to process the fact that I knew Jen was only calling me for money. A sad ending to this entire family's story.

"There are charity funds available. I suggest you look at them. I will not fund his burial. He was no father to me. I'm sorry if this is an inconvenience to you, but if you can't understand why your dad would never call me to bury him, that's on you. Even if hell had cell phone service and he could get through to me from below, I would be the very last person he'd call for money even for his funeral."

"You're pathetic. You paid for Mom's funeral."

"That was our grandfather's wish, and unlike Paul, I loved her. I loved you too, Jen. Paul would never allow you to believe that, though. I'm sorry he ruined our family."

"You ruined all of us. We don't need your money!"

The phone line went dead while I inhaled and stared at my friends.

"Did I hear you correctly on that call?" Jim asked.

"Yes. Paul's gone. He took his own life."

"Good God," Elena said. "How do you feel about that?"

I smirked at her. "Are we going into immediate therapy sessions every time a family member calls me and begs for money?"

"I'm serious, Alex. You're fresh out of therapy. We all agreed to go with you on these plans that you have to get back with Breanne. I never agreed to you waiting an entire week, but whatever. Now, you find out that Paul has killed himself? I have to know if this is bothering you."

"Truthfully?"

"Yes," everyone practically sang in unison.

I rolled my eyes and stood. "I don't feel anything. He's gone. He was a miserable man, and he died. If I *had* a relationship with him, I probably would've been there while he grieved his wife, but we all know the truth of my relationship with Paul O'Connor. There was none. I guess what I'm trying to say is, I'm sorry for those he left behind that this death will bring pain to."

"So, you're not relieved, sad, feeling guilty?" Elena asked.

"No, Dr. Brooks," I teased her. "But," I arched an eyebrow and gave her a crazy expression, "if you keep putting those things in my head, you might reverse the witchery that fixed my brain."

"You're such a dumbass," Avery said, walking over in her towel and hugging me. "I'm happy this isn't hurting you. It's so wonderful to have you feeling happy."

I leaned into her side hug. "Me too. Now," I eyed the group and then smiled, "if you are all worried about anything, it should be the fact that I need to get Bree's friends on board for my idea. I didn't spend almost a hundred thousand bucks on a ring for nothing."

Ash smiled. "She's going to be blown away. You do *your* part, and we girls will do ours. Saturday can't come fast enough."

"Does she know that this *birthday outing* is all your ladies' planning?"

"Yes, and you're welcome in advance," Elena smiled. "Given that we're *all* friends, it looks like Nat and Cass will gladly join us in Branson. Nat said to make sure there's good booze on the plane ride, though. She hates flying."

"She won't even know she's on a goddamn plane in that company jet," I grinned and wiggled my eyebrows. "Now to get into character, role play, and get my girl back in my arms."

"Such a romantic," Jake smirked, taking a beer from the outdoor fridge. "I can't wait to either live or die on this thing."

"You got the time off?" I chuckled. "Dude, your stupid ass kills me."

"We all did, dip-fuck," Collin chimed in. "None of us will miss this special moment. We're there, man."

"Well, let's hope I can run a tight game, and somehow, this all works."

CHAPTER THIRTY-NINE
BREE

*I*t was what I liked to refer to as March madness. Well, March Madness was already a coined phrase, but it took on a different meaning for me since, as Nat would say, it was my birthday month.

The twenty-first day of March was my birthday, and because of our fantastic new friendship with Avery, Ash, and Elena, Cass and Nat had managed to pull off a surprise trip to Branson, Missouri on Jim's company jet. It was the very same jet Alex and I had used to travel to Florida before our relationship fell apart, so that wasn't a detail that made me feel super happy.

Being on the private airplane was bitter-sweet because I couldn't help but remember mine and Alex's better times—everything that happened before the funeral had messed with him in ways that I could've never imagined. I'd inwardly accepted how much I missed him, but the drinks kept the pain of losing Alex over a month ago at bay.

I couldn't say precisely how long it'd been. I was certainly not one to count days, or I'd go mad. I just took things one day at a time, stepping one foot in front of the other until the pain got less and less —I was still waiting for that part, though, because the only thing that'd gotten less and less was my patience. I knew I had to get over him, but not a day—not an hour—had gone by when I hadn't thought about him and wondered how he was doing in therapy. I wanted him to be healthy and happy whether or not I was there for it.

I had my doubts about a hypnotherapy session, but Elena was convinced this was the road Alex needed to take so he could heal, given his specific issues. She'd heard testimonies of it working on patients when she called around to ensure it would help her friend, and she thoroughly researched the recommended therapist. Elena had said that this method may not work and reminded us that everyone was different with how they processed issues, especially the delicate matter of an adult dealing with repressed memories from childhood trauma.

Who knew what the heck was happening in London—where Alex still was, apparently—and if any of this therapy was helping him or not? I was primarily concerned about whether his memories would be conjured and do him more harm than good. I guess that was me and my big-ass heart again, worried more about an ex-boyfriend suffering than I was myself and how it'd ended badly between us. Alex was a total dick about it too.

I didn't care if this made me look like a big, empathetic weakling. I was in love with him. I'd never been treated as someone to be so highly valued, not in the way that Alex had treated me. However, as fate would have it, it turned out that it was *too good to be true* because our relationship wound up having an expiration date.

I just wanted to know if he was better or not, and now that this plane ride was bringing me to think about him nonstop, I was going to ask.

"So, you haven't heard anything?" I finally asked, sipping on my cocktail and looking at Elena. "He's been out there two weeks longer than he initially planned. I'm sort of worried things may have gone bad."

"Like I already told you," Avery answered first, "if things weren't going well, Jim said he would tell you. He knows very well that you need to know because, for one thing, Alex is your business partner, and two," she smirked, "we all know you're still in love with the guy."

"Let's just hope they fix him up nicely for our birthday girl," Nat chimed in, having started in on her cocktails early since she hated flying. "I *know* for a fact the sex was off the charts for Bree." She eyed me. "You glowed like a woman after microdermabrasion. So yes," she took a long gulp of her cocktail, "the sex was great, and you need that man back in your life."

"To keep a youthful glow?" I laughed at my ridiculous friend.

"And other things. It was phenomenal with him, wasn't it? You need him back in your life if only for that purpose alone."

Cass rolled her eyes. "Nat, we all are aware that *sex* is your fix for every problem, but seriously?"

Nat looked at me and frowned. "Cass is right. Mind-blowing sex with that gorgeous man was a shitty thing to bring up," she said. "It probably brought back memories that make it that much more painful, not knowing if you'll ever have it again with him."

"Slow down on the drinks," I smiled and shook my head. "And to answer you, my goofy best friend, that sex or not..." I paused and grinned, "I just want Alex happy and healthy. It's driving me fucking crazy that we're not together because I want to know how he's doing." I sighed. "I want to be there for him, and I can't."

"If it were Jake and me, I would want to know too. You're doing the right thing, though," Ash added with a smile. "If Alex comes out better in the end, I'm pretty confident he'll want to repair the issues that caused you both pain and ended your relationship."

"You two didn't end things because you stopped loving each other," Cass said. "It was his way of protecting you from him. Remember all of that shit that led him to go get help?"

"I just miss the hell out of him," I admitted.

"So, let's raise a glass, then," Elena beamed. "To days ahead when Alex is well and realizes that if he blindly found love with his business partner," she chuckled, "then he'll blindly fall in love with her again only with a healthier, new beginning this time."

I raised my glass. "A beginning that, if it happens, he'll never doubt himself being in *love* with me again." I sighed, knowing Alex and I may never get back together. "Well, in love with me or anyone else. To his happiness," I cheered, feeling a slow buzz coming on.

Nat rolled her eyes. "Are you serious? It's your birthday, and we're cheering to Alex's happiness with or without you as his lover? That's the lamest thing you've ever said, Breanne."

"Lame or not, I do love the man enough to concern myself with him being happy and with the right woman," I stated firmly.

"I'm not toasting to this. I'm laying down," Nat said. She was trying to remain firm, but we couldn't help but laugh at her tipsy state. "Wake me when we land, and don't think for a second that I missed that one hot pilot when we boarded. I'd like to personally thank him, as my life is in his hands."

"We'll be sure to do that," Cass said. "Go lay down and sleep this off because when we land, we're going directly to the attraction we set up for Bree. The rules were to drink, but don't get drunk, and now look at you?"

"God," Nat rubbed her forehead and meandered through the leather seating where we were in, "you owe me for this, Bree." She turned back to me. "Trust me, flying to an attraction in Missouri was *not* my idea of a thirty-something birthday party."

"No," I smiled, "I know *exactly* what your plans would've been. I'm glad we're going to Missouri instead."

"Wake me when the wheels are safely on the ground, please," Nat said.

WE'D CONSUMED plenty of food and water to soak up the cocktails we'd enjoyed on our luxurious flight, and after the plane landed in Springfield, Missouri, we loaded up into a party limo that was waiting for us. I should have been drawn to the party lights of this massive SUV, but instead, seeing the lime green grass and how beautiful the countryside was in the Midwest was more appealing. Of course, we had green grass for a small portion of the year in California, but nothing like this. California was sadly fighting constant droughts, and we didn't have the luxury of lush, green, rolling hills along the roadways we traveled—not like this, anyway.

When the party vehicle arrived at the destination, I pinched my lips together in humor and excitement. "Who would think to take me to a Titanic attraction? In Branson, Missouri, correct?"

"Correct," Avery said. "There was easier access to an attraction in Vegas, but I watched some ghost investigation show, and this is one haunted place. If we were doing this, then this was the place to go."

"You and your haunted attractions," I shook my head at her. "It was how you and Jim met, right?"

She laughed. "Yes, and since my hunt for ghosts on my tour of the Tower of London was a bust, I'm eager to find one now. That's why, in all of this planning, I boycotted the Vegas attraction, and now we're boarding a replica of the ship. I think this one might be a tad bit cooler."

"Whose idea was this anyway?" I questioned after we stepped out of the party wagon.

"You don't remember telling us that you compared losing the Sphere project to the ship sinking?" Cass said. "You were pissed you spoke those thoughts out loud in front of Alex on your way to save that project. You went off about it one night."

"No," I looked at the girls, questioning them with my confused expression alone. "Was I that insecure about it?"

"I guess you must've been, but you talk crazy when you're shitfaced drunk too," Nat said dismissively. "You blabbered on and on to us that you had mentioned it to Alex," she sighed as if this were the last place on Earth she wanted to be—and knowing Nat, it was. "You kept saying, '*I swear I'm cursed with that man. I say the stupidest shit around him.*' You told us how embarrassed you were that you'd compared that screwed-up job to the Titanic. Whether or not Alex thought you were crazy, we thought you were that night." She waved her hand up at the bow of the large, replicated portion of this ship. "Now viola. We're here for your birthday."

I couldn't help but laugh. "Well, thank God I talk while I'm drunk because I do find this ship fascinating, and I'm delighted to be here. I love that you all thought of this. It brings back the funny times I had when I wanted to prove that I was a *badass CEO*."

"A ship that sunk brings back *funny times* to you?" Nat looked at me like I was as crazy as I knew I sounded. "Breanne, people died, and we're here to celebrate your birthday at what I would imagine could be recognized as a sacred memorial."

"Well, look at you, Nat," I hugged her side. "You're all grown up, and now, we're the immature ones. I want to see this attraction, though. I'm thrilled with the idea I might learn something I never knew about this ship. I've always found it intriguing that it should've never gone down."

"Girls, our tour guide is waiting," Avery said. "Let's go learn about the RMS Titanic. I hear we get a boarding pass with the identity of one of the actual passengers, and we become those passengers on the attraction. I think we're about to get an intense history lesson on the sinking of Breanne's favorite ship."

"Let's go learn some history," I added.

As we were introduced to our tour guide, we fell into our roles as passengers aboard the Titanic, knowing the ship would undoubtedly meet its tragic demise, and only seven hundred or so lives would be spared. It was sort of eerie to journey into this, knowing it brought you more in-depth to that fateful voyage that could've easily been lost in history.

After we finished, I was blown away by so many things, not the least of which was the interesting fact that *linoleum* was considered to be a luxurious floor covering that only the wealthiest people could afford in 1912—the million-dollar grand staircase wasn't too bad either.

We were now leaving with the knowledge of the passenger we were and whether we survived the sinking of the ship or not. When we walked out, the girls' voices were hushed, perhaps because I was tuning them out while reading about the passenger that I'd been assigned. I was so consumed with the engineering and designs of the ship with my architect's frame of mind that I'd hardly considered the history of anyone who lived or perished on the luxury liner.

As it turns out, I was the passenger who was known as Lady Rothes, Nöel Leslie. Not only did she survive, but she was also pretty heroic, taking charge of the lifeboat—lifeboat number eight. She rowed it for more than an hour, in freezing-cold temperatures, before she handed that duty over to another so she could console a newlywed whose husband perished.

"What passenger were you?" Avery asked. "Mine didn't survive."

I told her who I was after learning about her passenger. "Check this out," I said as I read about the woman. "Not only did she row the boat for a solid hour, but she was also reported as caring for passengers who'd survived when they were aboard the rescue ship, Carpathia." I smiled at Avery. "I would have never known any of this. Strangely enough, I'm sort of bummed that I only cared for the architecture and beauty of the ship and was always upset it sank because it was reportedly flawed in design." I shrugged, trying to pull back from being somewhat emotional after coming off of that experience.

"That's crazy," Cass said. "Your personality is somewhat comparable to your passenger. I can easily see you doing what that woman did." Cass's eyes studied me. "Down to the fact that you saw past your wealth and gave it up to help everyone in your dad's company—"

"Whether she knew they were stealing from her or not," Alex said.

I nearly jumped out of my skin when I heard his voice as he finished speaking for Cass. I turned back and stared at his brilliant smile and his lighter expression, looking more handsome than I remembered.

"You're here?" I said, confused and in utter shock that Alex was here and joined by his closest friends.

"Well," he held up a boarding pass and pulled his sunglasses off to read the pass, "according to this, I'm not."

Did he go through this attraction too? Wait, this was Alex's idea. All of it, and my girlfriends did well in acting like it was theirs.

I smiled. "Third class passenger and didn't get a boat?" I tried to guess.

His eyes locked with mine. "No boat and my passenger gave up his life jacket. He was reported to be preaching to the ones who were going down with the ship." He read the information with a broad grin.

"Preaching?" I cocked my head to the side. "What passenger were you who selflessly gave up your life jacket to another and preached to help people cope with the fact that they might die?"

He glanced back down at his boarding pass. "Reverend John Harper, traveling to Chicago with his niece and daughter. I guess his heart was more concerned about consoling those meeting with the afterlife than his demise. It states here that some passengers heard him in the water preaching as they waited for help. The man didn't stop until his last breath."

"Wow," I said, blown away that Alex was standing there, looking so healthy and his face so soft that I wanted to step toward him and reach for his cheek just to feel him again. "It's surreal to learn about these passengers. I feel pretty sad that all I cared about was the ship's engineering flaws. Now, I don't think I'll ever forget about these passengers."

"Isn't that the point, though?" Alex asked as I ignored the girls, reuniting with their men behind Alex, most likely talking about their experience and who they were. I was more focused on Alex being in front of me with a new expression I'd never seen him wear.

"The point?" I questioned his eyes as they raptly studied mine.

"Yes, keeping their memories alive through an attraction such as this," he pressed his lips together. "I'll admit, the Titanic was never something I thought of until I met you. Aside from that and coming here, I feel it's intriguing to look past the ship alone and learn about the people who died tragically, and from what it appears, most heroically. Memories," he smirked. "They're such an interesting concept in combination with how our minds work, how we process whether they remain with us in history lessons or real life."

"I suppose so," I smiled at him. "I know I learned a good lesson, and that's not focusing on the structure of a flawed ship, but perhaps, like you said, keeping their memories alive."

He half-smiled. "Curiously, I can relate a bit to that now," he said.

"Strangely enough, this whole thing went another direction on me when I planned to surprise you with a visit to a ship you compared to the Sphere job."

"How so?" I stepped close to him, his expression more serious.

"Well, before I had someone dig into the secrets of my brain," he smirked, "my brother was just simply dead, and though I was wrongly blamed for that, my memories of him died behind the illusion of my flawed family." He slipped his hands into his pockets. "Maybe not all the same, but it struck me that my twin brother's life, and the life I shared with him, though short, had been stolen from me." He half-rolled his eyes. "I'm sure you know that Elena recommended hypnotherapy?"

"I do," I swallowed, knowing he *was* well and sharing part of his recovery journey with me. "It seemed to have worked. You seem very happy."

"It did. I was able to remember my twin brother, Albert. That was the grave I stood at when you found me the day of the funeral. Anyway, I remembered him and how much I loved him." He stepped toward me and ran his hand over my cheek. "I remember our history now, a history that was masked and practically overwritten by an abusive man."

"I'm so very sorry you lost your brother. How are you coping with all of that?"

He exhaled and smiled. "Rather well, believe it or not. I loved my brother, and while I was sad to remember how much I loved him, I also discovered that I tried to save him from drowning. More importantly, I know that I wasn't responsible for his death. I wasn't the evil individual Paul always led me to believe I was. With the therapy, I accepted Albert's death." He ran the back of his knuckles over my jaw, and I could only close my eyes to catch my breath, feeling how rejuvenating it was to have his touch against my flesh again. "I accepted the love I was always told I could never feel. I wasn't a monster, and that was liberating to learn on my own. It helped me understand I was capable of loving like most good people are."

"Loving?" I reopened my eyes. "Maybe, if you'd like to try it out, you can see if you can love me again?"

That was lame. I tried to lighten up both of us, or everyone watching us was going to tease our endearing moment, especially since he had his two doctor friends with him, Jake and Collin—the ultimate jokesters no matter what the occasion seemed to call for.

"Love you *again*? I never stopped, Bree, even though I thought I did at the time, I suppose." I saw the group gather around us from the corner of my eye. "I learned that the love I held for my brother was only brought up after being buried inside me because I accepted how I felt about you. Isn't it interesting how our relationship starts with me trying to save you, and in the end, after feeling love with you, it was you who saved me?" He nodded toward my boarding pass. "And *cared* for me, even though I tried to push you away. Cass is right. You do resemble that woman on your boarding pass, you know. A woman whose heart goes beyond worrying about herself: you're a woman who appears that her heart is bigger than..." he paused, and it seemed as though he was searching for words.

I smirked and decided to finish his statement for him. "My heart always seemed to prove it was bigger than my brain, in the aspect of trying to save my employees while they were stealing from me anyway?"

Suddenly, I realized why Alex didn't finish whatever he was about to say to me. A duo of men's voices hummed to the hit song that Celine Dion sang in the movie Titanic. I couldn't help but cover my smile. At the same time, Alex rolled his eyes and turned back to Collin and Jake—the two doctors I should've seen *this* coming from. Alex's reunion was shifting from the Titanic experience. The romance was beginning to swirl in the air between both of us, prompting the two jokesters to bust out the background music from that hit movie.

"What the hell are you two doing?" Alex said when he turned, and I laughed softly with the rest of the women who'd found the two men's humor just as entertaining.

"Well, I'm humming the tune for Coll to sing on key," Jake said, acting extremely serious. "Trust me. It takes a lot to keep Collin at that angelic level. And of all the songs he has to sing, it's got to be Celine Dion's song—the one we had to hear when we were forced to sit through the movie so we could *learn more* about the ship."

"I never told you idiots to watch a movie about this ship," Alex answered in confusion. "What movie?" He glanced between the two men.

"Titanic. Kate Winslet?" Collin stopped singing and answered. "Elena told me that you insisted we watch that three-hour movie." He looked around Alex and at me. "Speaking of which, I now will add my expert opinion. Leonardo DiCaprio's character was an absolute idiot, and *that's* why he didn't make it."

"Really? We're doing *this*?" Alex said. I could hear him trying to be firm, but there was humor in his voice too.

"Oh, hell yeah. We're doing *this*," Jake chimed back in. "Ash made me watch it too. She said *you* insisted that this was the best way to learn about the ship and appreciate what you were doing with Breanne. All of that said, Coll's right. Jack could've fit on that damn door. I would've managed it easily, and I wouldn't have died."

"Should we recreate it in the Pacific Ocean back home? I mean, we might as well see if you two are right or not?" I asked as the two doctors smirked and then looked at Alex.

"We should probably do that one song at the end of the movie. The one where the ship is sinking, sort of like Alex out here dying in the romance department," Collin eyed Jake, then smiled at Alex.

"Right. Let me get back into character again," Jake answered. Then both men started humming like violins as they switched their background music to a hymn from the movie.

This one was most likely accurate to the actual ship sinking as it was said the musicians played this particular song on the ship before it'd sunk.

Jim, who was previously in a humored conversation with Avery, became aware of the two doctors singing and trying to recreate the romance from the movie Titanic. I couldn't resist but find the silliness of it endearing. I missed all of us being together like this, especially with Jake and Collin's humorous gestures.

"Why are they humming a song?" Jim questioned with well-founded confusion.

"It's Jake and Collin. Why wouldn't they be?" Alex asked, folding his arms as everyone gave the two men our undivided attention. "It appears they're struggling to separate a movie from the attraction of Titanic we just went through."

Jim rolled his eyes and smiled at me. "You should've seen our guide's expression when they started singing Celine Dion's song." Jim looked at Alex. "You should've known this would happen after you told the ladies to make sure we all watch that movie about this ship."

"What movie?" Alex asked with a laugh. "I have no clue what you guys are talking about."

"You haven't seen Titanic? Have you been living under a rock?" I asked with a chuckle. "Why would you insist they watch it if you've never seen it?"

"This might come as a shock," Alex grinned at me, "but when the women get a chance to sit down their husbands for a romantic flick, they make up lies. It turns out that it's biting me in the ass when all I wanted was to beg you to forgive me and allow me a chance to prove I can never love anyone other than you. I love you, Breanne Stone. There's no doubt in my heart about that now."

Alex pulled out a Tiffany & Company box, and instead of gasping, crying, and impulsively grabbing Alex and hugging the man and never wanting to let him go, I was stopped in humor at how ridiculous his friends were behaving.

There was no way in the world I could get mad at any of this. It was as hilarious as it was beautiful, and I would never forget this moment. I watched in shock as Alex knelt and opened the box, and that's when Collin sang *loudly,* performing the part of the song where Celine Dion sings her heart out. Then I glanced down and watched Alex's eyes close and his lips tighten in humor. It was all priceless, and I couldn't help but join everyone in laughter.

Alex looked back at Collin. "Your heart will most definitely *go on* that damn jet if you don't stop singing," Alex tried to warn through a laugh.

"That was the part where you ask Breanne to—well, you know," Collin said with a grin. "I set that up perfectly for you. My voice didn't crack or anything. Celine Dion would've begged me for a duet if she heard it too." He shrugged. "Now, you ruined all of it. Talk about wasting your talent."

"Wasting *my* talent, or yours?"

"Ask Breanne," Collin said, putting his arm around his laughing wife. "She'll admit that was a nice setup for everything you had planned."

"It was epic," Jake fake-agreed with Collin, trying to keep a straight face. "Now, that ship has sailed, and you're stuck without Collin's vocals because, let's face it, you'll never hit those notes again, Coll." Jake shrugged.

"Never again. I'm still trying to accept that I nailed that, and Alex and Breanne aren't locked in some passionate kiss?"

"You know, Alex," I finally interrupted the men, "it's going to be *really* difficult to accept a proposal since Collin's voice is shot, and I don't have him on karaoke for your background music."

Alex rose and held my face between his hands. "I've got two failed marriage proposal attempts, and I'm begging you to forgive me for stopping my best *idiot* friend from singing as I attempted this proposal the right way."

"And now, I have to turn you down again?" I teased him, forgetting the soft laughter coming from everyone—including Nat's hushed squeals. Everything was out of focus, while Alex's beautiful green eyes were more beautiful and dazzling brighter than the huge rock that he held between both of us.

"I know this is yet another *not so ideal* proposal situation, but this time, my head is right. I know exactly what I want and why I want it. I need you in my life, and all of this," he waved his hand to remind me of the Titanic excursion again, "is when my heart knew that I was in love with you. My mind didn't grasp it all at the time, but it was *that* particular moment when you compared that faulty job to this ship that I knew I was in love with you."

"So, this whole experience wasn't so Collin could sing off-key to

Celine Dion? It wasn't about that romantic movie you never watched?" I grinned at him.

"Absolutely not," he admitted. "Being here, *on your birthday*, was just me, trying to bring it back full-circle to the day I unknowingly fell in love with you."

"I'll marry you on one condition." I arched an eyebrow at the man I loved and cherished more than I could sincerely express.

"Anything," he said. "You can play a sex tape at our wedding for all I give a damn. I just want you and only you in my life forever."

"Since you appear to be the only one who hasn't seen that movie..."

"Oh, hell," Alex looked at me with the most adorable and pleading expression. "I've watched every Grace Kelly movie with you, and Fred Astaire, and Carey Grant—all of the old romance films you've fallen asleep to in my arms."

I recalled how much I knew he hated watching old movies, but he watched them anyway.

"It counts for something, right?" he asked. "But I *can* watch *our* movie with you a hundred times, *Dorothy*, with my new heart you've insisted the wizard give me. I will gladly watch that movie with you." He kissed my ring finger. "But only if you put my outward expression of love on your finger."

I sniffed as I started to cry, officially caught up in the moment with the man I loved more than anything, and I felt more solid about marrying him than I felt about anything else in this world.

Alex returned to bended knee in front of me. "I humbly ask you to marry me or at least start over and date me until the day comes that you feel confident enough to become my wife."

"What if I told you that I felt confident enough that I would marry you now if I could?" I knelt in front of him.

"Well, that would put us all back on the plane and off to Vegas as your birthday evening stop, doing *that* Titanic experience," he looked back at Avery's grin, as she leaned into Jim's side, "and Elvis handling our vows."

I smiled. "Avery is on the hunt for ghosts. Give her a pass for that."

"Avery and Jim can remain behind to find Avery a ghost," Alex grinned at me. "Baby, I love you. We're going to have a massive-ass wedding, and I even had a lovely conversation with your Aunt Blaire about it."

"You talked to her?"

"Yes," his hand covered mine and slid the ring on. "She was a bit nicer than the last time I saw her." He kissed the ring he put on my finger. "She said you were thrilled about the wedding you had intended to have the first time, but you hated the idiot who ruined it all. Is she lying about loving the big wedding?"

I softly laughed. "I guess I was thrilled to have a big, beautiful wedding day. Marrying the wrong man was what ruined it all. That, and I'm never doing fashion week again. I'll *only* go to Paris because Theo's there, and I can happily shop for wedding dresses with him."

He held me close, and we clung to each other. It took me finally feeling Alex's soft and firm lips on mine to prevent me from laughing when Collin and Jake returned to their background serenade. Eventually, I couldn't help but giggle into mine and Alex's kiss.

"Sorry, I was thinking about how full my heart is, and then they're singing that song..." I shrugged to Alex's grin.

"So long as you and I will be married one day, I say let's get out of here," he said. "I have a hotel booked for you and me, and these party animals aren't finding out what room number we're in. Happy Birthday, baby. I love you so much," he said, and that's when a lovely luxury sports car came into view. "Don't ask. The guys insisted we rent these things, and the girls can drink in that party bus if they want to keep celebrating your birthday."

"Let's go," I said.

This was the perfect way to celebrate my birthday. Even though we had the doctor duo serenading us with a song that'd been worn out for decades, it was still excellent, and it all probably worked better than what Alex had planned initially.

Beyond the marriage proposal, I could sense a different side of Alex. He was more handsome, relaxed, and sincere than I ever remembered him being. The girls were right about when you find the right one—the other half of your soul. It felt like this. Even with our flaws, it worked because we *were* two souls that'd found each other. Alex's might have been worn when we came together but wasn't that our journey? To be the other half of each other and keep moving forward in life?

We were meant to face anything together, and now, we'd survive it because we were two bodies, but one strong force that felt an impenetrable love. Everything just got better, and we were complete with or without vows.

EPILOGUE
BREE

Part One

I guess when you're in love, time really does fly, or maybe time just flies when you're having fun? In my case, it seemed like both were the reason it'd been precisely two years since I first met Alexander—the man I knew at the time as *Mr. Grayson.* Allow me to rephrase that, it was two years ago in this hotel that, in some bizarre attempt to look cool in front of my douchebag of an ex-fiancé, I met a handsome man named Logan.

Later, I would come to know Logan as Alexander Grayson, the man who played me and forced me to send him on an adventure of lies in an attempt to save face because his company was merging with mine.

What a journey he and I had been on, and there wasn't a thing I would take back about any of it. Now, here we were on our wedding day, and luckily, there were no videos to play for our audience.

Throughout the months of dating that led Alex and me to pick the anniversary of our first meeting for a wedding date, I felt more love and adoration from him than ever. With work keeping us busy as usual—living in his home unless it was a girls' night that forced me back to the condo—Alex and I were insanely in love, and neither one of us could've been happier.

"Hold still, Bree," Cass said. She dusted blush on my cheeks as a stylist worked my hair into a fancy bun that would be complemented with a sparkling diamond tiara to match the jewels that were stitched along the bodice of my strapless gown. The dress was simple, really; it was long and shaped to flow nicely over the curves of my body, and the diamonds sparkled in all the right places. It was Parisian couture, and it showed. Theo and the designers in Paris insisted I wear the dress at first glance, and once I caught a glimpse of myself in the mirror, I couldn't have agreed more. It was stunning.

I was not the bridezilla Nat was sure I'd be. Instead, I was going with the flow, filled with gratitude that I was about to become Alex's wife officially. After the wedding, he and I were set to travel on the yacht he and Jim jointly owned—*Maiden Stone,* the one he'd named after me. He was incredibly proud of himself for naming the ship now because he said it represented our relationship—*Made in Stone.* The only thing we needed to do now was get to the boat after the wedding, which was anchored in the Sea of Cortez.

Alex still held an iron fist at work and with our employees, but this softer side of him led him down some silly romantic roads, so much so that I teased him that if our marriage *was* made in stone, he should probably take my last name and not the other way around.

"You look so goddamn beautiful," Nat said, walking into the room where I was dressed and fully prepared to walk down that aisle and become Alex's wife. "You're never going to believe what that gorgeous young doctor told me." She placed her hand on the hip of her pale pink gown.

"We don't have time for guessing games, so please tell us," Cass said, fiddling with my hair, proving that the hairstylist wasn't living up to her standards.

I pursed my lips and grinned. "Let me guess," I said, looking at Nat's flustered expression. "Dr. Brandt *still* won't date you?"

She rolled her eyes as Ash, Avery, and Elena walked in wearing their bridesmaids' dresses, perfectly coifed and ready to go. "No," she arched an eyebrow. "It turns out that even though Cameron's a player, he's not letting up on the fact I made the mistake of sleeping with Spencer Monroe."

I pinched my lips together. "At least you don't have to walk with Spencer. We put you with Cam instead."

"Yeah, thanks for *that* too. I'd love to say that it was a kind gesture. Now, it's just torture. He smells so delicious, and my female hormones will be raging by the end of this." She then smiled. "Are you seriously going to trust Zeus—a *cat*—to walk your wedding rings down the aisle and stay on course? Unless you've both lost your minds, you have to know that cat is going to lose it, climb some beautiful aisle of flowers, and freak out."

I stood and smiled at Nat, the only one who didn't get the memo that this was the joke we played on Theo. This is what she got for listening to gossip anyway.

"Alex has spent a lot of money, having Zeus trained to do this job, so whether or not Theo and *you* are okay with it, I'd hate to see Alex waste all that money."

"Breanne," she said with a sigh, "you realize there are quite a few gossipy guests out in your audience today. Don't be surprised at all if ninety percent of them are allergic to cats, and Zeus ruins this."

"Calm down," I hugged her. "Zeus is staying with Collin and Elena while we're gone. He's at their place with the sitter they hired for the little ones."

"That's another thing. Why don't you have a ring bearer or flower girl?" She eyed me. "I thought this was bordering a traditional-style wedding?"

"You crack me up. You didn't see Addison out there with Jim and little John with Jake?" I looked at Avery and Ash. "Tell me your husbands have chilled out a little? I'd like to hug my beautiful little flower girl before this whole thing starts."

Avery chuckled. "Jim and Jake are more worried about the kids being flawless than Theo is worried about you having a cat for a ring bearer. So, you've officially caused chaos over in the groom's area. I think Cameron is the only one who's fully relaxed."

"That's because he's got two weddings back-to-back; he's here for this one, and then the *real fun* begins for him next week when an old friend from med school gets married. He's groomsman of the month."

"Well, he's handsome enough to make it straight into a bridal magazine." Nat took a sip of champagne.

"Still trying to get over him turning you down because of Spencer?" Elena smiled at Nat, who was playing the part of *bridesmaid-zilla*. "Trust me. You can do much better than being turned down by that man."

"And Elena gives me a little consult?" Nat eyed her with a smile. "Too bad you're not a fortune-teller because I'd like to know how it turns out for me in the end."

I walked over and hugged her. "You'll know when the right one comes. It's all about the challenge you both go through to make it work out in the end. That awesome feeling of questioning *why the hell* you're in love with someone you didn't spend years getting to know." I looked around the room. "I would've married this man a year ago if I could've. Time has done nothing but hit warp speed until today when I walked into this hotel."

"Mommy," I heard my flower girl say to Avery, and I turned and smiled down at how adorable Addison looked in a tiny replica of my dress. "We're ready to *do this thing!*" she said and then skipped over to hug me. "Auntie Bree, you are so beautiful. Like a queen." She smiled, and her onyx curls sparkled with the jewels that were placed in them.

"You look beautiful, little missy," I teased her.

"Little John looks more handsome than even Uncle Alex does."

"Well, maybe that's because we're all ready for a beautiful day," I said.

"Theo's on his way with Clay and Joe." She motioned for me to bend down. "Uncle Jake said not to be afraid. Everyone from the crazy-farm is here."

"Sounds like something he'd say," Cass smiled at my flower girl.

"Have you told him yet? I figured that after our bachelorette party, you would," Ash asked me. "He's going to notice you toasting with sparkling apple cider and not the *real stuff.*"

"I don't know when to tell him. I mean, this is sort of my fault. I got back on the pill in case we wanted to start having children eventually, but after being so used to having that stupid IUD, I wasn't taking the pill right, and here I am."

"I told Jake on our honeymoon too," Ash smiled. "It was a fun gift to give him. You should take the same route."

"I feel guilty for not telling him when I first found out," I stopped and sighed. "I just opened up to you guys because you caught me not drinking at the bachelorette party."

"More like Nat caught you and wouldn't let up," Cass smiled.

"Well, figure it out because you're three months into this, and you're lucky it's your first pregnancy, so all you have is a little bump," Avery teased.

"There is an upside for Alex in all of this," Nat said as the girls all grabbed their slender bouquets of lilies. "There shall be no periods throughout the entire honeymoon, and of course, I hear that as time goes on, you get hornier, so the first six months of your marriage should be fantastic. All thanks to you getting knocked up right before your wedding."

I exhaled, feeling the nerves now. "Let's worry about getting through this day. My aunt has been faithfully attending that wedding book, and I'm going to dodge her. I can't cry."

"Ha," Elena chuckled. "Good luck with that. In addition to what Nat said, your hormones can kick in at random intervals, and you could be the blubbering bride up there with Alex today."

I eyed all of my bridesmaids as they chuckled. "Aren't you guys supposed to be my support crew or whatever it is that bridesmaids do on the wedding day?"

"We support you telling Alex when you're standing in front of that priest," Cass teased.

"All right," the door flung open. "Girls, let's get it going. You all look radiant and lovely," Clay said, walking in with Joe. "Joe, make sure the men know it's go-time. I've got fifteen planners in this building, and we're about to make some magic happen!"

I hugged both of Ash's best guy friends and thanked them, but it was Theo who made me crumble. All he had to do was stand in my dad's place, give me *that Theo smile*, and tell me how honored he was that I asked him to walk me to my future husband.

We had our moment, and in a monumental effort to not ruin Cass's perfect makeup job, I dried it all up. It was time to see my man and gladly marry him and love him with everything I was. Perhaps the girls were right. Maybe I would ask Alex if he would *marry us*, me and the twins—an unexpected surprise I found out about at my check-up two days ago. I wanted to be shocked, but with Alex being a twin, I knew it probably wasn't a stretch.

What would he think when he learned about all of this? There was only one way to find out, and I needed Theo to get me into that large hall in the Beverly Wilshire hotel, bringing me back to the spot where Alex and I first met in the most humorous way. What a journey we'd been on so far; however, with twins on the way, I felt this journey was just getting started.

Part Two

Alex

*(No sex tape played at our wedding,
and eight long months of carrying twins later...)*

"My God, how the hell can it be five-hundred degrees in the middle of flipping January?" Bree said, her legs kicked up on my lap as she reclined sideways on our sofa. "I hate these leather couches too. I'm literally sticking to them."

With extreme caution and love for this woman, who was overly vocal about her discomfort in the final days of her pregnancy with the twins, I rose and went upstairs to the linen closet to grab a cool, clean sheet for her to put between herself and the sofa.

I smiled when I passed the nursery, seeing the sailboat theme she couldn't resist having for the two boys. Yes, two boys. I was more blessed than a man should be. I had the best partner in business and life—aside from the occasional miserable, pregnant episodes that came and went in this final trimester—and I was receiving the most significant blessing possible.

When Dr. Allen announced that Bree was carrying twin boys, I was the first to shed a tear. That gave the doctor a chuckle since he'd known me for years from my position in the Saint John's Board of Directors, and he knew I could be *quite* the rigid prick. However, I beat Breanne in the emotional reaction department by a mile, and the best part was that I didn't give half a fuck what anyone thought about it either.

The only difference between my sons and Albert and me was that my boys would not be identical twins. Instead, the doctor noticed on the ultrasound that Bree was carrying fraternal twins, though, in reality, it was all the same to me. It was a miracle, and even though Breanne was miserable, I knew she was as elated as I was to meet our babies.

"This should work, dimples," I said with a smile, then I turned to the other sofa in our living area and spread out the sheet over the leather. "Let's get you onto a cool sheet and make you more comfortable."

She eyed me with *that* look, which told me instantly that I'd made a bad call, but I had no idea what I'd done wrong. There was a lot of that happening these days.

"I can't sit my lazy ass on *that* sofa and see the television. I hate where it's positioned anyway."

"Last I recall, my darling," I smirked at her flustered expression, "it was an exceptional architect who arranged this living area."

"Right," she glared, her jade eyes trying to level me with what I'd become bulletproof against. "God, I'm so sorry," she said, trying to sit up, prompting me to rush to her side to help her. "I'm the world's biggest bitch, and you don't deserve this crazy person I've turned into."

I took her hand and helped her up. "Hey," I kissed her soft cheek, "I love you more than the pregnancy mood swings." She preferred lounging in sports bras and soft shorts lately, and so I rubbed my hand over her exposed stomach. "And I absolutely *love* that you've given our children a nice, healthy place to grow until they're ready to meet us."

She looked up at me and smiled. "I love you, Alex," she said in the mood-swing shift I was expecting either now or tomorrow, whenever it came. "I'm hornier than hell right now too."

I bit back my smile. "Well, lately, your favorite position is riding on top. I'm down for killing time like that, and Dr. Allen did *approve* sex if you want to get this show on the road."

She exhaled. "I'm too damn hot for sex itself," she said as she switched gears again. I practically jumped when she turned and reached for my cock. "But," she gave me a mischievous smile, "I'm ready to get this over with, so I'm just going to brace myself on that wall, and you do your part."

"My part?" I tightened my lips because if there was one lesson I'd learned in this stage of the pregnancy with my lovely wife, it was to shut the fuck up, don't laugh, and do as she says. However, this was beyond humorous.

"Yes. Fuck me *hard*." She walked over to a wall in the living room, sighed in annoyance, and spread her legs.

"I have to admit, everything you just demanded of me can be a man's dream come true. However, this isn't exactly romantic."

"Fuck romance, Alex," she snapped into that gear again. "The romance is *dead* right now, and you're going to be dead if you don't get over here and help me get this going."

"Well, the doc said it was the sperm that triggered the pregnancy, so why don't we do this where it's a tiny bit more comfortable for you?"

"For me?" she turned back, and evil-Bree was in full swing. "Comfortable? I can't sleep—I don't even remember the last time I slept. I'm hotter than hell all of the fucking time, I fart when I least expect it to happen, my indigestion is killing me from all those tacos I can't stop eating, and as if all of that isn't bad enough, I pee myself when I laugh, cough, or sneeze. So, I ask *you*," she flashed her most challenging expression, "why would I give a shit about how or where we screw? Let's do our part and get these babies out of me before I burst at the seams."

I sighed, and my heart was sad that she was so miserable. I knew that we could get labor started through sex, but I felt terrible going through motions like this, especially when we had nearly perfected our sex life. I wasn't the *hop on top and have my way* kind of guy.

"Happy wife, happy life, right?" I said.

"Good God, I hate that fucking term."

"You hate a lot of things these days," I teased, then gently positioned Bree to take me and pray that I could keep my cock hard, doing the job that was required of me to get her moving into labor hopefully.

"Oh, fuck," she growled, her head rocking back into my chest. "Even while I'm miserable, I can't get enough of feeling you inside me."

That's all it took to keep me rocking my hard-on and staying the course for my wife. Now, all I could do was hope this got the job done because I didn't know how much longer Bree could survive feeling so miserable, and I didn't know how much longer I could keep dodging bullets.

"ALEX, I'M HAVING THE BABIES," Bree said to me, and we were standing at the altar again at our wedding.

I smiled at her, knowing this was a dream, but I loved this moment in time so much, and I love revisiting it. I watched as she stopped the priest, her bridesmaids all wearing ear-to-ear smiles, and she asked if I would marry her and the twins she was carrying. I didn't hear anything in the room, not even the reaction of the guests or my groomsmen. I felt my heart skip a beat or two, and I was *extremely* close to joining the bridesmaids with their shocked tears of joy. Breanne was a gift from the minute I first met her, and to learn we were having not just one child but two was double the blessing for me.

"Alex! Please, wake the fuck up, or I'm calling for the neighbor and leaving you here."

My eyes snapped open to see Bree, standing there in an oversized shirt, pajama bottoms, and the two braids I was proud I nailed when I braided her hair before we fell asleep.

"You're sure?"

"My water broke, so I think I'm pretty sure this one isn't a false alarm," she said, then bent over and held her stomach as I scrambled to get out of bed. I turned back and went to help as our birthing classes taught us. "Goddammit, grab our stuff," she demanded through her breathing. "I'm okay with the contraction." She blew out one last breath. "Whew. Maybe I'll be like Elena, and it goes quickly, and I won't have to wait long like *most* first pregnancies."

Thirteen hours later...

"I'm not doing this anymore," Bree said, fighting her contraction. "Go get Dr. Allen. I'm seriously done."

I rubbed a freshly cooled washcloth over her forehead. "Why don't we take Dr. Allen's advice and get that epidural so you can relax."

"Ohhhhhhhhhhh, shit!" she cried, and that's when her hand clutched the button of my pants.

As Breanne breathed through the painful contraction, I took a selfish moment to thank God that my belt had prevented her death grip from separating my balls from my body—something that would ensure she never had to go through this again.

Bree thought I was breathing with her, but not this time. This time my breathing was focused on keeping my dick safe and waiting for this severe contraction to end so I would never be in this vulnerable position again.

"How are our future parents doing?" I heard Cameron say, coming in, wearing his surgical scrubs.

"Dr. Brandt," Bree said, coming off of that contraction and relaxing back on the bed with an exhausted smile. "You're in pediatrics, right? Kids and babies," she questioned Cameron as he grinned at her.

"That I am," he said. "How are you doing, beautiful momma?"

She reached for his arm. "Listen to me. Get me the hell out of here, and get these two stubborn boys out of me," she said in that growl I was used to.

"As much as I'd love to help," Cameron grinned at me then her, "I'm not certified to deliver healthy pregnancies. Pediatric neurosurgeon protocols, I guess?"

"Then you have to go find Dr. Allen and tell him I need these babies out right now. I don't know what he's fucking waiting for." She looked at me. "Wait. You're on the board here, Alex. Go handle that doctor."

"I see labor and delivery is going well in here." Cameron stepped back just in time for another contraction. "Tell Bree she'll survive this. It's always worth it when you're holding your precious babies."

"Tell Cameron to get the fuck out of here if he's not going to put action into words with that," Bree panted out.

"Tell Allen or a nurse we could use a pelvic exam to see how dilated we are," I said to Brandt.

"*We*," Bree scoffed.

"Got it," Cameron said, then eyed all the monitors, "These are healthy heartbeats, and oxygen levels are doing great. You're doing awesome, Bree."

Cam left before Bree could throw one last jab, and thank God a nurse was quick to get in the room, close the curtain, and do Breanne's exam.

"Oh God, not another one," Bree said as another contraction came barreling down on her.

"We're ready to do this," the nurse said. "I'll go get the doctor, and we'll get this all moving along."

"Do you hear that?" I kissed Bree's forehead. "We're about to meet our sons."

Bree collapsed back into her pillows. Then her face returned to a pained expression coupled with another contraction.

"Let's keep these heart rates where they are and deliver naturally, Breanne," Dr. Allen said, pulling on his birthing gear. "If all goes safely, we're going to meet your babies soon."

I watched as nurses filed in and walked over to the warmers where the babies would go once they were born. I also didn't fail to notice the neonatal intensive care unit staff walk in as well.

"One more. I see baby number one's head," Dr. Allen explained.

"Would you like to watch?" the nurse asked Bree.

"God, no," she wailed out as soon as our first son's head made its entrance into the world.

WITH ALL OF Breanne's hard work, she safely delivered our sons. Both boys were instantly rushed to their warmers after I cut their umbilical cords, and just as Dr. Allen suggested, Bree's thirty-eight-week pregnancy could likely deliver two healthy baby boys. He was right.

Both babies passing the APGAR score made me exhale in relief at our two beautiful sons, who were now crying loudly for their mother. The group had all texted that they'd wait outside when Bree's contractions were more brutal, and it was only Cameron who had the balls to peek around the curtain to check on her before heading into surgery.

The nurses quickly wrapped both sets of dark-haired boys in their burrito-style blanket and handed them to Breanne after I walked to my wife. I kissed her on her forehead, her tired eyes peering up at me and her beautiful, dimpled smile lighting up the entire room.

"You did so well, baby," I kissed her forehead. "Our sons are healthy and on their way to you."

I watched, mesmerized, as Bree was handed a baby for each arm, and she smiled down at them. "Hello, my beautiful boys. You look so much like your daddy. Except you, little man." I watched, sitting next to her and allowing her to lean into my side some. "You have dimples, don't you?" She chuckled and smiled at me. "I love you," she said, and that's when I kissed her parched lips.

"There aren't any words to explain how I'm feeling. I'm so proud of you and more in love with you now than ever."

I glanced down, and the other infant popped the same dimples as the first one. I frowned and shook off any idea that Dr. Allen got this wrong with our boys being identical. There was no way in hell, especially with today's technology.

"Well, what the heck are we going to call you two?" I said, gently taking one of our sons from Bree's arm.

"Well, I've got Logan," Bree smiled at me with a tear in her eye. "And I think, if I'm correct, the beautiful little boy you're holding is Albert."

I looked at her in amazement. "You're *trying* to make me cry, and I won't," I said, arching an eyebrow at her while Dr. Allen continued to work, sewing up her vital area.

"I wanted to name our sons after two men who you loved and cherished. What do you think?"

"I love it," I said, kissing her. "And I love you. Do you want some ice chips or water? Your lips are parched, baby."

"I would love that," she said.

"Well, I certainly missed this," Dr. Allen said, examining what I could only imagine was the placenta.

"Don't tell me there are three?" Bree chuckled.

"No," Dr. Allen stood. "These handsome boys are identical twins." He smiled at Bree and me. "Congratulations to you both. When you're ready, you can have visitors. I can already hear Collin out there, so I'll have a nurse send your friends and family in whenever you say."

"Family?" I chuckled. "Did Jake say he was family again so he could come in first?"

"No," Dr. Allen looked at me. "A young woman said so. Her name is Jane O'Connor, I think?" he said, glancing back where the door had been closed for the delivery process.

"My sister is here?" I questioned him as if he'd understand why I hadn't seen to Jane since San Diego.

I hadn't heard from her since she said there was no way in hell she'd come to mom's funeral, and sometime between then and now, she was deployed. Apparently, she was back now.

"Surprise, daddy," Bree cleared my instant confusion with a lovely smile of adoration. "I sent her a text and let her know that we were going to have a baby at some point this month."

I kissed her forehead. "A baby? As in one?" I questioned. Bree had Jane's info since I threw it into her contacts as a joke, stating she was my first emergency contact if I didn't survive our deep-sea dive on one of our many honeymoon destinations.

"Go get her. I'm all tucked in and ready for everyone to meet these babies before the lactation consultant gets here and clears the room."

"You realize that, even though I love Jane, our friends are family to me too."

"Alexander," she used the one name she loved when she busted my ass—the married couple shit that happens, I guess. "She's your sister, and she's here because she loves you. Bring her in, and then we'll show her these handsome nephews of hers. The boys have the rest of their lives to spend with our family of friends—all the aunties and uncles and cousins that go along with it—but give your sister this. Our friends understand."

I cleared my throat and looked at baby Albert as he started to fight in my arms. "I'm not sure how to handle this, but I guess—" I glanced over at baby Logan in Bree's arms. "Well, I guess these two handsome men are a great conversation starter."

"They're a perfect way to start down a new and healthy road with your sister. I'm happily surprised she's here on the day they were born."

"Leave it to you to fix the last dangling issue in my family drama." I kissed her again, unsure if I'd ever be able to stop, given how happy I was.

I walked out to the comfortable waiting area, and Jim was the first to stand when he saw my approach. "We heard mommy and babies are healthy?"

"A new and very handsome dad didn't pass out?" I heard Jane as she walked up to me, smiles worn all around the room while the children were occupied in the learning and games corner of the room.

"Jane, I'm happy as hell that you're here," I said as she stepped back and smiled up at me.

"Well," she patted my cheek, "I've heard you're doing well from my sister-in-law. I texted Bree and congratulated her on your nuptials since your response was some BS thumbs-up emoji."

"I am." I grinned at how well my sister appeared. Her blonde, curly hair was loose around her shoulders, and she was dressed casually. She didn't have her usual stiff military look. "I'm happy you're here."

She jabbed me in my side. "You better be. Now, let's go," she said.

"Give us a second," I smiled at the group as Jane walked in to meet Breanne and our children for the first time, and the understanding smiles on my friends' faces were all I needed to see not to feel as though I was ditching them.

"Identical twins," Jane grinned at me. "I love the names, Alex. You're one lucky dad, you know."

"And you're one lucky aunt, eh?" I said, walking toward Bree's beaming smile. "We named them after our grandfather and our brother."

"It's a beautiful way to treasure both of them," she said. "Damn, I couldn't be happier for you," she looked at Bree, "and thrilled to meet a kind sister finally. Out of all the tragedy, it feels so freeing to let it all go and just be a *real* family."

"I think we're all a great family, now that you're with us," Bree added. "How'd you manage to get up here on this day of all days?"

Jane grinned, taking a seat, lost in baby Logan's eyes now. "I guess I got lucky. I left last night, made the six-hour drive after traffic cleared, and then Bree texted me when you guys were here."

"Yeah, well, she could have used your marine methods while she waited to deliver," I smirked. "This is all so surreal. I'm happy you're here."

Jane grinned at Bree and me. "I am too." She touched the dimple on Logan's cheek when he yawned. "Now, let's toughen these boys up and make them bad-ass marines, eh?"

"Fighter pilots?" Bree laughed.

"You know it," Jane grinned.

The rest of the gang filtered in, all smiles. Aside from meeting Breanne, falling in love, and finding my *true peace*, having everyone together in this room made me feel like the luckiest son of a bitch on the planet.

I loved the wholeness I felt. Over a year ago, Jane and I would've never been laughing or smiling like this—like the brother and sister we could happily be now. We went through hell together, and I was so thankful that I had my oldest sister after all was said and done.

Could I be the happiest man alive? Absolutely. I was the most content that I'd ever been, and I could say without reservation that I deserved this happiness, and I deserved the beautiful family I was blessed to have.

A painful past did make for a strong man in my case. When I asked Bree to allow me to be the last man she could ever love, she'd already honored that vow by giving me two more little humans to love unconditionally. And just like that, I had a family, and I knew I would never take any of this for granted—not for one damn day of my life. I was a man who'd been blessed a thousand times over.

THANK You for reading Mr. Grayson. I hope you enjoyed this one as much as I enjoyed writing it.

An included bonus of Dr. Brandt's intro to book 5 in the Billionaires' Series is next...

DR. BRANDT: SNEAK PEEK
INTRODUCTION

~

Description

Letting her go was a mistake. I *never* repeat my mistakes...

It was just going to be a quick vacation. A break from the demands of my job as a pediatric surgeon.

I never thought *she'd* be there.

Jessica Stein. *My* Jessa. The woman I left behind all those years ago is every bit as sexy now as she was then. I want her more than ever.

Too bad she doesn't feel the same way.

To her, I'm the guy who broke her heart and let her down. She thinks I'm the same player I used to be.

She's wrong.

But the only thing she wants from me is my medical expertise. See, her son is sick.

I'll do everything I can for the boy, and eventually, I *will* convince her to trust me with the secrets I know she's keeping. I need her to give me a second chance, because I *am* the man she's been waiting for.

All I have to do now is convince *her* of that...

~

Cameron (Cam) Sneak Peek...

This week in Jamaica was supposed to be a reprieve from the demand of my job as a pediatric neurosurgeon. What wasn't there to love about the white sandy beaches of the all-inclusive resort where we were staying? I was here for the sun and fun, but the latter had backfired on my ass.

I suppose I should've stopped the groom and questioned his *bright idea* of coming here after his fiancé dumped him a day before their wedding. Typically, however, guys didn't sit around and talk out their feelings. It was more common for us men to jump at the opportunity to turn a bad situation into a good one. You know, get each other's backs without questioning who was right or wrong in a relationship breakup—failed wedding or not. So, that's what I did.

I agreed to join the broken-hearted groom on vacation. Maybe Dennis would get laid and get over it; maybe he wouldn't. Either way, he requested that his groomsmen join him for a week, and I was happy to get away from work and Los Angeles for that time.

I felt pretty bad for the Dennis after he said that his ex-fiancé was taking her bridesmaids to Dubai on what should've been their honeymoon, so how could any of us say no to him? Little did I know this fuck-knuckle had played all of us, and *we* were the ones going on his honeymoon trip. I didn't know much about what happened before the wedding day fiasco, and since I was just a last-minute stand-in and not a close friend, I didn't plan on going too deep with him about it.

Dennis was a resident at Saint John's Hospital, and if it weren't for him bumping into me when I'd had a little too much to drink one night after two days on-call, I would've never agreed to be in his wedding. I don't even know why I agreed when I was drunk. I barely knew the guy, and I was quickly finding out how different we were.

He did things that, even in my younger playboy, reckless years, I would've never considered doing. A prime example of that being that he'd also invited his fiancé's married bridesmaids to join us in Jamaica—in our shared villa—for what was turning out to be some weird-ass sex fest. That was *not* my style. No fucking way. None of this was what I'd signed up for, yet here I was, fending off drunk married women all night every time they tried to sneak into my room.

This was a nightmare. I called down to the front desk of the resort and requested a private room outside of this villa, and all I could do now was wait for them to call with the good news that I had a spot away from this insanity. I still had four days left on the island, and I sure as hell didn't want to spend them like this.

I was pissed, and God help anyone who tried to downplay Dennis's role in roping us into his honeymoon, turning this room into some weird fuck parade between the dumped groom, his groomsmen, and the bridesmaids. Perhaps if I got caught up on my sleep, I'd laugh at myself for being stupid enough to jump on a plane with these strangers. Maybe I'd even laugh about it one day with my *actual* friends. However, at the moment, I wasn't laughing.

I took a sip of my rum and coke, trying to wake up since this cursed vacation had consisted of me getting cat naps in between women sneaking into my room all night.

"Look who's finally awake and joining the party," Dennis said as he gripped my shoulder and took the barstool to my left. "We thought you were sick or something."

His squeaky voice didn't match his graying hair, but that wasn't even the most annoying thing about him at the moment. I'd left the villa an hour ago and gone to the tiki bar, hoping to get away from the fools I'd come with, but here he was.

This would be my first conversation with the fucker since I learned the truth about what'd happened to ruin his wedding—*he* was the one who'd cheated on his fiancé, and not the other way around like he'd led me to believe.

"You said that your fiancé was the one..." I paused and eyed his smirk, and then I twisted and leaned into the bar to face him. "Why did you make it seem like your girl had cheated on you when it was your stupid ass who cheated on her? At the hospital, you said that *those days* were over for you. I don't get it. Why bother getting married at all if you still want to fuck around?"

"Oh, please," he rolled his eyes. "I'm not here to get lectured by a surgeon who was screwing a nurse in—"

I narrowed my eyes and held up my hand after I gulped down the last of my cocktail. "First of all, Gabby was my girlfriend. Second of all, just because she was an ER nurse doesn't mean that I was supposed to take a vow not to have sex with her."

"That's not what flew around the hospital."

"Thirdly," I continued, "I never cheated on her. When we ended things, she decided to make it appear as though I used her as my personal fuck-nurse. It nearly cost me my job, but fortunately, social media saved my ass when I had to deal with the board about her complaints."

"How so?" He frowned.

"Because she posted everything but nudes of us on Instagram. She'd blasted that shit all over her accounts, and it saved me in the end. So, lesson learned. I don't date co-workers at that hospital anymore, much less fuck them for the hell of it." The story sounded so stupid when I said it out loud.

"Why did you break it off? Were you bored with her? You see, I think that's what my problem is. I got bored with Kelly," he took a sip of a martini that was as dirty as he was, "and I cheated on her. I don't know, I guess I got cold feet, but after my bachelor party, I realized that I wasn't made to be a one-woman man."

"That shit went down at your fucking bachelor party?"

Who the hell was this guy? He'd always seemed to be a decent guy, but I'd gotten that character assessment completely wrong. I guess you learn more and more about people when you're stuck living with them in a fucked-up situation for a week.

"She caught me for the fourth and final time after she sent a friend that I'd never met to the party to spy on me. Her friend followed me after I left with a few of girls who'd shown up at the bar." He shrugged. "I couldn't lie my way out of having my picture taken while checking into a hotel with my hand on some chicks' asses."

"No shit?" I humored him in disgust. He wasn't an ugly guy, but never in a million years would I expect him to attract multiple women at once—unless he was paying them, anyway. "I don't know who to blame in this scenario, you or your girl, who'd known that you'd already banged at least four other broads before her friend caught you on your bachelor night."

"Kelly thought she could change me." He arched his eyebrow. "Marriage isn't the answer to that, you know. Maybe I'm a sex addict. Maybe I'm the one who needs therapy."

You think?

I tapped on my glass and ordered another cocktail from the bartender. "Does therapy really help a man who brings his fiancé's married friends to Jamaica for a massive orgy? And yes, you are a sick fuck." There went our working relationship. "Excuses and self-diagnoses or not, you realize that this whole thing is another level of fucked-up, right? All of us are here on *your* honeymoon? I thought this was part of your *broken-hearted* groom's getaway since your fiancé supposedly took her bridesmaids to Dubai."

He sighed. "You clearly got it wrong."

"Clearly," I said, taking a gulp of my new drink.

"I'm not going to sit here while you say that I'm the dick in this situation. It was everyone's idea to join me on the honeymoon that *I paid for*—no refunds—because she made me look like an asshole. Even her bridesmaids agreed that she handled it dirty. I mean, who stalks their fiancé like she did when she used her friend to catch me? Huh?

Who does that to their future husband and then calls off the wedding?"

Jesus Christ. This mother fucker is delusional.

"A woman who doesn't trust her man. Obviously, it was for a good reason. Listen," I spun around the ice cubes in my glass with my cocktail straw, "I'll keep my mouth shut about all of it if you make it clear to the married bridesmaids that they're not allowed in my room. I would at least appreciate it if you can get the word out to the rest of your wedding party that I'm not fucking any of them."

"So, now you're suddenly a prude?"

I rolled my eyes. "They're married and are here without their spouses. There were three of them in the span of one night who walked into my fucking room naked—drunk off their asses—and woke me up for some fun in paradise. I don't roll that way."

Instead of trying to negotiate my way out of being sexually assaulted all fucking night, I should've been at the front desk, begging for a private room. I'd pay for a broom closet if it meant I didn't have to worry about someone grabbing my cock in the middle of the night.

"You're being a stick-in-the-mud, Cam."

"Well, I think the honeymoon is over for me," I said dryly. "I'm out, man. I swear I'll sleep in a fucking cabana if one of those bridesmaids comes into my room for the third goddamn night in a row."

"Just chill." He shook his head like *I* was the one who was being unreasonable. I was no choir boy, but I also didn't like people in my space unless they were invited—and none of the people in that goddamn villa were invited. "I'll take care of the hotties who came with me and my guys. It seems like you're the only dick that's shriveled up for the week, eh?"

"How about changing shit up for the final four days that we're here? Instead of fucking every last *married* bridesmaid," my eyes widened as I took my drink and stood from the barstool, "you can just go fuck yourself?"

I briskly nodded and bowed out. Maybe when I was a dumbass in my college days, I would've been down for this type of shit, but obviously, I'd grown up a little, and this wasn't my game.

As I walked through the bar, fuck-me eyes were coming at me from all sides. A few of the bridesmaids were there from the villa—finally coming up for air, I guess—and it was almost like they were tracking me down. This *vacation* was fucking stressful. There was no way I was going to sleep with one eye open for the third night in a row.

"Cammy," I heard Tania call out, one of the more aggressive, naked bridesmaids. "Cam!"

I kept walking, hoping she'd be distracted by someone else on her hot pursuit to me. When I glanced back at her, she flashed her tits at me, making me run head-on into someone.

"Fuck!" I growled, trying to steady the woman I'd nearly trampled into the sand. "Holy shit! Jessa?"

"Cameron Brandt?" she chuckled.

"Oh, my God." I was in complete and utter shock.

I locked eyes with my stunning ex-girlfriend, and I couldn't help but smile when her bright blue eyes glittered as she laughed. I shivered internally at the welcomed sight of this lovely woman. She was the one who got away—and she was right in front of me.

"You look terrified like someone is chasing you." She smiled so sweetly as I stared in disbelief that I was looking into the eyes of the one woman I never stopped loving. "Are you okay?"

"I'm fine," I said in some foreign voice that I knew gave me away entirely. "This is quite a shock, running into you like this, and in Jamaica of all places…after all these years?"

An arm slipped around the back of my neck, bringing me back to my harsh reality. Fucking hell, how could I begin to explain *this* crazy-ass situation to the woman I'd crushed ten or more years ago? Why in God's name did I ever leave this beautiful woman? What the fuck was I thinking?

"Baby, you left me," Tania whined as she locked eyes on Jessa. "Who's this? Don't even think about it, girly. He's mine."

I wanted to throw the woman off me and catch up with Jessa, but I wasn't sure I had the right. How would Jessa trust anything coming out of my mouth when I vowed to love her and never leave her—yet that's precisely what I did.

Now, I was here with a drunk *and married* bridesmaid clinging onto me as if she and I were on our honeymoon, and I couldn't think so long as my Jessa's blue eyes were staring into mine.

"Is this your wife?" Jessa questioned with a smile, obviously eyeing the large rock the woman's left hand.

"No," I quickly answered. "She's married."

"But she's here with you?" Jessa looked at me like the dirty son of a bitch it appeared I was.

Tania stuck her tongue in my ear, and I nearly threw her to the ground. "Are you fucking serious?" I said to the married woman. "What the hell is wrong with all of you bridesmaids?"

"What?" Jessa looked at me with wide eyes, and I could only imagine what she was thinking from the smile on her face.

"You and I are taking the master bedroom tonight," Tania said as she grabbed my crotch. "We can share it with the others. You want it, Cammy. Stop playing around."

"Cammy?" Jessa seemed to bite back her smile.

If Jessa had ever prayed for my ass to be punished for hurting her, she was watching the answer to those prayers come true at this moment. I was miserable, trying my damndest to focus, and Jessa seemed to find it all extremely amusing. That's what this was all about, right? Karma biting me in my ass like I deserved.

If that wasn't enough, I was now fighting off this bridesmaid like a rabid spider monkey. "I'm getting another room, and you're going back to that wedding party. I'm done with this shit."

"Why don't I leave you two alone?" Jessa said with a curious smile. "It was nice to see you again, Cam." She looked at the woman who was hanging like a drunken idiot on my side. "Enjoy your wedding festivities, or whatever it is you're doing here."

"This isn't what it seems." I tried to smile while refraining from throwing a bridesmaid off my ass. "Trust me."

"Have a good one." She laughed and grinned at me.

"Jessa, can we talk?" I looked like an idiot with a drunk woman trying to lick me as she stumbled over her own feet. "I mean, do you have a minute or two?"

"I think you might be the busy one," Jessa chuckled, watching the bridesmaid that I was unsuccessfully trying to keep at arm's length.

"You think this is funny?" I grinned back at her, hoping I could get her to agree to meet with me.

"I've never seen anything like this before." Jessa looked at the girl, who was now sitting on the ground, holding onto my shorts like a toddler would cling to their parent.

"Neither have I," I said as I looked at Tania in disbelief.

"I really have to go." Jessa seemed weirded out about what was happening to me, and I couldn't blame her. I'd never been in a more ridiculous situation.

"I'll try to catch up as soon as I secure another room. The one I have now isn't working out."

"You do that." She winked before she turned and walked away, and I was instantly brought back to better days with my first and only love.

Thirteen years of college and med school taught me that resilience and good focus would get you what you want if you worked hard enough at it, and what I wanted now was Jessa. I hadn't seen her since I left early for med school, and I couldn't help but wonder what she thought of me after witnessing this scene.

I stood there—with an intoxicated, groveling bridesmaid holding onto my leg—and watched Jessa walk away. I'd had a lot of girlfriends and flings since Jessa, but no one had ever measured up to her. Now, I felt desperate to explain things to her and right all the wrongs I'd ever done. All I could do was hope to find her again and pray that she'd want to hear me out.

Coming this fall/winter...or sooner. Click here to preorder or learn more.

ALSO BY RAYLIN MARKS

The Billionaires' Club:

All books in the Billionaires' Club series listed below can be read in order or as a standalone. Each book has its own guaranteed happily ever after.

Book 1: Dr. Mitchell (Jake and Ash's story)

Book 2: Mr. Mitchell (Jim and Avery's story)

Book 3: Dr. Brooks (Collin and Elena's story)

Book 4: Mr. Grayson (Alex and Bree's story)

Book 5: Dr. Brandt (Release date coming soon, preorder here.)

Book 6: Mr. Monroe (Release date coming soon, preorder here)

ABOUT THE AUTHOR

Raylin Marks is the author of the Billionaires' Club Series and absolutely loves writing each and every love story with these billionaires and the ladies that bring them to their knees.

She is forever grateful to all her readers for all their support and encouragement as she ventured into this series and is excited to keep delivering more romance books to help give everyone an exciting reading escape.

Raylin's updates can be found on her social media pages. If you haven't followed her yet, the links are below.

Printed in Great Britain
by Amazon

39281519R00268